Tᴴᴱ
WINTER'S
SLEEP

Praise for **THE WINTER'S SLEEP**

'Spooky and compelling - a great debut.'
PETER JAMES

'A chilling modern ghost story for an age where we are
so haunted by debt that only the supernatural offers a
way out. A perfect book to read as the nights get darker.
Magical and frightening, I loved it.'
CARMEN MARCUS

'The writing is superbly vivid and tense. A brilliant,
riveting tale and an absorbing journey through modern
life, with its stress and debt, into crime and punishment,
and, ultimately, into a battle for a woman's soul.'
ANDREW CLOVER

'Monica Cafferky delivers a page-turner that keeps the
reader guessing until the very end. Filled with suspense and
chilling moments, *The Winter's Sleep* sprinkles elements of
surrealism inside this exciting debut novel. '
MACHEL SCHULL

'Really enjoyable - a spooky, surprising, rip-roaring yarn.'
DAISY WAUGH

THE
WINTER'S
SLEEP

Monica Cafferky

JASPERTREEPRESS.COM

Published by Jasper Tree Press
An imprint of *Not From This Planet*

www.notfromthisplanet.co.uk

ISBN: 978-1-912257-50-8

Cover Design by Michelle Gordon
Social Media symbols © Vecteezy.com

First Edition

For Tilly who loved Saltburn

PART ONE:
FIRE

Brigid

The herbalist shop stood on the outskirts of Leeds, the last in a row of Victorian buildings that had been earmarked for demolition. The other properties had already been boarded up, and the shop's lone yellow light spilled out onto the dark pavement casting ghostly shadows. The street was empty except for Brigid Raven, she walked quickly with her head down against the October wind.

When Brigid reached the apothecary she pushed open the heavy door. She'd been visiting her grandmother's shop since she was young, when she wanted to avoid her mother. The shop hadn't changed much over the last twenty-five years. It was still her favourite place to hide.

She breathed in the heavily scented warm air and took in the floor to ceiling shelves of jars and the worn blue counter. As though she had been summoned, Diana appeared from the back of the shop and wrapped her plump arms around Brigid in a welcoming hug.

'How was your day, poppet?' she asked.

'I'm fine, Gran, just feeling a bit drained. Long hours,' said Brigid catching a familiar whiff of lavender and rose. Brigid marvelled that her gran was in her eighties yet looked twenty years younger. Her face only had a few lines and her eyes were clear and not rheumy. Still, Brigid liked to pop round regularly to keep an eye on her, and at the weekends she helped clean her gran's flat above the shop.

Today, her grandmother's skin had an odd greyish pallor that Brigid hadn't seen before. 'Are you okay?' she asked full of concern. 'You look a bit peaky.'

'Don't worry about me, poppet,' said Diana with a wave

of her hand. 'I'm an old woman. I'm supposed to look this way. What about you? Are you still enjoying your job at that dog magazine? What's it called again?'

'*Canine World*. It's great, I love it, although it's non-stop.'

The only thing Brigid didn't love about her job was the pittance she was paid. But she didn't want to burden her gran with her money worries, so instead she chatted about her upcoming celeb interview with dog-loving Clare Baldwin.

Diana made some rosemary and parsley tea as Brigid talked about her job. From her years of helping out at the shop, Brigid knew that the tea was good for her asthma amongst other things.

'I'll just pop into the back for some shortbread,' said Diana. The herbalist stood up slowly, smoothed her pristine white apron and disappeared through the curtained doorway like a magician.

As Brigid waited she traced the outline of the star tattoo on the outside of her left wrist. She'd had the black inking done on her 21st birthday even though her grandmother hated them. She reckoned tattoos should only be seen on sailors and Hell's Angels. Brigid smiled. She loved her gran's old-fashioned view of the world.

Brigid pulled the cuff of her jumper down to hide her tattoo. As she looked up and glanced out of the shop's front window, the hazy figure of a young boy streaked past. The boy's outline was fluid, like a passing cloud, but the details of his body were distinct and unmistakable. He was a ghost. A cold shiver shot through Brigid's body.

The ghost child was wearing knee-length shorts and chasing a huge metal hoop. Although the snapshot from the past faded after a few seconds, the unexpected apparition still made Brigid's heart jump. The presence was like a silent shotgun going off in her body. The ghost was from the unseen world, the other place, and Brigid was glad to be separated from him by the shop's thick glass-front.

Brigid didn't see these spectres daily, even weekly, but often enough to know that she was different. Maybe even cursed. She rarely mentioned these encounters to anyone – not even to her gran. Her special sight, her so-called gift, made her feel like a freak.

Besides, nothing bad had happened since she'd encountered her first ghost in her bedroom when she was five years old. The old man had stood at the end of her bed, grinning at her, before he vanished into thin air. Brigid appeared to be merely an observer and never spoke to the spirits, they in turn never communicated with her either. As long as the two worlds didn't collide, she could live with this special sight. Just.

By the time her gran had returned with the shortbread, Brigid had recovered from her swift ghostly encounter and was fit to burst, despite her earlier vow not to bother her. So, when Diana said she seemed quiet, and asked if she was worried about something, out it spilled.

'I love dogs, but I can't write about squeaky toys and worming pills forever,' said Brigid with a sigh. 'I'm twenty-seven years old. I should be working for a woman's mag in London. But who's going to take me seriously when they see my cuttings about the best poo bags and a hero Chihuahua who saved his owner from a burning house?'

Brigid picked at the skin around her thumb even though it was sore. Her gran tutted, told her to stop fretting and said things would work out in the end. Brigid smiled, but her heart sank. When she was younger, her grandmother had always seemed to magically fix all her worries. But hugs and platitudes no longer quite did the job. Brigid changed the subject and asked her gran how she remembered all the complicated Latin names of the herbs.

'I lived above the shop when I was small, as you know. My mother used to blindfold me and put a different herb in each hand. I had to smell them and repeat their names.' As Diana talked, she held her palms open as if they were full of dried plants. 'It was the smell that helped me to remember, poppet.'

Brigid admired her grandmother so much. Not only did she know the value of the plants and their secret healing properties, she was also a woman who knew right from wrong and had a moral compass set from half a century ago.

'The world of nature is drifting away,' her grandmother continued. 'Folk think everything they need is on the internet. What they don't realise is that the internet is stealing their time. Isolating them. Technology even interferes with natural sleep patterns, poppet. Did you know that?'

'It's not technology that's keeping me awake at night, it's stress,' said Brigid. 'I wish I had a magic pill that could knock me out for a week.' Her gran's silence urged Brigid to continue talking. 'I'm suffocating, Gran. I can feel this invisible pressure pushing down on my head.'

Brigid closed her eyes briefly and confessed to the real cause of her concerns, 'I barely earn enough to support myself and I'm in so much debt I feel like I'll never pay it off. Josh is still out of work and I don't know how much longer we can last. I want to run away from my life. Just disappear. I lie in bed at night worrying and I'm exhausted from the lack of sleep.'

'It's only money, poppet. Stop fretting.'

Brigid realised her gran would never grasp the reality of her situation. How could she? She didn't know what it felt like to go to sleep worrying about money and to wake up with the same thoughts gnawing at her brain.

'Most people want to escape from something,' Diana said when Brigid didn't respond. She stood up and moved slowly towards the shelves on the far side of the shop. 'I've wanted to run away from this place for some time. But I promised my dying mother, God rest her soul, that I'd stay open and help people. But business was brisk back then, it was an easy promise to make. Now it's a difficult one to keep.'

Diana smiled at Brigid and picked up a glass jar. From inside the jar, the herbalist pulled out a newspaper ball and opened it to reveal a cluster of herbs, which looked like the dried jasmine you put in boiling water to make tea. But the flowers were smaller and a deeper purple. Diana showed the medicine to Brigid and explained that a small dose of the flower, just the one, would give her a good night's sleep.

'Like valerian?' asked Brigid. She'd heard this particular herb could help with insomnia and had been meaning to ask her gran about it.

'Better than valerian, and it's easy to take,' said Diana. 'You boil spring water, add one dried flower, and then let it steep for thirty minutes. The cooled mixture will taste bitter, and when you drink it be sure not to swallow the dregs. The flower is one of the *Aconitum* species. It's mildly toxic.'

Her grandmother counted out 11 purple flowers, 11

being Brigid's lucky number, and tipped the herbs into a white envelope. As she did so, Diana explained more about the herb's folklore. 'Tiny amounts of the herb are used to increase pitta, or fire, in Indian Ayurvedic medicine. In traditional Chinese medicine it's prescribed to help with a lack of Yang or coldness. In Britain the herb has been used since the 1500s as a sedative and sleep aid.'

'Does it really work?'

Diana nodded and added, 'Yes, but you do need to tackle the cause of your stress and not just the symptoms. The herb is not a cure-all.'

As she spoke, her gran's face was so close that Brigid could see the details of her right eye; the pupil dilated quickly reacting to an unseen darkness. It seemed to Brigid that her gran had reached inside her soul and pulled out her worry, but swiftly the moment was over. The brief connection left Brigid feeling somehow invigorated as if her gran had given her some of her strength.

'But heed my warning,' Diana repeated. 'Ingest the tea of three flowers or more and you will fall into a deep sleep, which will last for around 48 to 72 hours depending on your metabolism. Treat the flower with respect.' She explained that the mini-coma wouldn't kill Brigid but she would appear to have stopped breathing. 'Centuries ago people used the flower to fake their death but I've not heard of anyone using it this way for more than a hundred years. Even so, please be careful.'

'What's it called?' asked Brigid as she picked up the white envelope and tucked it safely into her bag.

'The plant's medicinal name is *Aconitum mortis*. But my mother, your grandmother, called it the Death Herb.'

Josh

Two hours later, and a mile and a half away from the herbalist shop, Josh Raven was about to put the key in the door of his smart terrace house where he lived with Brigid, his wife of three years. At six foot, Josh had to stoop slightly to connect his key with the lock. He shivered, the days were drawing in fast. He hoped the bastards didn't raise fuel prices again this winter.

As he fumbled with the key, his large fingers too big for the tiny piece of metal, Josh felt drained. He knew it was six o'clock because he'd just checked his Omega Seamaster. The watch had been a present from his mum and dad for passing his degree. It was the most expensive thing they'd ever bought him and he cherished it.

His gut twisted a little at the thought of having to sell his prized possession if his luck didn't improve. He'd spent another trying day searching for a job that didn't exist. What the hell was he supposed to do with a third in maths from Oxford for God's sake? Solve the world's problems with an algorithm? He couldn't even solve his own financial mess.

Six months ago, he would never have thought he'd be in this position. Whilst his job with HMRC at the local tax office hadn't exactly been challenging, it had given him a good salary. Then the treasury had decided to move operations on-line and his small branch had closed. Now he was redundant and broke.

Unlike his wealthy university friends, who he hadn't seen since graduation, Josh didn't have contacts in the city. Or the right accent. It was startling to already feel washed up when he wasn't even 40. Thank Christ he had Brigid. She was quite frankly the only good thing in his life. And he had his home. He'd paid the deposit with his inheritance from his grandfather. He knew if he hadn't invested the cash in bricks and mortar he'd have frittered the money away on dope or a new motorbike.

Josh's neighbour Mrs Adamski appeared in her front garden wearing slippers and an apron, she threw ashes from the fire onto her flowerbed. 'Terrible weather,' she called out over the fence.

The passing years had shrunken the 82-year-old and her head seemed too big for her tiny body. Josh knew Mrs Adamski was 82 because she usually shoehorned it into every conversation. He smiled and waited.

'Eee, this weather's not good for me old bones. I'm 82 you know,' said Mrs Adamski straightening up.

'Yes, I know you're 82, Mrs Adamski,' said Josh hiding his irritation. 'I'd get back inside and keep warm if I were you.'

He went inside before his neighbour could engage him in further conversation, and went straight to the kitchen to get a beer. Josh noticed that the lights in the living room were on, which he thought strange. His wife usually worked late.

'I told you, I had the afternoon off. I went to see Gran at her shop,' said Brigid. She was sitting on the sofa in her pyjamas. The wood-burning stove had been lit. The vibrant orange flames crackled silently behind the glass door.

'Not that nutty old witch,' Josh muttered under his breath. He didn't believe in alternative remedies, ghosts or any new age crap. But Brigid did, and he adored her and was prepared to overlook his wife's illogical beliefs.

8

Brigid heard his comment and told him not to be rude about her grandmother, then added that she ached all over. But she didn't think it was flu, more likely lack of sleep.

'I keep telling you to go to bed earlier and stop watching Netflix,' said Josh. He sat down and loosened his much-hated tie. So much for trying to look smart for his interview at the pretentious social networking company. He shouldn't have bothered. The wankers.

Josh looked at Brigid. Her green eyes stared at him unflinching, honest and innocent. Her face was open, without guile, and her Celtic pale skin and long red hair made her look transparent and ghostly, almost elf like. Josh noticed that she seemed paler than usual and he frowned.

'Is anything wrong?' he asked. 'You look like you've seen a ghost. Oh God, you've not had another weird encounter, have you, Bridge?'

His wife had revealed her 'second sight' one night, when blind drunk. They'd been married for a couple of months but Brigid hadn't confessed to her secret sooner because she was afraid he'd dump her. Josh, though, wasn't that easily discouraged from the things he wanted.

Brigid shook her head, said no she hadn't seen anything odd and avoided talking about her gift as usual. She insisted she was just feeling peaky from a lack of sleep.

Josh felt his shoulders relax. His thoughts returned to his earlier worries about money, and how he needed to find a job soon or they would lose their home. He probably had another month before he ran out of funds, then the bank would start circling them like a shark. Sodding fucking hell.

Brigid asked how the interview went, Josh slowly shook

his head to indicate it was a disaster. Christ, why did he bother even turning up to these things? He was always interviewed by some half-wit at least ten years younger, or twenty years older, who he could wipe the floor with intellectually.

Brigid crashed his thoughts by telling him about the powerful herb her gran had given her to help her sleep. When his wife said the herb was effective, but potentially dangerous, she had his full attention.

'What's so dangerous about it?' Josh asked before taking a swig of his beer.

'The herb gives you a great night's sleep. I might take some tonight,' explained Brigid. 'But I have to be careful because too big a dose slows down the breathing so much you can appear dead.'

'Oh, come on. What like some tantric yogi?' Josh had to stifle a laugh. This was one of the reasons why he loved Brigid. His wife cracked him up even when he was feeling totally shit.

Brigid ignored his mocking tone and said the herb could make the body temperature drop dramatically and the skin turn deathly white. 'Years ago, people drank a brew made from the flower to fake death and escape marriages or duels.'

'When you were doing your internship at *Woman* magazine didn't you interview a woman who woke up in a body bag in an ambulance?' asked Josh.

'Yes, that's right. So you do listen to me,' Brigid said punching Josh's arm gently. 'She'd been in a car crash. Claimed she'd had a near-death experience and saw her dead father in a tunnel of light.'

Josh remembered laughing about that story. He couldn't

help himself and laughed again. Life after death. What a load of arse. 'God, you're nuts,' said Josh aloud as he kissed the end of Brigid's nose. 'So apparently, even in these days of modern medicine, mistakes can still happen. But you know me, I don't trust doctors, MPs, lawyers, bankers, the police...'

'Josh, you hate anyone in authority,' said Brigid rolling her eyes.

His wife dug out the crumpled white envelope from her handbag and showed its contents to Josh. They both recoiled from the herb's pungent smell. The whiff only lasted a few seconds, and after it had vanished just some dried up old flowers were left.

'What do you do with the herb?'

Brigid rattled off the instructions. Josh was always amazed by her sharp memory. His own short-term memory was practically shot due to his years of dope smoking.

'Guess what it's called?'

'I don't know. The black flower?' Josh said dramatically.

'Warmish,' said Brigid. Josh suggested the death flower, she said that was even warmer.

'The death petal. Like a flower version of death metal?' Josh could hardly get the words out for laughing. The idea of a plant being able to put you to sleep and make you seem dead was totally ridiculous.

Brigid laughed too. 'Don't be daft. It's called the Death Herb.'

'The Death Herb,' Josh repeated slowly. 'How very medieval.'

After a Chinese take-away and a box-set binge, the couple went to bed just before midnight. Josh took off his watch carefully and placed it on his bedside table whilst Brigid drank a mug of her grandmother's sleep remedy.

Brigid snuggled into Josh's chest but within minutes she was asleep. His wife then rolled onto her back and fell into a deep motionless slumber.

Josh whispered her name, which would normally have woken Brigid but there was no response. He was impressed. Too often his wife lay awake for hours fretting about money, or puppy farms, or the destruction of the Amazon Rainforest. She was too sensitive for her own good. But since Brigid wasn't doing any worrying tonight he would instead, they were in a very worrying situation. They were drowning in debts and his redundancy money had practically run out. A fact he had kept from Brigid.

Frankly, they were in the sea and clinging to the lifeboat with wet fingertips.

Whilst Brigid continued to sleep like the dead, an idea came into Josh's mind. It involved the Death Herb and an insurance pay off. It might be illegal but they wouldn't be hurting anyone just taking money from a greedy bank who, everyone knew, only made its millions in profits by exploiting their customers.

As he lay in bed in the dark, Josh wondered if Brigid would be willing to go ahead with the idea. Was it too crazy to contemplate? He knew that even though he hated authority, she always toed the line. But she might be willing to do it for him? For both of them? Would she?

Josh totted up their debts. They both had overdrafts of about £1.5k each, which meant any income disappeared on the day it arrived in the account. Brigid owed £23k in student loans. His own student debts were higher and currently stood at £33k. Brigid owed around £17k on two credit cards whilst he was at least £11k in credit card debt and had a £12k personal loan – not counting that month's astronomical interest charges.

A quick mental calculation revealed their debt was approximately £99k. And that was without the mortgage. Christ.

A stab of horror pierced Josh's stomach. He whispered the figure in the dark. *Ninety-nine thousand.* It equalled their remaining mortgage.

How did this happen? They rarely went on holiday and seldom bought new clothes or even ate out. But he had bought a car, they had renovated the house and they did eat a lot of takeaways. Not to mention they were saddled with crippling student debts before they'd even entered the working world.

Quickly, Josh totted up the cash they could raise if they pulled off the scam. There were the two life insurance policies worth £320,000 together. The mortgage life insurance would clear the mortgage meaning the £220,000 or so from the sale of house would go to them. All in all, they could pocket around £540,000. A fortune.

They could pay off all of their debts in one go and be free of the stress of money worries forever, Brigid's debt would be written off and his could easily be paid off with the insurance money. They could start afresh. The figures rolled around in Josh's head until he dozed off.

Josh woke up in the early hours and shifted his position gently in bed not wanting to disturb Brigid. His crazy idea floated to the front of his mind and he thought about the sum of cash. Was it worth risking prison? And which one of them would fake their death?

After a moment of thought, he knew it would have to be Brigid. His wife was so honest that she wouldn't be able to lie and tell everyone he had died.

His Omega told him it was 4.44am. Josh rolled over and thought what his father, a retired tailor, would say if he found out that his son was in so much debt. He would be horrified.

But Josh had needed to take out the student loans to pay for his fees and his digs and all the other invisible things that suck money from your bank account. Then there was the issue of his credit card debt and loan – he'd spent most of his cash on renovating their house. They'd been so excited when Brigid had moved in with him three years ago. They married a few weeks later at Gretna Green telling everyone they didn't want a fuss, but really it was because they couldn't afford a big wedding.

In the dark, Josh listened to Brigid's soft breathing beside him and changed his focus to her instead of thinking about their money problems. He loved her red hair. Her laugh. Her devotion to animals. Her kind personality. Her tits. He adored everything about her. His dad was right – his wife was bloody fantastic. He knew that Brigid made him a better man. She shaved off his hard edges and her bright personality made up for his dreadful social skills. He couldn't be arsed whereas Brigid befriended people so quickly and effortlessly.

He glanced at his watch again. The illuminated hands showed 5am.

Josh placed his palm lightly on Brigid's shoulder. His long fingers touched her cotton t-shirt, the heat of her skin radiated out from the fabric. He left his hand there only for a moment, careful not to disturb her. But whilst his body was still his mind jumped ahead with a jumble of figures. There was no doubting the maths, if they could pull off an insurance scam it would be life-changing.

The odds of winning the lottery jackpot stood at 1 in 45,057,474. This plan had much better odds. Yes, there were variables that could affect the outcome, but when it came down to basic maths it was a fifty-fifty chance. They either pulled the plan off or they didn't. They either got caught or they didn't.

Then he told himself not to be so bloody stupid. It was a crazy idea. Although he had to do something to get them out of this financial mess. But what?

Brigid

The letter box clunked and a fan of envelopes landed on the doormat. Brigid flicked through the post quickly and spotted a letter from her bank, immediately she felt apprehension.

Reading her credit card statement, Brigid was horrified to see that she was only £250 off her limit. The bank had already told her that they would not extend her credit. Brigid read through the list again. Maybe some of the charges were a mistake and she could claim them back? But sadly, upon scrutiny Brigid could see that every item was correct.

There were no big purchases but numerous small payments under £40. All of them necessary items like supermarket shops and her bus pass. Brigid sat down on the bottom step, stared at the bill and felt her stomach churning.

She had two credit cards and the other card had reached its limit. Every month all of Brigid's spare money went on trying to pay off her debts, which often meant putting more items on her card. Watching her salary being swallowed up by an overdraft each payday was disheartening; it was a vicious circle.

Shaking herself out of the creeping depression, Brigid went upstairs to finish getting ready for work. Josh had already left the house. He was travelling to Manchester for a job interview at a tech start up.

'I hope he gets this job,' Brigid thought as she pulled on her tweed coat and yawned. She'd had another sleepless night. She was trying not to rely on the Death Herb, instead saving it for when she was totally exhausted. In the last twelve days, she'd only used the herb twice and it had worked a treat both times.

The morning flew by at work and just after lunch, Brigid's bank called her about her credit card debt. She fobbed them off with a promise of an extra payment at the end of next month, but heaven knew how she'd find the extra cash. Take out a payday loan?

At three o'clock a feature had fallen through so she quickly knocked up 900-words on dental care for dogs to fill the gaping hole. She gave the piece the headline 'All White Now' and the geeky subeditor had rolled his eyes at the pun. Brigid retorted, 'Any better ideas, sunshine?' which shut him up.

Before she managed to get another article finished, it was five-thirty and time for her meeting with her editor, Charlie Barrington. Brigid wove her way through the maze of desks that filled the open plan office saying hi to the teams in art and advertising as she passed.

Inside Charlie's office, magazines and newspapers were piled up on the editor's desk and a Barbour was slung over the only spare chair. Brigid hesitated before sitting down.

'Sorry, I'll take that manky old thing,' Charlie said stretching out her hand for the jacket.

The *Canine World* editor was in her mid-fifties with wild white hair and had an encyclopaedic knowledge of dogs. Rags, her ancient Jack Russell, snoozed under her desk.

'Right, ah yes. Performance review,' Charlie began, hanging the coat on the back of her chair. 'I'm really pleased with your work. So much so that I've created a new post for you. Deputy Editor. You will be my second in command.'

Without hesitating, Brigid grinned. 'That's fantastic news. Yes, I accept. Thank you.' A thought occurred to Brigid and trying not to sound too eager, she asked, 'How much is my

17

pay rise?'

With a nervous smile Charlie said, 'Sorry, I need to confess, Brigid. I can't pay you any more at the moment. I know I should, it's embarrassing, but advertising sales have been down again this quarter.' Charlie's computer pinged and the editor sighed as she opened the email. She typed a quick response with two stubby fingers. 'Brigid, sorry, that was the publisher breathing down my neck as usual. Okay, so the plan is that you do more of the celeb interviews, it will look good for your cuttings, and you can take on the hotel reviews. Who doesn't like a nice freebie? You can also have more input on the features. All good solid journalist skills.'

Brigid tried to smile, but found she couldn't hide her disappointment. 'It's a great opportunity, thank you,' she said flatly. 'Who knows? The sales might pick up.'

'Let's hope so or we might all be out of a job,' Charlie said, already focused on her screen. She glanced up to see Brigid still sitting there and said softly, 'Look, we can review the situation in a few months, I promise. If I can increase your salary I will.'

Brigid nodded, the meeting was clearly over. As she left she said, 'Thanks again for the opportunity. I'm really pleased.'

Back at her desk, Brigid thought, 'I will get that pay rise. I'm going to come up with some cracking ideas. I'll start tomorrow.'

It was time to head to the local animal shelter as she always did on a Thursday afternoon.

Hours later when Brigid walked into The Turk's Head, an 18th Century pub in Leeds city centre, she knew that she smelt of dogs but didn't care. She'd spent the last few hours cleaning out kennels and washing a mountain of dog beds and blankets. The hard work had helped to keep her mind off her financial issues, and her sort-of promotion.

One Staffordshire Bull Terrier, Georgie, a sweet little thing, had arrived at the rescue centre that day with fresh cigarette burns on her face. It was inhumane and upset Brigid terribly. She knew that unfortunately such cruelty wasn't an unusual occurrence. Brigid wished that she could click her fingers and make all animal abusers disappear into an abyss.

'I ordered you a double bourbon,' said Josh as Brigid sat down. Her husband had changed out of his interview suit and was wearing a blue jumper that made his sea-blue eyes pop.

The bar was busy considering it was a Thursday. Brigid had a soft spot for the place. The Turk's Head was where she had met Josh five years ago today, and so here they were celebrating. They didn't make a fuss about their wedding anniversary, which was in June. To them it was that first meeting that mattered.

Tonight the pub was decorated with carved pumpkins and fake spiders. Brigid had always loved Halloween, the time when the veils between the living and the dead were the thinnest, because people were more inclined to talk about ghosts; and although she never joined in the discussions, it made her feel less like a freak.

'How did the interview go?' asked Brigid. She shrugged off her shabby tweed coat and placed it on the back of her chair.

'They gave it to someone with more experience.'

Her husband forced a smile and Brigid reached over

the table to touch his hand. 'It's because there's a better job waiting for you.' She looked at her drink. 'Maybe we should economise a bit, cut down our spending. No more doubles.'

A flash of anger appeared in Josh's eyes. Her husband hated to be reminded that they were struggling, but she knew that his rage wasn't directed at her. It was their situation that bothered him. She kissed him on the cheek and his face softened. But she couldn't stop that sinking feeling in her stomach and the words tumbled out of her mouth, 'That job did seem like a dead cert though.'

'I know. I thought so too. Something will come up,' said Josh taking a slug of his whisky.

'But what if it doesn't?' Brigid asked, unable to stop herself. She wanted to console him, not make him feel worse, but the panic was rising in her body. 'I'm barely keeping up with my credit card payments. What if we lose the house?' Brigid heard her voice going up a notch and she took a deep breath to calm down. She didn't want to have an asthma attack, especially in the pub. She fished out her Ventolin inhaler from her bag and took two quick puffs.

Josh squeezed her hand and she felt calmer.

'I don't want to be homeless either, Brigid,' said Josh lowering his voice. 'But let's just enjoy tonight. It's our anniversary. We can talk about money tomorrow. Okay? Besides, I'm working on a plan.'

'Plan? You're not going to win the lottery so stop having that stupid fantasy,' Brigid said crossing her arms. 'We need to deal with our situation like adults. Tell our banks we're struggling.'

Josh's eyes narrowed, 'Brigid, you do not under any

circumstances tell your bank that you're struggling to pay the mortgage or debts. The house is our biggest asset. They'll take it away if they get a whiff of trouble. And the house could be the answer to our problems. Think about it.'

Brigid stuttered, 'Sell the house? Never.'

'Yes, sell the house.' Josh ran a hand through his thick dark hair and took a deep breath. 'Look, there's enough equity to pay off all of our debt and the mortgage, leaving us with just under £20k after estate agent and solicitor fees. We can move into a rented place while I focus on getting a job and we wait for your salary to increase and we can start saving for a house again.'

Brigid shook her head slowly. She didn't like the idea at all. Josh continued outlining his latest plan adding he wasn't going to tell her any of this until tomorrow, but his estate agent friend Henry had already valued their home.

'The house went on Rightmove today,' said Josh bluntly. 'I was going to see what kind of offers we received.'

'What the hell, Josh? How could you?' Brigid threw her hands up in disbelief. She was furious. This was a big decision and they were supposed to be a married couple who decided things together. Brigid felt betrayed. 'You are out of order putting the house up for sale without asking me first.'

'Calm down,' hissed Josh. 'If you think about it rationally this is the best way out of our situation. Don't you agree?' Without waiting for a reply, he stood up. 'I'm going outside for a cigarette. Have a look on your laptop at the listing, you'll be able to see the photos better. Tell me what you think when I come back.'

Josh avoided Brigid's glare as he picked up his coat. The bloody idiot. Her hands were shaking. Her home. Her beautiful home. How could he?

As Josh disappeared outside Brigid dug around in her handbag for her laptop's charger. She plugged in her ancient Mac and logged on to the pub's Wi-Fi. The estate agent's listing of their lovely home was easy to find.

'A truly impressive three-bed Victorian terrace with a small garden to the front and a larger garden to the rear. The property ticks many boxes and boasts a lovely mixture of contemporary living and original features. The accommodation comprises: reception hall, sitting room with original fireplace and wood-burning stove, dining kitchen with integrated appliances, first floor landing, three bedrooms and a bathroom.'

In the photos, their home looked bright and spacious. She felt like weeping. Brigid clicked onto another page and looked at the houses for rent. There was nothing decent in the area that didn't cost a fortune. Nothing. She clicked out of the estate agent's website and checked her bank account. It was even worse than she thought.

Josh reappeared and ordered another round of doubles. Brigid was too deflated to argue about the cost. Despite his nonchalant attitude, Brigid could see that her husband was vexed. He stood at the bar rubbing the side of his face with his palm. This non-verbal tick only appeared when he was anxious. She was really scared too. Her stomach felt like it was on fire.

'So, what do you think of the listing?' Josh asked as he handed her another drink.

'It's good but I don't want to sell our house. There must be another way out of our problem?' Brigid's voice trailed off. She felt broken and down-hearted. Her beautiful home was the one place she felt totally safe from the world. 'Can we go home after these drinks?' she asked feeling another fiery wave of fear wash over her.

Josh said okay and kissed Brigid on the lips. He tasted of whisky. Pulling away, he added, 'Henry just called me, when I was outside.'

'What did he say?' she asked.

'No interest yet. And his bloody boss says he's overvalued the house. He needs to knock at least ten grand off the price.' Josh rubbed the side of his face. 'Shit, I need another stiff drink or I'll never sleep.'

Brigid knew how he felt, she didn't think she'd get any sleep without some herbal help tonight. But her gran's advice was sound, as usual. She did need to sort out the cause and not the symptoms of her insomnia. And in that moment, as much as she hated to admit that Josh was right, their best and only hope out of this dreadful situation was to sell the house and use the equity to pay off as much of their debts as possible.

'There is another way,' said Josh moving closer to Brigid and talking in a hushed tone. 'We could pull off an insurance scam.'

'What?' Brigid said shocked. 'Commit fraud? Are you insane? I'm not a criminal. I drive at 25 miles per hour in a 30.'

'Hear me out, it's just an idea. We use the herb your gran gave you. We make it strong enough to make you appear… you know. Then we have an open coffin. Once everyone believes you're dead, I'll fill it with wood. Then we have a cremation.'

'Josh, that's a ludicrous idea.' Brigid finished her drink and put the glass down on the stained wooden table. What

23

was Josh thinking by coming up with such a bloody crazy scheme? He really was an idiot sometimes.

'Just listen. You hide out in the house until…'

'No, I won't listen. It's insane. You're insane.' Brigid was laughing now. 'Have you completely lost the plot?'

'It could work. Why not? You hide out in the house for a few months. Meanwhile, I collect the insurance money. Simple.'

Wanting to lift the mood on their disastrous anniversary, Brigid played along. 'Okay, so we collected the insurance money, and buy a house by the seaside. A cottage perched high on a cliff top overlooking the sea.'

Josh nodded and agreed, so Brigid kept going with the fantasy. She didn't believe that Josh was being serious.

'We could even get a dog,' said Josh, animated. For the next ten minutes they talked about their imaginary life and Josh explained his plan in more detail.

'So why do I have to be the one that dies?' Brigid asked playfully. 'You've way more experience of taking drugs and passing out in a coma.'

'Because it's easier to change your appearance,' Josh replied quickly. 'Women can cut and dye their hair. Wear make-up. Me? I'm stuck with my square jaw and it's a choice between a mullet or a crew cut. And darling, I am not changing my identity by sporting the hairstyle of a 1980s footballer. It's no contest I'm afraid, Bridge.' Josh leant back in his chair and added seriously, 'We just have to make it through the initial few months and hold our nerve.'

'But I've only been playing along,' Brigid said wide-eyed with disbelief. 'There's no way I could commit fraud and walk away from my friends. From my life. It's a stupid idea.

We need to deal with our debts like adults not criminals.'

'If we can't sell the house our only other option is to go bankrupt,' Josh said bluntly. 'But that would mean losing the house completely. And lose our credit rating. I'd never get a job in anything connected to finance ever again.'

'But we're not at that place yet, are we?' Brigid felt sick. If only she had a better paid job. If only Josh hadn't lost his job. If only, if only. Suddenly, selling the house didn't seem like such a terrible idea.

Her husband finished his whisky and wiped his mouth with the back of his hand. 'If we miss payments and the house is repossessed it's going to take us thirty years to pay off our credit cards and student loans. That's provided I get a decent job and we don't run up further debts. I'll be subscribing to sodding Saga magazine by then.'

'Josh, we've got to do *something*. My bank rang me at work today to talk about my credit cards. They want me to go in to discuss a payment plan. But I don't earn enough to pay the £250 a month they're asking for.'

'I'm sorry,' Josh said with a sigh. 'I wish I were earning so this wasn't all such a big problem.'

Brigid picked her thumb and said, 'Oh Josh, we're going to end up living in a hell hole.' She felt a lump of fear fall into the pit of her stomach. 'I need to go home. I'm sorry but I'm not in the mood for celebrating,' said Brigid holding back the tears.

As she stood up, and put on her tweed coat, one of her buttons fell off onto the floor. Josh bent to pick it up.

'Bloody leave it. I look like a tramp anyway,' Brigid muttered.

The couple headed home on the bus. As they rounded

the bottom of their street they saw two fire engines parked at the top. A police car and an ambulance were also at the scene.

'I wonder whose house is on fire,' said Josh as they walked towards the crowd of onlookers.

Some people say that time slows down when you're faced with a catastrophic event, and that's exactly what happened to Brigid. She saw their neighbour Mrs Adamski walking towards them in slow motion at the exact moment it registered that their home was the one ablaze.

Turning her head slowly away from her neighbour and Josh, Brigid watched the flames that were forcing themselves out of their roof and windows. The fire's orange and yellow tongues were beautifully primeval. Long whispers of flame and smoke danced seductively in all directions jutting out into the night sky.

Mrs Adamski's lips were moving but Brigid couldn't hear a single word. She was totally focused on the flames. They were stunning. She'd never seen such a wild fire so close and the high temperature was astounding and unexpected. Brigid had to turn her face away from the scalding heat but within seconds she felt compelled to turn back and stare at the raging flames burning down her lovely home.

Brigid looked at Mrs Adamski and said slowly, 'My home…' The rest of the sentence wouldn't come out of her mouth. She was mute with shock.

'I know, love. But it's just a house. At least you weren't inside,' Mrs Adamski said while putting a blanket around Brigid's shoulders.

Still stunned Brigid asked, 'Is your house okay?'

'Pah, it's time I downsized anyway. I'm 82. And I'm

insured with the Co-op, they'll see me right. Come on, love.' Her neighbour steered Brigid towards the steps of an ambulance.

Brigid was still in a daze, 'Where's Josh?' She felt like a robot.

'He's talking to the police,' said Mrs Adamski. 'Drink your tea. The sugar will help with the shock.'

The old woman lowered herself slowly onto the ambulance's steps and patted Brigid's hand. A paramedic with long grey hair tied back in a ponytail handed Brigid a hot mug of milky tea, one of the neighbours must have made it. The sugar kicked in quickly and Brigid returned from her daze and said thank you, pulling the blanket more tightly around herself.

'Do you have anywhere you can kip tonight?' Mrs Adamski asked concerned. 'I'm going to my sister's flat in Morley. I'd take you and Josh but she only has one-bedroom and...'

'I'm so sorry about your home,' said Brigid turning to face her neighbour. 'I really am truly sorry.' Brigid was starting to take in the stark horror of what was happening around her. Her house was burning down.

'Don't worry,' said Mrs Adamski. 'I'm still here. Worse things happened when I was a nipper. So, where will you sleep tonight?'

'My mother's house,' said Brigid in a monotone. She hadn't visited her mother for over a year but given the late hour she had no other place to go. They couldn't afford a pricey city centre hotel and booking an Airbnb was out of the question at this late hour.

'Right then,' said Mrs Adamski. 'Josh can drive you in

that old banger of his.'

Brigid explained they'd been to the pub and Josh was over the limit. Mrs Adamski tutted and said one of the neighbours could take them. She stood up slowly to organise a lift. The elderly woman wasn't wearing her obligatory headscarf, a sure sign she'd left her house in a hurry.

'Don't leave,' Brigid said grabbing Mrs Adamski's arm. Her chest was tight and she began to gasp for breath. She fumbled in her bag for her inhaler.

Mrs Adamski sat back down next to her and pulled the blanket up around Brigid's shoulders. 'There now, pet. I'm staying right here.'

'I'll get a taxi to my mother's.' Brigid realized that her whole body was shaking under the blanket. Her worst fear had manifested. She was homeless.

About half an hour later, the firemen got the flames under control and the crowd began to drift away. Once the flames were completely extinguished, black smoke continued to pour out of the gaping holes that were once beautiful wooden sash windows. Brigid had stopped shaking, but still felt overwhelmed with the shock of her home being destroyed. She wiped the tears from her cheeks and scanned the street for Josh. He was heading towards her with a young policeman.

'I'm sorry, Mrs Raven, but your house is not going to be safe to live in. Not for some time,' said the officer.

Then it hit her. Everything she and Josh owned was gone. All they had to their names were the clothes they were wearing plus her laptop and their mobile phones. It was a hard concept to process.

'What started it?' Brigid asked the policeman still shaking

with shock.

It was the obvious question. The policeman said he wasn't sure but it could have been arson or it could have been some kind of electrical fault.

'What?' Brigid was stunned. Someone might have deliberately set fire to their lovely home? Who? They didn't have any enemies.

'It's late. Someone will contact you tomorrow for a statement,' the policeman said putting his notebook in his pocket. 'Do you have somewhere you can sleep tonight? The locksmiths have been called to board up the doors and windows. I'm afraid that you won't be allowed access until the property has been inspected.'

'They're staying with family,' butted in Mrs Adamski.

'We're not going to Chapeltown,' Josh said crossing his arms. 'No way.'

'We can't afford a hotel,' said Brigid feeling utterly drained. 'Your parents are on holiday and it's too late to wake friends up. We're going to my mum's.'

Josh

The taxi stopped outside the terrace house in Chapeltown, Leeds, a mile north of the city centre. An old mattress, a fridge and sodden cardboard boxes were piled up in the middle of the property's patchy lawn. However, the neighbouring houses were much smarter and the area had changed vastly since it had shot to fame in the 1970s - thanks to the Yorkshire Ripper and his killing spree.

Taking a deep breath, Josh stepped out of the taxi and put on his mental armour. It had been a quiet journey with few words spoken. What was there to say? They had lost their home and everything in it. They had nothing. They were homeless. Josh knew that Brigid's worst fear was playing out and he felt powerless to stop the events that were unfolding around them like a horror show. And to top it all, he was having to ask his mother-in-law, Mrs Doran, for help.

Josh despised his mother-in-law. He'd visited her house just once, early on in his relationship with Brigid. Afterwards, he'd vowed never to repeat the experience. Since then Josh had seen Mrs Doran only a handful of times when she'd turned up at their house to borrow money from his wife. The loans were never, ever, repaid.

'She's at home,' said Josh. He'd half-hoped the silly cow would be out so they wouldn't have to stay at her dump.

Brigid knocked loudly on the front door. As they waited for a response, Brigid picked the skin around her thumb and flinched as she dug too deep. A spot of blood appeared by her nail. She licked it away.

'Don't do that,' said Josh gently as Brigid went to pick at the skin again. He took her hand and squeezed it.

Before Brigid could make an excuse, the bedroom window was flung open and a woman's gravelly voice shouted down, 'Who is it?'

'It's me and Josh, Mum.' Brigid took a step back into the garden so her mother could see her face in the light of the street lamp.

'What do you want?' her mother asked in a shrill voice.

Brigid said firmly, 'Mum, can you let us in please. It's urgent. I'll explain inside.'

Without answering, Mrs Doran withdrew the top half of her body from the window and slammed it shut. Shortly afterwards, she appeared at the front door and asked impatiently, 'Well, are you coming in or not?'

Mrs Doran was wearing a pink silky nightdress and Josh had a flash of his mother-in-law's unappetising flesh. He felt slightly nauseated. The woman's revealing choice of clothing always had that effect on him.

Josh indicated for Brigid to go first. He knew Mrs Doran was frighteningly unsober, he could see it in her eyes.

'Ever the gentleman,' she cackled. She left her visitors standing at the front door and walked along the hall into the kitchen on the right.

The couple followed her into the hovel. In the harsh light, Josh noticed Mrs Doran's face looked more haggard than when he'd last seen her four months earlier. She'd turned up at their house on a Sunday afternoon asking for money. Despite Josh's stern advice, Brigid had given her mother a cheque for £100 just to get rid of her.

Mrs Doran sat at her kitchen table, a thin stream of smoke escaped from the end of a cigarette that dangled from her thin lips. The front of her dressing gown hung open. It showed off her scrawny body kept slim by nicotine and a lack of food. Josh averted his eyes from the repellent sight.

'What's the disaster?' Mrs Doran spoke with a faint Irish accent. Brigid's family were originally from Belfast and moved to Leeds when her mother was ten.

'Why would you think something bad has happened?' Josh asked aggressively. She was right, of course. They would only show up at this late hour in desperation. God, he needed a cigarette. He reached across Brigid and took one out of a packet that lay discarded on the table.

'Help yourself why don't you,' Mrs Doran said sarcastically. 'So,' she persisted, 'why did you two love birds fetch up at this hour? It wasn't for tea and scones.' She laughed briefly at her own wit but the laughter quickly turned into a hacking smoker's cough.

'Our house has burnt down,' Brigid said matter-of-factly. 'We've lost everything.'

'Is this a fecking joke?' Mrs Doran looked at Brigid and then at Josh.

'No, Mum, it's not a joke. We're homeless.'

'What the hell do you expect me to do about it?' Mrs Doran asked, suddenly defensive and angry. 'If you've come looking for money I don't have any.' She pulled her dressing gown around herself, picked up her packet of cigarettes and tucked them in a pocket. 'If you need money,' she nodded at Josh, 'Sunshine here can sell his posh watch.'

Josh took a drag of his cigarette and looked down. He hated being at the mercy of other people, especially someone like his mother-in-law. The silly bitch. How dare she tell him what to do? He could never fathom how his sweet, caring wife had come from the womb of such a vile woman.

'Mum, we've not come for money. We just need somewhere to stay for a few nights and…'

'Look at you, you don't have a pot to piss in,' said Mrs Doran shaking her head. She lit another cigarette. 'The big shot journalist.'

Josh saw with shock that his mother-in-law was buoyed up by their misfortune. He knew Brigid would be making a determined effort to keep herself under control, although more than anything he wanted to slap his mother-in-law. But he too had to keep his emotions in check. Of course he would never hit Mrs Doran.

Sensing his anger growing, Brigid touched Josh's left hand lightly under the table and held his fingers. His wife's touch was cool and comforting.

'Like I said, we don't want money, Mum. We just want somewhere to stay for a few days until we sort things out,' Brigid repeated calmly.

Mrs Doran took another long drag on her cigarette, then slowly blew smoke at them. 'I suppose you could stay in your old room. It's full of my clothes. I've been meaning to sort them out but you know how busy I am,' Mrs Doran said with a fake smile.

'Yes, I know you're very busy,' said Brigid pokerfaced. 'Thank you.'

'And what do you say?' Mrs Doran asked Josh.

The woman was enjoying her illicit moment of power. Josh could never understand what had prompted Mrs Doran to begin an unwritten competition with her own daughter. It was pathetic.

'Thanks, Mum,' Brigid said for him. 'You're really kind.' Brigid held her mother's gaze for so long that the woman looked away.

Under the table, Josh balled his fist. Brigid tapped his closed hand with a finger and he unfurled his palm and held her hand gently. He felt the quiet strength of their unity. Not even his wife's evil mother could break their bond.

'There's some blankets in the airing cupboard,' Mrs Doran said, apparently tiring of the conversation. 'Might not be up to your standard mind,' she said with another cackle. 'Right, I need my beauty sleep.'

Josh followed Brigid up the stairs, his nostrils filled with the stink of damp and bleach. Brigid left him standing in the doorway of her room while she found some sheets.

The room was musty smelling so Brigid dug out a small electric fan heater from the bottom of the wardrobe, blew off the dust and switched it on. 'I bought this heater with my paper round money. I used to plug it in when she went out. It stopped me from freezing to death.'

Josh took his coat off, unsure where to put it. He couldn't believe they were back in the house that his wife had grown up in. He looked around and saw the threadbare pink carpet and the film of dirt on the windows. The place made him feel unclean.

His wife took off her tweed coat and put it on a pile of bin bags stuffed full of clothes. He put his own coat with his wife's.

'My mother's summer wardrobe,' said Brigid wryly.

'Bridge, I'm so sorry,' said Josh stumbling over his words.

'The fire wasn't your fault,' said Brigid stuffing a grubby pillow into a threadbare pillowcase.

'I'm not talking about the fire, my love. I'm sorry about your terrible childhood.'

34

Brigid

'Brigid,' Josh whispered in the dark, 'are you awake?'

'Yes,' said Brigid who hadn't slept all night. She leaned over the side of the bed and found Josh's watch on the upturned box that was acting as a bedside table. It was 4.37am. 'It's early, Josh, go back to sleep.'

Brigid shifted onto her side in the single bed and tried to get comfortable, but it was impossible on such a small mattress. In the half-light, Brigid saw that her husband's face was turned towards her. She knew that his beautiful blue eyes would be watching her in the darkness.

'I can't sleep,' said Josh. 'Bridge, do you love me?' He sat up, then cupped her face with his hands.

'Yes, you know I do,' she said puzzled. 'Why are you asking?'

Josh's hands left her face. 'I need to know that you love me because I've been incredibly stupid.'

'What's happened?' Fear rose up in her body like a tidal wave threatening to drown her. 'What have you done?'

She turned on a battered angle poised lamp and looked at Josh in the yellow light. Her first thought was that Josh had been unfaithful. How could he? And how could he tell her now? Right after their house had burnt down?

Josh pushed himself up and wedged himself into the wall to give Brigid more space on the single bed. 'It's not what I've done,' said Josh avoiding her gaze. 'It's what I forgot to do.' He paused, then said in a rush, 'Bridge, I forgot to renew the buildings and contents insurance.'

'You forgot to renew the buildings and contents insurance,' Brigid repeated. It took a moment for the meaning of his

35

words to sink in. She sat bolt upright. 'So we're...' Her thoughts were racing around so fast she couldn't form the words.

'Not insured for the fire damage,' Josh said finishing her sentence. 'We really have lost everything. I'm so sorry. I messed up. I can't believe I did this and I'm so...'

'When did you remember this fact?' Brigid felt like she'd been hit by a bus. No wonder he was so quiet earlier. They were completely ruined financially. This situation was a total disaster. Apocalyptic.

'I called the insurers when you were talking to Mrs Adamski.'

Josh looked like a small boy who had been found doing something wrong. Brigid felt sorry for him and furious at the same time. 'Didn't the policy renew automatically by direct debit from your account?' she asked confused trying not to raise her voice. She didn't want her mother to hear them arguing.

'No. I cancelled the old one and organised a cheaper policy through a broker,' said Josh. 'I was trying to save us some money, but I was waiting to get a new job before returning the insurance documents.' He swallowed hard to regain his composure.

'Right,' said Brigid in a whisper. She felt sick. Her chest tightened and she flipped back the covers and found her inhaler on the box next to Josh's Omega. As she took a quick puff Brigid thought about how panicked she had been earlier by their financial mess. And yet just a few hours later they were in an even worse situation. 'Without the house, and equity, we won't be able to pay off our debts. I can't believe this is happening,' said Brigid collapsing back on the bed.

'I'm a stupid idiot.' Josh put his head in his hands and groaned, 'I'm so sorry, Bridge.' He didn't look up as he added, 'I wish I could turn back the clock and make this right. But I don't have magic powers. None of us do.'

Brigid turned to Josh pulling his hands from his face. 'People forget to do things. It's okay. We'll just have to sell the house and use whatever we get to put towards our debts and…'

'Brigid,' Josh interrupted quietly, 'the house is practically worthless. But we'll still have to pay the mortgage for another 18 years. We are never going to be free from debt. Ever. We will spend the rest of our lives working to pay off our loans and a mortgage on a house we don't own. Then at the end, say in 40 years, we'll have nothing to show for it. Zilch.'

'Oh,' said Brigid. 'I see.' She was suddenly furious that Josh made such a stupid mistake.

She turned and looked out of the window at the moon, which hung low and bright, and fought back tears. The last time she'd cried properly was when she was nine years old. Her mother had given her cat away without telling her because it was too expensive to look after.

'There is one way out of this mess,' said Josh.

'What's that?' asked Brigid confused. With the house gone they had no options.

'The Death Herb,' whispered Josh. 'We have two life insurance policies that will pay out. And your death will trigger the mortgage policy. Clear the remaining mortgage debt.'

Brigid stared wordlessly at Josh. She chewed her lip and wondered if he was losing it. It must be the shock. It was a mad idea. She'd already told him as much in the pub. No

37

one had used the herb to fake their death for a hundred years, according to her gran. Who knew if the current strain of herb was even powerful enough to put a person into a deep coma?

'I promise if the herb doesn't work we'll forget the whole thing,' said Josh reading Brigid's mind. 'We'll declare ourselves bankrupt. It's our only other option.'

Still Brigid didn't say anything. She couldn't quite take in what was happening. It was 5am, she was in her childhood bed at her mother's house and her beautiful home had just burnt down. She was thousands of pounds in debt and earnt peanuts. She had no way of paying off her loans unless she sold her body. And she would do anything other than that. She wasn't going to follow her mother into the family business.

'Brigid, we're homeless. We're never going to get out of this debt. Our lives are over unless we take control,' said Josh echoing her thoughts. 'And we have to take control. I'm fed up of being pushed around by the banks, the money lenders. The wankers who make millions off working people like us who no matter what we do can never get ahead. Never.'

'I'm just thinking about the fraud. The implications. It's a bloody stupid idea, Josh.'

Josh shrugged his shoulders, 'It's not that stupid. It could work.'

'You're mad. And on top of that,' said Brigid, 'you're asking me to become a criminal. That's crossing a line that you can't come back from. And besides, I'm not leaving my gran. She's old, Josh, and she only has me. I can't do it.'

Josh

Four days after the fire, Josh and Brigid were still at her mother's house and still out of options. An officer had taken statements from them both, but the cause of the fire was still unknown. If the fire was arson, the police didn't appear hopeful they would catch whoever had destroyed their home. Josh could see that his wife was in a daze. She would be doing okay, doing something normal like the washing up, when suddenly she'd have to sit down as she realised, again, that her lovely home had burnt down.

When she glazed over, Brigid would take a few deep breaths and push herself to come back to reality. Force herself to continue with the mundane task. He could see the struggle in her body. His wife had stopped smiling and her shoulders had developed a slight stoop as if a heavy weight were resting on her back.

He felt the same burden on his own shoulders. Though his strain was caused by shame and hate for himself. What a mess. How could he have put off renewing the insurance? His reasoning that nothing bad had happened in the previous year, so a few months without insurance wouldn't hurt, seemed absurd now. That one little decision had altered the course of their lives in a huge way. Christ, he was stupid. Why didn't he just think? When it mattered the most he hadn't considered the possible consequences. This mess was all his fault and he had to put it right. He sighed and lit a cigarette.

Brigid was at her gran's flat having a hot bath and his mother-in-law was out somewhere. The house was empty and freezing. He had tried to light the gas fire in the kitchen but the meter must have run out. It was a long time since he'd stayed in a house that was so dilapidated. Wherever he looked something needed fixing or painting. The place was a dump. It was only a step-up from a squat. Sadly, the rentals in their price range were not much better and only a few streets away from Mrs Doran, which was way too close for his liking.

He knew that Brigid also hated the thought of living near her mother. Last night in bed she'd told Josh that she saw her mother's darkness seeping out of the house like black smoke, curling through the air and infecting the homes around it. He'd hugged her and said they were lucky to have somewhere to stay at all. There were growing numbers of people in Leeds, and other cities and towns around the UK, who didn't have a roof over their heads.

'There'll be a catch later. My mother never does anything out of kindness,' Brigid had whispered back in the darkness.

His mother-in-law was vile but at least she hadn't turned them away. His own parents were still on holiday, and he felt too ashamed to try and contact them to ask to stay at their house, and besides he didn't have a key.

Josh lit another cigarette and with the match still smouldering between his fingers he traced a circle on the sticky kitchen table. He mused about how much one event could tip you into a life you never imagined. Or wanted.

'If there is a God, help us to escape,' he said loudly. His words formed a cloud of white breath in the still room. 'Come on, you fucker, show me that you exist.'

Brigid

'It's not that bad,' said Josh looking out into the alley below.

He opened the bedroom window, lit a cigarette and blew the smoke out into the cold.

The freezing November air rushed into the room in an icy welcome.

'There's hardly any furniture and this light doesn't work,' said Brigid flicking the switch on and off. 'And I bet the boiler's crap.'

Unlike Josh, Brigid hated everything about their new house. The rental was dank and cold, and had a basement kitchen with woodlice in the corners. She was grateful that Josh's parents had lent them the money for the deposit and first three months' rent, but this new place wasn't much of an improvement on her mother's hovel.

Upstairs there was a bedroom and bathroom. The attic had been converted into a second bedroom but Brigid doubted it would pass building regulations. The woodchip walls had all been painted white recently but the brown carpets still sported stains, especially in the living room.

Josh threw his stub out the window and said brightly, 'At least we're not sleeping on the streets. Or still at your mother's. Let's get unpacked.'

The couple had spent the last few hours buying basics like clothes, towels and bedlinen.

As Brigid sorted through the shopping bags her mobile rang. It was Josie Augur, her closest friend who she'd met on her induction day five years ago at The Northern Magazines Company. Josie was 29 years old, slim, blonde and the exact opposite to Brigid who saw herself as a podgy Celtic redhead. But despite her good looks, Josie wasn't arrogant. She had a pure heart and was hyper-intelligent.

'Guess what? I'm *Vogue*'s new wellbeing editor,' said Josie in a rush. She currently worked on *Mind, Body Spirit Today* and was the deputy editor.

Brigid was taken aback by her friend's startling career leap. 'That's great news, you dark horse,' she said genuinely pleased. 'Did you wear your lucky crystal necklace? The one you found in Ibiza?'

'I did and the editor admired it, asked me where I'd bought it.'

'Get you. Why didn't you tell me you were going for the interview?' Brigid was slightly hurt that her friend had kept the secret from her. Usually they shared everything, good and bad.

'Sorry. I didn't want to jinx the job by blabbing.'

Brigid heard Josie's nervous laugh and forgave her friend immediately. 'I know what you mean. Tempting fate and all that. When do you start?'

Josie said she was leaving in two weeks, her editor was letting her go early. 'But I feel bad about moving to London when you're in crisis. You've just lost your home. I could stay a bit longer?'

'Go. We have a roof over our heads,' Brigid insisted as she sat on the saggy bed provided by the landlord. 'We moved in today. It's not that bad.' She hated lying to her friend. But she knew Josie would only worry about her otherwise.

'That's great. It will soon feel cosy.'

'I've called worse places home. I lived with my mother for seventeen years remember? Do you have time to meet up before you go?'

'I'm sorry, I don't. I have to work late to get ahead for the new deputy, get some copy in the bag so they're not left in the lurch. Then I need to go down to London to find somewhere to live, come back to pack and move. But I'll be back up north in a month or so and we can go out then.'

Brigid was disappointed but didn't say so, she didn't want to guilt-trip Josie into making time to see her. A small part of her wished it was her moving to London to start afresh, but she kept that thought to herself and instead told Josie, 'Yes, lovely, let's meet up when you come back.'

By six in the evening, Josh was cooking pasta in the basement kitchen and Brigid was running a bath. She had been right about the boiler – it had chugged out just enough hot water to fill a third of the stained metal tub before going cold.

She lowered herself into the lukewarm water, which barely covered her body. There was no central heating so the bathroom was freezing. Brigid could see clouds of her breath in the air around her face. But in spite of the lack of creature comforts, she did feel grateful to no longer be at her mother's house. Quite frankly, anywhere else was a bonus.

The shrill tone of her mobile made her jump, and she fumbled over the side of the bath for a towel to dry her hands before grabbing it from the toilet seat. Brigid was expecting the call to be from Josie, perhaps she'd found some time for them to meet after all? Sadly, no, she saw her mother's name flash up on the screen instead.

For a moment, Brigid hesitated then she realised the call had to be important because her mother never rang her. Brigid took a deep breath and tapped on the green arrow.

'Your gran. She's dead,' said Mrs Doran bluntly. 'One of the neighbours found her on the kitchen floor.'

There was no preamble. No tone of comfort. Her mother's words were harsh and cold. The two women had never got on and Mrs Doran's dislike of her mother-in-law was apparent in her tone.

Brigid sat up and shivered in the bath. 'What happened? How long had she been lying there?' The thought of her kind grandmother suffering alone, in pain, filled Brigid with anguish. She didn't deserve to die that way.

'A few hours. She had a stroke, most likely,' said Mrs Doran still speaking bluntly.

Despite her shock, Brigid teased out more details from her mother. A neighbour had popped round for tea, found the shop empty, gone upstairs and discovered her gran on the kitchen floor unconscious but breathing. An ambulance had been called but she died on the way to the hospital.

Shivering uncontrollably, Brigid couldn't bear to speak to her mother any longer. 'I've got to go, I'm in the middle of something,' she said. 'I'll call you about the funeral.'

Brigid put her phone back on top of the toilet seat and pulled her knees up to her chest in the now cold water. All she could think about were her gran's warm hands.

As a child, those gentle hands had plaited her hair, washed her school uniform, made her Bakewell tart that she'd eaten by a glowing coal fire. The fire at her gran's home was always a treat because after her dad died, when Brigid was nine, the gas and electric meters were always running out at her house. With Gran beside her, though, Brigid had been able to navigate through her childhood safely.

As the first tears formed and fell, Brigid hid her face with her hands and wished she'd been able to say goodbye and tell her gran how much she loved her. The woman's care had shielded her from neglect and her mother's rages. For her kindness, Brigid would be forever grateful.

'Why did it have to be Gran?' Brigid thought. 'Why couldn't you have taken my bloody mother instead?'

Inside her chest, Brigid felt a small ball of anger unfurl and burst open. Besides Josh and Josie, her gran was the only other person she truly cared about. Now it was just her and Josh against the world and the anger moved up her throat and burst out of her mouth.

'Fuck it!' shouted Brigid as she pulled out the bath plug. 'Fuck it all!'

Josh

The funeral for Diana took place on a Thursday afternoon. It was a sombre affair at the crematorium with only a handful of people, mostly elderly. Afterwards the mourners gathered at a nearby pub for a quiet wake.

Brigid had held up well during the service until the final hymn when slow tears had run down her face.

Josh had come prepared. He provided a fresh tissue for his wife and she'd taken it with a sweet smile that made his heart ache.

Surprisingly, Mrs Doran had turned up to the service. But immediately Josh had suspected is was only to borrow money from her daughter.

At the wake his suspicions were confirmed. He watched Brigid fish a £5 note out of her purse over the crab sandwiches. The bitch had been borrowing money from his wife since her first paper-round. Josh felt a flare of anger rise up, but he knew it wasn't the place or the time to vent it.

Back in their cold house, he hung up his cheap black suit, which he'd bought two days before, and had a fleeting image of pushing his mother-in-law down the stairs and her laying at the bottom in a crumpled heap with her neck broken. Shocked at how quickly the thought had taken form, he shook his head. Josh was appalled with himself. He wasn't a murderer. The idea was abhorrent and just plain wrong.

Yes, he despised Mrs Doran but he'd never actually kill the woman.

The disturbing thought was not something that he would mention to Brigid, and it wasn't the first dark idea that had crept into his mind over the last few weeks. He was afraid she would start looking at him differently, and what his wife thought of him was one of the things that mattered most to Josh. When he'd first met Brigid that night in the Turk's Head he'd been lost in a fog of dope, drifting through his life. His wife had changed everything. Nothing would ever turn his head away from her. Nothing.

Brigid was in the bathroom brushing her teeth. He heard her spit into the sink.

The house was freezing because the boiler had gone on the blink. They'd had no hot water or heating for 48 hours, not ideal in November. Sadly, the landlord didn't appear to be in a rush to get the issue fixed either. The attic room was the warmest space in the house, so with some difficulty the couple had already dragged the double mattress up the steep stairs and were now camped out on the top floor.

Josh checked that the attic's skylight was shut properly and threw a second blanket on the bed. It was going to be another chilly night.

Brigid

'We can't live this way, Josh. We're decent, good people. It's not fair.' Brigid took a puff of her inhaler to ease the tightness in her chest, no doubt caused by the damp in the house and the freezing cold temperature.

She pulled on a second pair of socks and shivered. It had been glacial all day, even changing out of her funeral clothes into her new pyjamas hadn't warmed her up.

'This is all we can afford,' said Josh in a raised voice before suddenly punching the wall. The impact left a dent in the bare plasterboard.

Brigid was taken aback by her husband's display of anger. He'd never behaved this way before. She felt the fear in her stomach rise and her heart quickened shortening her breath even further. She used her inhaler again and shrunk in on herself as the buried memories of her mother hitting her as a child resurfaced and floated around the room.

Josh dropped to his knees and took her face in his hands. 'I'm sorry. I didn't mean to lose my temper, Bridge. You know I would never hurt you, don't you?' Brigid nodded. 'It's the fire, our situation, the debts. Me being such a bloody stupid idiot. God, I'm so sorry.'

'I know you're sorry,' said Brigid putting her arms around Josh's neck. 'I feel like I'm losing it too. I'm exhausted. And having to say goodbye to Gran was more difficult than I could have ever imagined.'

Josh said sorry again and kissed her tenderly on the nose. Brigid knew that Josh would never hit her. Her husband wasn't that type of man. He was kind and caring like her gran. Josh always put her first.

The couple slid into bed and went over the day's events. Josh made Brigid laugh about her mum scrounging £5 from her at the buffet. Brigid admitted to giving her the cash just to get rid of her and agreed that her mother had no shame whatsoever.

'I had a missed call from the fire engineer while we were at the funeral,' Josh said. 'It looks like it was faulty wiring that caused the fire, not arson, so at least we know that no one was trying to kill us.' He was trying to be funny but it fell flat.

Brigid sighed. 'I spoke to the solicitor about Gran's shop and the flat. Turns out there was no equity. She had borrowed against the property so many times there was nothing left. She'd been living off her tiny savings this whole time, and she never told me.'

'Did you think she was going to leave you some cash?' asked Josh.

Brigid hated to admit it, but she'd half-hoped that her gran's legacy would bail them out. 'Yeah,' she said softly.

After a few moments of quiet, Brigid came to a decision that she hadn't even been consciously aware she was making.

'I'll do it,' said Brigid quietly. 'I'll fake my own death.'

She couldn't quite believe the words had come out of her own mouth. But she had never felt so low. She was broken financially, emotionally and physically.

Before Josh could speak, she continued. 'I can't take any more, Josh. My body is screaming with stress. I can feel my nerves jangling around my bones. They're humming as if they're on overload. I'm so tired. I'm not sleeping because I'm worrying about money. And my chest, I have this constant tightness, this ache. At times, I feel like I'm having to grab every breath out of my lungs. It's an effort just to breathe. Can you imagine how that feels?'

She took a deep breath and felt the ache again, deep inside her body.

Josh held her hand. 'Oh, darling. I'm so sorry.'

Her husband's fingers were warm and strong, Brigid clung to his hands. 'Josh, I've lost my home. My gran. And we will never, ever pay off our debts. I have nothing more to lose. Not a thing,' she was crying and pushing her words out between sobs. 'If it doesn't work, then we'll go bankrupt. But if we pull off the scam we can escape, create a new life with the money. It's worth the risk.'

'Really?' Josh spoke as if he couldn't believe what he was hearing. 'I thought the insurance scam was forgotten and buried. You said it was an insane idea. And you were right.'

Brigid knew she'd said these things, but she was past the point of caring. She was up to her neck in debt and sinking. Soon, only her nose would be sticking out of the swamp that had become her life. 'I'm just so sick of worrying about money, it's been consuming me.'

Josh tucked the hair behind her ear. 'We can find a way out of this, Bridge. As long as we stick together, we can do anything.'

'I want to do it, honestly, I just have one condition,' said Brigid tracing the outline of her star tattoo.

'Anything, just name it.'

'You have to promise to donate £10,000 from the life insurance money to the animal rescue.'

Josh was incredulous. 'Seriously? £10,000 to smelly mutts?'

'You said anything,' said Brigid crossing her arms. 'Plus, I want to say goodbye to everyone.' She found a tiny piece of loose skin by her thumb and picked the skin.

Josh covered her hand with his own and shook his head. 'You can't say goodbye. Your death has to be a shock for everyone. That way it's more real.'

'No. I want to go to London and see Josie, have one last big drunken night out together,' said Brigid with conviction. 'She's my closest friend.' The thought of not saying goodbye was a betrayal of their friendship. And she knew Josie would be devastated by her death and somehow, wrongly, blame herself because she hadn't been around to keep an eye on her.

'Absolutely not,' said Josh more firmly this time. He got out of the bed and paced. 'Yes to money for the dogs. No to a farewell shindig with Josie or anyone else. No goodbye phone calls either.'

'Why not?'

'Because you're too honest,' said Josh folding his arms. 'There's a risk you'll start blabbing and spill the beans.'

Brigid sighed. She saw the truth in her husband's logic but felt a sudden shock at the idea of never speaking to Josie again.

'No one is to know about this plan except for you and me. Agreed?'

'Agreed,' said Brigid reluctantly and kicked herself for not calling her friend that day. But now the decision had been made she knew that Josh was right, she wouldn't be able to speak to Josie because her friend would sense that she was hiding something.

'But there's nothing to stop the two of us from getting

hammered and celebrating,' said Josh checking his wallet. 'I'm going to the corner shop to buy some bourbon.'

Brigid

It was the morning after the bourbon celebration. Brigid had already been sick, twice, and she ached so much her bones hurt.

'I can hardly remember the last few hours before I went to bed,' said Brigid shielding her eyes from the sun streaming through the attic's skylight.

Josh kissed her forehead and told her she'd been hilarious. 'You insisted on singing along to an old *Top of the Pops.*'

Fragments of belting out Prince's *Sign 'O' the Times* filtered into her memory. Josh was still laughing as he left to go downstairs and cook a fry-up.

Ten minutes later, Brigid forced herself to get up and wash her hair. Even though the boiler was only spitting out vaguely warm water, she needed to get clean.

Lying in the tepid shallow bath, Brigid still felt nauseated and whilst she might not remember the night after the alcohol had taken hold, she recalled the conversation with Josh beforehand. Fear crept over her body like a black vine. Could she really go through with faking her death? What about her future? How could she have a future if she was dead? Did she really want to erase herself and become a non-person forever? But how else could they find the money to pay off their debts? Should they just declare themselves bankrupt?

The more she thought about the enormity of faking her death the more her throat slowly squeezed itself shut. 'In. Out. In. Out. In. Out,' she told herself and breathed evenly to try and calm down. She would not have an asthma attack.

'I can breathe. I can breathe,' she thought.

Soon her chest felt so restricted it was like someone was sitting on top of her body. When Brigid tried to catch her breath, she had trouble taking in enough air and her lungs let out a hollow wheeze.

Brigid knew that she wouldn't be able to hold a conversation, which was a clear indication of a bad asthma attack. Grasping the sides of the bath, she stood up slowly. It took all her strength to pull herself upright and she wobbled slightly as she put one foot, then the other, on the floor.

Weak from the effort of moving, Brigid slid down and sat motionless on the grubby lino. She tried to scream but she couldn't make a sound.

'Breathe, breathe,' she told herself.

As if he'd heard her internal screaming, Josh knocked on the bathroom door and called out, 'Are you okay?'

When she didn't respond, Josh burst into the bathroom and took in the situation quickly. 'How long?' he asked as he grabbed her dressing gown and wrapped it around her shoulders.

Brigid held up two fingers. Her chest was burning. Fire was rushing from her lungs to her throat, which felt smaller with every heartbeat.

'Okay, two minutes, so it's early. Listen to me. I'm going to take you to A&E. We can use this asthma attack to our advantage.'

Brigid's eyes widened in fear and she shook her head violently. In her mind, she was screaming, 'Are you fucking insane? Help me!' She tried to stand up but was too shaky.

Josh lifted her to her feet. 'We can get this asthma attack on record,' he said. 'Then you can have a follow up attack and that can be fatal. The cause of death.'

Brigid shut her eyes and tried to catch her breath to object. But it was no good. Her terror was making the attack worse. She motioned with her hands and mimed pumping her inhaler.

'No time. Trust me,' said Josh. 'We'll be at the hospital quicker than I could run upstairs and find your inhaler. The drive takes less than four minutes. I've timed the route.'

Josh

Josh checked his watch. Again. He had been waiting at the hospital for over three hours, then he saw his wife walking slowly towards him. Brigid's skin was even paler than usual, almost translucent, and she'd tied her dressing gown tightly around her waist.

'You okay?' he asked gently touching her arm in concern.

Brigid nodded, pulled her dressing cord tighter still and said quietly, 'I want to go home.'

Josh figured she felt self-conscious, which wasn't surprising given that she was naked underneath her robe. On her feet were thin hospital slippers that were too a size too big. Josh hadn't had time to grab her shoes.

'Come on,' said Josh putting an arm around his wife's shoulders. 'Let's get you out of here and warmed up.'

In the car, Brigid stared mutely out of the window then said in a whisper, 'I've not had an asthma attack like that for years. It was terrifying.'

'It's over and you're safe. We'll be home soon,' said Josh in a lively tone.

He wasn't really listening to Brigid, he was thinking about his plan and he couldn't believe that the first part had gone without a hitch. What luck. They were one step closer to the money. He planned to wait a few days and then tell Brigid how everything was coming together. What he needed to do for the rest of the day was act normal, keep things on an even keel. Not get her upset again, she didn't need to have another attack.

'I'll make you some crumpets,' Josh said as he indicated

to turn into their road.

Brigid said she wasn't hungry and stared out of the window. He let it go.

The house was cold and the air inside stabbed them with tiny icy daggers giving them no reprieve from the chill outside. Josh went to help Brigid up the stairs but she shrugged him off and walked up slowly holding the banister. In the attic bedroom, she kicked off the hospital slippers and eased herself into bed, still wearing her dressing gown. Josh tucked the covers around her like a child. Brigid ignored him.

In the cellar kitchen Josh disposed of a dead mouse that had appeared on the floor and then made Brigid two crumpets and a mug of black tea.

'I've brought you some food,' said Josh. 'I've spread the butter right up to the edges.'

Brigid pulled herself up in bed. Her nose was red, she'd been crying. It was to be expected, she'd had a big shock. But everything had gone exactly as he planned. Just as Josh put the plate on the floor his wife told him, firmly, that she'd said no.

Josh knew what she was talking about but he wanted to calm Brigid down so he made a joke out of it. 'What? You don't want tea and warm crumpets? Come on, Bridge, it's your favourite.'

'WHY DID YOU PUT ME THROUGH THAT? YOU WEREN'T TAKING ME TO HOSPITAL WITH A FAKE ASTHMA ATTACK. I REALLY *WAS* HAVING AN ASTHMA ATTACK AND I WAS TERRIFIED,' shouted Brigid.

'I thought you said yes,' said Josh calmly not looking at

his wife. He knew that little red spots of anger would be forming on her cheeks. But they would be gone within a few minutes if he didn't argue back.

'I couldn't speak and I shook my head to say no.' Brigid had stopped shouting but her voice was level and far more furious. 'I remember it distinctly. I asked you to get my inhaler and you refused. You fucking wanker. You could have killed me.'

It took a lot for Brigid to call him names and swear, but this time, Josh didn't really blame her. He did really need her to calm down though. He sat on the bed next to her. 'I swear, if you'd held up five fingers I wouldn't have chanced it. And besides, I had your inhaler in my pocket the whole time.'

'Oh, so that's okay then,' Brigid spat out. 'How could you?'

Josh sighed. What he said next was crucial to how his plan would pan out. 'I would never put your life at risk. Honestly.'

'You just *did*,' said Brigid turning her back on him and lying down.

Josh knew that he should just shut up and leave her to calm down. He figured his wife's anger would evaporate within a few hours so he crept away to the basement to tidy up. Half an hour later, still in her dressing gown, Brigid came downstairs into the kitchen to make a fresh cup of tea.

'I'm really so sorry I upset you, Bridge,' said Josh who was sitting at the kitchen table toying with a packet of cigarettes. 'I do feel terrible.'

He was genuinely remorseful. The idea to go to A&E had come out of nowhere when he'd seen Brigid on the bathroom floor. Without thinking too long, he'd acted on it. And it had paid off.

'I'm still angry. What were you thinking?' Brigid stood with her back to Josh at the sink washing a mug.

Josh spoke gently, careful not to anger her further. 'It's now on your medical record that you've had a severe asthma attack and you were rushed to A&E. When you have your next big attack, it won't be a shock that you died.'

'What?' said Brigid turning around still holding the mug covered in white bubbles. She put the mug down on the worktop with a bang. 'Explain, please do.'

'Of course, you won't really be dead, you'll be in a comatose state thanks to the Death Herb,' said Josh calmly. 'It's the perfect way to fake your death.' He couldn't believe how easily the scheme had all come together. If Josh had believed in such things he'd have thought the universe was lending a hand. It was a good thing Brigid had picked up a fresh supply of the Death Herb from her gran before she died.

'So you risked my life to make my fake death more realistic?'

Josh nodded. 'But I swear your life was not at risk, I wouldn't do that.'

Brigid made herself a cup of tea then sat at the stained kitchen table. 'I guess you better run the plan by me now, so that there are no more nasty surprises.'

Josh joined her at the table. 'We make up the herb. You take it and look dead. Then I ring your doctor and tell him I came home to find you'd had an asthma attack and were unresponsive. He comes here, examines you. Writes a Medical Certificate of Death. There won't be an autopsy

59

because you've recently had a huge asthma attack and been to A&E. You need to see your GP too, and soon, to get this attack on your medical records so the 14-day rule kicks in.'

Brigid frowned. 'How do you know all this?'

Josh explained that he'd checked the website of the Coroner's Office.

Brigid drank her tea. 'Okay so I'll see my GP, Dr Dixon, and get this huge asthma attack on my record. Ask him to examine me and check my medication. How do we make sure he's the one making the house call when you find me dead?' asked Brigid slowly. She felt sick at the idea of deceiving Dr Dixon, he had been her doctor since she was a child, and he had always gone above and beyond to ensure she was healthy and safe.

'You ask him casually when he's on call. He likes to chat. Find out some dates.'

'I can do that. It's a good thing he's still old fashioned enough to do house calls. And you're sure there won't be an autopsy?'

Josh nodded and smiled. 'I'm positive. You will have seen a medical professional within 14 days for the same health issue as the cause of death. It's perfect, Bridge. No one will suspect a thing.'

'You've got it all planned out, haven't you?' said Brigid looking down at her hands. She picked at the skin around her thumb.

Josh waited for her to speak again, afraid that he would put her off the idea. He could see she was beginning to warm to it.

'What happens then?' she asked.

'You lie low. I claim on the two life insurance policies.

We pay off the mortgage with the other policy and then we drive off into the sunset.' Josh held his breath, he could see his wife was taking in his plan, weighing up the risks. He was winning her around.

'It's an absolutely fucking crazy idea,' said Brigid rolling her eyes as she stood up to boil the kettle again.

'I know. But the craziest ideas are always the best. It's all slotting into place, Bridge,' said Josh unable to keep the excitement from creeping into his voice. He could feel the energy of the idea buzzing around him taking shape.

'What if Dr Dixon doesn't think that I'm dead? Have you thought of that possibility?'

Brigid's voice dripped with sarcasm. Josh ignored her tone and said, palms raised, 'Then we forget it. I promise. We take you to hospital for safety. I work out a plan B. We go bankrupt. We get second jobs. I do porn films.'

The porn comment raised a smile. Josh knew that his wife's anger was melting. Whilst she might not agree with the plan, he could tell she wasn't furious with him anymore, which was a relief.

'What would we do for money until the insurance paid out?' asked Brigid.

'I've got an extension on my overdraft. I've given the bank my parents' details as guarantors so they will cough up if I don't repay it.'

'Oh, Josh,' said Brigid with a sigh. 'But okay, I'll do it. I'll make an appointment with Dr Dixon and get the attack on my medical records. There's no harm in doing that at least.'

Josh smiled and said, 'The overdraft will tide us over until the real money comes through.'

It was underhand, he knew, but even so Josh took his top

off and threw it on the pile of dirty clothes on the kitchen floor by the washing machine. His wife glanced at his flat stomach and he watched her drag her gaze back to his face. She was so incredibly attracted to him physically. Their financial worries had dampened their sex life recently, but Josh could feel the flicker of desire returning.

'So that's settled. Sometime in the next fourteen days we're going to fake your death,' said Josh taking off his trousers and throwing them on the pile.

'I will decide the day,' said Brigid firmly.

Josh put his arm around Brigid's waist and slipped his other hand under her dressing gown and stroked the skin on her lovely, soft, naked bottom. 'Yes, you can decide the day. I promise,' he said before kissing her neck and cupping a breast in his hand.

Brigid

The sun shone through the attic window in a wide shaft and dust particles danced in the light like tiny jewels. Brigid turned away from the light and looked at her phone. It was 8.43am. She'd been awake for nearly three hours going over what could go wrong with their plan. Dr Dixon had given her a check-up the day before and prescribed her a new inhaler. But what if a different doctor turned up to examine her on the day and refused to write the death certificate? What if she really did die and her body was taken away for an autopsy? The list of what could go wrong was endless, and it frightened her.

Suddenly, Brigid couldn't stand the wait. She shook Josh's shoulder to rouse him, 'If we're going to fake my death let's do it today.'

Josh sat up and rubbed his eyes. 'What?'

'I can't sit here waiting,' said Brigid resolved. 'I want to take the Death Herb. Let's do it today.'

Josh was immediately awake and took his wife's face in his hands and kissed her on the mouth softly. 'If the herb doesn't work we go to plan B, I promise.'

'Deal,' said Brigid. 'Although there's one place I want to go before I die and get imprisoned in this house.'

'Anywhere, darling, anywhere. But first…'

An hour later they were dressed and heading out to the car. The Yorkshire Sculpture Park, near Wakefield, housed Henry Moore's sculptures of marble and metal. The beautiful shapes set in acres of parkland always made Brigid catch her breath. It was their sheer, enormous scale that astounded her. Her all-time favourite installation was a set of sculptures by Elisabeth Frink called Riace Figures. The human-shaped sculptures were positioned in a field and from a distance looked like men in white masks frozen in time.

'It's the human race constantly hiding from their emotions,' Brigid told Josh as they walked past the sculptures.

'No, Bridge. It's the power of man. His strength,' Josh replied. 'They're so obviously male.'

The hills were peppered with snow and they were bundled up against the frosty air in padded jackets and hats. They stopped and sat on a bench dusted with crusty ice. Brigid stared at the landscape climbing upwards from the nearby lake. The picture pulsed for a moment. She shut her eyes to ground herself. When she opened her eyes to the clear sky Josh was watching her and smiling broadly.

'Don't forget you're my moon and sun,' he said kissing her cheek softly.

'I know,' said Brigid.

'It's you and me against the world,' he added.

He kissed her softly again but on her mouth this time. Brigid kissed him back.

A pensioner and her yappy West Highland Terrier walked past. 'Eee, get thee sen a room,' said the old woman loudly.

Brigid and Josh burst out laughing. The woman puckered her lips and dragged her small dog away.

Her last day as Brigid Raven was nearing to a close. The couple were in the kitchen and nothing mattered from here on except the world that contained them both. Brigid opened the small black pouch slowly, so she didn't spill the contents, and carefully touched the Death Herb.

She put three of the dried purple flowers on a saucer. Brigid looked at Josh. She sensed an invisible silver cord glistening between them. At any moment the binding could snap but neither of them stepped back and so the cord didn't break. Instead, they stepped towards one another. Once drunk, the tea made from the Death Herb would bind them together far tighter than marriage. It truly would be for better or for worse. For richer or for poorer, and until death.

Josh put his arm around Brigid's waist. 'I love you.'

Brigid whispered the words in return then filled a glass with spring water. She tipped the liquid into a small pan. Outside it was snowing. The flakes were light and ethereal and disappeared when they hit the concrete in their tiny yard, the yard with its high walls that hid them from the outside world.

Whilst she was setting everything up to make the herbal tea, Josh closed the curtains by the small window above the kitchen sink. The kitchen was dark so Josh turned on the lights under the counter. The spotlights threw out a focused glow onto the worktop.

Josh asked Brigid how she'd calculated how much water to use and she replied that a glass would make exactly enough to drink. Josh said this was a sensible approach. They were calm and both knew the enormity of what they were doing. The energy of it passed between them silently, hidden, but ever present.

'I need to boil the water and add three flowers.' Brigid watched the pan. 'It makes sense to use the same method for the sleep aid but make it more concentrated.'

After a few seconds Josh said, 'The water is taking a long time to boil.'

'Let's look away. It might boil quicker.'

'It's not exactly scientific but I know what you mean,'

said Josh. 'When you wait for something it feels like time is passing slowly, but if you're busy or enjoying yourself it goes more quickly.'

'Is that the excuse men use in the bedroom?' Brigid teased.

Josh snorted. 'Probably. I've never needed that excuse though.'

'Are you sure?' Brigid asked with a sly smile.

Josh tickled her in protest until they were both laughing. She pulled away to check the water. It was just about to reach boiling point. 'This is terrible. How come we're laughing? I'm about to kill myself. Metaphorically.'

Still smiling, her husband said, 'Didn't you laugh at school when you weren't supposed to? Haven't you ever wanted to laugh out loud at a funeral? It's human nature. Laughing at the macabre.'

'I don't find death funny,' said Brigid adding the herb to the boiling water. Even though she had joined in with the jokes, she thought Josh was being a bit insensitive about death, especially as her lovely gran had only recently passed away. But then he'd never experienced a close death so he didn't know how much it hurt. How the grief dug chunks out of your soul.

'Death isn't funny,' Josh agreed. 'I'm sorry, I'm just nervous. How long do you have to leave it for?' He was finally composed.

'Half an hour.'

Josh peered into the pan and pulled his head back sharply and said the mixture smelt rank.

Brigid sniffed and said, 'I won't deny, it is rather pungent.'

Time ticked on. Neither of them were in the mood to joke about anymore.

'It should be ready,' said Josh looking at his Omega.

Brigid poured the sticky mixture into a glass before carrying it up the cellar stairs into the living room. She sat on the sofa and looked at the glass on the coffee table. Did she really have the guts to drink the murky mixture? If she swallowed the brew Brigid would be snuffing out her life with one breath like blowing out a single candle on a birthday cake. Her career would be over too, all those years of hard work rubbed out in an instant.

'You're doing the right thing,' said Josh. 'When we pull this plan off all our money worries will be over. Trust me.'

'I do trust you,' said Brigid eyeing the glass that looked similar to a hand-blown one Josh had bought her only the year before, when life in Leeds had been liveable, even enjoyable.

Her eyes filled with tears. Could she really fake her death and walk away from everything? Brigid looked down and whispered that she wasn't ready to die.

Josh told her not to cry, and added, 'Bridge, you need to do this. For us.'

But still she didn't reach out and pick up the glass. 'If I drink the tincture I'll look dead. But what if I really *do* die, Josh? How would you be able to tell?'

Brigid felt a little sick. The ramifications of what she was about to do hit her hard in the gut. Saying she would fake her death to save them both was one thing, but actually doing it was another matter. Josh was now looking at her intently. Brigid stared at his beautiful face, his eyes held her heart and she realised that if there was anyone she could die for it was him.

'Taking a larger dose of the herb isn't deadly. Your gran wouldn't have given you anything poisonous. And when you wake up I'll be here,' said Josh kissing Brigid gently on the lips.

Despite his words, Brigid didn't feel reassured. She felt faint. The room shrank inwards, strangely, like in a cartoon. She breathed in quickly as if the oxygen around her was disappearing. She counted her breath in and out.

Brigid wanted to stop time. To just have a moment to think. But she knew that delaying the next step wouldn't make it any easier. She also knew that by drinking the liquid she would rub everything out about herself except her body. Everyone Brigid knew, apart from Josh, would think that she was dead, she would be gone forever.

The thought made Brigid feel light. She could feel a cold winter's sleep entering her body and she felt the chill spreading from her torso and flowing into her arms. Her brain hummed with anticipation as she steeled herself to move her arm to pick up the glass and drink.

But she still hesitated. Fear had put a fist around her heart. What if the herb made her blind or put her into a coma? Or worse still, killed her? Where would she find herself then? Was she really prepared to fake her demise and risk actual death? To walk away from her life – for money?

Brigid counted to three, picked up the glass and took her first gulp. When the mixture hit the back of her throat it made her gag because it was so much more concentrated than her sleep aid. She took a deep breath, held her nose and drank the rest of the contents in four large gulps.

Josh stood and watched as she drank. He caught her eye

for a second then looked down.

Peering into the glass, Brigid saw that the dregs of the dark tea were thick and clumpy like hot chocolate. She remembered her grandmother's warning to leave them untouched.

Her future was rushing around her veins and she couldn't believe that she'd stepped through this window and frozen time. With the last swallow, Brigid realised that she no longer existed. She had erased herself.

Within seconds her face had gone numb and she felt a slight nausea. But it wasn't overpowering. She could feel her body temperature decreasing rapidly and her hands felt stiff. Finally, her fingers started to tingle.

The pins and needles sensation clung to her fingers and moved into her palms, up to her wrists, her arms and down her torso. She could feel her body slowly being enveloped by this prickly shadow.

The chilly darkness covered her limbs like an oversized jumpsuit, baggy and inescapable. Last to be covered was her head. As the pins and needles closed over her crown Brigid felt herself sinking into a deep sleep and she wondered if the slumber would last all winter. Would she ever wake up from the winter's sleep?

'What is it?' asked Josh. 'Do you feel okay?' He took a step towards Brigid but didn't touch her.

'No. I feel strange. Heavy,' mumbled Brigid almost incoherent now. 'Need… to shut… eyes.'

Brigid's mind was slowing down; her vision was darkening. There were no racing thoughts. No panic. She slumped onto her side and her eyes closed slowly. She could feel herself sinking into the sofa, becoming part of the material, blending with the fabric. Her body became nothing. Empty.

Brigid

Brigid hovered in the air in the living room. She was looking down at Josh who was slumped on the sofa staring into space. Her body lay still, next to him, curled on its side in the foetal position. She looked motionless, dead.

'What's happening to me?' she thought.

Terror rolled towards her in waves when Brigid realised that she was detached from her body. She had no voice, she was just pure, floating, consciousness. The sensation and fear triggered a memory of swimming as a child one Saturday afternoon.

Brigid was in the council swimming pool. She was in the deep end treading water and could see her body rippling under the warm blue water. Her hands were tiny and she wore her favourite swimming costume, the red one; one of her mother's boyfriends had bought it for her tenth birthday. Brigid knew what happened next.

To her right, she looked down and saw a boy's body crumpled on the bottom of the pool. He wasn't moving. Rigid with fear, Brigid didn't have the courage to attract the lifeguard's attention. If she shouted everyone would look at her.

What if he's just practicing holding his breath? What if he's not? Brigid floated above the body on the bottom of the pool hoping that someone else would spot the boy's dangerous situation. He didn't move and still no one noticed him. Ten-year-old Brigid spluttered, coughed and splashed her arms up and down as if she was drowning herself. Within seconds, the lifeguard jumped into the pool and swam towards her with his T-shirt bellowing behind him like a pair of angel wings.

When the lifeguard reached her in the water Brigid shouted, 'Help him! He's on the bottom.'

The lifeguard quickly grasped the situation and plunged to the bottom of the pool. Soon afterwards he brought the boy to the surface cradling his chin with one hand as he swam to the poolside with his free arm.

Brigid felt brave, but soon realised that she might get into trouble for faking her own drowning. It was like crying wolf. She quietly slipped out of the pool and stepped into the bleach footbath, which separated the changing room from the pool area.

When her right foot touched the tepid water, she found herself once again suspended in her living room in Leeds watching Josh.

Though she had no body as such, Brigid realised that she only had to change her mental focus and it changed her awareness.

Each time she thought about looking in another direction, for example at the living room window, Brigid's visual focus automatically shifted to the chosen spot. She looked at the mantelpiece and noticed some roses. The flowers had been bought by Josh the day before, they were beautiful.

Without warning it happened again. Brigid found herself in Roundhay Park, in Leeds, with Josh. It was two summers ago. The grass was full of daisies and they were laid down amongst the flowers cloud-watching.

Re-experiencing random moments from her life was an odd experience. Though Brigid was aware that she was replaying an event from her past, it seemed real but there was a slight feeling of falseness like being in a lucid dream.

She turned to look at Josh, he smiled at her as he lay on the grass.

'This isn't really happening,' she thought as Josh held out his hand. It was odd because her mind felt split into two. One half of her consciousness was experiencing the moment whilst the other half was watching it. She could feel the grass between her fingers and the air on her face. Brigid should have been happy but all she felt was panic.

'Will I be stuck like this forever replaying moments from my life? Am I in hell?' she wondered.

Without warning, Brigid was plunged into utter darkness. As the blackness engulfed Brigid, she heard voices. The voices cried out separately, each with its own plea. The sound merged together in an unholy chorus.

Brigid focused her awareness and found that she was no longer moving. 'I'm not really dead. I'm still alive. It's a mistake that I'm here,' she thought.

'It's a mistake that I'm here,' cried out a male voice. It was hoarse and sounded like it had been shouting into the darkness for eons.

Seconds later many other voices echoed in unison, 'It's a mistake that I'm here.' The voices became louder and nearer.

'But I'm alive,' said Brigid.

'But I'm alive,' cried out a single voice, and then another, and another until it sounded like a child's nursery rhyme with the phrase overlapping as the voices chanted.

'Who are you?' asked Brigid. She felt panic even though she had no body.

'Who are you?' shouted the many voices now in a single, ghostly echo.

The voices moved nearer. 'Go away,' shouted Brigid. But the voices circled her. She sensed their hunger. A tiny invisible mouth took a bite out of her. The pain was sudden and deep.

First one mouth, followed by another, and soon dozens of the voices were feeding on her. Despite having no limbs or torso, Brigid was acutely aware of the pain. The sharp teeth felt like hundreds of needles being thrust into her at once. She screamed out in agony.

'God loves me. God loves me. God loves me...' Brigid chanted intuitively.

Instantaneously as she thought these words an invisible force pulled her away from the voices. She fell deep into the heart of the velvet darkness and emptiness enveloped her. Brigid had no idea where this mantra came from but she continued chanting it in the utter blackness.

The mantra became one word, 'LOVE. LOVE. LOVE.'

If she focused on love the voices stayed away. If she stopped chanting, however, she sensed the voices moving towards her like a shoal of demon fish. She chanted.

Brigid floated for a short time in this sea of pain. Brigid floated forever.

A tiny light appeared in the blackness. It was a speck. A single pinhead. Yet it shone out brilliantly like the Pole Star.

Seeing the bright light in the never-ending darkness filled Brigid's consciousness with hope. She moved towards it. Soon, she was sucked towards the beacon and it exploded into a network of pulsating lights that were all interconnected. It was like looking at an endless patchwork of football fields filled with rows and rows of landing lights running parallel.

The expanse of it was too big for her to comprehend. The net of lights stretched onwards for infinity.

One of the lights near her glowed as big as the moon, brighter than the rest, and she was pulled towards this whiteness. The light expanded quickly into a tunnel. Brigid found herself being sucked inside the tunnel at supersonic speed still moving without control. Unexpectedly, she stopped halfway along the passageway.

For the first time, she had a moment to pause. Brigid took in the details of her new environment. The walls were made of what looked like metal and enclosed her like a tube. When she touched the surface her hand disappeared as if she'd dipped it into mercury. Brigid quickly drew her hand out of the wall, then realised that she had a body again. She felt her face, looked down and could see her feet. Joy filled her being.

Just at that moment of awareness Brigid felt another presence. It was a bright white light that shone over her body. It was so bright, so large and magnificent that she had to close her eyes.

A loud commanding voice asked her, 'Do you really want to die?'

The voice was neither male nor female. Brigid couldn't see a being but she sensed the love. It enveloped and cherished her. In turn, she felt like a naughty toddler who'd been caught peeping through the banisters at a dinner party below.

Brigid knew she'd stumbled somewhere that she didn't belong. She was humbled but not overpowered.

'No. I don't want to die,' Brigid replied telepathically.

As soon as she thought those words, she was aware of a voice shouting, 'Please don't leave me. I love you. I love you'.

She felt a hand grip her arm then she shot through a circle of light at warp speed and found herself floating in a living room. Looking down, she saw the body of a woman in an open coffin. Still and waiting.

Long red hair draped evenly over the woman's shoulders. The dead woman's skin was as pale as fresh milk and a tattoo of a black star was etched on the outside of her left wrist. A moment passed before Brigid realised that she was looking at her own body in the coffin.

The coffin was on a low stand and within touching distance of a man. He was sat on the sofa watching the coffin as if keeping a vigil. Brigid quickly recovered from the shock of seeing her own lifeless body and recognised that the man was her husband. Josh looked dreadful. Large purple bags were stamped deep and wide into the skin underneath his eyes. His dark hair was greasy and he was wearing dirty grey trousers and a baggy black sweatshirt.

Brigid moved nearer to Josh but he remained motionless. She tried to blow in his ear. Josh shivered, stood up and walked down the steps into the cellar kitchen. Brigid followed and watched Josh open the fridge and take out a beer.

It was light outside but she had no idea of the time or the day. Time had stopped. She felt confused and very frightened. In frustration Brigid screamed at Josh, 'WHAT ARE YOU DOING? I'M HERE. I'M NOT DEAD.' But no voice bounced around the room.

Josh went back upstairs into the dark living room and sat on the sofa in the same spot where she'd first found him. He popped open his can of beer and drank it slowly. Methodically. Only his moving arm and blinking eyelids betrayed that he was awake, otherwise he was a man with no life in his body. Brigid was aghast by what she saw. She rushed towards Josh and came to a stop next to his face. For a heartbeat, she pressed herself against him. Sadly, all Josh did was brush away an imaginary irritation on his cheek. He was cut off from everything outside of himself.

Brigid watched Josh work his way through several cans of beer. Eventually, he staggered upstairs and flopped onto the mattress in the attic – fully clothed.

As he lay in an alcohol-induced sleep Brigid explored their home. In the basement kitchen on the table she found a *Yorkshire Post*. The paper lay open amongst the detritus of dirty coffee cups and rotting fruit. A bold headline caught her eye: **Local Woman Dies from Asthma Attack**.

The short piece outlined how Josh Raven had come home to find his wife Brigid unconscious with an empty asthma pump in her hand. He'd phoned for an ambulance and her GP, who was on-call, but it was too late. Her doctor, who'd known Brigid since childhood, had pronounced her dead at the scene.

Dr Dixon was quoted as saying: 'She was a lovely, friendly, bright woman who cared very much about animals.'

The piece also mentioned that Brigid was a long-term asthma sufferer and outlined details of her previous severe asthma attack only days before – when she'd been rushed to A&E. At the end, the reporter added that Brigid had worked at a dog magazine. Brigid counted the words that summed up her life: 272.

'My life boiled down to the bones,' she thought sadly.

Another thought quickly ran across her mind. Maybe she really was dead? Fear filled her consciousness but she quickly pushed away this heavy emotion with the word 'love'. She repeated the mantra several times until she felt her equilibrium return. Her time in the darkness had taught Brigid that fear could clog her being and attract evil. She knew she needed a clear mind to function in this strange in-between world. The word 'love' was her only protection from the sea of hungry ghosts.

Still feeling perturbed, Brigid tried to make sense of her situation, 'How can I be dead when I'm aware and thinking? Is this what death is like? I can see Josh. I can feel his pain. So, maybe I'm not mentally dead, just physically at odds with my body.'

Winter rain hit the small window above the sink in the basement kitchen and Brigid wished she could rush outside and feel the drops on her face. She suddenly realised just how much she had taken for granted before. She made herself refocus on her predicament. 'Next question – does Josh think I'm dead?' Brigid pondered for a moment, 'I can't be sure what he thinks has happened to me. I need to observe him.'

Brigid became aware of her surroundings again. She scanned the space. Empty mugs and dirty plates waited to be washed in the sink and a dirty tea towel hung off the back of a chair.

Yet another part of the plan they had not considered was how Brigid would reconnect with her flesh. But then, they had assumed she would just be asleep for a while. Neither of them had imagined she'd be this in-between state with her consciousness outside of her body.

She floated back to the living room. The coffin was made out of dark wood and lined with cream silk. Her face was deathly pale, almost glowing white, and her arms were folded across her chest like a mummy. Her eyes were shut and even had pennies on them. Her body was clothed in the dress she had bought for her gran's service. It was ironic, Brigid never thought she'd be wearing the outfit to her own funeral.

It was dark outside, so it had to be the middle of the night. She heard Josh shouting upstairs in the attic bedroom and immediately an arrow of sadness pierced Brigid's soul. He was raging in his sleep and she was soaking up his emotions like a sponge.

Within seconds Josh's pain pulled her towards him. Brigid found herself in the bedroom hovering above the mattress on the floor where he slept.

She glided down near to her husband's body and noticed that she could see her hands. Looking down she noticed that her legs and feet were slowly materialising. Brigid had a body, albeit not a physical body, it was milky and hazy like the ghosts that she had seen herself.

'Am I a ghost?' she thought in panic. 'One of the undead?'

Brigid moved away from the bed and the ghostly outline of her limbs vanished. Moving back towards the mattress Brigid realised that when she was within Josh's aura an imprint of her body appeared.

'So away from Josh I have no spirit body. But near him I begin to have a body again. Interesting. I'm trapped but I don't think I'm a ghost because I can think. I can reason. I think therefore I am,' Brigid thought wryly.

Josh cried out in his sleep again and refocused her attention. His words were incomprehensible. The guttural sounds came from deep within his subconscious.

Brigid hovered next to him, her milky body fully visible, and stroked his forehead gently. 'Shh, shh,' she whispered in his ear.

Josh rolled onto his back and his snoring resumed. Brigid lay next to him. She was as still as the lifeless corpse in the coffin downstairs.

Brigid

As the sun chased away the moon Brigid heard the dawn chorus and it filled her being with joy. Whenever she heard the beautiful tweeting, even after all these years, she thanked the birds for saving her from her worst, and only, acid trip.

She'd been 19 and stupid enough to let her creepy boyfriend talk her into trying the drug. As the LSD had kicked in she'd thought werewolves were prowling outside her student house. She'd been too terrified to move out of her bedroom and had ended up peeing in her wash-hand basin. The dawn chorus had signalled the end of the terror and pulled her back into normality. Brigid had vowed never to take drugs again and had stuck to her promise.

Her mind froze. A stab of fear pierced her as she expected to revisit that terrible hallucinogenic experience. But she remained in the attic room with its sloping ceiling.

'This is a like a bad acid trip,' she realised, 'I just have to ride it out and trust that sooner or later it will end.'

Josh coughed, rubbed his eyes and hauled himself out of bed. She reached out to touch him. Her husband was still for a moment as Brigid made contact with his shoulder. He rubbed his face again and staggered down the stairs into the bathroom. Brigid hovered outside waiting for him. When he moved to the basement kitchen she followed.

After filling the kettle, Josh took a mug out of the cupboard. Brigid stood next to him and felt a swell of love as he performed the mundane actions.

Instinctively, she reached out and touched the knife on the breadboard. It moved slightly. Josh didn't notice. At that moment, he'd decided to rub his swollen eyes again.

Whilst Josh stared at the toaster Brigid pushed the knife for a second time. The piece of cutlery moved, but this time Josh had been looking out of the tiny window above the sink and missed the action again.

Inside, Brigid screamed with frustration. She felt weak, like a flickering light bulb, and realised that moving objects sapped her energy.

Brigid scanned the kitchen for something lighter that she might be able to work with to grab Josh's attention. On the worktop, she saw Josh's BMW car key. It was a single key attached to an electronic fob. She stared at the key and willed it to move; the act took practically all the energy Brigid had left. The key remained motionless.

Desperate, Brigid looked for something else. But a cup was too heavy as was a side plate. Crushed by her inability to move any more objects, and drained of her psychokinetic powers, Brigid went upstairs to sulk in the living room. Josh still hadn't opened the curtains but the dark seemed to help her recharge. For a moment she thought she could sense someone else with her, but then Josh came in the room and she focused her attention on him.

Later, the clunk of the letterbox snapped Josh out of his waking-coma but he didn't move. He sat still like a statue on the sofa.

'Can you hear me?' she whispered in his ear.

Josh turned his head towards Brigid's mouth.

'I'm here, next to you.'

Josh looked as if he was trying to catch hold of something that he couldn't name.

'I love you, Joshy Boy,' said Brigid using a nickname she hadn't ever uttered before.

Josh visibly shivered as if someone had walked over his grave. 'You're imagining things, Joshy Boy,' he said aloud and went down the cellar steps to make another coffee.

Brigid hovered behind Josh and peeped over his shoulder. She noticed a spoon on the breadboard and focused on it. For a second, the spoon didn't do anything but then it shot off the counter and onto the floor. Brigid was euphoric with her unexpected success.

Josh picked up the spoon and slowly placed the piece of cutlery on the worktop in the same spot it had occupied before its strange manoeuvre. He took a step back and stood absolutely still whilst looking at the spoon. Brigid tried to move the spoon for a second time but she was too exhausted.

'Bridge? Are you here?' asked Josh aloud looking around the kitchen. His eyes were wide with surprise and possibly panic.

Brigid felt a surge of so many emotions: love, joy, relief.

Josh ran upstairs into the bathroom. The bathroom contained the only mirror in the house although it cut the body off at the waist. Josh looked at his reflection and waited. Brigid had followed him quickly upstairs and was so close that she could hear his breathing. His breaths were short and rapid.

Trembling and with clenched fists, Josh closed his eyes and whispered, 'Come on, come on, Brigid.'

Pushing herself against Josh made Brigid feel stronger. Fuelled by Josh's vitality, Brigid looked at the mirror and willed for her reflection to appear.

Slowly she saw the image of her face forming in the mirror behind Josh. First her green eyes came into view, followed by her mouth, her red hair, and finally the rest of her face as if the missing details were being coloured in bit by bit.

The image faded away at her neck. She had no body. The couple's gaze met in the mirror before Brigid vanished. Eaten away by the air. She couldn't hold the image for longer than a few seconds before she was exhausted and felt her energy contract inwards, then collapse.

'I saw you,' shouted Josh. He spun around and said to the empty room, 'I know you're here.'

Hours later, Brigid lay on the attic bed spooning Josh in the dark. She felt his heat and love.

Josh's eyes were open. Although Josh couldn't see his soulmate he told her that he sensed her presence close to him.

Softly, he spoke words of love, 'You are half my soul,' he whispered, 'I can feel you. Come back to me, Brigid. Please promise you will come back to me.'

As his love crashed against her in powerful waves Brigid felt her spirit body being filled with energy. And as Josh kept on pouring his words of love into her she became stronger.

'You're my night star guiding me through life,' he murmured. 'You're my moon and sun. Without you I don't want to exist, Bridge. You are my reason for living, for everything that I do.'

With each truth, Brigid felt herself grow stronger. She felt hope and somehow believed that maybe she could escape from this living death. She just had to work out how.

It was sometime in the night. The birds were quiet and the only sound outside was the occasional passing car. Brigid hovered over her coffin.

She was desperate to be reunited with her flesh and bone

but didn't know exactly how to re-enter her body. She'd rushed down to her lifeless form and pressed her spirit against her skin so many times today, but as in her previous attempts it wouldn't let her in.

Out of nowhere she remembered a conversation she'd had eons ago with Josie.

Her friend's voice stretched across time and explained, 'The body's main sacred energy centre is found in the head, the crown chakra. The soul leaves the body at this point and, in certain circumstances, say after a near-death experience, it can re-enter at this location.'

Brigid moved to the top of her head and noticed a white light the size of a pea glowing on her crown. The more she focused on the glowing light the bigger it became until it was two inches across.

Feeling a sense of urgency, Brigid moved towards the now pulsating light. Seconds later, she was sucked into the brilliant whiteness. Pain shot through her, it was like nothing she'd ever experienced. The sensation felt like her skin had been ripped off her bones. Her body jolted and her head hit the side of the coffin.

'I'm alive,' was her first thought before retching.

Brown bile spewed out of Brigid's mouth in an impressive fountain and covered her dress. She wiped the sticky mixture from her face and sat up slowly, hanging slightly over the side of the coffin.

Brigid was dazed and exhausted, and her throat felt raw from vomiting, but it felt fantastic to be alive. To be breathing. She took in great gulps of air.

As though she had summoned him, Josh came running into the living room. He was wide-eyed with shock.

'What the fuck…?' he said with a grin before kissing Brigid on her sticky mouth.

PART TWO:
AIR

Brigid

The attic bedroom was dark except for the small circle of light that came from the metal side-lamp. Brigid sat propped up on several pillows with her wet hair wrapped in a towel. She wore a white night dress that revealed her milky skin. She was sipping Earl Grey tea from a mug.

'Jesus Christ I was worried,' said Josh shaking his head slowly. 'You've been out for three days.'

He pulled Brigid into his arms briefly then let her go and filled her in on the events since she had taken the Death Herb. She still couldn't quite believe what was happening. It was surreal. Josh explained that after she'd fallen unconscious he'd called an ambulance and her GP. He'd lied and told Dr Dixon that she'd suffered from another asthma attack.

'You looked dead,' said Josh. 'Dr Dixon couldn't find any signs of life. He was devastated and wrote out a Medical Certificate of Cause of Death there and then.' Josh outlined how the police had arrived soon afterwards and spoke to Dr Dixon who assured them of no foul play. 'One copper even lifted your body up to check that I'd not stabbed you in the back,' said Josh twirling a piece of Brigid's wet hair around his finger. 'That was a heart-stopping moment, but they left soon afterwards happy that I'd not murdered you.'

'What happened next?' asked Brigid. She pressed her cold feet against Josh's hot leg, and could feel the warmth returning to her toes slowly. But her body felt stiff and sore from being immobile for so long. The ache in her limbs felt like the flu and she wondered how long this side-effect of the Death Herb would last.

'There was no autopsy because of your history of asthma

and the recent attack and A&E visit, which was on record,' said Josh speaking in a rush. 'When I talked to the funeral director I insisted on an open coffin, I said your family followed that tradition.' Josh kissed Brigid and continued, 'You've cut it fine, Bridge. Your funeral is tomorrow afternoon.'

'That soon?' asked Brigid with surprise.

So, it was official. She was one of the undead. Her past life was over and a debt-free future lay waiting to be mapped out and discovered. The idea invigorated her. Josh interrupted her thoughts with talk of her family.

'My God, I forgot about your mother. She came to pay her respects. If you can call it that. She asked for your pearl and diamond engagement ring.'

'What? The vintage ring you bought me?' Brigid covered her hand as if hiding the ring would keep it safe.

Josh squeezed Brigid's shoulder and added, 'You're still wearing your ring, aren't you? I told your mother to piss off.'

Brigid shook her head slowly, 'Nightmare.' She would never have had the balls to lie to all those people, especially the police and her lovely doctor. Josh was right. She was the one who had to die. And yet she was alive. My God, she would never have a negative thought again. Life was so precious.

Josh laughed with relief, 'A few friends came to pay their respects but everyone was so freaked out by the open coffin that they walked in and out. What did it feel like being sort-of dead?'

'It was weird,' said Brigid. 'I was revisiting incidents from my life but then I was in this black nothingness, and there were these strange voices but I can't remember what they were saying. You know when you wake up from a dream and you have a sense of it, a feeling, but can't recall all the details? It feels like that.'

'Well, you had me worried,' said Josh kissing his wife's shoulder. 'I was beginning to think maybe you really were dead, and that your presence was in the house. Grief definitely messes with your mind. But I had to keep telling myself that you would come back. And thank God, you did.'

'I'm glad I came back too.' Brigid shivered. 'I'm not taking the Death Herb again, not even to help me sleep. It feels like I've been away with the fairies.'

'What do you mean?' asked Josh.

Brigid explained, 'In folktales, people who come back from fairyland can't remember what's happened to them. Their memory gets wiped. I've this strange feeling that I was in some kind of underworld. A place between the living and the dead.'

'You didn't visit the underworld, Bridge. It doesn't exist. You were in a deep coma and you're here now and safe,' said Josh. 'It was probably just a dream. A hallucination triggered by the herb.'

He kissed her neck. The touch of Josh's warms lips made her shiver slightly so she lifted his head and kissed him.

'What next?' asked Brigid pulling away.

'We're going to fill the coffin with logs and seal it up. You're being cremated so there won't be a coffin to dig up. And contrary to popular belief, coffins are not cremated one at a time, so when the jumble of bones are retrieved at the end of the day no one will have any idea that yours, my love, are not amongst them.'

91

'Nice,' said Brigid with sarcasm.

'I'm dying for a drink,' said Josh. 'Let's celebrate.'

'No thanks. I feel like death already. I don't want a hangover too.'

Josh

Brigid sat on the sofa and watched with a smile as Josh ran the industrial glue carefully along the edges of the coffin lid. Her knees were pulled up to her chest and she was wearing her white nightdress with a red cardigan.

'It's good to see you happy again,' said Josh wiping a splodge of glue off the dark wood. 'I don't think I've seen you excited about the future in a long while.'

'I just can't believe we're going to get away with the plan,' said Brigid resting her chin on her knees.

'I know. It's unbelievable.' Josh wiped his hands on some damp kitchen roll. 'I can't quite fathom it myself.'

What he didn't tell Brigid was that he was worried that someone at the funeral home might look inside the coffin and discover that there was no body inside. But to do that, they would have to prise the lid off with considerable force. It was unlikely, but possible. But who would open a coffin once it was closed? Wasn't there some kind of ethical funeral director's code? He pushed the thought away.

'Where did you buy the logs?'

'From a garage near Wetherby,' said Josh smothering his final thoughts of doubt. 'Come on, help me get this lid back on.'

Josh had packed the coffin with wooden logs. Every little crevice had been filled with newspaper. The coffin lid was heavy but the two of them were able to lift it into position. Josh went around and after tightening each screw he added more glue, carefully wiping away the excess.

'How do you know the wood will be heavy enough?' asked Brigid. She sat back on the sofa and huddled under a blanket for warmth.

The rental property was freezing just like Brigid's mother's home. Josh made a mental note to buy some oil-filled radiators. 'I weighed the logs using a luggage scale,' he said. 'The wood weighs around nine stone.'

'Surely that's not heavy enough?' Brigid asked incredulously. 'Look at me. I'm a size 14.'

Josh laughed. 'But the funeral director doesn't know that, does he? Time for me to get ready. They're collecting the coffin tomorrow at eleven.' Josh nudged the coffin lid with the heel of his hand. It felt solid enough to hide their secret.

'I forgot to ask. You're not having the wake here, in this house, are you?'

The worry on his wife's face told him that hiding in a house full of friends and family filled her with rightful horror. He laughed and said, 'I'm not having a wake. Full stop. I'm too devastated.'

'Good idea.'

Brigid was looking down, picking her thumb. He suspected his wife was thinking: this was not a game and there was no going back. No resurrection from the dead. 'What's up?' Josh sat down and put his arm around his wife. He might be wrong. She was so very mercurial.

'It's just hit me. I truly am dead. It didn't seem real before but looking at the coffin, and the death certificate, it's true.' She was holding a small piece of paper that up until that moment had been on the coffee table under the half-drunk bottle of bourbon.

'Oh, Brigid, you're not dead.' Josh took the death certificate and put it in his wallet for safe keeping. He'd need the precious document later for his meeting at the bank.

'To the outside world I am. Only you know that I'm here. I'm a living ghost,' said Brigid.

'You're not a ghost to me. There are so many things we have to look forward to.' Josh pushed a long strand of red hair away from Brigid's beautiful face. He suddenly had an idea. 'We could stay in a cottage in the Orkney Islands? I know that you've always wanted to visit that part of the world.'

Brigid nodded and smiled weakly as Josh set the scene for their trip. They would just have to wait until the money came through, then they could quietly vanish.

'We can drive to Orkney. Take the ferry. Imagine sitting under an unpolluted sky on the beach watching the stars.

'That would be fantastic,' said Brigid brightening up. 'What am I thinking? I've a whole life ahead of me without any money worries. How many people can say that?'

'Not many.' Josh was relieved that he was able to pull his wife out of her blues so easily. 'Once the insurance cash comes through we are free agents. We can move to the Orkney Islands. Or anywhere we want where people don't know us.'

'Perfect,' said Brigid with a sigh. 'You have a knack for making everything sound so easy and appealing. I need to stop worrying.'

'Yes, you do,' said Josh kissing Brigid's neck. 'I know you won't have a passport, unless we get you a fake one, but a holiday in the sun is the least of my worries. I need to focus on your funeral tomorrow.' Despite the normally sombre event he was preparing for, he felt excited. Buoyed up. For once, finally, it looked like events were going their way.

They chatted about the funeral. Brigid joked that she thought Josh was going to ask her to write her own eulogy.

'We're not having speeches,' said Josh. 'Just a poem and some music.'

'What poem? Hang on. This is weird. Shouldn't I be telling you what I want at my own funeral?'

Josh laughed and told her it was all in hand. The poem was *Advent* by Christina Rossetti and the music *Dirty Old Town* by The Pogues.

'The priest is going to say a few words but that's all.'

'Typical. Someone I don't know is going to sum up my life,' said Brigid rolling her eyes in jest.

'But it doesn't matter what they're going to say because you're not dead.' Josh squeezed his wife's thigh and added, 'You, my love, are very much alive.'

Brigid

The light was fading and Brigid peered into the street and watched the drizzle through a tiny crack where the bedroom curtains didn't quite meet. After a few minutes of silent observation, she made her way downstairs carefully navigating through the house's darkness.

Josh had shut the curtains in the living room and lit a candle. Brigid lingered in a half world where it was neither fully dark nor fully light. She didn't dare turn on the living room light, despite it being dusk, in case someone outside saw her outline through the thin curtains. The wooden coffin sat in the middle of the room like a huge sarcophagus holding lies and dreams of escape.

Brigid dozed with her eyes half shut and rested her feet on the trestle supporting her coffin. She was aware of external noises: the banging of a car door, a dog barking, Josh whistling in the kitchen. But the sounds seemed so far away. Disconnected, that's how she felt. Adrift and strangely tired. Since waking up from her mini-coma, her energy had been half its usual level and she had no problem slipping into this easy doze. All she had to do was close her eyes and drift. It didn't worry her, this lithium-like slumber. Why should it? She'd already lived a lifetime full of clocks and deadlines.

Brigid's reverie was interrupted by a knock at the front door. Two raps. Loud and firm. She froze, marooned in the living room, not sure what to do next. Who could be visiting them? Was it her mother? The police?

Quickly Josh appeared from the kitchen and took control. He motioned for Brigid to hide inside the cupboard that was built into the alcove. The space was empty and large enough to fit her body. Brigid bent double and thrust her knees to her chest just as Josh shut her into the darkness.

Through another crack, this time between the cupboard doors, Brigid could see the edge of her coffin and had a restricted view of the living room. She heard Josh talking to a woman in the hall and focused on the voice.

With horror Brigid realised that it was her friend Josie. When Josh walked into the living room, Brigid saw her friend for a brief moment through the crack. Even with only a short glimpse Brigid was able to tell that Josie had been crying because her face was puffy and red. Her poor friend. Someone she cared about was in pain because of her lie.

'I'm so sorry to drop by unannounced but I just want to see her before she…'

Josie broke down. Her friend was wearing a long black coat and standing next to the coffin. The fingertips of her right hand were resting lightly on the lid. She touched the polished wood as if it were a rare and precious thing.

Josh put an arm around Josie's shoulder. 'What about a cup of tea,' he said not waiting for an answer. Josie shook her head and pulled out a tissue to blow her nose.

Brigid noticed with slight alarm that she was breathing rapidly. She wasn't sure if it was being in a confined space, having her knees pressed up against her chest or the shock of seeing Josie.

She told herself silently, 'Breathe in, breathe out, breathe in, breathe out.'

The rhythm in her chest soon returned to normal, which was a relief because she didn't have her inhaler.

'I must leave one in here in case I have to hide again,' she thought.

Brigid looked through the crack and saw that Josie was still standing by the coffin. Her friend was mute and still. It took all of Brigid's strength not to jump out of the cupboard and shout, 'Surprise.'

Josh put a hand on Josie's shoulder. 'Say something, you idiot,' thought Brigid, 'you should be comforting her.' But Josh didn't speak. Either he was genuinely lost for words or wanted to give her friend space to talk about her feelings. Or he was worried about her falling out of the cupboard and ruining their plan.

When Josie finally spoke, her voice cracked with emotion. 'If only I could see her. I know it's weird but it would help her death feel real to me,' said Josie as she stared at the closed coffin. 'When I was in India people watched the bodies of their loved ones being burnt out in the open. Death is so restrained in the West. You don't get a chance to mourn. Not properly.'

'I'm so sorry, Josie, but the coffin stays shut. I did have an open casket but it freaked everyone out, including me,' said Josh. His deep and steady voice travelled into the cupboard.

Josh and Josie moved slightly. All Brigid could see through the long thin crack was part of her friend's back and the edge of her coffin.

'I know this is hard for you,' Josh added softly, 'but do you want to say a few words at the funeral?'

Josie completely broke down. Great heaving sobs came from her chest. Josh let her cry. 'It doesn't feel like she's dead. It's so strange,' said Josie between sobs. 'I can still sense her.'

Hearing these words, Brigid covered her mouth with her hand. She had to stop herself from crying out for a second time. Josh came back into view. He'd placed his hand on Josie's lower back and gently steered Brigid's grieving friend out of the room.

'Come on, let's sit down in the kitchen,' he said leading Josie away.

Brigid was left alone in the cupboard. She couldn't hear anything now because Josh and Josie were downstairs in the basement. Pins and needles sparkled up and down her legs and circled in her feet. Her back hurt from twisting sideways. However, she didn't dare move any part of her body too much in case she made a noise. She just had to wait.

After a while, Brigid heard movement. Josh led Josie out of the house and then the front door slammed.

Cautiously Brigid peeked through the slit. She was sure they were alone, but she was still afraid to open the door. Seconds later, Josh helped her out of her hiding place. Brigid stretched out her numb limbs and groaned with relief.

'That was a close call. We'll have to watch that,' said Josh raising his eyebrows and letting out a slow breath.

'More importantly, how was Josie?' asked Brigid. She felt guilty about her friend's distress. What she was doing was cruel and it caused her physical pain. But she had lost Josie, no matter what happened next, because if her friend found out about the situation, the scam, she would be disgusted by her dishonesty. Her closest friend would never speak to her again. The realisation made Brigid's face burn with shame.

Josh sat down and put his bare feet up on the trestle table, the exact same spot that Brigid had perched her legs. 'Josie is in shock. She even talked about handing in her notice and moving back up north.'

'She can't do that. She's only just started her new job,' said Brigid sitting down next to Josh on the sofa. 'Did you manage to persuade her not to move back to Leeds?'

'Yes. I told Josie that you wouldn't want her to give up her dream job. I said she had to teach those fashionista bitches about spirituality, which made her smile. She'll be fine.'

'You sure?' A knot had formed in Brigid's stomach and she knew it was intertwined with two emotions – guilt and concern.

'Positive. Stop fretting,' said Josh. 'There really is no need, honestly.' Josh pulled his wife towards him, put his arm around her shoulder, and said that Josie had offered to sort out some counselling. 'She gave me her mother's card, said I wouldn't have to pay for the session. I'm going to take her up on the offer.'

'Why?' Brigid was horrified and pulled away from her husband. What if Josh couldn't act bereaved? 'Do you think that's a good idea?' she asked voicing her concerns. 'You would be lying to Josie's mum. She's a top psychologist.'

'It would be odd not to take up her offer,' said Josh. 'I've just lost my wife.'

'Are you sure you can you lie convincingly?' asked Brigid looking him directly in the eye. She knew that Dr Augur assessed criminals for the Crime Prosecution Service. She would not be easily fooled.

Josh said in a firm voice that he could lie. No problem. Brigid shook her head, she wouldn't have been able to lie to someone she respected.

'Which is why I love you,' said Josh. 'You are so honest, but we need to tell a few untruths. You know that,' Josh tipped Brigid's chin up so she was looking at him. 'Okay?'

She nodded and felt a flutter in her stomach. Was it her conscience or nerves? She wasn't sure so she ignored it.

'What next?' asked Brigid pointing to the coffin. It was still in the middle of the room dominating the space.

'You're officially dead,' said Josh. 'All I have to do now is get through the funeral tomorrow and collect the insurance money.'

Josh

'Yes, the coffin's in here,' said Josh to the four men in black suits trooping into the house. He made sure his face was unsmiling and downcast.

One of the men walked into the living room, the most senior, Josh assumed. The other three men held back slightly, standing by the doorway, with their heads slightly bowed in respect.

The senior man coughed then said clearly, 'But tha's closed. I thought you wanted an open coffin.'

'I felt uneasy looking at her body,' said Josh. 'I shut the lid. My wife's family are a bit mad, I've no idea why they insisted on an open coffin.'

Josh saw the men exchange quick glances and he pretended not to notice. He pulled a tissue out of his pocket, bent his head and blew his nose to hide his smile. He thought the situation was farcical like some black and white Ealing comedy.

'Aye, lad, we understand,' said another man with large ears. 'We're going to take the coffin. Is that alright?'

Josh nodded, said thank you, and the men grunted quietly as they lifted the coffin and carried it out of the house. Josh heard the hearse door slam outside and felt relief and glee. They were another step closer to the cash, and not much could go wrong. They'd navigated the hard bit.

'It's okay, you can come out.' Josh opened the door to the house's unused bedroom where Brigid was sat on the floor. 'What are you doing?' he asked confused.

'I was trying to listen to what was going on downstairs.' Brigid stood up and her body cast a large shadow on the wall

103

behind her

'It wasn't exciting,' said Josh. 'They were surprised the lid was shut but everything's fine. There's no reason for them to open the coffin.'

Brigid kissed Josh on the cheek. 'You are clever. Deceitful but clever. I forgot to ask, who put me in the coffin when it arrived here?'

'The funeral home staff. I said you were a natural person and I didn't want them putting make-up on you.'

Josh stretched his arms over his head as if he'd just woken up. He was surprised by his own calmness. Brigid had been scared that the funeral director was going to smell a rat, but he'd had faith in his crazy plan. Why would anyone think that his wife was really alive and in a coma from some ancient herb? It was so ludicrous. And the only person who would possibly suspect foul play, Brigid's grandmother, was already dead and buried.

'It helped that I'd moved so quickly,' added Josh with a yawn. All this scheming was exhausting. 'I'd been given the death certificate only an hour earlier and no one asked any questions. Rigor mortis hadn't set in, that happens about three or four hours after death.'

'Nice detail. Thanks.'

Josh ignored his wife's sarcastic comment. 'I arranged the funeral, paid them there and then in cash, God knows how I got another extension on my overdraft. Then I just prayed that you'd wake up before your big day.'

'What would you have done if I hadn't woken up before the funeral?'

'I was going to lift you out. Fill the coffin with wood and wait for you to wake up.'

'What if I had really been dead?'

'Then, my love, the situation would have been slightly trickier,' Josh laughed.

'What a nightmare.' Brigid joined in with Josh's laughter. 'Imagine if they'd taken the coffin and you were stuck with my dead body at home.'

Josh felt suddenly euphoric. The tension of the past few weeks evaporated from his body. 'Bridge, we are going to pull this off. We're halfway there.'

Brigid smiled and Josh slipped his hands around his wife's waist and kissed her gently on the mouth. She kissed him back with soft little pecks that he'd trade in for something deeper later.

'I'm going to be devastated by my loss at the funeral,' he said pulling his mind back to the job. 'I plan to say as few words as possible. Hopefully no one will expect too much coherency from me. After all, I am the grieving widower.'

'I feel so guilty about lying to everyone,' said Brigid looking down. 'I can't shake it off.'

'I'd rather we didn't have to lie to friends and family too but it can't be helped.'

Brigid looked at Josh, 'I feel so uncomfortable about lying to people I care about. Some people have an antenna for deceit. Be careful, Josh.'

Josh raised his eyebrows. He knew who Brigid was referring to when she talked about an antenna. 'Ah yes. Your mother.'

'How's she been? I forgot to ask.'

Brigid was tracing the outline of her tattoo as if the five-pointed star could offer some kind of protection from evil. Josh hated how his mother-in-law made his wife feel, and the scam had the added bonus of meaning that he and Brigid could cut the dreadful woman out of their lives forever once the funeral was over.

'I rang your mother from Henry's landline, and I kept the call about your funeral brief,' he explained. 'She doesn't have my new mobile number, thankfully.'

'Was she okay with you organising everything? She didn't want to interfere?' Brigid asked. She was picking the skin on her thumb.

Josh nodded. 'Surprisingly, she was fine with me doing everything. Probably because she was worried I was going to ask her to contribute financially.' He laughed, but it wasn't very funny. 'She said she saw the piece in the *Yorkshire Post*.'

Brigid frowned. 'How did the paper get the story? It was published rather quickly.'

Josh breathed on his fingernails and polished them on his shoulder.

'*You* rang the paper?' asked Brigid. 'My God, you really do have balls of steel.'

'I thought it would be the perfect way to stop people asking questions,' said Josh pleased with himself. Yes, the idea had been a genius masterstroke.

'What did you say to the paper?' Brigid leant back on the sofa and made herself comfortable.

'I told the reporter my wife had died. I practically dictated the story. But I insisted that they didn't run a photo and surprisingly they agreed. I said it would be too distressing for your family. The reporter must have called Dr Dixon for a quote.'

'Yes, Dr Dixon. I hope my fake death won't get him into

trouble. Josh, he's a lovely man.'

'Trust me it won't, darling. Anyway, he's retiring next month.'

'True. I just don't want him implicated in our fraud.'

'No one is going to find out the truth, Bridge,' Josh said. 'And once the money comes through, we will leave Leeds and never return.'

'Okay. I'm sorry I worry so much,' said Brigid.

Josh felt quiet relief that his wife's concerns had been so quickly quashed. He pulled a blanket off the back the sofa and wrapped it around her shoulders. 'Still feeling the cold?' She nodded. 'Come on, have a nap. You look tired. I'll wake you up before I leave for the funeral.'

Brigid

Cold rivulets of air flowed into the hallway through the cracks of the badly fitted front door. Josh stood in his black suit ready to leave for the funeral whilst Brigid shivered slightly in her thin dressing gown.

Josh leaned down towards Brigid who closed her eyes and felt his kiss. His tongue was soft, yet urgent, and his warmth made her body pulse with life. A few moments later, Josh pulled away reluctantly.

Without speaking, Brigid stepped into the shadows of the living room so that she wouldn't be seen from the street when Josh opened the front door. She waited until she heard the sound of the front door being locked before going down the steps into the cellar kitchen. Opening the fridge, she saw the shelves were stacked with yogurts, salad and vegetables. She looked in the dry food cupboard and noted that it was full of baked beans and tinned tomatoes. There were no crisps, cakes or biscuits.

In disgust, Brigid reopened the fridge, took out a yogurt and ate it quickly. It tasted sour and made her face pucker up. As a paltry sugar substitute, she made a cup of tea with honey.

She sat at the kitchen table and switched on her laptop. Brigid was just about to go on Facebook when she remembered that she couldn't because she was dead. She didn't exist anymore in the outside world. So what had she become? A faint reflection of her previous self? A hologram? The thought troubled her momentarily but Brigid told herself to snap out of it. When she drank the Death Herb she'd signed up for this twilight existence, neither dead nor fully alive.

Brigid climbed the stairs to the top of the house. The door to the attic room creaked as she opened it. A strong scent of lavender filled the room. She knew it was coming from an unlit candle, but it almost felt like a visit from her gran. The sweet smell washed into her memory and gave her some comfort.

Brigid stood in the middle of the room and shut her eyes to let the past reclaim her thoughts. Her gran was leaning over the bath to check the water's temperature with her elbow. The herbalist, clad in a crisp white apron, turned to smile at five-year-old Brigid. The lavender salt baths were the highlight of her weekly visits because at Brigid's house there was never any hot water at bedtime.

Opening her eyes, the memory dissolved and Brigid stood on her tiptoes to look out of the skylight. Despite the cold weather, the nearby park was busy with tiny people and their dogs, mums and their pushchairs.

On the edge of the green space she spotted the church spire. Her eyes followed this point away to the far left, and beyond, where the crematorium stood surrounded by a clutch of buildings. Brigid wondered who'd turned up to her funeral.

She lay down on the mattress and fell into the stillness around her. She watched the clouds and thought about her funeral until the blue sky bled into a raging burnt orange.

Eventually, the fiery colours from the sky mingled with the swirling primary colours behind her closed eyes. Brigid drifted off into a restful sleep made up of more childhood memories of measuring out herbs and baking with her grandmother.

Josh

The chapel was simple. A long oblong space with white walls and high large windows running along either side. There were no pews but grey metal chairs in rows. A handful of the seats were already full. Josh silently took a seat at the front on the right side of the chapel and waited.

'Brigid would like this place. It's peaceful,' he thought as he sat down.

His parents arrived minutes later and joined him in the silence, and like everyone else they were wearing black. His dad's large round face was drawn and motionless. Josh knew he hated funerals, they made him feel uneasy. He noted that his father's suit was old-fashioned, the lapels slightly too big, but it was made of quality black Worsted cloth. The slight wet dog smell was distinct. Clearly the suit hadn't been out of his wardrobe in many years.

'She was a lovely girl,' said his mother in a hushed tone as his father looked down.

His mother's long white hair was rolled tightly in a tidy bun. Her pretty face was free of make-up and shone with quiet concern. Josh saw his mother's bent index finger, which was the result of a lifetime of sewing. Josh nodded, said yes, his wife was lovely. The three of them sat in silence as the chapel continued to fill up.

'Thanks for all your help sorting out the funeral,' said Josh in a whisper to his mother. He felt too awkward to stay silent. He had to say something.

'Don't mention it. Just you get through today,' said Mrs Raven patting his hand softly.

The Pogue's version of *Dirty Old Town* came out of the

speakers and Josh whispered to his mum, 'Brigid loved this song.'

His mother offered him a handkerchief, Josh took it and made a show of wiping his eyes. Christ, he felt terrible lying to his parents but needs must. He heard sniffeling and turned to see Josie with Natasha and Abigail, Brigid's workmates.

Quickly the seats filled up with people from Brigid's present and her past though Josh didn't recognise many of them. He saw Mrs Adamski arrive wearing what looked like a brand new black headscarf and a black coat he'd not seen previously. Josh made a mental note to thank her for coming and compliment her smart outfit.

When nearly all of the chairs were full, there was a commotion at the door. Josh turned and wasn't surprised to see that Brigid's mother was the source of the disturbance.

Mrs Doran was trussed up in a black dress that was too short, scruffy black stilettos and a rancid dark brown fur jacket. Her hair was piled high in her signature hairstyle.

Mrs Doran stumbled a little as she walked down the aisle, and her friend, another middle-aged woman who'd gone to seed, steered her into a seat and whispered something in her ear. Mrs Doran glared at the woman, who had ridiculous dyed black hair, and searched in her handbag.

The dark haired friend handed Mrs Doran a tissue but she pushed her hand away with a loud tut. In her other hand, Josh could see his mother-in-law held a hip flask.

'Wait till later,' hissed her friend who was dressed in a shabby blue coat.

'I'm burying my daughter,' said Mrs Doran loudly as she took a swig out of the flask. Her voice bounced around the stillness of the chapel.

'She's being cremated,' whispered the friend through clenched teeth.

Mrs Doran took another swig, then tucked the flask back into her tatty bag and asked, 'Happy now?'

The mourners stared, some open-mouthed, at the squabbling women. Josh had to suppress a smile and instead faked a coughing fit to gain his composure.

The friend leaned close to his mother-in-law's ear and growled something incomprehensible. Whatever it was, it made the dreadful Mrs Doran behave.

Once more, Josh was the one on show. He looked at the coffin straight-faced. Calm.

'Keep your cool,' he told himself. 'There's a lot riding on this performance.'

As the funeral celebrant, a thin middle-aged man with a bald head, began the service, Josh looked down. The man's words crawled over his skin.

Josh felt ashamed for the first time since putting the scam into action. He'd done a terrible thing, stealing Brigid's life, and lying to the people closest to them. But it was too late to change the cards that he'd dealt for them. Despite his guilt, Josh knew he was unlikely to see anyone at the funeral again – apart from his parents. He knew that his mum and dad weren't going to cause him any problems because they didn't like to pry. As far as they were concerned he was the grieving widower.

'I'll have to be careful about Mrs Doran. She might turn up with her hand out,' he thought. 'The last thing I need is her poking her nose into my business.'

When the service ended, Josh stood by the door and said his goodbyes. He made sure his face was a heavy, mirthless mask. After nearly all the mourners had filed out, Mrs Doran complained loudly about there being no wake. Josh turned his back on his mother-in-law and spoke to someone he didn't recognise.

Later, once everyone had finally drifted away, Josh headed home on foot. He was relieved. The pretence of the funeral had been more draining than he imagined. As he walked, the cold air slapped Josh's cheeks and he sunk down into his coat. He lit a cigarette and inhaled deeply.

He hadn't smoked for hours and his blood was fresh and receptive to the nicotine. Josh took another drag and a wave of wellbeing travelled down his arms in little ripples and lit up happy, addictive, pathways in his brain. Only now that the charade was over could he fully relax.

The funeral had been harder to witness than he had imagined. Raw and heavy emotions had slammed into him during the service. No matter how many times he told himself the coffin was full of wood, Josh still saw Brigid's lifeless body inside. Great big sobs had risen up from his chest, and he'd let them out aware it made the facade more real.

He knew without a doubt that he could never live without Brigid. Never.

Josh wondered if this whole scam had been constructed by his subconscious in a bid to bind the two of them together so that she could never leave him. He told himself not to be stupid. He was just feeling over emotional from the funeral.

Josh saw a pub in the distance. A blackboard outside showed The Cock and Bull was still open despite a flaking sign. A whisky would warm him up, and afterwards the fresh air would blow away his morbid thoughts about death as he walked the rest of his way home.

Brigid

The living room was lit only by the blue glow from the ancient gas fire and a few tea lights. Josh flopped onto the grubby sofa next to Brigid.

'What a day. The place was packed. You had a good show at your funeral, Bridge. Oh, and your mother arrived drunk with an equally shabby friend.'

Brigid's heart sank. It shouldn't matter how her mother acted, but it still hurt. The woman had no respect for anything, not even her daughter's passing. Brigid was pleased she'd never have to see her again.

'What did she do? Trip over in the aisle? Collapse in tears in her friend's arms and play the wounded mother?'

'Better,' said Josh laughing. 'She was bloody spectacular. The woman swigged from a hip flask and stumbled about the chapel.'

Josh recounted the funeral to Brigid in detail – even his urge to sob. He took a small urn out of a plastic bag and handed it to his wife with a wicked grin.

'Oh, Josh, you didn't,' said Brigid with mock horror. The urn was black metal and had her name in gold letters across the top. Underneath was a black and white photo of her, but the transfer distorted her face slightly and it looked cartoonish.

'Who knew that death could be so kitsch?'

'What do you expect me to do with this?' asked Brigid incredulous. She put it on the table and pointed at it, 'Well? What?'

Josh shrugged his shoulders. 'Nothing. I was going to put

it on the mantelpiece and light a candle every night, like a proper grieving widower.' He cackled and swigged his beer.

'Piss off,' said Brigid pushing his shoulder. 'Why are you laughing? This isn't funny.'

'I don't know, it's the relief,' said Josh running his hands through his thick hair. 'I'd no idea the funeral would be so exhausting.'

Brigid knew what he meant. Once he was back, the tension had oozed out of her limbs and into the air. She felt lighter. They were another step closer to freedom.

'It feels weird,' Brigid agreed. 'I don't know if I'll be able to get used to it. Being dead.'

'The concept will become normal eventually. Change just takes time to settle in.'

'Was Josie okay?' Brigid almost didn't want to hear the answer. She wanted her closest friend to be fine, but at the same time, if Josie hadn't been devastated at the funeral Brigid would worry that their friendship hadn't meant that much to her. Brigid chided herself for wanting to feel important.

'Josie was upset but she'll cope. She's strong.' Josh kicked off his black boots.

'I won't find a friend like her again,' said Brigid. 'She's such a caring and honest person.'

Josh told her she'd make plenty of new friends when they moved and to stop behaving like a baby. He sounded like a parent talking to a worried child about going to a new school.

Brigid couldn't stop herself and said angrily, 'But will I? I won't be able to tell them anything about my past or who I really am.' She paused then added, 'I've been thinking today. Everything that will come out of my mouth will be a lie.

How can you base a friendship on lies? I'm not a liar, Josh. Well, I wasn't until recently.'

'Things will work out,' said Josh pulling her closer. 'You just need to hide out here for six months and then we can move on. I've got a new plan that's going to help us.'

'Six months? That's a long time. And what new plan?' asked Brigid narrowing her eyes, 'Why haven't I heard of it until now?'

'I've only just come up with it, on the way home actually,' said Josh matter-of-factly. 'I think you need to change your hair.'

'Why?' asked Brigid. Her bottom lip stuck out slightly, she knew she could be childish sometimes, but she couldn't help it.

'You know I love your hair, but we're going to have to give you a new identity,' he said softly. 'Adjust a few things. It will make your re-entry into the world easier.'

'What else do you want me to change?' Brigid asked quietly. She couldn't help but feel hurt and suspected this plan involved a big physical make-over rather than just a few tweaks.

'You need to lose weight. Change your clothes. It makes sense to completely overhaul your look.'

'Oh, I see.' Brigid was crestfallen, taking no joy in the fact that her suspicion was right. Her husband's words stung and it felt like he was telling her she was ugly.

She had always thought he liked how she looked. Why would he want her to change? Then their current situation rose above her hurt feelings and she told herself not to be silly. This wasn't about sexual attraction it was about creating a new persona so that she didn't have to spend the rest of her life hiding behind a closed door.

'We need to give you a new name,' said Josh ploughing on. 'I was thinking of Anna. Anna Raven.'

'How did you come up with Anna?' Brigid felt uneasy again. Her first name had been her dad's choice, and it was her last link to her dead father.

'Anna was my sister's name. She died in 1998 when she was six years old. I was fourteen.'

This was the first time that Brigid had heard of Josh's dead sister and she was shocked. But then again, didn't everyone have secrets? Brigid had never told anyone about her Uncle Frederick who'd tried to touch her when her mum went for fish and chips. She was just ten years old.

Josh opened his wallet and pulled out a yellowing birth certificate, which he unfolded slowly. He didn't notice that when he took out the document another piece of paper, with Josie's new London address written on it, fell out of his wallet and on to the floor. But Brigid saw the paper fall and she pushed it slowly under the sofa with her foot.

'I adored Anna,' said Josh. 'She was so funny and an amazing dancer. Anna could watch a dance routine on the TV and pick it up immediately. She used to dance her way around the house, she was never still.'

Brigid was silent as she took the birth certificate from Josh. The document looked flimsy and small in her hand. The years had carved deep lines into the yellow square of paper, cut a grid across the faded black ink.

'Anna was playing hopscotch on the pavement outside the corner shop when she was hit by a car. It mounted the pavement and crushed her against the wall,' said Josh.

'Oh, Josh, that's so sad. Why have you never told me?'

Josh continued, tears in his eyes, 'No one in our family ever talks about Anna including me. Ever. Anna was a good girl, she deserved better. The driver only got three years. I stole her birth certificate when I was sixteen.'

'Do you miss her?'

'Sometimes. Other times it's like she never existed.' He paused and wiped his cheek with the back of his hand. 'I have a jumble of memories of Anna that are fading.'

They talked more about losing a loved one. How unless you've been through it yourself you had no idea of the impact. The slow shock that turns into disbelief and anger. Josh raised his beer to his mouth and Brigid noticed that his hand was shaking.

'Did you go to her funeral?' Brigid asked softly.

'No. My parents thought it would upset me too much. I could have forced my way in but who gate-crashes a funeral?'

'It must have been hard.' Brigid handed back the faded birth certificate, and her husband folded it carefully back into his wallet. A thought occurred to her. 'Is Anna's death why you don't believe in God?'

Josh nodded. 'I stopped going to church after that, so did Dad. Mum kept up with it, though. I could never understand how God could let an innocent child like that die.'

'I'm glad that you've told me.'

Josh shrugged his shoulders. 'I'm sorry I kept it a secret.'

'I understand, it's fine,' said Brigid, 'but I'm not sure I can take…'

'Brigid, this is the perfect solution,' said Josh taking hold of his wife's cold hands. 'You were born in the same year. In a strange way, you'd be helping me because it finally means that something positive will come out of my sister's death.'

Brigid didn't answer immediately. She could see his logic, but a dead child's name?

Josh waited for her response in silence. Brigid could practically hear his brain ticking over and planning.

He was right, of course, it was a good idea. She sighed and said quietly, 'So how do we make this work?'

'We can use Anna's birth certificate to create a new identity for you. Not to apply for a passport or anything like that, but it will come in handy,' said Josh kissing her forehead. 'Maybe we could call you Annie to stop it from being so weird?'

'Okay,' Brigid paused. 'Are we going to use the name Annie in private?' Brigid stumbled over her new moniker. It felt unfamiliar and alien on her tongue.

'That's a good idea, it means there will be less chance of us slipping up in public. If that's okay with you?'

'Do I have a choice?' she asked. Brigid knew the answer was no. Josh had thought it through and his logic was sound. 'Who will I be though? Your sister? Or your wife?'

'My wife, of course. No one will link me to her death it was years ago. And yes, you have a choice, I'm just trying to make sure this all works for both of us. If we get caught out, we will both go to prison.'

Josh avoided her gaze as he filled up his glass with more whisky.

Brigid said nothing and a moment later stood up and announced that she agreed and she was going to completely change the way she looked. The challenge would give her something to focus on. She was already getting bored hiding away in this dark house and it had barely been a couple of days.

'I knew you'd come around, Bridge,' said Josh smiling. 'Want a drink?'

'No thanks, too many calories, and from now on you need to call me Annie.'

The sooner she took up this new identity the quicker she could mould it into her mind and body. In a way, it would help her cope with her situation.

After all, Annie hadn't taken part in this fraudulent scam. That had been Brigid.

Annie

Three days after the funeral, they were sat at the kitchen table and Annie was tucking into her dinner. Josh asked why she wasn't having any potatoes.

'No carbs for me. Just protein and veggies,' she said loading up a fork with greens. Annie estimated that she was eating around 1,000 calories per day. 'I reckon I can shift around two stone in two months if I keep this up. The weight loss will change my appearance dramatically.'

'I'm proud of you,' said Josh.

Annie said she'd be at the low end of the scale for her height, but she would be fine.

'Well, if it makes you happy,' said Josh. He continued to watch *Look North* on the old portable TV perched on the end of the table whilst he ate.

Irked by his flippant remark, Annie threw down her cutlery and said, 'For God's sake, I'm not doing this for me. It's *you* that wants me to change how I look.'

'I know it's hard, but you are going to have to trust me,' said Josh dragging his attention away from the TV. 'Come on, Brigid, it's not for long.'

'Annie. My name is Annie,' she said sarcastically.

Josh's gaze returned to the screen. She picked up her fork again, and they ate the rest of their meal in silence. Annie knew that Josh thought she could be tiresome at times. But didn't he see how many sacrifices she was making? And now she was on a bloody diet, of all things.

After scraping the remains of her dinner into the bin, Annie turned to Josh and said quietly, 'It better bloody be worth it.'

The full moon lit up the attic bedroom through the skylight. In the ghostly light Annie could see Josh's chest rising and falling in a quiet ebb and flow of air. He was sleeping deeply and although it was hours since she'd lost her temper, Annie was still seething. She wanted Josh to acknowledge the effort she was making. Her anger gave Annie a deviant courage.

Quickly, and silently, Annie slipped out of bed, scooped up her clothes and dressed on the landing. In the darkness, Annie stretched out her hand and used her sense of touch to move down the stairs, along the hallway and then navigate into the basement.

Inside a kitchen drawer, Annie found a small torch. Like a burglar, she used the thin beam of light to guide herself around the room until she located the second item on her wish list – a pen. She rummaged through the pile of newspapers and magazines on the table and found a blank postcard that had come free with a house magazine.

The postcard of Saltburn-by-the-Sea, in North Yorkshire, depicted a Victorian cliff lift heading down towards a busy beach on a summer's day. Annie quickly scribbled a message on the back of the postcard. Just as she finished writing she remembered an old book of stamps in her purse. Fate was looking out for her.

Moments later, Annie slipped silently out of the house and walked down the road towards the post box, which was only fifty yards away. Despite the lack of light, the ungodly shapes in the trees and shrubbery didn't scare her and the open air was sharp against her skin. It felt fantastic, liberating, to be out of the house after being cooped up in the attic. For a moment, she almost felt normal and like her old self, like Brigid.

Whoosh. She felt the cold breath of death pass through her body and she jumped. A ghostly jogger in sweatpants and his panting Collie ran past her. Neither of the pair had feet, their legs faded away a few inches above the pavement. A cold shiver ran along Annie's body in a wave as the wispy white duo disappeared around the corner.

'Silly sods,' she thought. 'Who goes running in the dark? I bet they got hit by a car and that's how they died.'

When she reached the post box, Annie was calm again although her hand hovered momentarily in the gap causing the postcard to be suspended in mid-air. But her need to connect with her best friend was so strong that she flung the postcard into the box. She was still angry with Josh and he would never find out what she'd done.

Josh mumbled, but didn't wake up, as Annie slipped back into bed and pulled the duvet over her shoulder. She let out her breath slowly and soon crossed over into the other world.

Her dreams came in fits and starts, gently at first but soon she was dragged into a nightmare. Trees reached out to grab her and she was sucked into the ground. A dark voice called Annie's name and grabbed her arm, pulling her deeper underground. Her throat was filled with soil as she scrabbled to get free, but the hand held her there, refusing to let her escape. She tried to scream but no noise came out of her mouth.

Annie woke up with a start. It took her a millisecond to register that she'd been dreaming. Relief pulled her heart down from her mouth and back into her chest.

Typically Josh slept on, undisturbed by her disturbing

dreams, as she tried to arrange the jumbled memories of her nightmare into coherence. Annie tried to separate what was real and what was her subconscious. Being buried alive had definitely been a dream but what about the postcard? Had she really sent the card or had she dreamt that too?

In the shadows, Annie saw the torch on the floor.

Leaning over the side of the bed she pushed it underneath her pile of clothes and took comfort from the fact that she hadn't signed the postcard.

Josie

When Josie Augur saw the postcard, she looked at the Victorian image of the seaside, turned it over and read the message.

'Your intuition is usually right. Trust it.'

There was no signature on the card. It was addressed to her home, but her name wasn't on it. The writing was in capitals in black biro.

'That's odd,' she thought. 'Cryptic. Must have been intended for a previous tenant.'

Before throwing the bright card in the recycling, Josie re-examined the photo of Saltburn-by-the-Sea more closely. She knew the place. She had gone on holiday there as a child with her parents. The town had one of Europe's oldest cliff lifts and a restored pier.

Josie smiled at the memories the image stirred, and instead of throwing the postcard away, she stuck it to the fridge door with a magnet.

Maybe the postcard was a sign from the universe that she needed to go there on holiday? It certainly would be nice to get out of London. She hadn't lived there long, but she already found the city claustrophobic at times.

Josie glanced at her watch and swore. There was no more time to think about the postcard or possible holidays because she needed to rush for the tube. She had a meeting with the deputy editor about a mindfulness special and she wanted to be fully prepared.

As she dashed out the door, the heavens opened and Josie swore again.

She would definitely be booking a holiday later.

126

Annie

The light coming through the skylight woke Annie up. The attic was the only room in the house where the windows weren't permanently covered, and as a result Annie spent most of her time in this space watching the clouds, reading or exercising. It was a few days after Christmas. The holiday had been a quiet affair without gifts or rich, stodgy foods - just the usual TV shows. Josh had received a card with a much needed cash boost from his parents, and even a note from Josie.

The days were short but endless and Annie had an uneasy sense of freedom. She rarely checked the clock. What was the point? She was an outlaw of time and space. No more tick tock, tick tock.

But as the days had passed, Annie's confinement was beginning to make her feel like a hostage. Annie couldn't shake off the sensation that she was waiting for something to start. Or was she waiting for something to end? Despite all of the paperwork being filed, there was still no cash from the bank. She tried not to bring up the subject, she knew that Josh was beginning to grow uneasy over the delay.

Annie flipped back the duvet and sat up on the edge of the mattress. Josh had got up hours ago. She thought back to the middle of the night. She'd woken up in a cold sweat after having yet another nightmare. The bad dreams had been coming almost nightly since the funeral, and they were so vivid she could still smell and taste things from them when she woke up. She wondered if the night terrors were a product of her enforced confinement or an after effect of the coma.

127

She wasn't sure, but Annie was certain about one thing – the dreams were terrifying.

In the latest nightmare, Annie had found herself inside a closed coffin and experienced an acute sensation of being trapped. Rats licked the moisture from the corners of her eyes and nibbled her hands. The animals' small, wet tongues made her flesh crawl and she couldn't shake them off her body. Just as they had starting eating her flesh she'd felt another presence in the coffin. The unseen evil had covered her mouth and suffocated her. At this point she'd woken with a jolt and lay trembling in the darkness whilst Josh continued to sleep next to her like one of the undead.

Even now the memory of the dream made Annie's palms sweat and her chest tighten slightly. Annie didn't know what the presence was but it was evil. The word 'demon' was too medieval, even though it felt like the most accurate description. But who believed in demons in the 21st Century?

'It was just a stupid nightmare,' she told herself as she dressed. 'Everyone has bad dreams.'

Annie heard Josh before she saw him because the attic stairs creaked. He put a cup of peppermint tea on the bedside table and said he was going out later. Annie stretched and didn't mention the nightmare. It didn't seem important now that she was fully awake, in fact it almost seemed childish.

'I'll get you some newspapers if you want?' added Josh blowing out a match.

Her husband had just lit the lavender candle, knowing that she liked the smell, and the dead match's black smoke spiralled into the air. Annie felt her skin crawl at the sight of the smoke because it reminded her of the dark presence.

Again, she said nothing. Instead she told Josh to save his money, she didn't need any papers.

'I'll be downstairs reading,' said Josh kissing her forehead.

Annie nodded and launched herself out of bed and walked past the exercise bike and weights, which Josh had bought from a car boot sale, and went into the bathroom. She stood naked on the scales. The dial showed she'd lost 8lbs.

Looking in the mirror Annie noted that her pyjamas were loose around her bottom, they used to be skin-tight. Her boobs were smaller and her stomach flatter. She felt pleased but still wanted to lose more weight. Not for vanity's sake, but because every pound lost meant she was changing her appearance and moving closer to her goal of transformation.

'I want to throw off Brigid's skin,' she thought as she headed back to the attic and climbed onto the exercise bike.

She planned to complete a five-mile ride before breakfast and do another cycle later on. The bike, she'd discovered, was a great way of killing the endless hours and keeping her mind off the nightmares.

It was sometime later in the afternoon, and Annie was spread out on the mattress staring out of the skylight. She was watching the puffy clouds pass overhead and imagining what it would be like to float on one.

Josh popped his head around the door and asked, 'What are you doing?'

'Watching the clouds. These ones here are Cumulus.' Annie pointed to the woolly shape that was floating a mile or so above the house. She'd just finished reading a book on cloud formation. Cumulus were not found above 6,500 feet.

'Interesting,' said Josh not even glancing at the sky. 'I'm going to the bank for my meeting.'

Annie turned to Josh and took her chance. 'Why? Is there a problem?' He hadn't mentioned his appointment and this made her uneasy. Was her husband hiding something?

'The meeting is nothing to worry about, I promise,' said Josh buttoning up a clean shirt. 'Just crossing the T's and dotting the I's.'

Annie turned back to stare out of the window. 'We'll soon be rich,' she said flatly watching the clouds. 'I hadn't realised quite how boring death would be.'

Annie felt cut off from the world, rather like the ghosts she had encountered. She was of this place but not really part of it.

'Sorry, I've no time to chat,' said Josh checking his appearance once last time in the bedroom's new mirror.

The small reflection cut his handsome face in half. Annie saw that he had to move his head to see the right side of his reflection.

'That's how I feel. Like my body is split in two,' she said. 'Two parts neither fused nor whole.'

Josh ignored her comment and said he had to dash. When Annie heard the front door slam, she jumped up and pulled her laptop out from her holdall and pressed the power button. A bit of internet surfing would cheer her up. Annie only tended to go online whenever Josh was out, but it wasn't because she had anything to hide, she just didn't want him to think she was lazing around.

While looking at various social media sites, using her

fake accounts, Annie saw numerous posts from Josie about a recent trip to Mauritius for *Vogue*. It was weird. It felt like she was spying on her friend, then she realised that was exactly what she was doing. It was an odd sensation, this separation from the world. She wondered if this was how lonely people felt? Cut off and isolated? The world flowing around them while they remained hidden away.

At least they could reach out if they wanted to. Annie could speak to no one but Josh. And she was beginning to wonder if that would be enough.

Josh

The walls of the bank's staircase were made of an impressive marble. It seemed to take forever to arrive at the top of the building where his meeting was scheduled. Josh, despite being fit, was breathing rapidly when he reached the final landing.

He touched the marble wall to steady himself and left an incomplete handprint. The outline of moisture from his sweaty palm was barely visible on the cold stone. He paused to catch his breath as he stepped into the wide expansive foyer. Josh noted the leather tub chairs arranged in a corner and the free coffee machine.

'Don't get drawn into any long discussions. You're here to get the money,' he told himself.

Opposite the chairs were private glass-walled meeting rooms, a handful of which were occupied. Josh helped himself to a black coffee while he waited. He wanted something to do with his hands. Clearly, he couldn't smoke inside this building.

Josh hadn't told his wife that he was anxious about this meeting. After he'd phoned the bank about her death he had been sent various claim forms, which had been easy to fill in. But now he was worried that he'd been called in for a follow-up interrogation.

What could they be suspicious about and on what grounds? Why was there a delay in paying out? He took a deep breath and sipped the bitter black liquid.

From his time at the tax office, he knew that the best approach was to play dumb. Only answer the questions asked. Don't offer any extra information.

The door to one of the cubicles opened and a tall man wearing brown brogues stepped out into the waiting area and said Josh's name. The man introduced himself as Donald Lawrence and he gestured for Josh to take a seat inside his cubicle.

'Please call me Lawrence. There's another Donald at the branch.'

Josh smiled to mask his thoughts. The man was too posh for a high-street bank. He should be working in the City. Something must have gone wrong in his life.

'I'm very sorry for the loss of your wife…' Lawrence glanced at his notes, '…Brigid.'

Josh wondered if the gold signet ring on Lawrence's little finger was real. Or was the family crest a fake imagined by an artisan jeweller in Hoxton? Oxford had been full of people like that, who thought that a new accent and expensive trinkets somehow elevated them. But he'd learnt to listen for the flat Northern vowels that sneaked in and gave their game away. Lawrence had flat vowels.

'Thank you,' Josh replied politely.

'So, your wife had two life insurance policies with us totalling £320,000.'

Josh said yes. Nothing more. With unease, he wondered where this conversation was going.

'I see you own a house in Roundhay? But it was involved in a fire recently,' said Lawrence consulting the forms again.

'Yes,' repeated Josh still poker-faced.

'The life assurance alone is a rather large amount of money to come into,' said Lawrence leaning back in his chair. 'A rather large amount indeed.'

'I've not really thought about it, what with the funeral and everything else…' Josh let his voice trail off.

'Yes, yes of course,' said Lawrence. 'I'm sorry, it must have been a dreadful shock to lose your wife. And so suddenly.'

Josh wouldn't be smoked out. He waited calmly for Lawrence to move his next piece.

The man leant back into his chair, and rested his hands in his lap. Josh copied Lawrence's posture. He'd read somewhere that imitating a person's body language made them trust you. There was more silence for a few seconds. Lawrence fidgeted and shuffled his papers. Josh still sat with his hands in his lap.

'And you contacted us…' again Lawrence consulted his paperwork, 'the week after your wife's death?'

The man was not on the ball, and this wasn't an investigation. Josh felt his tense shoulder muscles relax a little.

'That's right,' said Josh not betraying his relief.

'And you're still living in your temporary accommodation in Chapeltown?'

'Yes, I'm still living in Chapeltown. For the moment.' Josh maintained his calm exterior.

'Ah yes, unfortunate that you didn't renew the house insurance,' said Lawrence half-smiling.

'Smug fuck. So, you've done your homework,' thought Josh. His shoulders tensed again, he willed himself to smile back and not allow the man to affect him.

'What is your house worth now, Mr Raven?'

'Around £80,000,' lied Josh. 'An estate agent valued it recently. I also took advice from a specialist surveyor.'

Lawrence smiled again. Josh noticed that the banker's

mouth was stretched into a half grimace, the type of smile that switches on and off in the middle of a sentence.

'A politician's smile,' thought Josh.

'What are your plans for the property?' asked Lawrence. He leant forward and added, 'Will you renovate or sell?'

Josh stumbled for the first time during the meeting. He was taken aback by this unexpected question. 'I've er, not really thought about it. I'm still trying to process everything that's happened and…'

Lawrence cut him off mid-sentence and said, 'That's understandable.' He cleared his throat and added, 'You're probably wondering why I asked you to come to this meeting?'

The man spoke in a hushed tone and put on what he thought was a sympathetic face. Josh saw right through him. All Lawrence cared about was money. Josh sensed a pitch coming.

'To be honest, I want to talk to you about your investment options once your policies are paid out,' explained Lawrence.

'Bingo. I was right,' thought Josh. 'The man is a vulture.'

'I know it might seem insensitive but the bank has a number of fantastic investment opportunities,' said Lawrence who was speaking brightly now. 'These offers may be withdrawn at any moment, however, if you were to apply for the products today it would constitute an application. And, you would be eligible even if the products were removed from the market at a later date.' Lawrence beamed as if he'd just done Josh a huge favour.

'Oh right. I see,' said Josh. He shifted in his seat and tried to decide how to turn the man down as quickly and politely as possible.

'Let me be frank,' said Lawrence aware that he was possibly losing a sale. 'A colleague who was processing your claims forms gave me your information. It's standard practice these days to cross-reference between departments. We can offer you some great investment opportunities. I hope you're not offended.'

Josh kept a neutral face, nodded, and said thank you. He stood up and held out his hand. 'I'm not offended. Not at all. But it's too early for me to be thinking about investments. Can I contact you at a later date once the money has come through? By the way, do you know why there has been a delay?'

Lawrence's mouth dropped slightly. He couldn't hide his disappointment. The man was clearly put out by Josh brushing him off so firmly, and quickly.

'There's a backlog due to staff shortages and the holidays,' said Lawrence. 'I know that your claim is going through because I spoke to the department only this morning.'

Josh smiled, murmured his thanks and headed towards the door. He didn't care about Lawrence's feelings. He wanted to get out of his office and fast.

Lawrence had to respond in bank mode so he smiled, gave Josh his business card and said thank you. But he spoke in clipped tones, it was clear he'd expected an easy sale. Josh didn't flinch at the man's frostiness. In one smooth motion, he took Lawrence's business card then said goodbye and left the room.

As he walked away from the bank Josh sensed that he was being observed. He'd seen this part of the street out of Lawrence's window during their meeting and for good measure he made a show of tucking the man's card into his wallet.

He would throw the card away later.

Annie

January brought with it a chilly frost that seeped into the house and into Annie's bones. As she tidied the bedroom, whose décor was as barren as the skeleton trees outside, Annie went over recent events in her mind. She was relieved that the trip to the bank had turned out, in Josh's words, to be 'a posh tosser just trying to sell investment products', but it bothered her that it was still taking so long. Even taking into account time off for Christmas and New Year, the claims were going through without any issues, so why hadn't they paid out?

Aside from the money issue, another thing gnawed at Annie's mind. The bad dreams. Last night she'd had the rat nightmare again. Her body had been crawling with the tiny beasts and she'd screamed and clawed against the lid with bleeding fingers whilst trying to escape the coffin. When a presence had joined her in the confined space, she'd woken up.

Annie moved on to cleaning the bathroom and hoped that all of this wiping and mopping would wash away the shadows from her dreams.

By the time she'd reached the kitchen, Annie had shaken off the unsettling memory. She opened a kitchen cupboard, emptied it, wiped the shelves and put the tins back in neat rows. On another shelf, Annie repeated the process with the dried goods.

'What I wouldn't do for a piece of cake,' she thought. 'I'd run naked down the street.'

Annie erased the image of the cake in the same way that she had pushed away the nightmare. She turned her full attention to getting every part of the kitchen spotless. Perhaps, if she was completely physically exhausted tonight she wouldn't have the dreams.

The weight had continued to drop off her and Annie found that she liked her new body shape, so no matter how much she wanted cake she knew she wouldn't eat it. A fresher version of herself was emerging ready for her new life.

Even Josh agreed. 'You don't look like Brigid anymore,' he'd told her last night, 'It's quite astonishing.'

Brigid would have been hurt by Josh's comment but Annie was pleased. If she was to succeed in creating a new identity then she'd have to transform herself beyond recognition. Josh telling her that she didn't look like Brigid meant her metamorphosis was working. The food denial and the long attic bike rides, that took her nowhere, were paying off.

Turning her husband's words over in her mind, Annie mopped the kitchen floor. She focused on her new identity.

Her name became a mantra. 'I am Annie Raven. I am Annie Raven. I am Annie Raven.'

When the words merged into one she let her mind go blank and gave into the rhythm of moving backwards and forwards with the mop. It was relaxing. Cathartic.

Downstairs cleaned, she moved upstairs to the living room and automatically went to open the window to air the space. With her hand outstretched, Annie stopped herself. Josh continued to ban her from opening any windows and from even looking out of them – even at night.

'We don't want people to see you,' he'd explained. 'It's too big a risk. Remember, you're dead.'

Once again, Annie left the curtains drawn. The strict rules about the windows meant Annie was living in a cocoon. The light came through the windows in different colours and intensity depending on the time of day, but she could never feel the fresh air.

When it was bright she longed to go outside. She'd forgotten what it felt like to breathe clean air into her lungs and feel the wind on her face. She had cabin fever. The stale air suffocated her, especially as the house was so depressing with its dated brown décor and woodchip wallpaper.

When Josh went out she often sneaked upstairs to their attic bedroom and opened the skylight wide even though it was winter. After she had finished cleaning the living room, she went up to the attic bedroom and did just that. She stood under the open window with her eyes shut smelling the breeze. Annie felt the icy air and she didn't care if the draft froze her head and shoulders and made her shiver. The open window recharged her body with positive ions.

Feeling refreshed, Annie flopped down on the mattress and opened her laptop. Without hesitating, she visited the rescue charity's website where she'd volunteered in her other life. She wanted to see which dogs had found forever homes and was delighted to learn that Crystal, a West Highland Terrier, had been reserved as had the Staffordshire Bull Terrier who'd arrived with facial burns. But several other dogs she knew were still looking for owners.

'Please God find someone who will love them,' she prayed quickly.

The dogs were well cared for at the centre, but she hated the thought of them sleeping at night in the kennel block, afraid, and having nightmares as scary as her own.

Josh

It was after six and dark outside. Annie was wrapped up in bed reading her tatty copy of the *Children's Encyclopaedia of Dogs*. She'd found the book at her mother's house in a dusty cupboard and taken it with her, God knows why.

'I've been thinking about what type of dog would suit us,' said Annie resting the book down.

The room was ice cold and he could see his breath. Josh turned on the fan heater and said, 'Hang on, we need to move first.'

Josh kissed his wife softly on her lips and wished she wasn't quite so obsessed with dogs. He'd string her along for a bit and they'd get a mutt when he was good and ready.

Annie picked up her book and flicked through the pages nosily. She was angry at him, again.

'Don't sulk, Bridge. We can decide on the breed nearer the time,' said Josh rubbing his hands together. He kicked off his black boots and trousers and scooted into the warm bed.

His wife screwed up her face, 'It's Annie. And you smell of alcohol. I knew you'd go to the pub before you came home.'

'I met Henry for a pint. He's been a good mate. If we ever sell that wreck of a house he's only going to charge us 1.5 per cent.'

He knew his wife wouldn't be cross with him for long.

Annie put the book down and frowned, 'I was thinking about my own friends earlier, about what they've been doing since I died. I'm worried about Josie, she's so sensitive.'

'She'll hold up,' said Josh avoiding her eye. Shit. Best

keep his wife off the topic of her old life or she'd soon spiral downwards. Keep her mind focused on the future. Josh added breezily, 'Don't fret, Josie's new job will stop her thinking about your death. And you have so much to look forward to. A dog for one thing. A warm house with a real fire.'

'I suppose so,' said Annie biting her lip. 'It's just so hard. I feel so cut off from everyone. From life. I'm lonely, Josh. I didn't expect to feel this way.'

'You have me. Everything will work out. And when we move, you can make new friends.'

Josh flipped back the duvet and got out of bed. Lonely. She was sodding lonely. Didn't his wife know how lucky she was compared to all the other worker bees? No more commutes, no more sitting in boring meetings with some arsehole breathing down your neck about your performance and targets. He didn't mention these thoughts, of course, but wondered why couldn't she just get on with things and see the bigger picture? She was always moaning about something. Christ, they were rich. Or they soon would be rich.

'I'm going for a bath,' he said picking up a damp towel from the chair.

It was the coward's way out, he knew. Excusing himself from the situation to avoid a fight. But they had to get on with one another and she was winding him up with all her bleating. Best to remove himself for an hour or so, let her get her head back in that silly dog book.

Like he'd told his wife numerous times, it was the two of them against the world. A new life would soon unfold, ready to mould into whatever shape they wished.

They just had to hang on to the dream for a little while longer.

Annie

The living room curtains were shut. The only light that lit up Annie's face was the glow from her laptop. She was flicking through photos and smiled at a selfie taken with Josie the previous year on holiday in Ibiza. They were in a bar, faces flushed, holding their cocktails aloft like prizes. It had been a fantastic trip. She'd only been able to afford the holiday because Josie's aunt had lent them her villa. All she'd had to pay for was her cheap flight. She'd never be able to have a holiday abroad again. Not unless Josh bought her a fake passport, but that meant more lies, more risk and it wasn't worth it. She needed to stay low, become invisible.

'You shouldn't look at old photographs. They'll make you maudlin,' said Josh flopping down on to the saggy sofa.

Annie frowned. 'It's not good to forget people.' She was still smarting from Josh's comments the previous evening about how Josie's friendship didn't matter. The friendship mattered to her. She cherished her memories of them together, and at times it felt like she was grieving for her lost friend. Annie missed Josie every day.

'You're not going to forget Josie,' said Josh putting an arm around his wife's shoulders. 'Or any of your other friends.'

'I just feel closer to them when I look at photos,' said Annie looking at another image. 'Makes me feel like I'm still alive.' She smiled at the last picture taken of the two of them together at Josie's mother's house, they were grinning and both making the peace sign.

'You *are* still alive.' His exasperation was clear in his voice. 'And you have me. You don't need anyone else.'

'It's not that your company isn't enough, I just, I don't

know, I feel cut off.' Annie was surprised that her husband didn't understand how she felt, but then how could he? He was out in the world whist she was stuck inside. 'I can't talk to anyone or call anyone. I can't go outside. I'm trapped in this in-between place.' Annie didn't mention her brief trip to the post box for obvious reasons.

'I'm sorry, it won't be for long. You'll just have to put up with just me for a while,' said Josh jokingly. He grinned at her and leaned in for a kiss.

'I'm being serious,' said Annie pushing him away. She knew her husband was trying to lighten the mood but it made her feel like he was making fun of her feelings. 'Don't you understand how I feel?'

'Yes, and I think it's amazing what you're doing for us.' Josh was suddenly serious. He took Annie's hands, turned the palms over and kissed them. 'You are so brave.'

'I'm not brave. Soldiers are brave. People who fight cancer are brave,' said Annie. 'It's been too easy. Something *has* to go wrong.'

'Be positive. You've read enough of those crappy books about the law of attraction.'

He smiled and the corners of his eyes crinkled. He knew that she couldn't resist his smile. She smiled back and felt her anger begin to fade.

'Let's activate the law of attraction,' he said throwing his arms wide. 'Everything is going to work out exactly as it should,' said Josh raising his eyebrows. 'We will get the life we deserve.'

'Okay, okay, I'll try to be positive,' said Annie laughing. She caught Josh's high mood. He could always make her instantly feel better with his infectious energy.

'Good. I loved you curvy, by the way. But you do look fantastic now. You're like a Northern supermodel.'

'You're so corny,' said Annie laughing again. He was flattering her, the silly sod.

'I don't care. It's true. Once you've cut your hair you'll be unrecognisable.'

'Cut my hair?' Annie felt her good mood fizzling away and touched her long red ponytail, she presumed Josh had just expected her to dye it. Her mother had hacked her hair off over the kitchen sink when she was a child for being cheeky, it had taken forever to grow back, and she'd promised herself never to have short hair again.

'Obviously, you need to cut and dye your hair before we move. I thought you knew that.' Josh added quickly, 'You can always grow it back later.'

Annie didn't know what to say. The thought of dyeing her beautiful red hair had been bad enough, but cutting it all off too? Before she could say something she might regret, she went upstairs to find a jumper. The room had turned suddenly chilly.

When she came back downstairs, Josh was stood with his arms folded by the fireplace. His jaw was clenched and it was clear that he was furious about something.

'What have you been doing?' His words were spat out one by one.

'What do you mean?' asked Annie taken aback. She had no idea what had made her husband so angry so quickly. Had he found out about the postcard? How?

'You've been on Facebook. Twitter. Pinterest and God knows what else. You've even been on tarot websites and asked "Will we pull off the insurance scam?" I can't believe you've been so bloody stupid!'

Annie looked at her laptop on the coffee table and winced. She'd never imagined Josh would snoop and so she hadn't thought it necessary to clear her history. Even though she knew it had been wrong, her laptop was her final link with the outside world. And the invasion into her private space made the anger rise up inside, she swallowed it down.

'Every single key stroke… Every single web search. Every time you log onto a site it's recorded on your hard drive,' said Josh. His face was red and he was slowly shaking his head.

'I thought if I erased the history on my browser the information would be wiped out,' said Annie calmly, maintaining control.

Josh's face had now turned puce with rage. 'You've not even done that,' he shouted. 'What if the police had arrested us today for fraud and seized the laptop? For crying out loud.' Josh ran his hands through his hair.

Annie remained silent. This wasn't the first time her husband had been this furious with her. And she knew that if she let him burn it off he'd soon calm down. He was like that – boom explode – then it was all over. No good would come of them screaming at each other, which is why she had to be the bigger person and squash her resentment.

'We agreed no access to social media,' said Josh still furious. He pointed to the computer, 'That is a fucking time bomb.'

'I swear I've not posted anything.' Annie made eye contact with Josh and tried to lighten the mood. 'I created a fake profile and I've just been looking at people's posts.'

Josh ignored her excuses. 'You're not to go on any social

networking sites again. Understand?'

Annie nodded. She knew it was best to stay silent. He ranted about how she'd worked in the media and should have known better. How some silly bloody searches could have ruined everything. Josh took a deep breath and Annie was relieved to see his rage visibly draining away.

'I'm sorry I lost my temper,' he said blowing out the last of his anger. The rage left his body and he smiled. 'It's just that we're so close. We have to be careful. Stick to the rules. No opening the curtains. No browsing on social media. Agreed?'

Annie said she was sorry and understood why he was so livid. She felt a mixture of humiliation and shame. Josh was right to be angry. How could she have not realised the consequences of her actions? It wasn't just the money at stake, it was their freedom too because if they were caught committing fraud they would more than likely go to prison.

She wondered briefly how on earth they had got to this point. How two basically good, decent people had ended up as what? Criminals?

It was a crazy chain of events that had pushed them into this terrible position and Josh had taken control. Could she have stopped it? Could she have said no at any point? She could have said no to taking the Death Herb. No to putting wood in the coffin. No to faking her funeral. No to hiding out in this awful house.

But she hadn't said no.

Which made her just as guilty as Josh.

Josh

The psychologist's practice was situated in a tastefully decorated Georgian mansion down a quiet side-street in Leeds city centre. In the waiting room Josh sat with one other person. The middle-aged man had a shaved head and was wearing a grey suit, he was hooked up to an ancient iPod and was well-built with hands the size of side plates. He gave off a subtle odour of violence.

'I should have arrived just before my appointment,' Josh thought as he pretended to read a battered car magazine. 'That guy looks like he's going to kick off at any moment.'

The two men sat in silence whilst the receptionist tapped on her computer keyboard.

As the minutes ticked by, Josh's mind wandered to his argument with Annie the day before. He was still shocked by his own rage and her naivety concerning her computer's history, but he'd said his piece, and his wife had promised to delete her fake social media profiles and he had to trust her. Even so, he'd double-check her laptop when she was in the bath or asleep. Too much was at stake for any more cock-ups.

Eventually the receptionist looked up. 'Mr Darkere,' she said to the man with the headphones. 'Mr Bennett Darkere,' she repeated more loudly.

The man removed an earplug. The Elvis track *Jailhouse Rock* blared out of the tiny pod.

'Sorry, I've made a mistake,' said the receptionist. 'Dr Augur was expecting you this morning. Didn't you receive the message about changing your appointment?'

'No, I didn't,' said Bennett Darkere calmly. He waited

for the woman to speak again as his tinny music filled the room.

In his peripheral vision, Josh saw the man had clenched his right fist. Actually, he had a point. Why had the receptionist made him wait?

The receptionist rescheduled the appointment for later in the afternoon and said he was lucky there had been a cancellation. The man unfurled his fist. Josh turned another page. He knew the man wouldn't lose it here.

Bennett Darkere put the earplug back in his left ear and left. The pretty receptionist called Josh and said that Dr Augur was ready for him.

The clinical psychologist Dr Elizabeth Augur shook Josh's hand as he entered her office. All of his thoughts were on the job in hand.

The psychologist was in her late fifties and wore a black tunic dress over black tights with brown knee-high riding boots. Around her neck hung a chunky silver and amber necklace. On her fingers were several large silver rings, and no wedding ring. The therapist managed to give the impression of being professional and hip at the same time.

'I bet she likes a toke,' thought Josh, 'The old hippy.'

'I'm so sorry for your loss,' said Dr Augur shaking Josh's hand. 'Brigid was a dear friend to my daughter Josie. I thought very highly of your wife. She was an honest and cheery person with a steely determination. Anyone who escapes her kind of background has real strength.'

Josh said thank you and reminded himself he needed to refer to his wife as Brigid and not by her new name. More mentally prepared, he sat down.

Josh noticed that hung on the wall behind the psychologist

were strange masks, some of the distorted faces looked frightening with their large screaming mouths. The masks were made of wood, some were painted, and all had holes cut to represent eyes and noses giving them an eerily life-like appearance.

Real human teeth appeared to be attached to one particular mask and the tiny yellowing tombstones created a gaping hole that drew in his eyes. Were they African? One thing was certain, they gave Josh the creeps even though he didn't go in for any of that voodoo rubbish.

'You've noticed my little collection,' said Dr Augur turning briefly to admire her masks. 'I have a deep interest in the human psyche and the masks we create for ourselves. Masks help us to navigate through life and hide our true feelings.'

Josh smiled slightly and thought, 'How true, doctor, how true.'

Dr Augur turned over a clean page on her notepad and said, 'That brings me to why I invited you for these free sessions. Grief can be a debilitating emotion, Josh. I want you to feel safe. You can remove your mask in my office. Tell me, how have you been coping since your wife's death?'

Annie

A week later, Annie hunted through the clothes on the attic floor for some clean jeans and spotted a plastic bag containing a packet of permanent hair dye. Josh must have bought the box earlier that morning when he'd gone out to buy a newspaper.

Seeing no point in putting off the inevitable, Annie picked the box up and headed to the bathroom. She set the box down on the sink, grabbed a comb and two elastic bands and divided her hair into two bunches. With a few brutal hacks, her long red locks were soon cut to jaw length. After a few more snips, she had cut a short fringe.

The discarded hair fell into the basin. Annie took a deep breath before daring to look at her new reflection in the mirror. She was surprised, the end result didn't look too uneven.

Josh knocked on the bathroom door, 'Are you okay?' he asked.

She was glad she had locked the door. Annie wanted the results to be a surprise for Josh. 'Yes, just washing my hair,' she said still looking at her new reflection.

Annie unboxed the dye and the instructions.

'I'm going for another session with Josie's mum. Wish me luck,' said her husband through the bathroom door.

'Luck,' Annie called back.

The whole house shook as Josh exited and the irritation curled in Annie's stomach. How many times had she asked Josh not to slam the front door? Tutting, she quickly read the instructions then squeezed the dye onto her head. The black mixture slid across her crown like an oil spill. Annie rubbed the dye vigorously into her hair and worked it into a thick lather.

As she let the hair dye take, Annie went to make a cup of tea and hunted out the radio from their bedroom.

Soon the soothing tones of classical music swirled around Annie as she washed the sludgy lather off her head into the wash-hand basin. Then she stepped into the half-full tub. The warmth and music sucked her into relaxation.

For the first time in weeks Annie's mind wasn't chattering and she floated in nothingness. She'd not had a nightmare for two nights and felt rested.

'Everything will work out,' she was thinking, 'it's just the stress.' Vivaldi's Four Seasons was playing on the radio when the music crackled, then cut out.

Annie sat up to investigate and just as she reached for the radio on the floor she saw something move out of the corner of her eye. The bathroom was door ajar, she'd not closed it after finding the radio, and she saw a black shadow streak past. The apparition was too quick for her to take in any more details. She shot out of the bath, water sloshed onto the floor.

'Josh, is that you?' she shouted. The goosebumps on her arm, however, let her know that what she'd seen had not been a living person. Even so, she wanted to be sure.

Naked and dripping water, Annie poked her head around the bathroom door to check the dark landing. Her heart was pounding. She hadn't heard her husband come back into the house.

'Josh?' she called again quieter this time, mindful that she didn't want the neighbours to hear her. 'Josh,' she called a third time. Still no response.

Shivering, Annie grabbed a towel to dry off, put on her dressing gown, and went out onto the landing. She turned on the hall light and leant over the stairs. The house was silent, she was definitely alone.

The radio suddenly burst back to life. She jumped at the unexpected noise and went back into the bathroom. She turned the radio on and off a few times, but it seemed to be working fine.

Annie shook her head. It had been so long since she'd seen any spirits that she'd forgotten how much the encounters freaked her out. Too jittery to relax in the bath again, she pulled out the plug and went to get dressed.

'I'll be seeing fairies next,' she mused slipping a t-shirt over her head.

Hours later, Annie's new hairstyle made Josh's mouth drop open.

'I hardly recognise you,' he said.

'Does it make me look like a Goth?'

'A very sexy Goth.' Josh kissed the end of her nose. 'Or Louise Brooks.'

Josh dumped his coat on the stairs and kicked off his boots. He'd been gone for a few hours and Annie felt relieved her husband was home and she was no longer alone. She still felt creeped out by the dark shadow.

'How was the session with Josie's mum?' she asked turning up the gas fire.

'Fine. I talked about my grief but said that I wouldn't be going back. I needed time to come to terms with everything. I think I'm in the clear, Dr Augur won't harass me for a follow up session.'

Annie put her arms around his neck. 'You are a bad man,'

she said then kissed him and felt a fluttering in her loins.

Josh pulled back to look at his wife.

'You look like a completely different person compared to two months ago.' He hooked his fingers into her knickers and said, 'Let's see if the blinds match the curtains.'

They passed the hours of the afternoon in bed. Josh had smoked two joints and read a car magazine before falling to sleep. Annie was wide awake, so she logged onto her laptop and deleted all her fake social media accounts. She'd promised to wipe them after their row but was only getting around to it after much pestering from Josh.

It took a while for Annie to navigate Twitter, all sorts of warnings flashed up. Her email addresses were easy to dump though. Slowly with every keystroke, she wiped out her digital presence and committed cyber-suicide. Now her only footprint on the net was her Facebook legacy account, which she couldn't look at because she couldn't log in as herself so she had no access to it.

Annie felt a lump in her throat. It was strange to have such a strong emotional reaction to her death on the net. It was unexpected. Suddenly Annie realised why she felt tearful. The outside world from her past no longer existed, from here on it really was just herself and Josh. Her past had been erased forever and obliterated.

Of course, Annie Googled herself afterwards and the odd hit came up for *Brigid Raven* but when she clicked on any of the links, for example her staff profile on the magazine, it said things like 'Page no longer available' or 'Sorry there is a problem and we're trying to fix it'.

It was official, with no digital presence she no longer existed. The last cord to her old life had been cut.

Josh

As Josh waited outside the estate agents he sucked on his cigarette. He'd been meaning to cut down on his smoking, but what with the stress of losing his home, his lack of a job and all his money worries, kicking his nicotine addiction didn't seem that important any more.

In fact, the cigarettes kept him calm. For the last few weeks he'd felt on edge and more prone to losing his temper than usual. That outburst with Brigid over social media was just the tip of it and it scared him. Where was the rage coming from?

It was the pressure of the scam, he told himself. He wasn't a bad person. All the waiting for the cash to come through would be enough to send anyone over the edge. As usual, he was being fucked about by the overlords. The bloody Masters of the Universe. Once things were sorted with the bank, and the house was sold, he'd be back to his chilled self.

Taking a final drag on his cigarette, Josh promised himself he'd give up smoking once all the stress was over and he was far away from Leeds.

Checking his watch, Josh noted that it was four minutes to nine. Henry should be here opening up like the other retail workers who were hurrying up Briggate with freshly applied make-up and coiffured hair.

Why was he always late? It was one of the things that irked Josh about his acquaintance. He wouldn't call Henry a friend because he didn't confide in him. But Henry wasn't exactly an enemy either, and they did meet occasionally at the Turk's Head for a pint.

Should he have checked out a few other firms before

giving Henry the sale? It was the quickest option at the time, and he'd taken the easy route like he always did. Josh chided himself, that was another change he'd make once they left Leeds. He'd be less lazy.

Josh spotted Henry rushing towards the shopfront. When he was a few metres away, Josh noticed a small piece of white tissue stuck to the estate agent's face.

'What are you doing here?' asked Henry producing a bunch of keys, which he used to unlock the door.

'Did you cut yourself shaving?'

'What? Yes, shit is the tissue still on my face?' Without waiting for an answer Henry rubbed his cheek. The tissue disappeared and a small red cut appeared in its place.

Inside the branch, Henry flicked on all the overhead lights. The room filled with light and the quiet hum of electricity.

'Have you come for an update?'

Josh nodded. Of course he'd come for a sodding update. He'd not schlepped into Leeds through the rush hour traffic to chat about the weather.

'You could have rung,' said Henry turning on the computers. 'Saved yourself the journey. Sorry, there's been no interest in your house but it's still early days. The other staff are in at 9:30 today, I'll get them to ring round some developers.'

'Is there anything I can do to help?' said Josh with a fake smile. He was feeling that rage again and swallowed it down. Didn't this moron realise how important it was to sell his house quickly? Hadn't he gone over it a dozen times?

'No, the price is spot on. Don't worry, we'll get you a sale,' said Henry hanging up his coat.

'I'm counting on you, mate,' said Josh still smiling. 'Don't forget, if you let me down I'll break both your legs.'

'Very funny,' said Henry laughing as he sat down at his desk. 'You crack me up, Josh.'

'I'm not joking, Henry.'

'Right, got it,' said Henry shaking his head and smiling. 'You used to say you'd shag my wife.'

'I'll do that too,' said Josh as he left the estate agents.

Outside, Josh sighed deeply. He was so frustrated with having to let someone else control a key event in his life. Why was he surrounded by so many bloody idiots?

'The house will sell. Everything will work out,' he told himself as he lit another cigarette and felt the tension melt away from his body.

Annie

The days merged into one another seamlessly. Sometimes, Annie missed the structure of her previous life. She felt lost, as if she was stuck on a desert island surrounded by a murky sea that stretched out into infinity. That was how she felt today. Marooned with her thoughts whilst the rest of the world was out of reach shimmering in the distance.

Annie forced herself to think of something pleasant. She lay back on the mattress in the attic and imagined living in a cottage on a cliff top. The living room had white plastered walls and logs were stacked beside a wood-burning stove. From the window, there was a spectacular view of the sea.

'I've brought you some breakfast,' said Josh.

He was holding a tray and had appeared from the depths of the house. On the tray was a mug of black tea and a bowl of chopped fresh fruit.

'The breakfast of dieters,' said Annie.

Josh put the tray down and said he was going to meet Henry in an hour.

'I haven't heard from him since we spoke the other week. I want to see if I can move things along a bit. God knows what lunatic would buy our wreck of a house, but he says there's a market.'

'I'm sure Henry knows what he's doing. When do you think that the insurance money will come through?'

What Annie really wanted to know was how much longer she would have to stay imprisoned in this house bathed in darkness? Outside it was bright and the winter sun streamed into the attic bedroom. She longed to crunch through the snow.

'Within a month or so,' said Josh putting on a warm jumper.

'Have you heard from the bank?'

'No, and no news is good news.'

Josh handed Annie the bowl and a spoon and sat on the bed. Annie toyed with the fruit. She couldn't help but think the worst.

'Don't worry,' said Josh. 'The hardest bit was faking your death and I couldn't believe how easy that was to pull off.'

'I'm not as cocky as you.'

'Just as well,' said Josh tweaking her nose. 'I'm going out, remember no lights.'

Annie nodded and wished he wouldn't leave her alone because she'd seen the shadow again in the middle of the night. Annie had just come out of the bathroom when she felt a sudden and unexplained nausea, the thing then appeared in her peripheral vision again, only a few feet away. The shape was about six feet tall and quickly merged into the darkness in the hallway.

When she'd woken Josh up and told him about what she'd seen he'd teased her. He'd said it was the night playing tricks with her eyes and told her to go back to sleep.

Annie had spent the rest of the night awake and terrified that the thing, whatever it was, might come back. It wasn't like one of her normal sightings, those ghosts were always of people or animals, mostly dogs, and the humans wore clothes and fitted into a story somehow. It was the lack of detail, the nothingness of this black shape that disturbed her. She couldn't link the presence to the environment and explain its existence.

Annie climbed onto the exercise bike and put her

headphones into her ears. Her legs pumped to the beat. As she peddled and watched the sky, she could feel her muscles working and the heat rising in her face.

Annie was lost in the music when she experienced a strange sensation on her skin. Pins and needles pricked her neck and the sensation spread upwards across her scalp. Her body was alerting her to a danger that consciously she wasn't even aware of yet.

Annie pulled out her earphones and listened. She stilled her legs on the pedals and became motionless like a small animal being hunted in a wood. Outside was silent, but Annie could sense danger, so slowly, and quietly, she climbed off the exercise bike.

Quickly, she crept downstairs to the next landing hoping that she wasn't going to have another sighting of the dark shadow. She waited in the hall frozen to the spot.

After a few seconds, Annie's ears picked up a sound. Someone had opened their metal gate. She heard a knock on the front door. He or she didn't wait for an answer. They were letting themselves in with a key.

'That's not Josh. He wouldn't knock.'

Annie's instinct was to launch herself under the double bed in the empty bedroom. A large white sheet hung over the side of the bed and hid her from view; she'd thrown the sheet on the bare mattress to air the day before.

Curling inward to make herself smaller Annie's mind raced. Who could it be?

'Anybody home?' shouted a voice with fake cheer. It was her mother.

How did she have a key? In a flash, Annie remembered. Her own set of keys to their new rental property had vanished hours before they'd moved in. She thought Josh has mislaid them.

It was clear what had happened. Her mother had stolen the keys from the kitchen table.

Downstairs, Annie heard her mother clattering around. The woman was like a whirlwind going through the house's few objects.

Her chest felt tight. Annie realised she was holding her breath. She let out the air in a thin stream and concentrated on regulating her breathing. The last thing she needed was an asthma attack.

Long minutes passed. Outside on the landing a light was switched on, Annie saw a beam of yellow squeeze under the door. She waited, Annie wouldn't have been surprised if her mother had shouted, 'I'm coming to get you.'

Her mother went into the bathroom but didn't shut the door. Annie heard her mother's pee hit the water in the loo, which made her skin crawl. The loo flushed.

Annie felt the panic fluttering in her stomach. At any moment, the woman might come into the spare bedroom. What if she looked under the bed? Annie silently willed for her mother to go back downstairs.

But the door of the bedroom was pushed open.

Annie saw her mother's scrawny ankles. The woman's feet were so close that Annie could have reached out and touched the scuffed heel of one of her stilettos.

'Go away. Please make her go away,' pleaded Annie to whichever God was listening.

Just then, the front door closed with a bang. The whole house shook. A bunch of keys was thrown on to the hall table.

'Mrs Doran?' shouted Josh. 'Why are you in my house?'

She must have left her fur coat on the banister.

Her mother's scuffed shoes froze for a moment then Mrs Doran shouted back, 'Yes, it's only me.' The feet vanished out of the room.

'What the hell do you think you're doing?' shouted Josh from downstairs.

Annie took a deep breath and smiled. Josh would chase her mother away.

Josh

'Don't get your knickers in a twist,' said Mrs Doran.

Josh watched his mother-in-law walk slowly down the stairs, he was surprised by the level of hatred that he felt towards the woman. How dare she come into his home unannounced? Thank God she clearly hadn't found her dead, but very much alive, daughter.

Annie must be hiding somewhere. Clever woman.

'I was only popping round to make sure you were okay,' said Mrs Doran raising her chin.

'And you thought you'd have a snoop whilst I was out.' Josh could not believe his mother-in-law's gall. He had to fight to keep himself under control.

'I wasn't snooping,' said Mrs Doran wide-eyed with innocence.

Josh stood at the bottom of the stairs and replied, 'So what were you doing exactly?'

The woman was such a liar. He could see it written on her craggy face.

'I've been worried about you,' said Mrs Doran as she scooped up her rancid fur coat from the end of the bannister.

Another lie. The woman only cared about herself. And drink. Josh stood to his full height and his mother-in-law had to tilt her head again, this time to look up to him. Her upturned chin gave her a superior look that didn't sit well with her shabby clothes.

'I let myself in to make sure you hadn't topped yourself,' she added with a shrug.

'As you can see, I'm still breathing. Keys,' said Josh as he held out his hand.

'I only…' Mrs Doran hesitated and the keys remained in her hand.

Before she could raise any objection, Josh calmly pulled the keys from her hand.

'There's no need to be so rough,' said Mrs Doran rubbing her wrist. 'That hurt.'

'Is that what your daughter said when she was little?' asked Josh feeling the quiet rage bubble up and fill his body.

Mrs Doran said nothing. Josh leant closer and smelt the rancid bag's cheap perfume.

He whispered in her ear, 'These days you would be put in prison for what you did to your child.'

Mrs Doran pulled away, 'What about the will? I have a right to the money.'

'You have no rights. My wife left everything to me.'

'I'll see you in court,' replied Mrs Doran.

Josh blocked her path. 'You don't have the money to litigate. But if you do take this to court, I'll make sure that every bit of your sordid past is revealed. Your secrets will be splashed over the local papers, probably the national press too.'

Mrs Doran cackled, 'What dirt do you have on me?'

Josh smiled. 'My wife found her old diaries when we stayed at your house. She'd hidden them under a floorboard. I still have them in a safe place.'

Mrs Doran sneered and said, 'Brigid was a child, who would believe her word against mine.'

Josh shook his head in disgust. 'My wife told me how you used to strip her naked and lock her in her bedroom when you went out. You left her for hours. And that's the tame stuff.'

'You've not seen the last of me,' said Mrs Doran as she turned on her heels.

Josh opened the front door. 'Yes, I have. Go on, fuck off.'

He physically pushed his mother-in-law out onto the path.

Mrs Doran stumbled and turned to have the last word but Josh waved her away and shouted, 'Don't come here again.'

He slammed the front door and thought, 'So much for keeping a low profile. And so much for keeping my anger under control.'

Annie

A few days had passed since her mother's uninvited visit and the house had settled into stillness once again. The curtains were drawn and the world remained remote. The gas fire provided a small amount of warmth as the temperature dropped further outside.

Josh was sat on the living room floor eating a pizza. Annie was on the sofa slurping homemade soup from a mug, still on her diet.

'I really don't know what I would have done if my mother had looked under the bed,' said Annie out of the blue although she'd been thinking about it off and on all day.

Even now, the thought of discovery made her stomach flutter with nerves. Her mother's intrusion was not a factor that either of them had remotely contemplated and the woman had nearly blown their plan.

'What would you have said?' asked Josh. He wiped his greasy hands on a napkin and added, 'Just for fun, let's imagine she found you. And…?'

Annie couldn't stop herself from laughing. The whole situation was so ludicrous. 'I would probably have just said, "Surprise" and crawled out from under the bed.'

'Can you imagine what an absolute disaster that would have been?' said Josh. He joined in his wife's laughter and when they'd calmed down added, 'I really hate her. I know hate is a strong word, but I mean it. Your mother is evil. I bet if she had found you, she would have blackmailed us for the insurance money.'

Even though Annie knew he was probably right, and she didn't like her mother very much either, it was still upsetting to hear Josh talk about her that way so Annie told him her feelings.

'It's not nice to be so negative about people,' she added. 'I know my mother's not a good person but when we talk about her like that it makes me feel like I'm pulling her darkness towards me. I've spent my whole life trying to protect myself from her.'

Josh said he was sorry and changed the subject. He asked if she wanted to go somewhere for a holiday?

Annie felt a rush of excitement, 'Really? When?'

'It will take me ten days or so to tie things up in Leeds,' said Josh topping up their wine glasses.

'Can we go to the seaside?' I really want to walk on a beach. Smell the salty air.' Annie couldn't believe she was going to be free and re-join the world. She would take off her shoes and run screaming down the beach with joy.

'I don't see why not. We need somewhere remote,' said Josh with a grin. 'I know just the place. I saw it on a postcard once. It looks perfect.'

'Can you buy me something little to celebrate?'

'Anything,' said Josh.

'I want a cupcake with pink icing from that bakery on the corner near the Corn Exchange,' said Annie.

It was a long time since she'd had a sugar rush and she deserved the treat after being cooped up in the dark.

Josh

'What do you want?' Josh asked the stranger on his doorstep. The man was beefy-looking, an ex-marine or a copper, and his shaved head only added to his menacing look.

'I'd like to speak to Josh Raven,' the man replied calmly.

An old woman in the street walked past. She was pulling a shopping trolley and paused outside the house to shout, 'Now then, Josh Raven, it's a grand day.'

'Yes, it's a nice day, Mrs Flint,' Josh replied loudly looking annoyed.

The man smirked and Josh examined his face again. He looked vaguely familiar.

'I'd like to ask you a few questions, Mr Raven.' The man, who was wearing a tight-fitting grey suit, took a step towards the front door.

'Why?' asked Josh even though the bald man intimidated him a little. 'Who are you?'

'I work for the bank and the insurance underwriters. Just want to cross the T's and dot the I's,' he said with a smile that didn't reach his black eyes.

The man's right foot was lodged in the door so Josh couldn't close it.

'Oh, yes of course, come in,' said Josh in a friendly tone as he stepped aside. Even though the panic was jumping around in his head, he asked casually, 'Is everything okay with the claims?'

'Why wouldn't it be?'

'It's just taking longer than I thought,' said Josh standing in the hall. 'Is it usual for bank employees to make unannounced house calls?'

'Not always, and don't worry, everything's fine,' said the man as he walked past Josh uninvited into the dimly lit living room. The man surveyed the space, his gaze rested on the mug on the table and Annie's half-eaten cupcake with pink icing. 'Cupcakes?' he asked surprised.

'I know, not very manly. It's my secret addiction,' said Josh quickly, relieved that Annie had dashed up the stairs to the attic when the man had knocked at the door. Josh picked up the cake, took a huge bite and made an exaggerated 'Mmm' noise as he chewed.

The man raised an eyebrow but didn't comment. 'You had a house fire at your home and then you moved here? And you're selling up?'

'Yes,' said Josh, throwing the overly sweet half-eaten cake back on the plate. 'The house is a wreck after the fire. Besides, it holds too many memories. I want to move on.'

'Houses can make you feel like that,' the man said in a condescending tone.

The man stood in the middle of the room with his legs spread apart like a cowboy, as if he owned the place. The stranger was really giving Josh the creeps. He combed through his memories and tried to think why the man seemed so familiar. Josh came up with nothing.

'Is there anything specific you want to know?' Josh asked turning on the charm and hoping he sounded sincere.

'No.'

'Sorry, I didn't catch your name?' added Josh.

'That's because I didn't introduce myself.'

The man walked around the room and without a word went down the cellar steps into the basement kitchen.

Josh followed him, shaken, and watched the man survey

the mess, wondering why he wanted to check out the house. This behaviour wasn't normal. In fact, the man was menacing. Was he looking for clues? Did the bank suspect fraud? But how could they? Brigid was dead. He'd given them her death certificate. Even so, Josh's heartbeat sped up again, and he tried to stay calm but his hands were sweating slightly.

'Never been that good at doing dishes,' said Josh lightly. He started piling the plates up in the sink for something to do.

'Bit of a dump,' said the investigator.

'Beggars can't be choosers,' said Josh. The washing machine beeped, it had finished the cycle. Josh jumped and said, 'I hate beeping gadgets. They always startle me.'

The man flicked through the piles of papers on the kitchen table. Josh felt hot. He was feeling trapped in his own kitchen with this man whose name he didn't know. Was he even from the bank?

Without warning the bald man moved closer, thrust his face close to Josh's, and asked, 'Did you fake your wife's death. Or kill her? Tell me.'

'What the hell?' asked Josh in a raised voice. He took a step away from the man and shook his head. 'No. Of course I didn't kill my wife. I loved her.'

'Just having a bit of fun, son,' the man said deadpan.

He handed Josh his business card and made his way upstairs. Josh followed him and said to the man's back that he couldn't just walk around his house.

They were in the middle of the living room. The man turned around slowly. He stood still and said nothing to Josh. His face was neutral, a mask.

'I would like you to leave,' said Josh firmly. He crossed

his arms. 'Please.'

The man's eyes scanned the room again and he asked, 'What are these?' A pair of red knickers lay on the floor by the arm of the sofa. He nudged the underwear with the tip of his shoe. 'You're a quick worker. Your missus hasn't been dead five minutes.'

'They're mine,' said Josh without missing a beat. 'I like to wear women's underwear. It relaxes me.' Josh picked the knickers off the floor and shoved them into his back pocket.

'Are you a fairy?' asked the man laughing. 'You don't look the type.' He was standing by the mantelpiece. The tension between the two men appeared to be broken.

'No, I just like to wear women's clothes. It's called being a transvestite. When a man is sexually attracted to another man then he's gay…'

'I know all about the gays. We had a bent copper's club when I was in the force.'

The man shook his head in disbelief. Josh was intrigued to hear that the man had once be a policeman. Though he had an air of authority about him, he also had the air of being a criminal. The man turned to glance at a photo of Josh and his wife on the mantelpiece. It had been taken on their holiday to Malta years ago, Josh was kissing Brigid's cheek. The photo wasn't in a frame, though, instead it was propped up against the wall.

'Red knickers. Fancy cake. You're not a man in mourning, my friend.'

'How do you expect me to act?' asked Josh, his anger flaring up. He knew he needed to stay calm, but he really just wanted the man out of his house before he got caught in a lie.

'Not like this. You're too, what's the word. Jaunty.' The man was unruffled as if he was chatting to a friend.

'Jaunty?' asked Josh confused. 'Jaunty?'

'Yeah, jaunty,' he said. He picked up Josh's Zippo lighter from the mantelpiece and flicked it on and off.

'I am upset,' said Josh aggressively. 'Exactly where are you from again? Your card just says WOM Ltd. There's no explanation about the company.'

Outside a car alarm went off. The man threw the lighter on the floor and rushed to the window ignoring Josh's questions. He pulled aside a grubby curtain to see two local kids bouncing up and down on the bonnet of his Jaguar. 'You little…' he said and dashed out of the house without another word.

Josh followed the man out into the street. 'If you wish to speak to me again don't hesitate to contact my solicitor,' he said coolly. 'And if you really are from the bank, I assume you will have the contact details.'

Before the man could reply, Josh turned and went back into the house and locked the door behind him. Leaning against wall, breathing heavily, Josh examined the man's card again, which he was still holding in his hand.

On one side WOM Ltd was printed and on the other just the name BENNETT DARKERE and a mobile number.

When he heard Bennett Darkere's Jaguar rev up and drive away, Josh exhaled loudly.

Being here no longer felt safe. They needed to leave today.

Annie

The front door slammed. Annie heard Josh run up the attic stairs. He pulled their new travel bags down from the top of the wardrobe.

'What are you doing?' asked Annie. She'd been hiding in the attic since the doorbell rang and she was confused. Why all the panic?

Josh told her they were leaving, she needed to pack quickly. He wasn't looking at her as he spoke. Instead, her husband was throwing clothes and shoes into his bag.

'I thought we were leaving in ten days,' said Annie. 'What's the sudden urgency? Who was at the door?'

'An insurance investigator, I think,' said Josh. 'I mean it. Get your stuff together. Now.'

Although she was excited at the thought of re-entering the outside world, Josh's tone was scaring her and Annie didn't move. 'I don't understand. Why do we have to leave suddenly?'

Josh stopped packing and took hold of his wife's shoulders. She could feel his fear, it came off him in small waves. She had never known Josh to be afraid of anyone.

'He's a psycho,' said Josh still holding her arms. 'He'd murder you in the woods. Trust me. I know. I've bought drugs from people like that. Come on.'

Her husband dropped his grip and he was soon scooping up his phone charger and gadgets from around the room. Neither of them had many items to pack.

'Was he from the bank?' asked Annie. 'Why would the bank be employing psychopaths?' She was confused and still rooted to the spot.

'No. I think he's a private investigator hired by the bank,' explained Josh. 'But he's an ex-copper and I can tell he has no scruples and he won't stop.' Annie didn't move so Josh told her firmly, 'Pack. Please, darling.'

'What should I take?'

Annie was overwhelmed. Suddenly, the real world had come crashing into her bubble, and she felt flustered. She was unable to keep up with the speed that Josh was making decisions. Her life had become so slow and timeless since her death.

'Just pack everything you need,' said Josh. 'We're not coming back here again.'

'Where are we going?'

'Just do it,' Josh pleaded. 'I don't have time to explain. I've got calls to make.'

Annie was stunned to hear this information but knew that she had to trust Josh. He clearly felt they were in jeopardy. So, they would run. She opened the wardrobe, which was practically empty thanks to her few belongings. She pulled out a vintage green leather jacket she'd bought soon after the fire and began to pack.

It was over three hours since Darkere's visit. Josh had spent that time in the kitchen making calls and had then gone out to buy a burner pay-as-you-go phone. When he came home he found Annie in the attic sat on the mattress surrounded by bags.

'Sorry, but we're going to have to sell your laptop and our mobiles,' he explained. 'A house clearance company is coming in an hour.'

'Why have you sold our stuff to a house clearance company?' Annie threw her hands up. Apart from a bagful of clothes, all she had was her laptop.

'We need the cash and quickly. And we don't have time to put it on eBay, do we?' said Josh sarcastically.

Annie hid in the attic when the house clearance man arrived, she could hear Josh haggling loudly in the hallway downstairs and explaining that the furniture wasn't for sale, only the tech items. The man said something about using the loo and minutes later he appeared at the top of the attic's stairs. Annie was sat on the bare mattress, their bedding was packed, and she jumped in surprise at the intrusion.

The man in overalls was just as stunned to see her and he quickly retreated and mumbled, 'Sorry, I thought the bathroom was up here.'

'How much did he give you?' asked Annie once the man had left. She didn't mention seeing him, it didn't seem important. It wasn't like they would ever meet him again.

'£480. In cash,' said Josh. He looked drained.

'£480 quid?' said Annie raising her voice. 'Is that all? For my laptop and the phones?'

'We were lucky to get that amount at such short notice,' said Josh. '£480 can go a long way if you're careful.'

'You're right,' said Annie with a shrug. She calmed down quickly. It was done and there was nothing she could change. 'What next?'

'We wait for it to get dark,' said Josh. 'But I have one more visit to make before we leave.' And with that Josh slipped out of the house.

Annie was wrapped in a blanket when Josh returned from his mysterious trip an hour later. He was grinning. Unlike her husband, she didn't feel like smiling.

'Josh I'm scared. I don't know why you look so happy.'

It was true, she'd never felt so afraid. Annie didn't know where they were going, where they would live. And whether their whole scam would be found out. The uncertainty was crushing.

'I've got a surprise for you. Cheer up.'

'Josh, I feel like I'm jumping off a cliff into the unknown.'

It was true, Annie had a knot in her stomach that she'd not felt since before her death, when her bank had been chasing her relentlessly for money.

'I want to stay here. I don't want to go on the run,' Annie pleaded.

'We can't stay. It's not safe.' Josh held Annie's cold hands and spoke softly. 'I've sorted everything out. Our old house is already on the market. I've set up a PO Box for our mail and the rental agent is going to sort out our bills. I've asked my solicitor to liaise with the bank about the insurance policies. As far as the solicitor is aware I'm going away for a break following a bereavement.'

Annie let out a long breath. 'I'm sorry, I'm just…'

'I know. But it's time to leave. We can't risk another visit from that man. We'll wait a while, then leave in the early hours.'

Annie nodded and lay back down on the mattress, with the blanket wrapped tightly around her.

She fell into a dreamless sleep, and was woken by Josh a few hours later. Annie followed her husband down the stairs. In the hall, she took a deep breath. Josh squeezed her hand. The house was in darkness except for a single bulb above them, which threw out an unnatural large glow. Josh opened the front door and the cold air hit their faces.

'What about being seen?' Annie pulled back momentarily and hid behind her husband.

'It's 3am. There's no one around.'

Annie relaxed. Parked in front of the property was a second-hand Land Rover Discovery.

'I really wanted a Range Rover but the budget didn't stretch to that,' said Josh jangling the keys. 'That's where I went earlier, to trade in my BMW. Christ knows how, but I managed to get the shortfall on finance. Come on, scoot.'

A cloak of darkness hung around them and Josh told Annie to hop in while he loaded up. The interior smelt clean and the heater soon warmed up her frozen feet. Annie let herself sink into the large seat as Josh slammed the boot of their new car that meant more debt. But at this point Annie didn't care. She was out in the world and stepping into the next part of her new life and new identity. Brigid was truly dead.

The roads were quiet as Josh drove the Land Rover through the night away from the city. At first, Annie watched the skies and the lights of passing planes taking unknown people to mysterious places.

Eventually her head fell to the side, and she gave into tiredness and slipped into an easy sleep.

PART THREE: WATER

Josh

Just after 6am they reached Northumberland. Josh pulled over into a lay-by on the A1 and killed the engine. Annie was still in a deep sleep, he touched her knee gently.

His wife murmured and he felt a stab of guilt. How had he manoeuvred them into this terrible mess? The past few months were a crazy blur, and at times, he wondered how he'd reached this point. Had he really faked his wife's death and committed fraud? Was he really on the run?

With limbs that felt as if sandbags were balancing on them, Josh reached behind and grabbed his coat. He fished his gear out of his pocket, rolled a joint then wound the window down slightly so he could blow the smoke out.

Using his new burner phone, Josh text Henry for an update on the house. He left a message, covered himself with his coat and closed his eyes. Josh let his body go limp and switched off. Despite being on the side of a busy road, just before rush hour, for the first time in months he felt himself fully relax.

Two hours later Josh's mobile alarm beeped. Annie stirred but stayed asleep and he decided not to wake her. Not just yet.

He searched her face and realised he could still see Brigid in the fullness of her lips, the shape of her elfin jaw. Her features were more defined, and the dark hair disguised her previous self and made the mask complete. As Annie she was much stronger, her slim body was tougher and leaner, and she had the air of being able to hold her own.

He had no words for how he felt about her, how much more he loved her because she'd taken his hand and jumped off the cliff with him. Brigid was dead to everyone but him. He hated to admit it, even to himself, but he wasn't sure if he could have made the same sacrifice. Yet she had sacrificed herself. The realisation made him feel ashamed. Silently, he promised Annie that he would never let her down.

'What time is it?' asked Annie with a yawn. She stretched out in her seat.

'Just after eight,' said Josh still holding the hidden secret of his remorse.

Annie stretched again and added, 'I'm hungry.'

'I think I saw a sign for a roadside café about a mile away,' said Josh starting the engine.

A few minutes later they pulled into the café's empty car park and were soon tucking into breakfast. The café was stark with Formica tables and chairs but the portions were generous. Pushing her half empty plate away Annie said she was full and picked up a discarded tabloid. She turned the pages looking for the stars.

Josh put his hand on the paper. 'Don't,' he said.

Annie asked what he meant.

'Don't read your horoscope or mine. If they're positive you'll feel great but if they're crap you'll start to worry.'

'No I won't,' said Annie shrugging off his hand. 'It's just a bit of fun.' She read the stars silently.

Josh sighed. 'Why do you read horoscopes? You're smarter than that.' It confused him how his intelligent, educated wife, could be compelled to believe in such superstitious claptrap.

A yawning waitress brought extra mugs of tea and plonked them on the table. The couple stopped talking.

Once the waitress was back behind the counter Annie

repeated, 'It's just for fun.'

'But it's not, is it?' Josh stirred his tea noisily to indicate his irritation. Annie continued to flick through the newspaper. 'Forget it,' said Josh. He was eager to get back on the A1 and put more distance between them and the investigator.

'No, let's talk about it. What's wrong with astrology?' asked Annie closing the paper and putting her elbows on the table. 'Out with it.'

Josh sighed, his wife wasn't going to back down so he told her the truth. 'I thought you'd weaned yourself off horoscopes when you stopped reading the papers. It's all fairy tale shit,' he said stirring more sugar into his tea.

'So, you're saying there are no unseen forces at work? Everything happens by chance?'

'That's right. There's no hidden mystery,' said Josh bluntly. 'You live. You make choices. Sometimes stupid ones. Then you die, and that's it.'

Annie glared at Josh. He was on thin ground, they rarely argued about the metaphysical because he knew her strong views on the subject. But he couldn't stop himself, he was tired and tetchy, and she had pushed him.

'So there's no bigger meaning to our existence? We're specks crawling around on a tiny planet hurtling around space?' asked Annie folding her arms.

'Pretty much,' said Josh with a shrug. 'You know I feel this way, and the sooner you accept there's no omnipotent universe or God looking out for us the happier you'll be. It's just you and me,' he said flinging his spoon down on the table.

Annie was quiet. He noticed that his wife was looking down and tracing the outline of her tattoo slowly with her index finger. She thought the five-pointed star kept her safe. He thought it was ridiculous.

'Look, I'm not attacking you,' said Josh feeling irritated. 'Money protects you from life's uncertainties, not hocus pocus.'

'You really don't get it, do you?' His wife looked up. 'There are two universes. You're living in one and the other is unseen, unpredictable. Sometimes the two realities overlap. You have less control over your life than you think.'

Annie sat back and Josh knew that was the end of the conversation. He was being dismissed. Any further comment would be ignored by his wife. Nothing he could say would make her drop her belief in this unseen world.

'I'm sorry,' said Josh. He really didn't want to fight. They were only arguing because they were both exhausted from the lack of sleep. 'I didn't mean to upset you. Let's get going.'

He was truly sorry and he loved Annie more than life, he told himself, but it didn't stop him from thinking that her view of reality was naïve. Who still believed in God in the 21st century? But he couldn't, and wouldn't, rely on some unseen universal power to sort out their problems.

He had to make sure that everything went to plan and nothing, and no one, was going to stop them getting their hands on that money.

Annie

The countryside flashed by the car window and the smell of the cows crept into the car through the Land Rover's air vents.

'It's good to see animals in the fields,' said Annie.

'Look,' said Josh, 'the Northumberland Coast.'

The sea had just appeared on the horizon and the blue sparkled with splashes of white. Tankers sat in the water far off in the distance small and toy-like.

'It's beautiful,' said Annie. She watched the floating dots of seagulls. It was surreal to think that only the previous night she'd been confined to the house in Leeds.

'Do you miss it?' asked Josh changing the subject. 'Your old life?'

'No,' said Annie shaking her head. 'In an odd way, it's like my previous life never happened. The fire and my death. Hiding away for the last few months severed any links to the past. That's what it feels like anyway.'

Annie had already moved on from their earlier row at the café because she knew that Josh was never going to agree with her point of view. But she did see the dead, and just at that moment Annie spotted the ghost of a small girl standing by the side of the road. She was 30 feet away and wore a short dress from the 1970s. Annie stared straight ahead as they passed the ghost girl and didn't make any comment.

'Are you sure you don't miss your old life?' asked Josh again keeping his eyes on the road.

Annie fiddled with the radio as the ghost child was left behind. 'What? No. It was too stressful.'

Josh glanced at her briefly and smiled. Annie's stomach

185

flipped. Even after all this time together, a glance from him could still make her body tingle.

'Are you happier?'

'There's no comparison.' Annie drank in the view, it was so many different shades of green and blue. 'Besides, from this point on anyone I meet will know nothing about me. I can become the person I've always wanted to be.'

The miles faded away and the only noise came from the radio.

After a while Annie asked, 'Where are we going?'

They were still on the A1 but the landscape had become barren, rural, and yet even more beautiful. Josh said their route and final destination was a surprise. Annie said she liked his surprises.

The causeway that linked Holy Island to the mainland came into view. The road was raven black and Josh drove along it slowly, sand stretched out on either side.

Annie saw the wooden poles for the walkers to the right; the poles marked a safe route across the wet beach to Lindisfarne Priory. It was difficult to imagine that later the road would be completely submerged under the high tide. But twice a day, the tide totally cut the island off from the mainland and marooned it in seawater.

Josh told Annie that people regularly got caught out but they weren't going to make the same mistake. He'd checked the tide table.

The Land Rover rumbled as they headed onto the island. In the near distance, Josh and Annie spotted Lindisfarne Castle, it stood high and majestic on the rock. Nearby were the ruins of Lindisfarne Priory.

'I've always wanted to visit this place,' said Annie. 'Is this our final destination?'

Josh turned the Land Rover into the island's small car park. 'No, I wanted to bring you here as a treat. We're booked into a B&B just around the corner, we're too early to check in. Let's go for a walk.'

The couple strolled around the holy place and took in the mismatch of grey cottages and grander Georgian homes. Lindisfarne Priory, tall and half-standing, dominated the village.

Josh and Annie walked silently across the weathered and smoothed gravestones around the priory. The stone's dates had been rubbed off by time. Annie thought, with a tinge of sadness, that eventually everyone faded away and no one remembered your name.

Annie stopped to appreciate the view of the sea and castle and told herself not to be maudlin. She felt stunned and overwhelmed to be outside in the open after nearly four months of hiding in the dark. The world felt infinite.

'I'll get the stuff,' said Josh when they returned to the car.

He lifted out their bags and Annie followed him silently as they snaked their way around the thin streets to a B&B called *The Sea Bird*. The property was a large Georgian house with square windows and a generous front door painted apple green. The door was unlocked. Josh shouted a greeting as they entered the spacious hallway.

'It's perfect,' said Annie.

The hallway had a wooden floor and white walls. It looked like a palace compared to their rental dump. Annie was looking forward to a roaring fire and soaking in a full bath.

'You must be Mr and Mrs Raven,' said a voice from one of the rooms. A trim man appeared. He was wearing a crisp white shirt and jeans.

'Good journey?' The B&B owner was friendly.

'Yes thanks,' said Josh and Annie in unison.

'I'm Patrick. My husband Alfie is buying supplies. The local bakery does crumpets and pastries to die for.'

'Fantastic, thanks,' said Annie. 'I love crumpets.'

The couple followed Patrick up the wooden stairs and into a large bedroom with a king-sized bed made up with white linen and a fake fur throw. An old trunk sat underneath the window. Annie said the room was lovely, really welcoming. Patrick beamed but didn't leave.

'The bedding's nice,' said Annie. She picked up immediately on why the B&B owner was still in the room.

'It has a 400-thread count,' said Patrick stroking the cotton lovingly. He raised his eyebrows.

Annie realised he was waiting for more praise. 'The linen curtains are stylish,' she said enthusiastically. 'The carpet, one hundred per cent wool, nice on your bare feet. And I love the original fireplace.' All the praise was genuine. The place was heaven.

'Thank you,' said Patrick. 'The fireplace took me forever to strip. What a mare.' He rolled his eyes.

Annie continued, 'I adore the wall colour.'

Behind Patrick's back Josh mouthed, 'What the fuck?'

Annie ignored her husband. She walked into the en-suite and put her hands on her hips and said to Patrick, 'This is the best bathroom I've ever seen in a B&B.'

It was true. The place was sparkling clean with a white roll top bath and a huge a walk-in shower. For a moment,

Annie thought the B&B owner was going to hug her. She was ready to hug him back. The room was pure luxury.

Patrick puffed out his chest and said, 'You're welcome. If you need anything just shout.' As he shut the bedroom door he paused and added, 'Enjoy.'

Annie collapsed on the bed with a contented sigh. 'This is bliss.'

'Why did you encourage him?' asked Josh laughing. 'I thought he was going to get into bed with us.'

'Why not? Anyway, it's true. This place is gorgeous. Don't be so British about complimenting people.'

'Whatever. I need to relax.' Josh flopped onto a chair and put his feet up on the trunk.

'Your solicitor won't tell the investigator where we've gone will he?' asked Annie. The thought had suddenly popped into her head.

'My solicitor doesn't know where I am,' said Josh, 'but he's knows one thing. I hired him to keep his mouth shut.'

They unpacked, and had another walk around the village, then went to the pub next door to the B&B for a meal.

Later on, Annie and Josh relaxed in the quiet living room that smelt of beeswax polish. Annie took a deep breath, the scent took her instantly back to her gran's flat. She missed her deeply.

'Do you want Earl Grey or coffee?' asked Patrick interrupting Annie's thoughts.

'Earl Grey, black please,' said Annie. It was turning into the perfect evening.

Patrick arrived with a trolley stuffed with cups, saucers, a milk jug, sugar, plates, napkins, a tea pot, jam and a plate of crumpets.

'Supper for you, my dears,' he said with a flourish.

'This looks amazing, thank you,' said Annie. She could feel her mouth watering despite being full from her evening meal.

'We'll never eat all of this,' said Josh incredulously once Patrick had left. He poured himself a coffee with milk and three heaped spoons of sugar.

Annie looked at him and raised her eyebrows. 'Want to bet?'

'Take it easy. You look great since you've lost weight.'

'I'll eat what I want. One day of pigging out isn't going to make a difference.' Annie reached for a crumpet and slathered it in jam. 'I deserve a treat after all the stress I've been through.'

It was 9pm and the light had faded hours ago, Annie stood looking out of the bedroom window at the stony beach. She watched the moon reflecting on the sea. It was a lovely vista but she couldn't appreciate it because she felt uneasy. It wasn't all the food she'd eaten, it was another uncomfortable sensation. Something or someone was watching. Her neck felt hot and prickly.

'Stop scaring yourself,' she thought. 'There are no ghosts here. You're safe.'

The strange feeling persisted as she quickly undressed. Shaking her head, Annie told herself for a second time to forget it. She was alone and Josh was just in the en-suite. She turned back to the glorious view of the moon.

A cold breath blew an icy blast onto her cheek.

The unexpected sensation made her jump. Annie turned and in the corner of the room she saw a shadow. The dark ghost was a swirling black mass that reached from floor to ceiling.

Annie's whole body was prickling with fear but she didn't have time to react before the darkness collapsed in on itself, seeped into the wall and disappeared. The whole encounter only lasted seconds, but Annie looked down and saw that her hands were shaking. She felt deeply unnerved.

This entity was not at all like one of her normal ghosts that were merely holograms from the past. No spirit had ever made contact with her body in a physical way before. Her cheek was burning as if she'd been branded.

Annie looked in the mirror above the dressing table and was shocked to see that a tiny red mark had formed. A welt. She touched the small circle on her cheek gingerly with two fingers and smarted. The spot, less than half an inch, was red raw.

Unnerved, Annie didn't want to be alone so she barged into the en-suite and dropped her dressing gown. Without saying anything, Annie stepped into the frothy bath. Josh made a comment about her lovely breasts but she ignored him; she wanted to think.

Despite the heat, Annie shivered. She was miles away from Leeds and yet it seemed the dark ghost had left her nightmares and followed her to this island. How could a spirit do that? And why had it marked her face?

'You're shaking,' said Josh. 'Are you coming down with flu?'

'Josh, I've just seen it again.'

'Seen what?'

'The dark ghost. The one from my nightmares. It was here minutes ago in our hotel room. Look, it did this to my face.'

Annie leant towards Josh and showed him the red welt that was already fading. He touched the mark gently, said she must have scratched herself and not noticed.

'Josh, I didn't scratch myself. I know what I saw.'

'Okay. Slow down. Tell me exactly what happened,' said Josh sitting up in the bath and taking hold of his wife's cold hands.

Annie took a deep breath and gave Josh a blow-by-blow account of her encounter. From the expression on his face, she knew her husband didn't believe her. She was right.

'The dark ghost, or whatever it is, is being generated by your imagination,' said Josh stepping out of the bath and wrapping his lower-half in a towel. 'It's called The Third Man Syndrome.'

Josh explained how Sir Ernest Shackleton had experienced the presence of a third man during his treacherous Antarctic expedition as had many other Arctic explorers, and mountaineers in far off places.

'Isolation can trigger extreme stress,' Josh added confidently. 'In such circumstances the mind can create the delusion that a presence is with you. You've been isolated for months. It's no wonder that your mind's playing tricks. Once you're out and about again, it will go away.'

Annie sighed and pulled her hands away. She knew he was just trying to comfort her in his own weird logical way. But the ghost was not a figment of her imagination. It was real. And its presence was getting stronger.

Despite her fear, Annie resolved not to mention the encounter to Josh again because there didn't seem to be any point. He would never believe her or see her point of view. She would put it in her box marked 'private' along with the sightings of her holographic ghosts. This was a mystery she was going to have to solve herself.

Hours had passed but the memory of the dark ghost made it impossible for Annie to sleep. The unsettling encounter lingered in her thoughts. She touched her cheek and felt that all traces of the red mark had gone. Maybe she had scratched herself? But she'd definitely seen the ghost.

Annie wanted to think about something else, and sensing that Josh was awake she whispered, 'Josh, I know it's a surprise, but where are we going?'

Josh rolled over to face her and placed a hot hand on her hip. 'Tomorrow we're doubling back and heading to Saltburn-by-the-Sea,' he said. 'You showed me a postcard of the town once. We're booked into a holiday let for a week, which will give us some breathing space to find a rental property.'

Annie's heart skipped a beat. That was the postcard she'd sent to Josie. The thought of her best friend made her feel sad. Her old life was long gone and buried.

'Is that okay?' Josh asked when she didn't respond.

'Yes,' Annie said. 'It sounds perfect.'

Darkere

The envelopes had only just arrived and contained various bits and pieces all relating to the Raven case: copies of the couple's birth certificates, marriage certificate and all the original application forms for the insurance policies and the mortgage from the bank.

It wasn't necessary, but Darkere liked to be thorough and call in extra paperwork. You could find interesting leads in unusual places, and he'd read the fresh information through several times.

Afterwards the investigator went outside and walked his father's unploughed field to think. He had a lot on his mind.

When Darkere had started in this game ten years ago, after retiring from the police, he'd had an office in Boston Spa. Investigating insurance fraud had been a lucrative business. But the rise in information online meant a decline in the need for men like him. For the last two years he'd worked from home to cut down on overheads. Home was a ruinous farm on the outskirts of Wetherby left to him by his parents. The animals were long gone, but the rusting machinery lay discarded in the yard in front of the house. The place was quiet and isolated, which suited Darkere.

When he wasn't busy with cases, and it was race season, Darkere went to the track. Recently, he'd had an appalling run on the horses and, despite backing a few winners, he'd lost money continually since the start of the season in November. The run of bad luck meant he owned Scott Mac £20,000.

The amount wasn't a fortune, but it was a fortune if you

didn't have it. The farm was already mortgaged to the hilt. Darkere couldn't see how he was going to raise the cash to pay back the loan shark. There had been a few friendly phone calls from Scott Mac's second-in-command, Little Andy. So far he'd kept the exchanges upbeat. As far as the lender was concerned, he was liquidating a few assets and pulling the cash together. But in truth, Darkere had nothing to liquidate.

He kicked a clod of grass and made a decision. There was no way he was going to let this case go. No matter what. He had to find the answers and put all the pieces of the puzzle together. His boss had promised him a bonus of £15,000 if he proved the case was fraud. He would scrape together the remaining £5,000 for Scott Mac and get himself off the hook.

Darkere felt more buoyant as he climbed over the stile that divided the lumpy field from the path to his farm. To solve the case all he had to do was follow his usual method. Get inside the claimant's head. Work out what skills he had that made him different. This information would give him the key to unravelling the tricks of Josh Raven's deceit.

Darkere already had motivation, thanks to his friend at the credit reference agency. It seemed the couple were up to their eyes in debt just like himself. The irony wasn't lost on Darkere. But he would pay his debts back without becoming a criminal. Unlike Josh Raven who already had a record for selling drugs.

Josh's suspended sentence was from years ago, when he was 19, so technically it shouldn't still be traceable. But computers no longer wiped out information they only added the details to their records like cyber gods tracking every move online.

Darkere was still thinking about the couple, specifically Brigid Raven, as he drove his Jaguar up Otley Road, in Harrogate. His train of thought was interrupted by the sign for Crag Lane. Darkere turned right. He was meeting an American spy at a country pub near Harlow Carr Gardens.

The spy liked to be called Donald Duck, or Donald for short, and he wasn't an Ian Fleming kind of operator. He was an espionage lurker. The American worked at Menwith Hill on the moors outside of Harrogate, which was a joint RAF station and US Air Force Base. The base's hi-tech link up of satellites and computers could eavesdrop on any phone call, text and email sent from anywhere on the planet. Donald spent his working days, and nights, monitoring digital communications from around the globe.

Officially, this espionage hub didn't exist. But it was an open secret amongst the worldwide military and the locals in Harrogate. Darkere had met the American when he'd been seconded to the American base as police security. He approved of its spying activities because on the whole the investigator didn't trust the public or the cyber geeks who could paralyse a company (or country) with their hacking demands. If the public had nothing to hide what was the problem with a bit of surveillance?

He arrived at The Dog & Gun. Before he locked his car, Darkere picked up a flat cap from the passenger's seat.

At the bar, Darkere ordered a black coffee. 'Make sure it's hot,' he told the barman.

The tables were full of young couples sipping lattes accompanied by dogs and children. A handful of mature couples were enjoying lunch.

Darkere found Donald sat by a window. The spy's skin had an unnatural yellow pallor, which was a result of the hours spent out of daylight with computers. The spy was wearing blue jeans with a crease down the front, a white t-shirt, a blue anorak and white hi-top trainers. He looked like a Yank in casual attire.

'The first time I tasted English tea I thought it was disgusting,' said Donald when Darkere sat down.

'It's an acquired taste.' Darkere's own coffee sat untouched.

'I'm thinking about going on holiday to Mauritius,' said the American. 'I hear it's good for diving.'

Darkere didn't know if the story about the Mauritius holiday was fake or real and he didn't care. 'The Red Sea is another good diving spot. Although I doubt it's safe these days.'

'You got that right, buddy,' said the American.

The men looked at one another but didn't say anything more. Donald's mobile beeped, he checked the message.

Darkere knew that it was a pre-set reminder for his contact to leave the pub.

'Nice bumping into you,' said Donald draining his cup. 'Take it easy.' The American picked up Darkere's flat cap and left the pub.

Inside the hat was the favour he owed the American and a rip in the lining, which had been sewn up with neat stitches. The lining contained a piece of paper with two mobile numbers printed carefully in Darkere's small, neat writing.

One of the mobile numbers belonged to Brigid Raven. The other number belonged to her husband Josh.

Josh

After a leisurely breakfast, Josh paid the bill and packed up the Land Rover. It was just starting to spit from black clouds as they drove across the causeway towards the mainland.

Soon the rain was coming down in thick round drops and Josh had to turn the windscreen wipers on full. He was glad he'd checked the wipers were working when he'd looked over the car at the garage.

Several miles of watery countryside passed before the storm eased up. Just as the sun came out of the clouds Annie asked him how much money they had left.

Josh had been waiting for this question since breakfast. His wife did tend to fret.

'The house clearance made us £480, but we've spent £100 on the room, £60 on diesel, and £35 on food and drinks. That leaves £285,' said Josh.

Annie's body slumped down in her seat. 'What are we going to do? We won't be able to afford to live on that amount of cash for long.' She was close to tears.

Josh understood his wife's worry and revealed he had £1,000 in an emergency fund. He kept his eyes on the road as he spoke.

Annie shot up in her seat. 'Where did you get the money from?'

'I sold my Omega.' Josh indicated his empty wrist. He was surprised his wife hadn't noticed.

'You sold your watch?'

Josh nodded. 'I took it to the dealers by the market. He gave me a good price.'

'Won't your parents be mad you've sold it?'

Josh shrugged and said, 'I'm not going to tell them.' He looked at Annie quickly. She was staring at him, 'What?' he asked.

'You always come up smelling of roses,' said Annie shaking her head. She reached over to touch his bare wrist. 'I know how much the watch meant to you. When we get the money through, you should go get it back.'

Josh shrugged. 'It was just a watch. You are more important to me.'

He didn't need to glance over to know that Annie had tears in her eyes. But he wasn't just saying it to keep her happy, he meant every word.

Annie

To reach the rural town of Saltburn-by-the-Sea, on the edge of the North York Moors, Josh had double-backed from Northumberland and followed the A1 down the North East coast. The main route into Saltburn was straight like a Roman road. As they approached the town's outskirts, passing row after row of Victorian terraces, Annie caught a glimpse of the sea again in the distance with the imposing cliff that hung over the beach and dominated the view.

'No one will find us here,' said Josh. 'It's a tourist place so we can blend in easily. And there are loads of other places to visit nearby like Runswick Bay and Whitby.'

'You don't have to sell it to me, it's perfect,' said Annie feeling hope return.

Fresh place, fresh start. Annie felt determined to release the past, including her most recent spirit encounters. She made a silent promise to be positive and not go hunting for things in the shadows. The darkness was no longer her friend, she was free to be outside and enjoy the light.

Josh reached the end of the main road and turned left onto a street that followed the seafront. Ahead, Annie saw the towering cliff more clearly and she felt a jolt of awe. The rock stood ragged, cut out of the landscape, and jutted into the wet sand below creating a cove. Annie knew that at high tide the sea kissed the cliff's feet.

Moving upwards, the top of the cliff was covered with grass and further inland became farmland. In the distance, a row of white cottages perched on top of the cliff and stood solid like a one-walled fortress.

Annie had just minutes to take in the vista before Josh

turned the car sharp right down a steep hill. The Land Rover followed the twisting road but they didn't stop at the beach at the bottom. Instead, Josh drove on past the seafront cafes, the surfers and dog walkers and up another steep hill away from the town.

After half a mile, Josh turned left down a gravelled farm track. The Land Rover bounced slowly towards the row of white cottages.

'Are we staying here?'

Josh nodded looking smug. Annie took a sharp intake of breath. 'Wow.'

When she opened the car door the tangy air hit her. The salty taste was sharper up on the cliff top. Below them, the sea wasn't too choppy. Small waves rose and fell.

There were ten cottages and each property had a long garden at the front and parking by the back door. Some of the gardens had vegetable patches whilst others housed sheds or clusters of bedding plants.

Josh opened the outer door of a porch at the back of one cottage and said, 'There's a key safe somewhere.'

He found the small black box at floor level by stacked wood, punched in six numbers and retrieved a keyring from the safety box. The key turned smoothly in the lock and the back door opened directly into the living room. Josh flicked on the light switch.

The first thing that Annie noticed was the stone fireplace with its large wooden mantel. Logs were stacked neatly in the fireplace on either side of the wood burner.

'Fantastic, a proper fire,' she said.

'It heats the radiators, so we need to get it going,' said Josh. 'The place smells like it's been empty for a while.' He

201

went back out to the car leaving Annie to look around.

'It's so cosy,' Annie said aloud to herself. She was thrilled. Opposite the fireplace was a leather chesterfield with mismatched floral cushions. To the right of the sofa, under the window, was a Queen Anne chair that was covered in faded chintz fabric. Annie loved the cottage already and she could see herself living there.

Josh reappeared with a bag. 'What?' he asked and dropped the holdall on the living room floor with a thump.

'It's lovely.' Annie popped her head into the kitchen, which was just off the lounge, and noticed the faded floral curtains at the window and wooden worktops battered with age.

Josh shrugged. 'Vintage tat. But I knew you'd like it.' Josh disappeared to pick up more bags from the car.

Annie smiled. He was right. The cottage's shabby décor made her feel relaxed. But it wasn't grubby, it was a worn look that made her feel like she could relax on the sofa and not feel guilty. Its comfort held the promise of smothering her secret worry that the presence would follow her here. But she brushed the fear away again like she had in the car.

As Josh dropped the last of their bags on the floor, she went over and kissed him.

'It feels like home. I love it.'

'And that's all that matters to me,' said Josh kissing her back. 'Personally, I think it's a dump, but we're only here for a week.'

Josh

'In 1861, says local legend, Henry Pease was walking on the beach and he had a vision,' read Annie aloud. 'On top of the cliff he saw a heavenly city with angels. The entrepreneur, and Quaker, took this vision as a sign to build a town and called it Saltburn-by-the-Sea.' Annie let the book rest on her lap. 'It was fashionable to have visions in the Victorian era,' she said.

'Mmm,' said Josh.

His wife didn't half prattle on sometimes. Darkness had covered the cliff and out at sea he was watching the swaying lights of two fishing boats. Josh wondered who was mad enough to be on the water in the rain and cold at this ungodly hour. He was glad to be inside in the warmth, it was cold on the cliff top. He turned from the window to watch Annie. She was wearing her red cardigan and sat in the chintz chair with her bare feet hanging over the side of the arm to catch the fire's heat. Josh would melt if he sat so near the flames.

Annie picked up the dusty old book she'd found in a cupboard and continued. 'By 1870, the resort rivalled other well-known spa towns such as Harrogate and Bath. Bathers enjoyed the sea water whatever the season and had special huts that propelled them out into the water.'

'Those Victorians certainly knew how to have fun,' said Josh as he turned back to the window.

'Yes, they did. By the way, Josh, I've searched through my stuff but I couldn't find my favourite photo of us, did you pack it?'

Josh wasn't really listening, but replied with a grunt.

'Could you look for it tomorrow?'

Josh grunted again. The boats looked like they were in the same position. 'They must be anchored,' he thought. Josh pulled himself away from the window and put another log on the fire. Annie had thrown lemon peel onto the embers earlier and the blackened skins gave off a powerful citrus smell. Josh poked the fire and just as he stood up there was a knock at the back door.

Josh and Annie looked at one another. Annie inclined her head to the door. The person outside knocked again loudly.

Josh opened the door. A woman in her seventies thrust a hand towards him.

'Swain, Margaret,' she said in a loud voice. 'Own the cottage. Live next door.'

'Do you want to come in?' asked Annie immediately.

Josh wanted to glare at his wife but instead shook Margaret's hand a little taken aback. He would never have booked the cottage if he'd known that the owner lived next door. Why did Annie have to be so bloody friendly? What was she thinking inviting the woman inside?

'Bitterly cold out,' said Margaret as she stepped inside in a sprightly manner.

The woman was bundled up against the weather in a hodgepodge of clothing: a red scarf, a worn beige raincoat, purple trousers and a yellow wool beanie. Tufts of bobbed grey hair escaped out of the edge of her hat. Strangely, she'd carefully applied red lipstick that seemed oddly glamorous given the rest of her get-up and the time of day.

'All shipshape?' asked Margaret beaming.

'Great thanks,' said Josh.

Small drops of water were dripping from her raincoat

onto the stone flags but Josh didn't want to say anything because it was her cottage.

The woman nodded to the stove. 'Good little burner. Been in since I bought the place.'

Margaret not only talked like a sergeant major from the 1930s but she also had the same body language. She stood erect with her hands clasped behind her back. Josh mused she must have had a parent in the armed forces.

'It's a lovely cottage,' said Annie. 'Really cosy.'

Josh didn't invite Margaret to sit down. That would lead to a longer conversation and he didn't really want to talk to the woman. Surely Annie realised that chit chat was dangerous? It would lead to questions and questions were bad. People who asked questions wanted to know: where you were from originally, where you lived now, what you did for a living, the type of car you drove, what you paid for your house, how many children you had, and so on.

'Know how to work everything?' asked Margaret. She stayed rooted to the spot by the door.

'Yes, thanks,' said Josh and Annie together.

'Ah, jinx. Born together and ripped apart together,' said Margaret with a smile.

Josh and Annie looked at each other. He was struggling to make sense of Margaret's last comment.

'Twin souls,' said Margaret. 'I carry your heart with me?' The last line was spoken as a question.

'Ah, e.e. cummings,' said Annie.

Josh was impressed. He couldn't quote a single line of poetry.

'Very good,' said Margaret. The woman grinned and after an awkward pause said, 'Right ho. Must be off.' As she touched the door handle Margaret froze and turned back. 'Oh! Nearly forgot why I popped round.'

The woman commanded the room. She had Josh and Annie's full attention. Josh had no idea what she was going to say or do next.

'People in after you have bailed. Blasted nuisance. Cottage is free for an extra three weeks if you want it?' she was standing with her hands clasped behind her back again. 'Thought I'd ask on the off chance. Know you young 'uns often work from home these days.'

'That's great,' said Josh looking at Annie who was nodding enthusiastically. 'We'll take it.' He pulled out his wallet from his back pocket.

'No need.' Margaret put up her hand. 'Will come back at the end of the week. Cheerio.'

When she was gone, Josh said, 'What the...'

'She's eccentric.' Annie flopped back into her original position by the fire. 'I like her. Besides, we've somewhere to live for a month so it takes the pressure off.'

'She's clearly mad,' said Josh careful not to talk too loudly. The old bat probably had supersonic hearing.

'The woman's harmless,' said Annie slightly annoyed. She rose up and went into the kitchen to make a cup of tea.

Soon the old kettle was whistling on the gas stove. When Annie returned, she picked up the conversation and said, 'Margaret's not going to guess our secret so stop being horrible.'

'Let's hope not. All I need is some batty old crone ringing the police,' said Josh fiddling with an FM radio that didn't work properly. 'This place is a time warp.'

'Let's not be nasty about anyone from now on. Let's be

206

positive,' said Annie. She sat next to Josh on the sofa and picked up his hand.

'Okay,' said Josh not wanting to upset his wife. 'I'll play nicely.'

But Josh didn't feel positive. They had enough money to last five weeks at a push; the holiday cottage was costing them £150 per week and it was an absolute steal at that price. But even so, after six weeks or so, they were going to be broke. Again. If he'd lived in the 19th century he'd be worrying about being thrown into the workhouse.

He could claim benefits, but he wanted to keep out of the system as much as possible. Benefits meant giving photocopies of his bank statements, a permanent address and details of when he'd last had a pee.

'Damn it. What was taking the bank so long to pay up?' he wondered for the millionth time.

Darkere

The Pump Room Museum in Harrogate stood next to a cluster of smart shops and was opposite the park. A tap outside the small museum was supposed to issue a jet of foul egg-smelling water for passers-by to drink; taking the 'cure' had been popular with the Victorians. Darkere pressed the button a couple of times but no water came out.

'The council turned the tap off some time ago,' said a haughty woman. 'For health and safety reasons.' She wore a camel coat and had a halo of white hair. Her white poodle modelled a similar bouffant.

'Typical,' said Darkere scowling, 'Don't you just fucking love health and safety.'

'Quite,' said the startled woman. She walked away briskly pulling the poodle behind her.

The American spy appeared from the small side street behind the museum. 'I see you're still full of charm,' he said laughing.

Darkere turned around. 'Piss off,' he replied with a smile.

'Walk with me,' said the American quietly.

Darkere and Donald walked briskly over the zebra crossing towards the empty park. A crow in a tree broke the silence by squawking. The spy mimed shooting it.

'A Weatherby SAS?' asked Darkere matter-of-factly.

'Remington 870.' Donald put his hands back in the pockets of his black MIA bomber jacket.

The two men continued in silence on the winding path that ran alongside the stream. The Valley Gardens was well kept and free of litter. When the men neared the café by the boating pond Darkere asked the spy what he'd found out.

'The SIM card on Brigid Raven's mobile is dead and has been for a while. I can't access that info,' said Donald. 'Josh Raven's SIM is also dead, but it was only killed six days ago.' The spy glanced around to make sure they were still alone as he continued walking. 'I've got you a week of his calls.'

'A week?' Darkere couldn't keep the irritation out of his voice. 'Do you have a location at least?'

A location would save him having to track down Josh Raven old school style, cut down on his leg time.

'Nope. With both SIM cards out of action I can't give you a location,' said Donald shrugging.

'That's it?' said Darkere. They had nearly reached a bench near the main gates.

'Yep.'

Donald fished a packet of cigarettes out of his pocket, lit one for himself and sat on the bench putting the packet between them. Darkere didn't smoke but he casually put the cigarettes into his coat pocket.

'Can't you go back three or four months and get transcripts for all of their mobile phone conversations? What about a print of their texts and emails?'

The American laughed. 'No way, man. Any searches involving live voice tracks and digital hacks require special clearance these days. Your two people terrorists?'

Darkere shook his head and felt angry. What was the point of having all this hi-tech equipment if the military didn't use it?

'Or world leaders?' asked Donald half smiling.

'What do you think?' Darkere didn't bother to hide his annoyance. 'I need this information. This case has got under my skin. It's become personal.'

'It always gets personal,' said the American. The spy walked away from Darkere and out of the Valley Gardens without saying goodbye.

Back at the farm, Darkere examined the printout of calls made from Josh Raven's mobile and tapped a pencil rhythmically on his clutter free desk. A repeating number caught his eye because it had been called three times in quick succession, and only hours after his own visit.

'I bet Brigid Raven was hiding in the house. I know she's not dead,' Darkere thought with annoyance. He had a sixth-sense, a copper's intuition, and he wasn't going to discard the gut feeling, no matter how unlikely, that had served him well over the years.

The investigator did a quick internet search. The repeating number was for a holiday letting agency. He'd put money on odds of 2-1 that Josh Raven had already booked a holiday let.

The Ravens had no idea but they were following a typical pattern. Commit fraud then vanish to a hideaway somewhere. He just hadn't expected them to run before the money came through.

Darkere wondered if the couple had left Leeds already. Perhaps they were staying in a holiday home booked through that letting agency? They couldn't go abroad because Brigid Raven would no longer have a valid passport. Unless, of course, she'd got hold of a fake one.

Darkere clenched his fist and slammed it down onto his desk.

He needed to see Brigid Raven in the flesh. Finding out the truth had become an obsession, this case had burrowed under his skin like a tropical insect. Darkere had to discover the real facts and he couldn't let it go. It was haunting him. He woke up in the morning thinking about Brigid Raven wondering if she was dead or alive. He went to sleep thinking about all the ways the woman could have faked her death. Her ghost was always with him whispering in the far reaches of his thoughts, and he had nothing. No explanation. No leads. It was a first for him.

Darkere knew that his best chance of cracking this case was to gain photographic evidence that the woman was still alive. An image was crucial because the GP was above suspicion, the death certificate was genuine in itself, although flawed, and Brigid's so-called body had been cremated so there was no proof rotting six feet under.

But he was struggling on the photo-front. Before he'd spoken to Josh, he'd already done several stakeouts at their home during the day and night. Nothing. All he'd caught on camera was Josh coming in and out of the house at various times. The curtains remained permanently shut, although this was a red flag it clearly wasn't proof that Brigid was still alive.

Darkere sifted through their file and plucked out a list of addresses. His first job tomorrow, after another stakeout tonight, would be to visit the couple's workplaces. Colleagues were well-known for being loose lipped if you asked the right questions.

If the Ravens had already gone on the run, Darkere would find them.

Josh

Josh put down a basket of kindling by the fire just as his mobile rang. It was Henry with the news that his boss was insisting they put their old house up for auction for £40,000 - although a young couple was interested. The couple wanted a renovation project and were willing to offer £32,000. Josh wasn't impressed and voiced his displeasure about the low figure.

'My advice is to take the couple's offer,' said Henry quickly. 'Your home does look like it's been nuked. It's a miracle someone has even put in an offer, mate.'

Josh opened the living room window a few inches to let in some fresh air. 'I'll take it on one condition,' he said as the cold sea breeze blew into the room.

The estate agent let out a sigh of relief and said, 'Honestly, the buyers are really keen. What's the condition?'

'I want the deal done within four weeks. No excuses.'

Josh lit a joint and inhaled deeply. The couple were getting an absolute bargain. They knew it. He knew it. Henry knew it. At the very least the sale should go through quickly. He'd inflate the price a bit when he gave his wife the news to stop her from worrying about money.

'I'll make sure it's fast,' said Henry brightly. 'You can trust me, mate. To be honest, I'm desperate for the commission.'

'Business slow?' asked Josh not really interested. He blew a long plume of smoke out of the window then picked up the binoculars for a better view of the sea. It was dark but in the distance Josh could see the lights of a fishing boat bobbing on the waves.

'Like a graveyard. I've had one viewing besides yours in

three weeks. I'm sure my boss would have sacked me if I didn't close a sale this week.'

'Well done for finding me a buyer. I appreciate it,' said Josh. He didn't want to chat, he wanted to finish his joint and watch the sea traffic. 'Hey, look I've got to go,' said Josh focusing on a Dutch tanker in the distance. 'Give me a call if you need anything further from me.'

Josh was surprised by Henry's honesty and frankly quite embarrassed. His experience of estate agents was that they usually crowed about busy viewings and rising markets. Was Henry just saying that things were desperate to get Josh to accept a lower offer than the auction valuation? The paranoia hit his brain. But Josh ignored this idea. The bottom line was that they needed the money and he would take thirty-two grand over nothing right now.

'Tomorrow I'll ring the solicitor,' he thought. 'Find out what's going on with the insurance payments. Better that he chases them up, I don't want to make things look fishy by being too desperate.'

He finished his spliff and went to the bedroom where Annie was drying her hair. She was naked under her dressing gown which was open slightly. Her damp hair looked blacker than it did when it was completely dry. Josh still couldn't believe her transformation at times. It was like being married to a different woman. Her beauty was breath-taking.

'I've got some news,' he said over the noise of the dryer.

She switched off the hairdryer and looked at him. 'What? Has the cash come through?'

Josh put his arms around her waist and pulled his wife closer. 'No, but it's still good. A couple moving up from London are desperate to buy the property. They want to renovate it.'

'That's fantastic.' Annie smiled and kissed him.

He caressed the soft skin of her back under her robe and felt a zip of pleasure. Finally, after his monumental cock-up of forgetting to insure the house, he felt like he had finally done something right. Not that he had done much. Henry had done all the work. Josh kissed Annie back, then fetched a bottle of bourbon and two glasses from the kitchen. He re-joined Annie who was sat on the bed.

'Looks like our luck is changing,' he said as he filled the glasses. 'It's a good offer considering the state of the property. They're willing to pay £50,000.'

'Wow, that's amazing,' said Annie. 'Well done. Have you contacted any letting agents about a rental property further north?' She tucked her legs underneath her.

'Not yet. But I'm happy with that offer and so should you be.' Josh sipped his bourbon and noted the curve of his wife's breasts and wondered if they might have sex tonight. It had been weeks.

'I am happy,' Annie said sipping her own drink. 'The sale will help us out until we get the insurance money.'

'The cash will do more than that,' said Josh, 'it will get us out of the workhouse.' He stroked his wife's naked thigh, and she yawned.

Annie put her unfinished drink on the bed and got up to finish drying her hair.

'No sex tonight then,' Josh thought reading his wife's cues. But he didn't say anything. Instead, he went back downstairs to the lounge and rolled another spliff.

Darkere

The trees in the park were thicker than Darkere had expected and he would need to use his Night Owls to navigate through the twisted branches. The night-vision binoculars were an expensive piece of kit and ideal for a stakeout such as this one.

Darkere lay down on his stomach on a ground sheet with his elbows resting on the damp grass. It was his first night watching the Raven house from this angle on the edge of the woods.

The Night Owls took a few seconds to adjust, but once in focus the binoculars gave a green monochrome image that was sharp and clear. His eyes quickly adapted. He spotted a big male fox by a bush. It was eating something.

Adjusting his vision, Darkere moved to the left and brought the row of terrace houses into sight. He knew which property he wanted to view. The one with the skylight.

As he watched the still, dark house, Darkere pondered the Raven file. It was the most interesting job that he'd had for a long time. There was no way he was going to leave it unsolved especially if what his gut told him was true. Besides, he needed that bonus. If he didn't pay back the twenty grand, and soon, it was only a matter of time before Little Andy paid him a personal visit, and that wouldn't be fun.

He just had to work out how the Ravens had faked Brigid's death. The young lad at the funeral home had confirmed there had been no autopsy, which set off big alarm bells.

Or was she really dead? Had Josh Raven somehow murdered his wife for the money and got away with it?

'Nah. His balls are too small,' thought Darkere still looking through the Night Owls.

There was plenty of motivation for the fraud - considerable debt. Josh had lost his job. Brigid's salary was pitiful. They had much to gain from the insurance policies. Financial freedom being their number one benefit.

'You think you're clever,' thought Darkere with a smile. 'But I *will* work it out and I *will* find you.'

It was past midnight, but he wanted to be one hundred per cent certain that the Ravens had fled before he stopped surveying the house.

Another hour had passed when Darkere registered that his feet were getting cold. He tried to ignore the numbness that gripped his toes but it was no good. He stood up, stretched and stamped his feet lightly. Years ago, he could have held the same position for hours. He was getting old.

'What yee doing?' boomed a Scottish voice.

Darkere twirled round quickly and came face-to-face with a tramp. Startled, the investigator said, 'What the bloody hell?' He took off the night-vision goggles and tucked them in his pocket.

It took Darkere's eyes a few moments to adjust and when they did, he could make out the features of the man in front of him. Although he could smell the tramp better than he could see him. The aroma was a mixture of whisky and unwashed skin.

'Ah asked yee a question, sonny,' said the tramp more loudly.

The man was wearing a long overcoat and though Darkere couldn't make out the details he suspected that beneath the coat were layers of dirty clothing. The old tramp was clearly drunk and confused.

He figured it was best to humour him. He didn't want the old boy shouting and giving the game away.

'I'm watching someone,' said Darkere as if speaking to a friend.

'Oh ay. Who?'

The tramp stepped closer. His stench rolled off him in waves.

'Just someone,' said Darkere casually stepping further back into the trees.

The tramp followed him. 'Don't play games with me, sonny,' said the tramp loudly. 'Who yee watching?'

'Shh, shh. Okay, I'll tell you,' Darkere spoke quickly and quietly hoping to get rid of the vagrant. 'I'm watching a man and a woman in one of the houses opposite.' The lights from the street were out of view and the branches stretched around them forming a circle of wood.

'Is this a new type er dogging?' whispered the tramp. He had a hint of humour in his voice.

'Do I look like a pervert?' asked Darkere unamused. His patience for this interruption was gone. The smelly old tramp was annoying him.

'Well, yer hiding in the woods in the park… with night-vision goggles,' said the tramp. He laughed and repeated, 'Hiding in the dark.'

The tramp was making fun of Darkere and he felt a flash of anger. 'I am not a fucking pervert. I am a policeman,' he said, his voice raising in volume.

The tramp laughed and said loudly, 'Yer a liar. Yer nay a policeman.'

'I am not lying,' said Darkere firmly.

The man called him a liar again and Darkere felt the red mist rising. He told him to shut up. The tramp laughed. Darkere was furious, livid. The smelly vagrant was going to blow his cover. He told him again to be quiet.

'Are yee gonna make me, big man?' asked the tramp. 'Are yee gonna make me?'

In a swift move, Darkere hit the man with his right fist square on his nose. He felt the bone break. The tramp's hands automatically covered his bleeding face. Without thinking, Darkere hit the old man in the stomach, hard. All he wanted to do was make the Scottish drunk shut up.

The tramp crumpled to the grassy floor. Darkere kicked him three times in the ribs as the tramp lay on the ground groaning.

'Yeh've a bad soul,' wheezed the tramp. 'A bad soul.'

Instinctively, Darkere kicked the tramp's head a couple of times until the man went still. He heaved from the exertion. Even in the half-light he could see the trickles of blood flowing out of the man's nose and ears. He nudged the old man's shoulder with his foot but the body was unresponsive.

'You should have stayed quiet,' muttered Darkere. 'And you shouldn't have called me a liar.'

Swiftly he picked up his kit and stuffed it into his rucksack. Darkere tramped around the grass to hide any signs of the fight and made a skid mark near where the tramp had fallen.

'You're just an old drunk who slipped in the woods and froze to death,' whispered Darkere as he walked away.

Annie

The bedroom was black, shrouded in night, and Annie's eyes struggled to focus in the darkness. She felt a sensation of weight on top of her body pinning her down like a fallen tree. She lay immobile unable to even twitch her arms or legs.

Was she awake or dreaming? Terrified, Annie lay with her head turned to the left side. She listened to the hissing breath of the presence only inches from her right ear.

Annie willed the presence to vanish and quietly chanted the Lord's Prayer. 'Our Father, who art in heaven. Hallowed be thy name…'

At the sound of the holy words, the dark ghost vanished into the inky black of the night.

Annie finished the prayer and felt relief. As the final 'amen' left her mouth she woke up suddenly. It had been a dream.

This wasn't the first time she'd had a nightmare at the cottage. They'd begun last week and each time she'd woken Josh in the middle of the night and he'd tried to comfort her. But after the fourth successive night he'd hissed sharply in the dark, 'I've told you, it's your sodding imagination. Go back to sleep.'

With a slightly shaking hand, Annie turned on the bedside lamp. The room felt warmer and less threatening, but she noticed that the bed was empty next to her. Josh was either still out or sleeping downstairs on the sofa.

But it didn't make any difference that Josh wasn't there because Annie wasn't going to tell him about the night terror. There was an obvious note of boredom in his tone whenever she brought up the issue.

His stock response over the last few mornings had been, 'It's just your imagination.'

Wide awake, she thought about her attempts the previous day to get help with the presence. She'd rung a local Catholic Church but it was a small parish and an answer phone message had said the only priest was away in Africa on a charity trip. She was too embarrassed to leave a message or to call the number for the nearest Catholic Church in Whitby as had been suggested.

Where else could you go for help with dark spirits? She didn't know the answer. In all her years of seeing ghosts she'd never met anyone like herself. Annie wished she could talk to her grandmother. She still missed her every day. Her calm manner and soothing herbs had always brought her comfort. But Annie had no one. No one except a husband who drank and smoked too much and didn't have the patience to comfort her.

Annie decided her best line of defence against the presence was holy words. A prayer was what a priest would have used to help her anyway.

She picked up the book on her bedside table, but after trying to read the same paragraph three times, she gave up.

It was no good. The terror of the dream filtered back into her mind. She wouldn't get back to sleep again and thoughts of the dark ghost scared her. Annie slipped her dressing gown on.

Downstairs, Annie tiptoed past a sleeping Josh in the living room. Her husband had taken to leaving the cottage around 3pm and returning in the early hours. He said he didn't want to wake her, which is why he often ended up sleeping downstairs.

The explanation was that he'd been at the pub, and judging by the smell of him Josh was telling the truth. He was drinking their money away when they should be watching every penny. They had rowed about his budgeting several times. Why couldn't he be content with a few beers at home? His love of the pub meant she was often alone and she spent hours walking along the windy cliff top. And they were in danger of becoming trapped by debt again.

Annie sighed and went into the kitchen. The floor tiles were cold on her bare feet. Outside an owl hooted and Annie shivered. Holding one bare foot off the floor Annie put the kettle on a gas ring.

Pouring the boiled water into a mug, she decided to think of the dark ghost's visits as merely night terrors. It was the only way she could cope with them.

Annie carried her black tea into the living room and put her mug on the mantelpiece. She knelt on the hearth rug, poked the orange embers in the stove and added a log.

Josh was still asleep on the chesterfield. An empty glass and general mess littered the low coffee table. As Annie collected up the glass and empty crisp packets Josh stirred.

'Leave it. I'll do it in the morning,' said her husband sitting up.

He rubbed his eyes and yawned. He was still dressed and the smell of alcohol oozed from his pores and crumpled clothes.

Annie continued to tidy up. 'The place looks like a pigsty,' she said. 'What if Mrs Swain were to come around in the morning before you'd cleaned up?'

'Who cares what the old bag thinks,' said Josh. He stood

up, stretched and added, 'I'm going to bed,' His face was ashen, vampire white.

'Don't be nasty about our landlady,' said Annie. She couldn't stop herself and followed her husband into the hallway. 'You look dreadful,' she said. 'You need to stop staying out so late and cut down on the drinking and dope.'

Josh told her he could do what the hell he liked. Coughing, he climbed the stairs slowly hunched over like an old man.

Annie didn't like their skirmishes, which were happening too regularly. It was just because of their close proximity and the fact that they'd been so isolated. She needed to widen her world and make some friends.

But how? What would she tell people about herself?

The bedroom door banged shut and Annie wished Josh wasn't so exhausting. Was the dope triggering his mood swings? She really would have to talk to him about it again, and his drinking.

She had hoped that once the money came through things would improve. But she wondered if it would just make things worse; Josh would have free reign to blow as much cash as he wanted on the things that were bad for him.

Josh

The hot bath felt like heaven. Josh's hangover slowly melted away as the steam curled around him. He'd spent hours in the pub the night before, longer than he'd anticipated, but the beer was good and it was nice to just chill without Annie badgering him.

He hadn't meant to fall asleep on the sofa again when he'd come home but the fire had lulled him into nodding off. Josh didn't see what all the fuss was about. Couldn't his wife understand that he was under a lot of stress?

As he got out of the bath he pondered everything that had happened. He'd mastered-minded their brilliant scam. All they had to do was sit tight and wait for the money. Yes, it was taking longer than expected for the cash to come through, but banks were notorious for dragging their feet where big pay outs were concerned.

'If there was a problem I would have heard about it by now,' Josh thought coming down the cottage's narrow stairs. He was dressed and shaved but his hair was still wet.

Annie appeared from the kitchen carrying scrambled eggs on toast and said he could have it, she'd make some more.

'She can't be that mad at me,' thought Josh picking up his cutlery and digging in.

'Why don't we go for a drive to that retail park this afternoon? It's only twelve miles away,' said Josh between mouthfuls.

Annie, who'd just sat down with another steaming plate, was looking out of the window. She turned to Josh and said, 'What? We don't have any money. We can't afford it.'

Josh wiped his plate with a piece of bread and explained

that the bank had extended his overdraft on the premise that the insurance money was to be paid out soon. Annie said she couldn't be bothered traipsing around the shops and that they should save their money and be sensible.

Josh knew what his wife really wanted to do was walk on the beach and search for driftwood and interesting pebbles. A large pile of sea-sanded wood stood by the back door. The different sized pieces were balanced against one another and made a gnarled tepee of twisted wood.

An old glass jar by the kitchen sink held her stones from the beach. All useless shite.

'It will be fun,' Josh persisted. 'And you need to get out and about again.'

Annie groaned and gave in after further persuasion. She admitted that he was right, she was shying away from crowds and noise.

'Until I died, I never appreciated stillness, now I crave it,' she said looking out of the window at the sea.

'Well, darling, sooner or later you're going to have to re-enter the real world, and that means shopping,' said Josh. He clapped his hands once and added, 'Fantastic. You can't beat a retail buzz.'

Annie

The retail park was crowded and hot. It had been a long time since Annie had been in such a busy place and all the people overwhelmed her; she was drowning in a sea of noise.

'Why don't we split up?' asked Josh. He looked around. 'I'll meet you outside Costa at twelve for lunch?'

Josh kissed her on the cheek and before she could protest the crowd of shoppers swallowed him whole.

Annie hesitated for a moment unsure of where to go then spotted a book shop nearby. The shop was a welcome haven and she weaved her way through the islands piled high with 'two for one' paperbacks.

In the gardening section Annie found a hardback on roses. Only yesterday Margaret Swain had mentioned her pink roses and said the bushes bloomed in late May or June. Annie decided to buy the book, it would be a nice surprise for her landlady. Then she picked up a leather journal with a flaming heart on the front.

Making her way to the till, Annie saw a man as she passed through the classic cars section. He was reading a book on Cadillacs. His face was tanned, clean shaven, and his mouth could only be described as a Cupid's bow.

The man sensed Annie watching him and glanced at her. The book was still open in his hand. A smiled passed between them.

Annie turned away first, her face felt hot. She pretended to root around in her bag.

'He's a stranger,' she thought walking towards another aisle. 'More to the point, I have a husband.' There was a queue at the till and she joined it.

'You dropped this?' said the man politely a few minutes later. He smiled and held out a white linen handkerchief.

Annie jumped and thought, 'Oh please, God no.'

Close-up, the man's cropped blonde hair had lighter strands and he looked like a GI who'd been surfing all summer. His body was strong, healthy and pulsating with life. Annie froze.

'Well do you want it?' asked the handsome man. She detected a soft American accent.

Annie felt herself blush and she said thank you and snatched the handkerchief more sharply than planned. The linen was white with the initials BR embroidered on it, it had been a present from her Gran years ago. She kept it in her handbag as a good luck talisman. It was one of the few objects she possessed from her previous life.

'I'm Duke Bailey,' said the American with a perfect white smile.

He held out his hand. Duke's grip was firm and his skin unusually warm. She hoped her own hand wasn't too cold. Josh often said her hands were the same temperature as a bag of frozen peas.

'You're American,' said Annie fumbling to make conversation.

'Yes, I am, ma'am,' said Duke with a laugh.

He was staring at her. Annie found his gaze unnerving.

'I'm British,' she squeaked and immediately kicked herself for her banality.

'I know you're British. What's your name?'

'It's, it's…' for a moment Annie's mind was blank.

'You've forgotten your own name?' Duke laughed.

'No, of course I know my name. I'm Annie Raven,' she

stood up straight and hoisted her bag onto her shoulder.

'Well, nice to meet you, Annie Raven,' said Duke. He bowed his head slightly and walked away.

Annie remained rooted to the spot and watched Duke's slow and measured stroll. Without turning around, he put his right arm up and waved just before he vanished into an aisle of books. He had beautiful hands. The fingers were long and graceful.

Outside the shop, Annie raised the handkerchief to her nose. It had a new smell. A faint odour of cinnamon and musk.

'For God's sake,' she told herself and stuffed the handkerchief back into her bag.

As Annie waited for Josh outside Costa she re-ran the encounter with the American in her mind. There was only one word to describe him. Hot. She used to feel that way about Josh.

But when was the last time they'd made love? She couldn't even remember.

Darkere

The stakeout in the woods had been a risky waste of time, but there'd been no mention of the tramp on the local news, and there was nothing to link Darkere to the man's death, so he reasoned he was safe. Besides, the tramp wasn't important, what he needed to focus on was the job in hand. The Raven case.

The house had been dark and silent and Darkere suspected that Josh, and Brigid if she was alive, which he thought she was, were on the run. Darkere was hoping for a fresh lead by the end of the day, all he needed was a single nugget from one of Brigid Raven's colleagues. Time for a visit to the woman's workplace.

Leeds City West Business Park, the home of Northern Magazines, had a smart reception that led to four lifts. Darkere was given a pass and made his way up to the third floor and *Canine World*.

Outside the lift, double glass doors led to a large open plan office space with floor-to-ceiling windows that overlooked the gardens and parking area below. A glass cubicle stood opposite the main door and it was empty except for a desk and chair. Pinned up on one wall were rows of the magazine's front covers – this was obviously the editor's den.

Darkere made his way towards one of the occupied desks. Several people were tapping away on computers. Around the room were waist-high piles of magazines and newspapers interspersed with plastic boxes filled with items such as dog books, coats and toys. He even spotted a half-full box of dog toothpaste and toothbrushes.

'Looks like a jumble sale for pets,' thought Darkere.

Strangely, the investigator couldn't see any evidence of real dogs, which he thought odd. He presumed a pack of smelly mutts would be running about the place pissing in the corners. He was glad there weren't any though. He wasn't a dog lover.

A thin woman who was sat at the desk nearest the editor's office put down her juice carton. She didn't hold out her hand.

'I'm Abigail, the deputy editor. And I'm very busy,' she said rudely. 'The editor's out at lunch. What do you want?'

'I was hoping you could help me with some information about Brigid Raven,' said Darkere calmly. He'd love to slap the snooty look off her face. 'I'm investigating Brigid's death.'

He was on several CCTV cameras in the building and having given his real name to the guard on reception thought it best to be honest – up to a point.

Abigail opened a new juice carton and sucked on it loudly. Darkere ignored the noise and continued. 'Did Brigid do or say anything out of the ordinary in the days running up to her death?'

Abigail shook her head, 'No. Her life was basically the magazine and her volunteer work with rescue dogs. She went to the kennels every week. She was a bit sad really.'

Out of the corner of his eye the investigator saw a younger woman in glasses sat at a nearby desk. She was listening intently to the exchange between himself and Abigail.

'Did Brigid talk about any plans to go away?' As he spoke, Darkere turned his body slightly so the younger woman could hear him better. 'Maybe there was somewhere special in the UK that she always wanted to visit? Or liked to go?'

'Let me think,' said Abigail enjoying the attention. 'Where did she want to go? She liked beaches. And cities.'

'I don't see what connection Brigid's holiday plans have to do with her tragic death,' interrupted the young woman in glasses. She had come out from behind her desk and hovered in the space between Abigail and Darkere.

Darkere could see the tears in the woman's eyes. He could tell she had been close to Brigid. He turned his back on Abigail and introduced himself to the friend, her name was Natasha Hopper.

Abigail tutted and sat back at her desk and resumed tapping away on her keyboard.

'Brigid had an asthma attack and died. End of story,' said Natasha. 'Who do you work for exactly?'

'I'm a private investigator who's been hired on behalf of the couple's bank,' said Darkere with a smile. 'Just crossing the T's and dotting the I's, that's all.'

'I thought you were with the police,' said Abigail.

The deputy editor's head was poking out from the side of her computer, she didn't hide her surprise. Her eyes were wide and her mouth hung open for a second too long. Darkere wanted to fill the space with his fist and choke her. Shut the silly bitch up.

'I'm sorry but I don't think we can help you,' said Natasha. 'I'm not sure why you're here. Brigid's death was a tragedy and a loss to everyone who knew her.' She glared at Abigail and addressed Darkere bluntly, 'Perhaps security can show you out?'

Natasha picked up her handset and began to dial. A big fat tear rolled down her cheek. She wiped it away quickly.

'I'm leaving. Thanks for your time,' said Darkere. 'If you think of anything please let me know.' He handed Natasha his card.

Driving home, Darkere decided his next line of investigation would be another visit to the couple's rental property but during the day this time. He would chat to the neighbours. Find out for certain if they'd moved out. There was bound to be some nosey old biddy who knew all the street gossip.

Until then, he decided to push on with the other two cases for WOM Ltd. The files were straightforward and he could progress them quickly and get his invoices filed and get paid. He'd let the Raven investigation stew for a few more days.

After years in this game, Darkere knew that if you took a step back interesting leads bubbled up to the surface like dead bodies in a pond.

Annie

An old Western film was on television, and the gunshots blasted out into the living room. Annie flinched at the unnatural noise. Her head was groggy thanks to a lack of sleep. For several nights she hadn't dropped off until the early hours because of her fear of the dark ghost. Thankfully, the spirit hadn't manifested last night but she was still feeling delicate.

'Can you turn it down please?' she asked Josh.

Without saying anything, Josh crouched by the TV and lowered the volume. There was no remote control. He flopped back onto the sofa.

'This TV should be in a museum,' he said sulkily.

Annie ignored him. She was cutting up vintage comics, which she'd found in a charity shop - Saltburn had several. The scissors moved deftly in her hand. In another life, she'd have been a surgeon or a dressmaker depending on the century.

'How's it going, Blue Peter?' asked Josh still watching the screen.

'Fine.' There was a loud knock at the back door. Annie was puzzled because they had no friends in Saltburn. Surely Jehovah's Witnesses wouldn't trek all the way up here to the cliff top?

Josh sprang up. A courier in a brown uniform with a yellow emblem on his breast pocket greeted him.

'I've got a delivery for,' the courier consulted his clipboard and added, 'Josh Raven. Where do you want it?'

'Just in here,' said Josh.

The courier moved backwards and forwards between the

van and cottage. Annie didn't want to start an argument in front of the stranger so she waited until everything was unloaded.

'What on earth have you bought?' asked Annie as the courier drove off. She was shocked by the large pile of boxes in the middle of the room.

'It's just a few things we need. A new laptop, TV, DVD player…' Josh ripped open a few of the plastic bags to jog his memory. 'There's bedding,' he added, 'and some sofa cushions and a wool throw for you.' Josh pulled out a tartan throw and handed it to Annie.

'I admit, the throw looks good. But we can't afford this stuff. Not yet, anyway. Or has the money come through?'

'Didn't you know it's a basic human right to have a large flat screen?' Josh ripped open the TV's box as he spoke.

'No, it is not,' said Annie. She hated how Josh turned everything into a joke. 'What's this? A new phone?' She was rooting around in the bags herself.

'Yes. I bought you a pay-as-you-go.'

'I don't need a mobile. Josh, seriously, how much did you spend?' Annie pointed to the packaging.

'Not that much,' said Josh.

Annie pushed him again and Josh admitted that the total came to about £2,000.

'Two grand!' shouted Annie. 'We don't have that kind of money. Are you insane?'

She was furious. Josh was supposed to be good with figures. The bloody idiot. What was he thinking spending all that money?

'The house has been sold and the insurance money will come through soon,' said Josh nonchalantly.

'But how did you pay for it?'

'I put it on new store cards and used the address of our old house in Leeds. The sale's not gone through yet.'

'Josh, that's dishonest. And we can't afford the direct debit payments.'

Josh said it was fine, no one would know.

'I've been worried sick about how we're going to afford to live and you've gone and bought all this crap. You're insane.' Annie was trying to keep her voice down but was too angry to worry about the neighbours hearing her.

'It's really not that much…' Josh trailed off.

'I need a home where I can put down roots. Not a flat screen TV.' Unable to control herself Annie shouted, 'I don't know what has got into you.' She grabbed her coat from the peg rail and opened the door.

Annie was full of rage. She'd never been so annoyed with Josh. How dare he spend so much money without consulting her first. They were supposed to make all their decisions together. She stomped down the stony path towards the cliff, and the more she examined what had happened the angrier she felt.

At the bottom of the cliff path she panted slightly from the exertion. Even so she carried on walking briskly and went down the slipway and on to the beach. The sand glistened with little pools of water. The tide was out. In the distance gulls bobbed on the sea and behind her clumps of kittiwakes cried out from the cliff.

Annie walked all the way up the beach, and whilst she pushed her feet into the damp sand she pondered the events that had led her to this place. She knew what she'd signed up for when she'd agreed to the scam. It was going to be a new start. But as Annie looked out to sea she realised that she'd underestimated how much her death was going to steal from her life.

With startling clarity, and a hint of fear, it hit her that she was utterly dependent on Josh – and she had no control over his whims. Previously, his rash behaviour had been curtailed by having a job. There was always Monday morning to think about or so many weeks until payday. Now her husband had no boundaries.

What would happen if she fell out of love with him? If she could no longer tolerate his behaviour, or his drinking? How would she survive? She was technically a nobody. They hadn't even looked into securing her any fake documents.

A chill went through Annie's bones, she hoped it was only a blast of wind from the sea. Even so, she still looked around but didn't see any fading images of the holographic ghosts that projected from their past into her present. There were no dark shadows either. Annie heaved a sigh of relief and sat for a long time on a rock staring at the sea before finally walking slowly back up the cliff path.

The empty boxes and packaging were still piled up in the porch, but Josh had been busy. Her husband had wired up the TV and DVD and tidied up. Books were back in the small bookcase by the alcove, the backgammon set had been put away. Even the coffee table was clear of clutter and had been wiped. The soft throw hung neatly over the back of the sofa and fresh logs were stacked in the basket by the fire. Everything was in its rightful place.

Josh came out of the kitchen. 'I don't want to argue,' he said. 'I'm sorry, I thought I was doing the right thing. I thought you'd be happy.'

'I don't want to fight either.' Feeling drained, Annie collapsed on the chintz chair.

'You've been gone ages,' said Josh sitting on her chair arm. 'I was starting to worry.'

'I walked all the way along the cliff path. The cottage looks great, by the way.' It was then that she noticed her husband was grinding his teeth. 'Are you okay?'

'Mr. Speedy helped me with the tidying.'

'What?' She couldn't believe what she was hearing. And where had he got amphetamines from? He didn't know anybody that sold drugs in Saltburn.

'Don't freak out,' said Josh. 'I just purchased a bit of speed in the pub the other night.'

Annie noticed that he was fidgeting. He was fiddling with the buttons on his shirt and having trouble keeping his hands still.

'What were you thinking?' said Annie raising her voice. 'The dealer could have been an undercover policeman. You idiot.' Annie was stunned and her anger quickly resurfaced.

'I promise in future I'll go to the dealer's house.' Josh directed her to the table in the corner of the living room. 'Sit down, I'm cooking dinner.'

'I'd rather you didn't buy any drugs at all,' said Annie. 'And you need to cut down on your drinking. You look so pale and unhealthy. You've lost weight too.'

Josh said it was the stress and he promised to stick to just a few pints. Annie couldn't be bothered to argue anymore. She'd talk some sense into him when he was straight. It was useless trying to have a proper conversation with her husband when he was wrecked.

'I am your slave for the rest of the day,' Josh said with

an exaggerated bow. He disappeared into the kitchen and came back out with a pot of tea and some French fancies on a plate.

Annie ate a few mouthfuls of a cake. 'Please don't do that again. Don't make a decision that affects us both without discussing it first. I don't like it.'

Josh nodded. 'Okay, I promise.'

Annie pushed her half-eaten cake away and looked around the room. She had to admit that the throw and cushions made the place look even cosier.

'Pity we can't stay here, I love this cottage,' she said.

'Yeah, it's a real pity,' said Josh unconvincingly.

Josh

Josh heard Annie loudly set her book down and he inwardly sighed and paused his new Xbox.

'Are you a fast rider?' asked his wife.

Josh was sat on the floor leaning against the chesterfield. Annie was curled up in the chair by the fire and had been reading some bloke's memoir about Vietnam, which she'd found upstairs in the bedroom. At least it wasn't a ghost book, and she'd not mentioned any dark dreams for a while, which was a relief. Even so, she obviously wanted to chat. He didn't. He would rather see how fast he could finish the circuit.

'Mmm. I'm okay,' said Josh trying not to encourage her. He picked up the controls and re-started the game. 'Why don't you go out for a walk?' he said without looking at his wife whilst negotiating a difficult bend. He pushed down the throttle and the bike raced ahead on the large new TV.

'I'll pop round to see Margaret,' said Annie. 'The noise of that game is driving me mad.'

'Make sure she doesn't put you in her cauldron,' said Josh with his eyes still fixed to the racetrack. He didn't like the old bag. She was too close for comfort.

'Why are you so nasty about her?'

'She's from an army background. Those types always follow the rules,' he explained with disdain. 'The woman would shop us to the police if she knew our secret.' He froze the computer game and turned to Annie. 'Why do you like her so much? You have nothing in common and there's decades between you. You haven't told her about our secret, have you?'

He felt a wave of fear rush through his body. The paranoia buzzed in his brain as his mind jumped ahead to an image of him being arrested by the police and led away in handcuffs.

Annie looked puzzled and said, 'I like her, she's interesting. And you're being paranoid. I haven't told Margaret anything.'

Josh relaxed. The paranoia was no doubt caused by the drugs. He definitely needed to lay off the dope for a day or so. Have a few days hash free.

Turning to Annie, he added calmly, 'Listen to me.' Josh was pointing his index finger at his wife, behind him his motorbike was still frozen on the screen. 'Don't tell her anything. In fact, I'd rather you didn't spend any time at all with the old bag. It's too much of a risk. She's bound to ask you questions about your past.'

'How could you even think I would blab about the scam to Margaret? I'm not stupid.'

Annie was incensed but quite frankly so what? His wife's feelings at this moment were less important than the end game. And she needed to receive his message loud and clear.

'Just don't forget it was me who came up with the idea,' said Josh restarting the game for a second time. 'Listen to what I say. Keep your bloody mouth shut.'

It was true. If it wasn't for him they'd still be living in that dump in Leeds in thousands of pounds of debt and working like slaves. Why couldn't his wife show some gratitude for his brilliant plan? It had worked.

'Fuck you,' said Annie grabbing her coat and bag storming out of the door.

'Shit,' thought Josh.

He immediately regretted being so direct with Annie. It was the stress of waiting for the cash and their arguing wasn't helping matters. Every time they spoke they seemed to be butting heads. What was wrong with her these days?

Christ, he needed a hit. Sod it. He dug out his stash tin from the cupboard by the fireplace and began to roll a joint.

Annie

Fuming, Annie slammed the back door. Just listening to Josh's drivel about masterminding the scam made her want to explode.

He was so rude when he talked to her. Who the hell did he think he was speaking to? She was his wife. Since coming to Saltburn, the worst parts of her husband's personality had been exaggerated by his increased drug taking and drinking. His paranoia was at an all-time high. He didn't seem to trust anyone. Not even her. He stayed up late, surfaced in the afternoons and had no structure or shape to his day. Her husband couldn't see that he was spiralling out of control. But she could.

'I'm not equipped to deal with his problems,' thought Annie as she knocked on Margaret's door.

She waited a few minutes, but there was no answer. Typical. Her first social call to her landlady and she was out. Annie decided it was probably a good thing given her state of mind. She decided to walk on the beach and call again in half an hour. She didn't want to go back into the holiday cottage, not after storming out.

On the beach the trumpet calls from the kittiwakes were loud and drew in Annie like a mermaid's song. She sat down on a large rock in front of the Ship Inn to soak up the stillness. The sea air washed out her insides and made her feel clean but the bubbling anger that lingered in the back of her mind stayed stuck like splattered blood on stone.

After a while, a dog ran up to Annie. She had her eyes shut with her face to the sun so she heard the animal first, the rhythmic panting of its breath. When she opened her eyes, a silky black Labrador was sat in front of her wagging its tail.

Annie held out a hand. The dog sniffed her skin and pushed its wet nose up against her fingers. Annie stroked its head. The pooch barked for more fuss when she stopped petting it.

'He's lovely,' said Annie to the dog's owner. She felt her anger bubbling down slightly. 'What's his name?'

'Daniel. He's such a softy,' said a woman with long blond hair and slim legs like a greyhound.

She was wearing faded blue jeans, brown leather boots and a short tweed jacket. She appeared to be in her early thirties and had a calm, friendly air.

'What a great name. Hey, Daniel.'

Despite her anger softening, Annie still wanted to be left alone. But the dog was so sweet and the woman so friendly that it felt unthinkable to be rude.

The dog crouched down into a play position. The woman pulled out a grubby tennis ball from her pocket. Before the blonde had even thrown the ball, the dog had run 100 yards down the beach.

'Daniel,' said the woman in a high-pitched voice to catch the dog's attention. 'Here, Daniel.'

The dog stopped, skidded in the sand and lolloped back with his tongue hanging out. Just when he was a few yards away the woman threw the ball.

The ball arced high in the air, landed on the wet sand and bounced creating sprays of salt water. Daniel caught the ball and stood with it half hidden in his mouth, then dropped it and ran back to the woman.

'Fetch it. Go on fetch the ball,' said the woman. The dog

looked at her blankly. 'He's trained me well,' she said and walked off to retrieve the ball.

Once they'd gone, Annie walked up to the far edge of the cove where the cliff jutted out towards the sea. Any last froths of anger were teased out of her body by the beating pull of the water. But Annie could feel that the latest row with Josh had scooped out yet another tiny piece of her heart.

The beach emptied of dog walkers, couples and errant youths and reluctantly, after watching the waves for a while longer, Annie walked back up the cliff path. She remembered the book she had bought on roses, and decided to go back into the cottage to get it. That way, she had an excuse to pop in to see Margaret.

Josh was so wrapped up in his game that he didn't even notice her slipping into the kitchen, picking up the shopping bag and slipping out again.

She wasn't sure how her elderly neighbour would react to her unannounced visit, but as she raised her hand to knock on Margaret's back door it opened.

'Annie. Nice surprise,' said the old woman beaming. 'Come in.'

Margaret Swain was wearing a green corduroy skirt and a purple polo neck. An unbuttoned blue quilted body warmer hung loosely around her top half and grey tights covered her legs. On her feet were black furry ankle boots.

Annie held up the plastic bag. 'I saw this book the other day and thought of you.'

Margaret took the bag and ushered Annie inside. The place had the same mismatched style as the rental cottage although it was smarter. The white walls were newly painted, which surprised Annie.

'Shut the door. Keep the heat in,' said Margaret impatiently.

Annie closed the door behind her and followed Margaret into the lounge. She sank on to the sofa. A fire blazed in the hearth and the high flames were alive with salamanders.

'Better than watching TV,' said Margaret poking the fire making it burn even brighter.

Annie realised that the only piece of technology she could spot was an old AM/FM radio.

'Time for a cup of tea,' said Margaret standing up with no sign of stiffness.

'Let me,' said Annie.

Margaret nodded and settled back down in her chair again.

In the kitchen, Annie lifted up the lid on the cream Aga. Josie's mum, Elizabeth, had an Aga and she remembered making toast with Josie on the hot plates late one night. At the memory of her friend Annie felt a little pang and took a deep breath. She rubbed her tears away before they came and carried on making the tea.

Whilst the kettle boiled Annie took in the room. It was the same size as her kitchen next door and was what designers called 'freestanding' and 'eclectic'. The range cooker took up the middle of one wall and to the right of the Aga stood an antique pine dresser. The top part of the dresser was full of blue and white striped Cornish ware plates, mugs and bowls.

Underneath the pine shelves was a double cupboard. Annie was sure it housed 'the best crockery' bought with money that had been saved up week-by-week and not on credit. She itched to have a look inside the cupboard but thought it rude. Instead, she took two mugs from one of the dresser's open shelves.

Opposite the Aga was a row of kitchen units with a wooden worktop. The units stretched the length of the room. An assortment of items sat on the worktop: a jar of tea bags, a blue teapot, olive oil, bottles of pills, some garlic bulbs, and a large dish of salt. It reminded Annie of her gran's flat above the shop. She smiled and plucked two tea bags from the jar.

'Biscuits in the tin,' boomed Margaret. Her voice carried easily between the two rooms.

Inside the tin Annie found jaffa cakes, bourbons and chocolate digestives. She hesitated, which biscuits should she choose?

'Bring a selection,' said Margaret.

Annie heaped a pretty plate with biscuits and found the milk jug. She carried the tray carefully into the living room.

'Marvellous,' said Margaret when Annie appeared.

Annie went to put the tray on a small table at the side of Margaret's chair but her neighbour tutted. Annie lifted up the tray and in one swift move, Margaret moved the side table and put it between them. Without a word, Annie put the tray back on top of it.

'I'll be mother,' said Margaret pouring the tea and handing Annie a bourbon on a dainty side plate.

They drank their tea silently but it wasn't awkward. Annie wondered if it was okay to dunk her biscuit in her tea. Oldies could be such sticklers for manners.

'Go on. Dunk it,' said Margaret.

Smiling, Annie dipped her bourbon and savoured the

soggy texture as it hit her mouth. The sweetness was slightly offset by her black tea. It was heaven.

'Good eh?' said Margaret with a chuckle. 'Have another. Go on.'

'Thanks,' said Annie. 'Tea and biscuits are one of my favourite things.' It was true. It had been hard to give up the sweet treats.

'So, what's this?' Margaret asked as she reached inside the bag. The plastic crinkled as Margaret pulled out her present. She folded the bag neatly and set it on the arm of her chair and turned the book over to read the blurb.

'You mentioned your roses and I thought…' said Annie.

'Lovely present,' said Margaret smiling. 'Really lovely. Know about the world's oldest rose?'

'No,' said Annie shaking her head.

'It's a thousand years old,' said Margaret. 'Grows on the wall of the Hildesheim Cathedral in Germany.'

Margaret told Annie all about the ancient rose and the flowers that had grown in her mother's garden.

'When I was young I used to make perfume out of them,' she chuckled. 'Course it wasn't really perfume.' Margaret poured more tea. She had a firm grip of the teapot but Annie noticed a small patch of red scaly skin on her fingers.

'Eczema,' she said. 'Comes and goes. Make my own potions with herbs from the garden to soothe it.'

Annie was surprised. 'Are you a herbalist?'

'No. Farmer's wife. Country people knew about plants, back when. Why?'

'My gran was a herbalist.' Annie told Margaret about helping out in her gran's apothecary when she was small. 'Gran was the best. She was kind and a good listener. I miss

246

her. You remind me of her, Margaret.' Annie trailed off.

'Thank you. Dead, is she?'

'Yes, she died last year. She had a stroke.'

'Always hard losing a loved one,' said Margaret brushing the crumbs off her lap. 'Might not be flesh and blood, but I'm here if you ever want to talk.' She tapped her nose with her finger. 'And Mum's the word. No loose lips in this house.'

Annie said thank you and Margaret casually asked how long she and Josh had been together. Annie said they'd met five years ago and been married for three and a half.

'Doesn't seem your type,' said Margaret bluntly. 'Seems a bit spineless to me.'

Annie felt immediately defensive and explained that Josh had been under a lot of pressure recently. That he'd lost his job last year and been a bit depressed. Annie stopped herself from saying more as she remembered Josh's warning.

'Kissed a prince. Turned into a frog,' said Margaret with a chuckle.

Annie managed a half smile. 'It's not like that, really. It feels… I mean, I think…'

'Out with it.' The old woman offered Annie another biscuit.

Annie hesitated and chose a jaffa cake. Sitting here with Margaret gave her the same feeling of being with her gran and she was desperate to talk to someone about her and Josh's crumbling marriage. However, it was difficult to explain the situation without going into too much detail, detail that would reveal their secret. She also really needed to talk about the dark ghost, but Margaret didn't strike her as the type to entertain the idea of the supernatural.

Just the previous night Annie had experienced another

frightening dream. She'd been in her lovely home in Leeds, before it had burnt down, and a dark shadow had appeared behind her in the bedroom mirror. As she froze, the darkness had hovered close on the edge of her vision and then turned itself into a stream of black smoke that had curled around her mouth and nose. The smoke expanded rapidly, covered her face with a black film as thin and soft as silk, and then it had slowly suffocated her. The liquid shroud had seeped into her nostrils and pushed into her mouth.

Annie had woken up gasping and clutching at her face trying to free herself. She hadn't mentioned the nightmare to Josh. She couldn't bear for him to tell her it was nothing to worry about. It was easy for him to say. He wasn't being haunted.

'I'm not sure Josh and I want the same things,' said Annie letting the dream fade in her mind, deciding to confide in Margaret about her relationship.

'Why?' asked Margaret. She was genuinely interested. 'Go on. Won't tell a soul. Promise.'

'I feel distant from him,' said Annie in a rush. 'There's a huge cavern between us and I don't know how to cross it. But I can't leave him.' Annie stopped herself.

'Don't be so weak, girl,' said Margaret hitting her knee with her hand. 'You can walk away anytime. Just leave the bugger if you're not happy.'

Annie looked down. Margaret said sorry, she could be too blunt sometimes.

'No, it's true. I should walk away but I can't,' said Annie.

She knew she was teetering on the edge of saying too much, but she hadn't spoken to anyone properly for months, other than Josh, and the words tumbled out of her mouth.

'Modern disease of relationships,' said Margaret as she selected another biscuit.

'What do you mean?'

'Women give it away too soon.'

'I don't understand,' said Annie confused.

'Always hold some part of yourself. In here,' said Margaret. She tapped her chest where her heart beat beneath her wrinkled skin.

'You shouldn't hold back if you love someone,' said Annie frowning. It was a statement and not a question. And she believed her words to be true.

'Fragile things. Hearts. A person can die of a broken heart. How's yours?' asked Margaret without any trace of malice.

'Not broken. Just bruised.' Annie went to fill her mug to deflect another question but the teapot was empty.

'Where are you from exactly?' asked Margaret.

Her guard carefully back in place, Annie said slowly, 'We did live in Leeds but we're in the process of relocating. I told you about my husband losing his job. And we recently lost everything in a house fire.'

'Sorry to hear about the fire. Must have been traumatic. Have you money to pay the rent?'

'Oh, yes, don't worry about that, cash isn't a problem,' Annie hoped that this conversation was leading where she hoped it was leading. 'Josh has some... inheritance coming soon so we can live off that whilst we look for work.'

Annie looked down. She was ashamed of lying to her new friend.

'You're in luck. Too old to be prattling about with

holidaymakers. Want to rent the cottage? Longer term? For cash?' Margaret tapped her nose again with a finger.

Annie grinned. 'That would be fantastic, thank you.' Annie threw her arms around Margaret and hugged her gently. 'You're an angel.'

Margaret looked surprised but smiled. 'Cottage needs to be lived in. Be nice to have some company.'

'Thanks again,' said Annie. 'I must go and tell my husband.'

Annie grabbed her bag and coat and dashed out of Margaret's house with all fear of the recent dream quashed by her exciting news.

Darkere

The farm's old wooden door was being battered by a violent hand. Darkere heard the noise from the living room. It was rare for him to have a visitor at his home and so late. Whoever was outside at 11pm was obviously not making a social visit. The caller could only be Little Andy. Scott Mac didn't make his own house visits.

Darkere shouted, 'Who is it?' He was using the extra few seconds to compose himself.

'Scott Mac,' said a loud Glaswegian voice from behind the door.

'Fuck,' thought Darkere. The man himself. 'I'll just get the keys,' he said.

'Hurry up,' said Scott Mac. 'I've wasted enough time on you already.'

Darkere's hand shook slightly as he unlocked the door. He breathed deeply and put on a smile.

'Nice place,' said Scott Mac pushing past him followed by Little Andy. 'Very nice place.'

'I was going to ring you,' said Darkere calmly.

'Were yee now,' said Scott Mac. The gangster walked over to the bureau and ran his finger along the length of the large collection of Elvis albums. He pulled out a dog-eared record called *Double Dynamite*, which showed the King in a jewel-encrusted jumpsuit. He turned the record sleeve over and read the track listing.

'I've got your cash,' said Darkere.

Scott Mac's eyebrows shot up slightly. He pushed the album back into the collection and broke into a wide smile. Darkere could see the man's gold front tooth. He also noticed the black leather jacket that hung off his shoulders like a cape.

'That's a thing you don't hear often is it?' said Scott Mac turning to Little Andy, who was anything but little. His bodyguard, come-driver, come-torturer, was 6ft 5' with the build of a man who took steroids.

'Aye, boss,' said Little Andy.

'Just give me a minute,' said Darkere. 'The money's upstairs.'

Without waiting for a reply, Darkere ran up the stairs into his bedroom. He opened the drawer on his bedside table and took out two rolls of notes held together by rubber bands. One bundle held £8,000 and the other £4,000. £8,000 short of what he owned Scott Mac.

Darkere turned to the wardrobe and grabbed at the shoes in the bottom one-by-one, pushing a hand into the toes of each before quickly flinging them over his shoulder. All of the shoes were empty.

'What yee doing, fucking printing the money?' Scott Mac shouted up from the bottom of the stairs. He laughed at his own joke.

'I'll be down in a sec,' shouted Darkere. He took a deep breath and holding the bundles walked down the stairs with a straight face.

'Here you go,' he said holding the cash out to Scott Mac. 'I was lucky on the horses yesterday. It's a bit short but I've a work bonus coming. I'll get the rest to you in a few days.'

The loan shark didn't say a word but tipped his head towards Little Andy. Darkere handed him the cash, which the tank of a man counted quickly.

'Eight,' said Little Andy. He counted the next bundle as

the room was silent. 'Four,' he added.

'You're eight grand short,' said Scott Mac. He whistled, 'That's not small change, laddie.'

'Come on,' said Darkere with his palms turned upwards. 'I'll have it soon. I promise.'

Scott Mac tutted twice. 'That's what yee said last week and the week before. I've been generous wi yee given our long history but I cannae wait anymore. Money is tight for everyone,' he said. 'It's a fuckin' recession despite what the government shite says.'

Darkere protested, 'I've always paid you back and my luck's turned on the horses.'

But the loan shark held his hand up. 'Give Elvis a wee bit of a shake, rattle and roll,' said Scott Mac as he turned to leave without a backward glance.

Little Andy led him to a chair in the kitchen, Darkere knew better than to protest. If he fought back he'd be likely to end up in little bits in a disused quarry.

The first punch hit the right side of Darkere's face and knocked his head back. He didn't wince. 'Punches like a girl,' Darkere thought even though he knew it wasn't true. He was trying to harden himself up for the beating.

The second punch hit his mouth hard and a sliver of blood appeared in the corner like a baby dribbling milk. 'Ignore the pain, focus on something else,' Darkere told himself sternly.

But the pain shuddered through his whole body, and after the seventh punch Darkere was wheezing slightly.

Suddenly, Little Andy punched him in his heart hard, twice. Darkere felt a sharp stab dance across his chest and up his arm. The shock of the pain made him gasp and his eyes watered.

Seconds later, Scott Mac's henchman left without a word. The front door slammed but bounced back and was left ajar. Darkere didn't notice. His body was shaking with an adrenaline rush and he sat on the sofa to calm down.

'That was bloody lucky,' he thought taking deep breaths. 'Good job I won at York yesterday. I might be missing a few fingers otherwise.'

As he felt the lingering touch of relief he became aware of another sensation, a shortness of breath and a slight light-headedness. It was odd and unexpected, but soon Darkere experienced a wave of pain travelling from his chest to his arms. His jaw felt oddly sore.

With horror Darkere realised what it meant and he felt panic rising. He just made it to the phone in his office and dialled 999.

A voice said, 'Which emergency service do you require?'

'Ambulance,' Darkere spluttered out the words. He was gasping like a drowning man.

Without waiting for more instructions, Darkere gave his address in a clear monotone.

'Heart attack,' he whispered. 'Having a heart attack.'

Darkere couldn't fight the pain any longer. His head fell forward onto his chest and the investigator collapsed onto the floor and fell swiftly into darkness.

Annie

Last night Josh had mumbled an apology when Annie had come back from visiting Margaret. But it hadn't been the right time to mention their landlady's offer of renting the cottage long-term – or the fact that she'd already said yes. Josh had said he was sorry, but he was still monosyllabic and stoned.

Maybe here and now was the ideal moment? They were walking in the woods near the beach. It was late afternoon and deathly quiet except for a clutch of noisy crows in nearby trees. As they passed underneath the birds squawked loudly.

'Noisy buggers,' said Josh laughing. He turned to Annie, smiling. 'Are you happy? I would do anything to make you happy you know.'

Annie squeezed Josh's hand and sensed that it was an opportune moment to bring up their living arrangements. Her husband was in a good mood, not drunk, and she hadn't seen him smoke any dope so far today.

'Margaret has offered us the cottage to live in long-term. I said yes,' she blurted out.

Annie badly wanted Josh to say it was a brilliant idea. She couldn't imagine going back to the smoke of the city. The sea air let her breathe more easily and she hadn't suffered a single asthma attack since coming to Saltburn. Her asthma pump was gathering dust in her bedside drawer, which was just as well as she hadn't registered at a GP surgery yet although Josh had assured her she could do so with only a birth certificate – his dead sister's.

The smile quickly fell from Josh's face and his features

contorted. 'I'm not living in the bloody cottage forever. It's a hovel.'

'But it's cheap and I love it,' said Annie exasperated. She was determined to win this argument.

'Tell her thanks, but no thanks,' said Josh angrily pulling a leaf off a tree branch.

'It's the ideal home for us. Remote, low overheads and it's fully furnished.'

'I don't want to discuss it anymore. End of. We are not staying in Saltburn. When the four weeks are up at the cottage we're leaving.'

'It's my dream home,' said Annie desperation creeping into her voice. 'And the sea air is good for my asthma. You just said you'd do anything to make me happy.'

It was too late, she could feel a whisper of hatred towards Josh resurfacing. He could be so selfish sometimes.

Josh said quietly, 'I want to move to Edinburgh. I've found us this fantastic penthouse flat.'

Annie shook her head. 'I don't want to live in Scotland. I want to live here. It's peaceful. I feel a real connection to the countryside, the sea. Look at it, the place is beautiful.'

Josh stopped and folded his arms. 'I'm not living in this toy town.'

'What about what I want? I don't exist anymore because of you. And you won't even let me have a say in where we live, that's not right.'

'Shh, not outside,' Josh hissed. 'Someone might hear, and stop being so dramatic. There's no need.'

Annie lowered her voice a fraction. 'I am not being dramatic. I like it here.' Annie was finally speaking her truth. Margaret had put fire in her belly. 'I'm only just starting to

256

realise that when I wiped out my past I also wiped out my future.' She folded her arms. 'I'm a ghost in my own life. I can't enrol to study new things, or get a job, or even volunteer somewhere. I'm a shadow, and you did that to me.'

'You don't mean that,' said Josh looking hurt.

'I do. And you're behaving like a selfish dickhead.'

Josh's mouth fell open. She could tell he was stunned. Annie never spoke to him this way, and she was always the one to roll over first. But not anymore.

The crows in the trees above them were still squawking loudly and Annie felt like they were backing up her righteous rage.

'Living here is all I need to make me happy,' Annie said. 'Who knows, Margaret may even sell the cottage to us? But no, you want some flash flat full of gadgets. Before we know it, we'll be in debt again. It's not happening, Josh. I want to stay in Saltburn.'

'I didn't realise living here meant so much to you,' said Josh rubbing the side of his face. 'Do you really want to live here?' he asked softly. 'Really?'

The light was fading. Annie nodded, feeling calmer. 'I feel stronger. My asthma's hardly affecting me. It's the fresh air.'

'So, we'll stay,' said Josh shrugging his shoulders. 'How much does she want in rent?'

'I forgot to ask.' Annie was amazed at how easily Josh had given in to her demands. But whilst the argument was over the silence continued to hang between them as they snaked through the trees, along the beach and back towards the town.

'Did you really mean what you said about not having a

future?' Josh asked.

They were halfway up the cliff path that led to the cottage.

'Don't you understand?' asked Annie. 'My life was frozen the moment I drank the Death Herb.'

'No, I don't understand why you're so upset. Our financial worries are over. I'll get a part-time job, eventually, but we're free. We can do whatever we want.'

Annie didn't reply. She could see that her husband didn't understand or see her point of view. And perhaps he never would.

'Margaret's right,' she thought, 'It's time to put myself first.'

Mander

Sandra Denning knocked on her boss's door at WOM Ltd. The secretary relayed the information to Andrew Mander without any fuss. The freelance investigator Bennett Darkere had been rushed to Leeds Coronary Care Unit after suffering a suspected heart attack at home.

'The registrar found his WOM Ltd business card in his wallet,' explained Sandra, 'He wanted to know about next of kin.'

'He's single,' said Mander with a sigh thinking he'd have to organise someone to mop up Darkere's cases. 'His only daughter lives in America but I don't know where.' Mander narrowed his eyes. 'What else did you tell them?'

'Very little. I'll call the hospital back and repeat exactly what you've just said to me.'

'Good, and thanks,' said Mander turning back to his computer screen. He didn't like people poking about in his business.

The secretary quietly closed the door. Mander saved the document he was working on, a letter to his bank about extending his company's overdraft, and clicked into the database which listed all the cases under investigation.

All active files were stored electronically. The MD could log into any case at any time and check on its progress. The only person who still used paper files was Darkere, the stubborn sod. He sent his updates in via snail mail because he had 'concerns about internet security', and Sandra had to painstakingly decipher his handwriting and upload the information onto the internal system.

But Mander liked Darkere despite him being annoyingly

old school. Perhaps the heart attack had come at the right time? It would give him an excuse to let Darkere's work dry up with no unpleasantness. He would give him a small bonus, of course, and Darkere had his police pension. There was no need for him to feel guilty.

Files popped up on Mander's screen. Working his way down the list, Mander saw three recent cases – one of which was the Raven file. The other two had been completed.

'Damn,' thought Mander.

He'd forgotten about the Raven investigation and that ridiculous bonus, which he clearly couldn't afford. The MD realised that his memory wasn't as sharp as it once was and he pressed his phone to speak to his secretary.

'Did Darkere send any updates about the Raven case before his heart attack?'

'Yes, it came in the post last week. I've been meaning to put it on the system. I've been really busy and…' replied Sandra.

'It's fine. I'll do it, please bring it in.'

The manila file was light. Mander sighed and put the file on his desk. He'd been working out the cash flow for the business this morning. He really would need to crack the whip. Things were starting to get slack and the company reserves were dwindling, especially after the re-fit.

Mander scrolled down the full database of pending cases and shook his head. Some investigations had been running for over six months. Six bloody months. Back in the day, he'd have been sacked for letting a case dribble on for so long.

He picked up the manila file, opened it and tutted when he looked at Darkere's paltry research for the Raven case.

Darkere had photocopied a few bits of paper and posted them to Sandra. That was the total extent of his research.

Mander quickly read the newspaper story about Brigid Raven's death. He double-checked for any mention of an autopsy and could see that her GP had pronounced her dead at the scene and issued a Medical Certificate of Cause of Death. The report stated that she'd visited A&E a few days before her death with the same health problem and had received treatment, and she'd seen her GP.

So legally, Mander deduced, there was no reason for an autopsy and it was clear she was a genuine asthmatic. Darkere had scribbled notes to this effect in the margin of the news story – and underlined the words 'no autopsy'. He had also checked out the A&E visit and confirmed this had taken place. Mander didn't want to know how he'd gleaned this information but he trusted that it was accurate. Darkere didn't make mistakes.

Flicking through the insurance paperwork Mander saw that the payments for both policies were up-to-date. He read a letter from the bank which confirmed that Mrs Raven had clearly declared her asthma on her original form, she'd even attached a separate covering letter about her illness.

'Very honest,' thought Mander.

The amounts for the pay-outs were large, he mused, but this was an open and shut case in his opinion.

What the hell had Darkere been doing dragging this investigation on for so long? It was straightforward. Woman dies from asthma attack. Doctor pronounces her dead. Husband claims on life insurance.

The hands-on MD updated the file on the database himself. He pulled up a 'final recommendation form' and input the research.

His conclusion read: *Following a detailed investigation by my team I can see no irregularities with this claim. I strongly recommended that all the insurance monies and claims be paid out in full to Mr. Josh Raven.*

Mander scanned in a copy of the Death Certificate, the *Yorkshire Post* newspaper cutting and bullet pointed the circumstances for when an autopsy normally took place for background research.

Smugly, he noted that it had taken him less than twenty minutes to close the Raven case and list the job on the outgoing invoice run.

PART FOUR:
EARTH

Josh

It was official. They were staying in Saltburn and had rented the cottage from Margaret Swain. Despite being pleased at the result, Annie still hadn't spoken to Josh much since their big row in the woods, so Josh had decided to spruce the place up as an olive branch.

Over the past week, he'd painted the front and back doors, cleared the garden of weeds and filled pots with tiny onion-like bulbs and lavender plants. Soil clung to his hands as he worked the earth. Until he'd dug the garden, the ground had been hard like stale cake.

The next task was painting the living room pale blue, which Josh was doing. Annie had chosen all the colours for the makeover: blues, browns and greens. She told him the tones echoed the landscape. He thought the colours were dull but he'd kept his mouth shut.

Painting the living room walls had taken three hours so far and made his arms ache. After a break to allow the walls to dry he was on the second coat.

'I'm not as fit as I used to be,' thought Josh as he struggled to move the decorating ladders he'd found in the outhouse. He hoped that this DIY would make Annie feel more settled because he was sick of all their bickering.

'So what if we can't live in Edinburgh at the moment? We can always move next year,' he told himself as he slapped more blue paint onto the wall with a roller. 'Just because we're staying for now doesn't mean we'll live here forever.'

When the walls were dry, Josh planned to hang neutral linen curtains in the living room and a roller blind in the bathroom. For some reason, Annie liked the handmade curtains in their bedroom, so they were staying, although he thought they were horrible.

For phase two he'd written a list of all the DIY jobs that needed doing like fixing wobbly doorknobs and re-enamelling the roll top bath. Josh was running through a quick mental list of today's tasks when he heard a familiar booming voice.

'Anyone home?'

Josh put on a cheery smile for Margaret Swain. He'd stupidly left the door open to air the room whilst he decorated.

'First rate job,' said Margaret hovering at the threshold. 'Splendid work.' As his neighbour spoke she rocked backwards and forwards on her heels with her hands behind her back.

'Thanks,' said Josh standing back to admire his work. 'The colour's nice, isn't it?' he lied. Josh would have preferred white. More importantly, why was Margaret poking her nose in? She seemed to be dropping into the cottage unannounced every bloody day.

'Annie in?' asked Margaret cocking her head as if she was listening for movement upstairs.

'No,' said Josh. 'She's gone for a walk along the cliff top to Whitby.'

Christ, she was a nosy old bag. He picked up the paint roller to indicate he must get on and finish the job. No time to chit chat.

Margaret stepped into the room and poked her head in the kitchen. 'Well done, young man. Having a big clean up I see.'

'Annie scrubbed the floor tiles yesterday,' said Josh not

turning around.

'Marvellous,' said Margaret. 'Must be off. Just wanted to say hello and see how the work was going.'

Margaret left and Josh wished they didn't live next to their landlady. Then again, the cottage was dirt cheap. The price meant he'd had enough money to splash out on this makeover and still treat himself to a few pints every night.

Josh thought about disappearing for a swift pint at The Victoria & Albert later when he'd finished. The pub served real ale. The pub landlady also made her own pickled eggs, the spicy delights floated like biology specimens in a jar on the bar.

Annie hated the pub and had only been there once. She said it was full of crusty old men. But Josh loved it. If he could, he'd spend all day in the place.

He pushed the thought of The Vic out of his mind and sighed. 'No rest for the wicked,' he said aloud as he finished what he hoped would be the last coat on the annoyingly uneven walls.

Annie

The path followed the edge of the cliff from Saltburn all the way to Whitby. A sheer drop on this stretch of the Cleveland Way led to the beach and the rocks below.

'If I fell I'd break my neck,' Annie thought. She moved as close to the edge as she dared and peered over the solid mass of rock. 'What would it be like to fly free into the air, then cross over to the other side?' She wondered if it would hurt. Or would death be instant?

A gull cried overhead, Annie blinked and backed up from the edge quickly and pushed the unsettling idea away. Suddenly, a blast of wind rushed around Annie's head and she was sure her name was being whispered. She froze to listen better to the strange low hum, but as quickly as the voice appeared the mournful sound vanished leaving her slightly shaken.

Was the voice the dark ghost? She shook her head as if to dispel the idea and moved further away from the jagged edge and back onto the worn cliff path.

After only a few steps, Annie reasoned that the sound was her imagination and nature playing tricks in the vast open space, she comforted herself with the thought. But a lingering unease remained.

She'd dreamt about the spirit again last night and had woken up bathed in sweat and feeling sick, but she didn't tell Josh. In fact, Annie had stopped mentioning the strange dreams to her husband altogether. Josh didn't listen to his intuition or see signs and patterns in life's events, so he was of little help to her.

There must be a way to stop the dreams. But how? She

could understand the initial nightmares after her experience of waking up in the coffin. But surely enough time had passed for her subconscious to work through any buried fears?

A bench on the cliff top path came into view. Annie sat down, shut her eyes and tried to empty her mind. Below her she could hear the waves beating against the rocks.

'Daniel! Daniel!' shouted a voice nearby.

It was the slim blonde with the black Labrador. They'd met a few times on the beach but never chatted for long. Annie didn't even know the woman's name.

The dog owner came into view on the path. Annie shielded her eyes from the sun and was relieved to see another person. The human contact made her morbid dreams seem less scary and real.

'How's Daniel? Has he been behaving?' asked Annie stroking the dog's head.

Daniel flopped down on the grass at her feet. He panted and half shut his eyes.

'He's been chasing the seagulls. He never catches them, of course.'

Annie laughed and the woman put a lead on her dog. 'Phew, it's warm,' she added sitting on the bench next to Annie.

'Yes, it's lovely,' said Annie. 'I hope it stays like this all week.'

They chatted about the weather, dogs, and the gorgeous view. The long vista stretched across the beach to Whitby Abbey in the distance.

'I'm Echo Ivy, by the way.'

The woman put out her hand. Annie shook it. Her skin

was warm and soft.

'Mad name, I know,' said Echo with a shrug. 'My parents were hippies.'

'I'm Annie Raven. I have a strange name too.'

'Annie Raven is a nice name,' said Echo giving Daniel a drink.

The talk turned to work. Echo asked Annie what she did for a living.

'I used to be a journalist but I was made redundant.' The lie burned Annie's mouth. But she was good at keeping secrets.

Echo said she was a holistic therapist and then glanced at her watch. 'Blimey, I better go. I have a client booked in.'

Echo offered Annie her mobile number, said to call her anytime if she wanted to meet for a cup of tea and a dog walk.

A genuine smile lit up Annie's face as she waved goodbye to her new friend. She felt thrilled but was worried about telling Josh. He'd already made it clear that they needed to be careful about becoming too close to people.

But Annie couldn't see what harm a bit of chit chat could do and decided to keep the news to herself. Josh's paranoid mind would only imagine her blabbing and revealing their secret, which would never happen.

Annie left the bench and meandered down the path. Behind her, the cliff towered above majestically like a cathedral. The kittiwakes, which lived high in the rocks, called out incessantly and created a wall of sound whilst below them shallow pools around the beach glistened in the sun.

Despite the beautiful surroundings, and thoughts of her

new friendship, Annie's mind jumped back to her troubles. She was worried about her rocky relationship with Josh. A paint job did not repair a marriage. And she was bound to him for life – whether she wanted to be or not.

Annie sat on a smooth boulder and wondered how she was going to solve her issues with her husband. He was drinking and smoking more, increasingly paranoid, and his behaviour was so erratic and unpredictable it was like living with a complete stranger at times. And this was the man she was dependent on for her survival. Could she trust him? Did she have a choice? Hopefully, her husband was turning over a new leaf what with all the DIY, a pathetic hope, she knew, but what else did she have to cling to?

Then there was the dark ghost. It both scared and intrigued her. Its energy was repulsive. She wanted the spirit to leave her alone, but she also wanted to find out why it was haunting her.

Maybe Annie was going to have to open her mind to the ghost. Let it inside her.

Josh

Josh cracked open the living room window and lit up a joint. The sky was particularly clear today but he took no joy from the view.

The endless blue was boring. There was nothing to do in this tiny town but drink or watch fatties on the seafront eating ice creams.

'God, I miss the city,' he thought. 'The buzz. The people. The noise.'

Josh turned his mind to more pressing and important events. The sale of their house in Leeds had gone through without a hitch and it was completion day today.

Josh willed his mobile to ring, but it remained quiet on the mantelpiece above the unlit fire.

'Fuck it,' he thought, 'I'll clear up.'

Half an hour later, when Josh had finished packing the decorating stuff away, his mobile finally trilled. Josh answered the call immediately. It was the solicitor. The money from the sale of their house was in his account, and as luck would have it, the cash from the insurance policies had also come through. His bank balance would be looking extremely healthy.

'I can't wait to tell Annie,' thought Josh putting his phone down. 'The news might even lift her dark mood.'

Josh mused for a moment and decided to let her know face-to-face. The news was too big to waste with a text. He wanted the full reaction, and the glory, if he was honest. And he deserved it. Out of nothing, a bloody nightmare situation, a total disaster, he'd created this pot of money. Only his big balls had turned their luck around.

Okay, things had been strained between him and his wife recently but it was only their money worries. That issue had been dealt with so they could start planning, and properly. Stay in Saltburn for six months, maybe a year at a push, sod the agreement with Margaret.

'It's important not to get attached to a place. Or people,' thought Josh re-lighting his joint.

He knew this frame of mind and approach was important, but did Annie? She was so friendly. It was one of the things he'd liked about her when they first met. She was open, he could read the emotions on her face.

But given their situation, openness and friendliness were not qualities to be praised or cultivated – they could only lead to questions. And questions lead to lies, and lies were never a good thing in a small town. People always hunted out the truth.

Come to think of it, Margaret Swain was getting a bit too friendly. He really would have to nip that relationship in the bud; he just needed to chip away with a few snide remarks, make Annie feel uncomfortable about visiting the old crone.

'It's for the best, really, in the long run,' thought Josh as he walked to the pub. They had to keep their life small and simple.

And that meant no space in their world for anyone other than himself and Annie.

Annie

Josh was out when Annie arrived home. 'So much for him cutting back on his drinking and staying out of the pub,' Annie thought dumping her bag on the chair.

The air was muggy in the dark cottage and she lit a candle to get rid of the lingering paint smell. Annie had to admit that the place did look lovely.

After eating a light supper, Annie did the dishes and tidied the cottage. Hours had passed since she'd last seen Josh and though part of her wondered who he was talking to in the pub, and feeling jealous that he would rather spend time with strangers than with her, part of her didn't care. She didn't have the energy for more confrontation, not today.

After all, he wasn't going to divorce her, was he? She was dead. Maybe he just needed to drink the stress out of his system. She was sure that things between them would improve once the money came through. It was supposed to be completion day today but no text from Josh, so maybe it had been delayed. A few more days waiting wasn't going to hurt.

Dusk came and went with a brilliant display of oranges and yellows over the cold North Sea.

Yawning, Annie headed up the cottage's narrow stairs.

She was rubbing cream into her face in the bathroom and looking at her reflection when she saw the dark ghost behind her. The outline of a dark human shape was reflected in the mirror. The thing had no eyes or other facial features and the edges were hazy, fuzzy as if its blackness was bleeding into the air.

The hair all over Annie's body prickled in terror. She was

frozen to the spot, paralysed with utter fear. The blackness pulsated as if it was a living, breathing thing.

The dark ghost took a step closer to the mirror, and towards Annie. The image remained faceless but present and only inches from her own body.

Annie remained rigid with terror. A cold breath caressed her neck.

In the mirror, she saw the presence step back and a long thin tentacle form from the middle of the mass. The unnatural prong grew and stretched out towards her. As Annie watched the tentacle swaying around her head, she held her breath.

The tentacle touched her hair softly then moved to within an inch of her right cheek and formed into a sharp point. She watched from the corner of her eye as the sharp edge of the prong hovered only millimetres away from her skin.

Suddenly, her mobile sprang to life. Her bedtime alarm flashed up on the screen, which she'd set in an attempt to improve her sleeping patterns. The loud jingle of bells bounced around the room and at an incredible speed. The dark ghost rushed past Annie and dived into the mirror leaving an invisible trail of cold air.

The encounter had only lasted seconds but Annie was left disturbed and scared. How had the presence used a mirror to vanish? Where had it gone and where had it come from? Had the alarm scared it off? Would it come back? And why was it here at all?

Mustering courage, Annie took the bathroom mirror off the wall and hit the plaster with the palm of her trembling hand. Her skin slapped against the wall like a dead fish landing on a marble slab. The wall was solid.

Still shaking, Annie went downstairs to the kitchen and had a drop of brandy to calm her nerves. Then she went to bed and left the light on.

It was pointless ringing her husband's mobile because she knew it would be switched off. Another one of his new habits. He was still fed up with hearing about the dark ghost. The last time they'd argued about the presence he'd suggested that the Death Herb had affected her neurologically.

'The drug's triggered hallucinations,' he had shouted. 'It's all in your bloody head.'

Although frightening, this latest sighting would be her secret. Josh didn't understand her terror, and she had the feeling that he didn't want to either.

Unable to relax enough to sleep, Annie picked up the book on her bedside table, which was a collection of near-death experiences. She was hoping to glean some information, maybe find out if other people had seen the dark ghost when having an NDE? But so far there had been no mention of the dark ghost in the book – or any other clues on how she could deal with the strange phenomenon. She read a few pages and then tried to settle down to sleep.

Sometime in the night Annie woke up. She tried to move but couldn't. Her limbs felt like stone.

'I'm paralysed,' she realised.

Fear filled her every pore. Out of the corner of her eye she saw the outline of the dark ghost. Its shadowy form stood a few feet away from her bed. For the first time, she made out the distinct shape of arms and legs fully formed, not just a fuzzy shape.

Her heart sped up and she struggled to move her body but no part of her would budge. The dark ghost took a step towards her. Cold icy air hit her face.

The room was bathed in night so it was hard to make out any features, but Annie was aware the thing's whole attention was on her. The dark ghost took another step closer and stretched out a black arm, long thin fingers touched her right wrist gently.

The shadow's touch was so cold it felt like her flesh was being sliced open. The icy grip then tightened around her wrist and it was agony like no other pain she'd ever experienced. Her instinct was to cry out but her mouth wouldn't move and no sound would form. She was mute.

In the next instant, Annie was no longer in her bedroom but being dragged through endless darkness. The darkness was so black that it felt like she would be lost forever.

Without warning, she found herself on a rocky plain. Grey lumps of stone stretched ahead of her in all directions for eternity. A dark hole, a cavern, appeared a few metres away and the dark ghost dragged her towards the gaping depths.

A searing heat emanated from the hole. She felt the flesh on her body begin to melt slowly like candle wax.

As they moved even closer to the cavern's entrance Annie saw that the hole plunged deep into ground. No vegetation, no animals, no other living thing was around the hole or anywhere else on this lunar-like landscape. There was only rocks and emptiness, the cavern and the dark ghost.

Annie was terrified. If she fell into the hole there would be no return. She would die here, and her body and soul would melt and disappear in the intense heat for eternity.

Then Annie remembered the voices in the dark the last time. The mantra.

'God loves me. God loves me. God loves me,' she chanted. 'Our Father, who art in heaven…'

The shadow suddenly relinquished its painful grip. Annie immediately found herself back in her bed in the cottage.

A film of sweat covered her body. She was gasping for breath and angry.

'In the name of Christ I demand you leave me alone!' she shouted.

Still trying to catch her breath, Annie wondered if it had all been a dream, or had she really been taken to a barren landscape?

She looked down at her wrist. A faint red line was visible, the mark cut her star tattoo in half. But the redness was disappearing before her eyes. Within seconds the otherworldly branding had vanished completely.

Downstairs, Annie heard the TV in the living room switch on. Had Josh come home?

In the narrow hallway, the window suddenly burst open and swung backwards and forwards in the wind. With a shaking hand, Annie pulled the window shut.

With her palms tingling, and feeling her stomach flipping with nerves, Annie walked slowly along the rest of the hallway and crept down the stairs.

The living room was still and empty. Relieved that the ghost wasn't there, but disappointed that neither was Josh, Annie turned off the TV and told herself it must be faulty. She sat on the sofa, covered herself with the throw, and waited. Nothing moved. Silence wrapped around her. She felt her heart slow down and the sickness fade.

Just when she was thinking of returning to bed, a pile of books flew off the table and scattered on the floor. She screamed and grabbed the iPod from the coffee table and cranked up the sound on the Bose speaker. The random track that blasted out was *Kashmir* by Led Zeppelin.

Annie sunk to the floor in the corner of the room by the fireplace and drew her knees up to her chest. Her eyes were shut tightly and her body was curled in on itself, she had made herself as small as possible as the drumbeat swirled around her. Something was in the room with her, Annie could sense it. She was being watched.

Josie had told her once that ghosts didn't like loud music. She really hoped her friend was right.

The drums vibrated through her body and Annie felt the fear being pulled out of her limbs and chased away by the music. She lifted her head. Annie was alone in the room. The presence had gone. Finally.

The next track started and Annie saw movement out of the corner of her eye. She looked up to see Margaret standing by the sofa wearing a quilted dressing gown and a frown.

Margaret took a few steps into the room and pulled the plug for the speaker out of the wall. The room went quiet.

'What's going on?' asked Margaret sternly.

'I'm sorry, I didn't mean to disturb you,' said Annie.

'Bit late for a disco,' said Margaret raising her eyebrows. 'All by yourself?'

'I'm sorry. It was just…' Annie burst into tears.

Margaret sat on the sofa and patted the space next to her, 'What is it?' she asked gently.

Annie climbed onto the sofa beside her neighbour and said she'd felt something strange in the cottage, something unholy.

Looking into Margaret's eyes, Annie explained further.

'There was a presence here, just before I put on the music. I didn't see it but the thing was watching me.'

'Just your imagination,' said Margaret booming.

'No,' Annie insisted. 'It was real.' Annie rubbed her wrist but said no more.

'Never thought this place was haunted,' scoffed Margaret. 'What happened exactly?'

Annie told Margaret about the dark ghost first appearing in the cottage in her dreams, leaving out her earlier encounters, and moved onto her experience in the bathroom mirror. There was no mention of the hot cavern or the red mark on her wrist, she didn't want to scare her friend too much. Or give the impression that she was insane.

'Impressive,' said Margaret. 'And spooky.'

Annie said she knew it sounded silly and looked down. Margaret said that if she was frightened it wasn't silly.

'What does Josh think?'

'He thinks it's my imagination.'

'Umph,' said Margaret. 'Don't know much about ghosts. But if you think you've had an encounter then I believe you.' She paused for a moment and then clapped her hands. 'Salt will keep it away. Grandmother swore by it. Used to scatter it over the doorways of the farmhouse and barns. Stopped the animals getting spooked.'

'Of course. Salt. Why didn't I think of that?' Annie hit her forehead with her hand.

Annie and Margaret sprinkled salt at the front and back doors. They also filled little bowls with the mineral and dotted them around the cottage. Any thoughts of wanting to make contact with the dark ghost had vanished. It was too terrifying.

Margaret pulled out a small picture of an angel with a sword from a drawer in the coffee table and hung it up near the mantelpiece. 'Not a religious person. But I like Archangel Michael,' she said. 'Can't do any harm.'

'I like angels too,' said Annie. 'I had no idea that picture was hidden in there.'

'Roman Catholic?' asked Margaret.

Annie smiled. 'No, but I've always liked angels, or at least, the idea of them.'

'Me too.'

'Thanks, Margaret. I'm feeling a lot calmer.'

'Good,' said Margaret wiping her salty hands on her dressing gown. 'If the spirit comes back we call a priest. Ask him to flick some holy water about the place.'

'Hopefully that's the last time I'll see it. Thanks again,' said Annie. 'I'm sorry again for disturbing your sleep.'

Margaret waved away her apology and let herself out of the cottage, quietly shutting the back door behind her. Annie locked it then retreated back upstairs to the bedroom.

In the early hours as the light trickled through the curtains from outside, and Annie lay alone in bed wide awake, she promised herself that it was time to stop being afraid of the shadows.

'I need to step away from the darkness and fear,' she thought. 'I can beat this thing. Whatever it is.'

Josh

Five days ago, various small bowls of salt had appeared around the cottage. The salt was in the bathroom, bedroom, on the landing and the mantelpiece next to a weird picture of an angel.

Annie was fanatical about refreshing the bowls every other day. She'd told him the salt was good Feng Shui. It was strange, and slightly annoying, but at least she wasn't talking about that weird 'black presence' anymore, which was a huge plus.

As far as Josh was aware she'd not seen the ghost recently. Though even if she had, he knew it wasn't real. Her experiences were simply a product of her imagination, the Third Man Syndrome. He was fed up to the back teeth of his wife talking about spooks, and if they were off the agenda that was great.

All he wanted to do was to be left in peace to enjoy his life. No stress. No hassle. Enjoy a smoke, and go to the pub for a pint. That's exactly what he was going to do today, as soon as he could slip away.

He could hear Annie in the kitchen. She had decided to do some baking and was banging around in the cupboards looking for the ingredients.

Josh was sure his wife was creating the racket on purpose because of his thumping hangover. Each crash was torture.

'Please be quiet for God's sake,' he thought as Annie banged yet another cupboard door. He couldn't see why she was so angry. All the house and insurance money was safely in his account. They were rich in comparison to the general populace, and the idea made him feel slightly giddy.

'Aren't you pleased?' Josh asked his wife for the umpteenth time since completion.

He was leaning against the doorway to the kitchen. Annie was dusting a Victoria sponge with icing sugar. No doubt she was going to take a piece of the cake to their nutty landlady.

'I've told you already, the money took so long to come through that the excitement has gone,' Annie said washing the bowl.

'You don't really feel that way. Do you?' Josh was incredulous. Her reaction was quite frankly disappointing. 'Our debts are all paid off and we have no cash worries for the rest of our lives.' His wife was acting like he'd won £10 on the lottery.

Annie looked out of the window and paused, her hands were lost in the white bubbles. Not looking at Josh she replied with a shrug, 'I'm tired of talking about money.'

Josh could see that she was watching the birds in the garden on the feeder she'd put up that morning. Birds were not more important than money. He was annoyed by how blasé his wife was about their turn of fortune.

'The money is what we've done this for,' Josh said trying to keep calm. 'I'll have to find a job eventually, but if we're careful then we're set up for life. You can have anything you want.'

'Like what, exactly? What do I need?' Annie spoke loudly and folded her arms. Wet suds dripped onto the kitchen floor. 'I have a lovely home. Food. Warmth. And I'm safe. What else do I need? Tell me.'

'I don't know. Shoes? Shall we buy you some new shoes?' Josh wondered what the hell was wrong with his wife.

'I'd rather go to the beach for a walk.'

'I've never heard of a woman turning down the offer of a new pair of shoes,' said Josh snorting. The sodding beach, she was obsessed with it. It was the same every day. He couldn't see the attraction. Sea, sand, so what?

'From now on we should only spend cash on the essentials,' said Annie firmly. She turned back to the washing up. 'I didn't give up my life, my identity, to buy new shoes. We need to be careful with the money because I won't be able to work to replenish it if you spend it all on pointless stuff.'

'Fine. But make sure you keep your mouth shut with that mad old bat next door. I don't think she's all there,' said Josh as he shrugged on his jacket. 'I don't want Margaret Swain blabbing about us to her cronies and blowing our cover.'

The idea of his wife revealing their secret to the landlady made him suddenly so furious. The old bat could ruin everything. What did they say in the war? Loose lips and something. Whatever. He needed to get out of the cottage and away from his infuriating wife.

'We should be celebrating, not arguing,' thought Josh as he stomped down the cliff path towards the town, and the pub.

Annie

The weather turned warmer as spring flew by and the days edged towards summer. Thankfully, the dark ghost had stayed away and Annie was convinced the protective salt was working. After a few objections to the bowls, her husband had dropped the subject and retreated back into his world of computer games, drink and dope.

They were both sitting in the lounge, but while she was trying to read a book, Josh had his headphones on and was lost in his virtual world of speeding bikes.

They hadn't really talked since their row over money when she'd been baking. Annie sighed and turned back to her book but she couldn't concentrate. She was worried about their lack of communication. Last night, she'd spent the evening on her own again. Josh had said he liked to go out alone. When Annie had asked if she could tag along her husband said no, she didn't drink anymore so what was the point? She'd just be a killjoy.

He'd arrived home at 2am but slept downstairs on the couch. They hadn't had sex in months. Annie was beginning to wonder if he really was just going to the pub.

Perhaps they could go for counselling? But that would mean official records about their personal details, which might invite more questions than would be safe.

Staring out of the cottage window Annie tried to convince herself that they didn't need external help. Things would improve. Josh was just stressed.

It seemed that living in Saltburn didn't help. Josh hated the view. The small doorways. The immersion heater, and the fact the cottage was situated on a cliff. They had to drive or walk down the steep hill to get anywhere. Her husband had even had a rant about the small windows.

'Everything is scaled down by a third,' he'd complained yesterday. 'It's like living in a house built for a bloody Hobbit.'

But despite their relationship trouble and Josh's complaints, Annie was insistent on living in the cottage. Especially now the dark ghost was staying away. She loved the cottage, the sea air, her walks on the beach, and her new friends. She was not going to back down on her decision because she'd developed a relaxing rhythm to her days.

She started the mornings with a breakfast of fruit and yoghurt, then went for a walk on the beach. If she bumped into Echo they'd go for a cup of tea on the seafront.

In the afternoon, she read or took a longer walk along the cliff path. Sometimes Annie scoured the charity shops for novels. In the evening, Annie watched a film or read. She usually dropped in on Margaret Swain every day too, only for an hour or so, although sometimes the visits lasted longer. The old woman was good company and didn't pry. Josh had been wrong about their neighbour.

If only Josh could be as content. It felt like they no longer wanted the same things in life.

'Josh is like the invisible man. He's never at home,' Annie said to Echo glumly. They were sat outside a café near the train station. Annie had given up on her book and left Josh at home still glued to his Xbox.

'He's probably just going through a phase. You know, after being made redundant,' said Echo licking icing from her fingers. 'I'm sure he'll settle down. He wasn't like this when you first met was he?'

Annie shook her head. It felt like a betrayal of her marriage saying more so she didn't expand. But Annie couldn't hide her worry from Daniel, the dog looked up and whined softly.

'Oh, don't fret, Daniel, I'll be all right,' said Annie stroking the Labrador's head. 'I've faced worse things.'

'He's telepathic,' said Echo feeding Daniel a tiny piece of sponge. 'He uses mind control to make me give him treats. The greedy little piglet.'

Annie laughed, leant down, and in a deep voice said to Daniel, 'Does this puppy have special powers?'

Echo laughed. Daniel thumped his thick tail in delight because he was the centre of attention.

'He also uses telepathy to wake me up in the night if he wants a pee,' said Echo. 'I swear, I sit bolt upright and I can see the outline of his head in the dark.'

'Really?'

Echo nodded and said it was uncanny and had happened too many times to be a coincidence.

'Doesn't Harry ever wake up?' asked Annie.

'You are joking. He's never once let Daniel out in the middle of the night.'

'He's a nice bloke though, Harry. He's reliable and honest,' said Annie mentally comparing Harry's stability to Josh's kamikaze approach to life.

'Harry's great. I'm not so sure about the honest bit. I mean, he's honest with me and his customers at the garage but…'

'What do you mean?' asked Annie surprised. She had never heard her friend talk in a negative way about her husband. She was intrigued.

'I shouldn't have said anything,' said Echo, suddenly finding the menu interesting not making eye contact with Annie.

'What? Who am I going to tell?' said Annie. 'You have to spill the beans.'

Echo put the menu down and said, 'Harry has a record.'

'He's been in prison?' said Annie shocked. 'What for?'

Echo said it wasn't for her to say. But he didn't murder anyone and he wasn't a paedophile. Echo was speaking in a whisper.

Annie lowered her own voice and asked, 'How long was he inside for?'

'Nearly two years. That's why he trained as a mechanic because his criminal record made it difficult to get a job. Then he opened his own garage.'

'I never would have guessed,' Annie said. 'But I'm not going to judge him. I don't do that.'

Echo shrugged. 'I think everyone has their own dark secrets.' Annie blushed and Echo raised an eyebrow. 'Do you have a criminal record too?'

Her tone was teasing, but Annie's cheeks burned hotter still. 'No, nothing like that.' Although she had committed fraud and broken laws, she hadn't been caught, so it didn't count. 'I can see ghosts. Spirits.'

As soon as the words were out of her mouth Annie regretted it. It would have been easier to say she had a criminal record. More acceptable somehow, certainly less mentally unstable.

Echo lowered her voice and leant forwards. 'You do?'

Annie nodded slowly and told her friend about the first time she'd seen a ghost at the age of five. 'They can pop up anywhere. I'm used to it, sort of,' said Annie. 'Although I haven't seen one of those ghosts for weeks. And they never do anything, they don't talk to me. They're trapped in their own little world.'

'You're speaking as if there are other ghosts,' said Echo frowning. 'What else do you see?'

Annie hesitated but her friend didn't appear to be mocking her, so she continued. 'There is another presence. A dark ghost. But it doesn't have human features like the other spirits. It looks like a black shadow.'

'Does it have a shape? Does it speak?' Echo was interested. 'I've never seen a ghost but I was obsessed with them as a child.'

'The presence has a human outline but it's not human. It's like an energetic copy and it's pure evil. I can sense it,' said Annie.

Annie told Echo about her experiences, her lucid nightmares and the fact the dark ghost never appeared to Josh. She told her friend everything except for the details about the Death Herb and her subsequent coma.

'How many times have you seen this dark ghost?' Echo's face conveyed a mixture of sympathy and fear.

'I've lost count,' said Annie looking down. 'Many times, and it's always terrifying. I've scattered salt around my house, for protection. And it seems to be keeping it away.'

'It doesn't sound like an ordinary ghost,' said Echo shaking her head. 'A ghost is supposedly a recording of a person that repeats on a loop. A discarnate entity is another matter entirely.'

'What are you saying?' said Annie slowly. She reached out to stroke Daniel for comfort and he licked her hand.

'I'm no expert but I don't think that your shadowy visitor is a ghost. I think it's a dark entity. People used to call them demons,' said Echo lowering her voice.

'Stop it. You're scaring me,' Annie whispered back. The hairs on her neck stood on end and she felt a fluttering of fear in her chest.

'Sorry but if I'm right the salt won't keep it away forever. It will be rebuilding its energy, drawing off your fear or the negative energy of someone in your home.'

'You mean the thing's going to come back?'

Echo nodded slowly. 'Highly likely if it's an entity. And to stop it you need to find out exactly what it wants and why it's haunting you.'

'I've thought the exact same thing,' said Annie surprised and relieved that her friend was taking her seriously. 'But in all honestly, I'm lost. I don't know where it comes from let alone its reason for appearing in my home and dreams.' Annie explained that she'd tried to do some basic research, but none of the paranormal books in Saltburn Library had any mention of this strange phenomenon. 'I've read all six books cover to cover and I couldn't find anything on the net either.'

'How about this,' Echo said looking at her phone, 'an intuitive is giving a talk on dreams at the Saltburn Wellbeing Centre next weekend. The blurb says she's studied with shamans in South America and Norway. Why don't we go and see if she can chat to you afterwards? She might have an idea of what's going on.'

'Do you think she will be able to help me?' Annie wondered if the intuitive had ever met a dark ghost, a demon. And if not, how would the woman know how to tackle one?

'It's worth a try,' said Echo with a shrug. 'If she can't get rid of it, she might at least know someone who can.'

'That would be great, thank you,' said Annie genuinely relieved. 'You won't tell anyone about this entity, will you? Not even Harry?'

'Cross my lips and hope to die,' said Echo gently. 'I know you're worried about coming across as bonkers but you're not. You're very stable. And lots of people see spirits even dark ones.'

Annie visibly relaxed. 'Thank you. Okay, so I've told you my big secret. Now you have to tell me yours.'

'I already told you,' Echo protested.

'That was Harry's secret, you must have one of your own?'

Echo sighed. 'Okay, but only if you promise never to utter a word to anyone?'

'I promise I won't tell another soul,' said Annie crossing her heart.

Echo covered her face with her hands and said, 'When Harry took on his new mechanic I had a crush on him.'

'Does Harry know?' This was not something she'd imagined. Echo struck her as the faithful type.

'Not likely,' scoffed Echo. 'It was a silly infatuation that lasted a few weeks.'

'No stolen kisses?'

Echo said no, the grass was never greener. Daniel had moved to her side and Echo rubbed his ear. 'I told pooch all about it, of course, but who's he going to tell?'

'All the other dogs on the beach?' said Annie laughing.

Echo put her hand to her mouth. 'Stop it,' she said in mock horror.

Daniel barked loudly to show he was in on the joke.

Later that evening as Annie dried herself after a hot bath she wondered if Echo's comment about the dark ghost was true. Would it come back? Was it really a demon?

She hoped the intuitive might be able to help her before it returned.

Darkere

Nine weeks had passed since Bennett Darkere's heart attack, but the offices of WOM Ltd looked the same from the outside. The cars were parked in their designated places and thin trees still sprouted from patchy grass.

The refit, however, had transformed the interior beyond recognition. Glass tables had replaced the wooden desks and the magnolia walls had been painted a sharp lime green. In reception, a large modern painting in blood red and white hung above a leather sofa.

'The place looks like an art gallery,' Darkere remarked to Mander's secretary, Sandra. She laughed and made him a very hot cup of coffee.

As he sipped his drink, Darkere noticed that he was kept waiting for his meeting for fifteen minutes. He'd never had to sit that long before and it made him slightly agitated. He found it hard to sit still for long periods of time.

Darkere watched the phone on Sandra's desk and waited for it to ring. He wanted to smash the thing to pieces. He took a few deep breaths. Getting angry wasn't good for his heart.

Eventually, the secretary's phone buzzed. With a smile, Sandra told him to go through to Mander's office.

Darkere stood up slowly. He needed to appear calm, in control and ready for work. His funds were running low and yesterday's trip to the bookies had been a disaster. He still hadn't settled his full debt with the loan shark Scott Mac, and he doubted their goodwill would last much longer. They hadn't called him, yet. But they would. Darkere needed this job, but there was more to it than that. No one had ever escaped him before and the stakes were high on this case.

Mander was on his mobile and he gestured to Darkere to sit down. It was a minute or so before the managing director of WOM Ltd finished his call.

'Sorry about that,' said Mander putting down his phone. 'Feeling better?'

'Fine,' said Darkere making sure he sounded upbeat.

'I thought you would be taking it easy?'

'I'm bored. You know me,' said Darkere. 'And I like my job.'

He didn't want to come across as desperate and concentrated on keeping his manner light and breezy.

Mander fiddled with a pile of papers on his desk. 'I don't think we have any freelance cases at the moment. Sorry, Bennett.'

Darkere was perturbed by Mander using his first name. They never used first names. 'But I haven't finished the Raven case, and there must be others too. You always have cases.' Darkere did his best to keep the weakness out of his voice. He wasn't going to plead.

'Not this time,' said Mander turning back to his computer. He tapped a few buttons. 'No, sorry. Definitely no freelance work at the moment. And the Raven case is closed.'

'What are you talking about?' asked Darkere trying to rein in his anger. 'The case stinks. It's fraud.'

Mander looked down as if he was disappointed and said, 'No. It was cut and dried. The wife had a massive asthma attack and died. I'm surprised it took you so long to investigate. What kept you hooked in? That's not like you.'

Darkere shook his head slowly and ignored the question. 'We should re-open the file. I don't know how, but Brigid

294

Raven faked her death. She's alive. I'm sure of it.'

'Do you have any proof? Because all the evidence suggests that she is dead and there was no foul play. I'm not about to risk my company's reputation for one of your hunches,' Mander looked through a folder on his desk.

'I've always been right in the past,' said Darkere firmly. 'And you know it.'

'Sorry, it's too late. Our invoice has gone through. Just let it go.'

'She was put in a coffin at home only hours after her death,' Darkere persisted. 'When the coffin was collected it was sealed shut. I think they faked her death to collect the insurance money and pay off their mortgage. Their home was in a fire weeks before she died. They had no building's insurance.'

'Fucking hell,' said Mander coolly. 'Have you told anyone else about this?' Darkere shook his head. 'How did they fake her death?' Mander raised his eyebrows. 'How?'

'I don't know. That's what I was working on before I had my heart attack.'

Mander slammed his palm on his desk to indicate his word was final, 'Darkere, it's done. Just drop it. Even if you're right, I'm certainly not going to tell a high street bank, and my biggest client, that I made a mistake. They'll never use my company again. So stop digging.'

'What if I don't? What if I prove they committed fraud and I happen to accidentally tell the bank?'

Mander hesitated then asked, 'Are you blackmailing me, Darkere?'

Darkere shook his head. 'No. Blackmail's something criminals do. How about we have a gentlemen's wager? If I win the bet you'll give me my job back.'

Mander visibly relaxed but frowned. 'There's no job to give back. Things have changed.'

'What are you talking about?' Darkere was confused. 'The place has undergone a refit but the business is the same.'

'Jesus, you're the only investigator who doesn't update his records on the network. The way you work is ten years out of date. I know you're a first-class investigator, but still…'

'If I prove without a doubt that the couple committed fraud, will you put me back on the team?' asked Darkere.

Mander sighed, 'And if I don't say yes?'

Darkere stood up and looked out of the window. 'That particular high street bank is your most prestigious client isn't it?'

'Okay, okay,' said Mander angrily. 'I thought we were friends?'

'We are,' said Darkere smiling briefly. 'Which is why I'm not going straight to the bank or the police.'

'You don't have enough evidence. And why do you care so much?'

'I just don't like the fucker. Josh Raven,' said Darkere. 'It's as simple as that. Plus I've never let a fraud slip through my fingers. If I win the bet you'll give me the bonus you promised and I'll learn how to use your sodding networking system.'

Mander forced a smiled and shook Darkere's hand. 'If you lose the bet?'

'You won't see me again and your young dickheads can rule the roost.' The men's hands fell apart.

'Let's be clear,' said Mander. 'I'm not going to act on any information that you give me, and you won't ever inform the bank or the police. This is just a gentleman's agreement?'

'Agreed. It's a bet only between ourselves.'

Annie

The rain had been coming down like a monsoon since the early hours, and the sodden earth had left the air with a slight chill. Even so, Annie didn't want to put off her morning walk; she needed to get out in the fresh air to clear her mind.

Josh was snoozing on the sofa after another bender at the pub. She closed the door quietly so she wouldn't disturb him. It wasn't that her husband's sleep was precious, Annie wanted to avoid awakening the beast. With a hangover, Josh was even grumpier and she just didn't have the energy to shrug off his snide comments, not today.

The grass along the track from the cottage to the cliff path was wet and soaked Annie's trainers, but she didn't notice. Her mind was focused on the intuitive. Annie was wondering if the woman would be able to answer her questions about the disturbing dreams and encounters. The thought of the night terrors starting again left her feeling anxious, and she felt a slight dizziness and breathed deeply to kill the unpleasant sensation. She'd been sleeping so well since the house had been protected by the salt. It would be exhausting to fear bedtime again like a small child.

'I have to stop thinking about the dark ghost or I might draw it to me,' she told herself sternly remembering Echo's advice.

With effort, Annie thought of food instead and what she would cook for dinner that evening. Perhaps a vegetable lasagne with salad and crusty bread? She would see what was on offer at the supermarket. She had already implemented a budget for their weekly food shop. Josh seemed incapable of managing their money.

In the chilled aisle, Annie bought some Greek yoghurt, it would make a change from her usual choice for breakfast. She also picked up the dinner ingredients and some sandwich making essentials for lunch.

On her way home, Annie stopped by the Victorian cliff lift and her eyes travelled to the cove in the distance and the row of coastguard cottages perched high on the cliff where she lived. It would be hundreds of years before the soil crumbled away and reached Margaret Swain's doorstep. The land here wasn't like the soft earth of Scarborough that threw hotels into the sea.

Annie breathed in the salty air. The view was beautiful especially in the bright sunlight. The pier stood black and solid on spindly legs of metal. Beneath the pier, the sea moved backwards and forwards in a perfect rhythm and the incoming tide crept further up the sand.

'Woof,' Daniel announced himself at the top of the steps. The dog wagged his tail and Annie bent slightly to pat his head. Moments later Echo appeared.

'I've been walking up these steps for years and they never get easier,' said Echo.

'I know they're a killer. How are tricks? I haven't seen you for what, oh, a whole day.'

Echo laughed. 'It's a small town. I'm good thanks.'

'Fantastic.' She reached down to stroke Daniel's furry head.

'Slightly odd question but I've been meaning to ask you – how come you're not on social media? I've looked for you but there's no Annie Ravens that look like you or live in Saltburn. It's as if you don't exist online.'

Annie felt her palms tingle and she willed for her cheeks

not to glow red and make her look guilty. She said the first thing that came into her head. 'The whole social media thing makes me feel uncomfortable. It's living in a goldfish bowl.' As she spoke Annie rubbed Daniel's shoulders vigorously and the dog shut his eyes in bliss.

'It's a good way of keeping in touch with people.'

'I prefer real human contact. Each to their own, though,' said Annie truthfully.

Just then, two women appeared on the other side of the funicular. They stopped by a bench to look at the view. They were a hundred yards away and the bright sunlight bleached out their features.

Annie was still thinking about Echo's comments regarding social media when she heard one of the women laugh. She froze. Annie would know that laugh anywhere. It was unmistakable, it belonged to her best friend Josie.

Annie remained crouched down, her heart thumping as she clung to Daniel. The dog wagged his tail delighted with the extra attention.

'Are you okay?' asked Echo with a perplexed look on her face as Annie continued to kneel close to her dog.

'Of course,' said Annie in a quiet voice. What was she going to do? Josie could not see her.

'Are you sure?' asked Echo confused.

'I'm hiding from those two women,' Annie whispered. Echo went to crouch down next to her. 'Don't bend down too,' hissed Annie.

Echo straightened up quickly. A gull swooped low above them, and Daniel barked furiously at it.

The unexpected noise pulled the women's eyes away from the sea and made them look in the dog's direction. Annie felt her face burning. She wanted to run over to her friend and hug her but she couldn't, instead she had to hide. Her freedom depended on it.

'We need to leave,' she whispered to Echo.

Echo played along smoothly and said loudly, 'Come on pooch, time for some grub.'

Her friend blocked any view of Annie with her own body. Annie stood up and they turned and walked briskly away from the seafront and the two women.

'Oh, God. I don't believe it,' thought Annie her mind racing. What was Josie doing in Saltburn? And how would she explain her need to hide to Echo? Was it still safe to stay living at the cottage? So many questions, but the brisk sea air offered no answers.

Josh

'Josie? You saw Josie? She's in Saltburn?'

Josh looked out the window, half expecting to see his wife's old friend coming up the path to the cottage.

'Yes,' Annie said. 'But she didn't see me, I'm sure of it.'

'Why on earth would she even come here? Is this somewhere she visits often? Is that why you wanted to stay here? Was this your plan all along?' Josh felt the muscles in his neck tighten as the anger bubbled away beneath his skin. Why wouldn't his wife just bloody well listen to him and do what he asked? It was so simple. Lay low, reveal nothing and keep her mouth shut.

'Oh, Josh,' Annie sighed, dipping her tea bag up and down in her mug. 'Don't be so ridiculous. I have no idea why Josie is here.'

Josh frowned at his wife. She was too nonchalant, and there was an odd note in her voice that made him doubt that she was being entirely truthful. It was disconcerting. He seemed unable to read her so easily recently, but his distrust was probably the paranoia from all the dope he was smoking. She would never lie to him or keep secrets. They were a team. It was them against the world.

Josh made a snap decision. 'We can't risk being found out,' he said abruptly. 'Maybe we should leave. We could go tonight or tomorrow at the latest. We don't need to give the old bag any notice. I'm sure we can still get that amazing place in Edinburgh – or somewhere like it.'

Annie rolled her eyes. 'We're not at risk of being found out. You're being paranoid. Besides, you know that I love it here. Do you realise I haven't had an asthma attack since we arrived in Saltburn? I've never been fitter, and I don't think I would feel this good in the city. There's too much pollution.'

Josh knew from his wife's stubborn tone that she wasn't going to back down, but he could use this potential problem as leverage. Get her on side again and back under his control.

'You must have said something to Josie at some point about this place otherwise she wouldn't be here,' said Josh curtly. 'It's too much of a coincidence.'

'Come on Josh, don't be…'

Josh put up his hand to silence Annie. 'No, I mean it. Listen to me. No more cosy chats with Mad Margaret and back off from that Reiki nutter and her fat dog.'

'Daniel is not fat. Besides, the dog can run faster than you.'

'Be that as it may,' said Josh without any hint of Annie's humour, 'I forbid you from seeing Margaret and Echo. It's too risky.'

'You can't forbid me from doing anything, Josh,' said Annie spitting out the words as all mirth evaporated from her voice. 'I'll be friends with whoever I want. And all this crap about me coming here to meet Josie. You're the one who chose this place, remember? Christ, listen to yourself. You sound like a lunatic.'

That was it, he wasn't going to be insulted in his own home. 'I'm going out,' said Josh grabbing his wallet and keys.

It might seem like the weak option, to run away from an argument, yet again, but he was fuming and the safest course of action was to leave the cottage. He needed to walk

303

away before he really lost his temper with his wife and did or said something that he would later regret.

Annie

The sky was a painter's blue but the air was crisp, and the North Sea breeze seeped into the cottage. Annie covered herself with a blanket but she didn't close the window because the salty air was good for her chest.

Shivering slightly, she wondered where Josh had slept. Annie hadn't seen her husband since last night after their row about Josie. What an earth had he been doing all this time? Probably passed out drunk on Ethan's sofa – the new best buddy she'd never met. Her husband's hypocrisy irritated her. Josh could have friends but she couldn't.

A prickle of pins and needles shot up her right leg. At the same moment, Annie felt relief about hiding the fact that she'd sent a postcard to Josie. It was obvious to her why Josie had visited the small seaside town, and it was only likely to have been a day trip. Her friend wouldn't waste a valuable week on the North East Coast. A yoga retreat to Bali or Ibiza was much more Josie's style.

Annie shifted her position on the sofa. She'd been sat in the same spot since coming home from a walk hours ago when she'd bumped into Echo.

Echo, she knew, could never replace Josie but she was a turning into a good friend. As they'd strolled on the beach earlier, she'd been honest about her relationship worries. She and Josh had grown apart. Annie couldn't remember the last time they'd have fun together or when a chat hadn't ended in an argument. And his drinking and drug taking was out of control.

'It sounds as if Josh needs professional help,' Echo had said concerned.

But Josh didn't think he had a problem and that was a problem in itself, even though his behaviour when he drank was awful. He morphed into a different person. Drunk, he was sarcastic, unemotional, incoherent, and he made Annie's stomach turn with disgust. But the morning after, he was always full of remorse until she suggested he was drinking too much. Then he'd turn nasty. Only last week he'd told Annie to keep her big nose out of his business.

'Maybe if Josh didn't have so much free time he wouldn't drink so much?' added Echo. 'I've never asked you this before, but how come neither of you work?'

'Inheritance.' Annie had said quickly.

Hours later, Annie still felt the shame crawl over her body as she recalled the rest of the conversation. Echo had laughed and said she thought they were lottery winners.

'Would it have made a difference if I was?' Annie had answered sharply. She winced at the memory.

But as ever her friend was gracious. 'Do I look like the kind of person who cares about how much money people have?' said Echo as Daniel put wet paws prints on her jeans.

Echo's parting words had been to look on the internet for advice. Maybe contact AA and see if there were any local meetings.

Annie had spent the last few hours researching drinking problems. She was shocked to see that Josh was following a well-known addiction cycle where he drank too much, was abusive then sobered up and promised to change. But of course, he didn't change and the cycle started all over again. And he was using drugs in the same way.

If she broached the subject of professional help with her

306

husband she knew that Josh would lose his temper. He'd just argue that he wasn't doing anything wrong and he was in control.

But clearly he was not in control. Whereas Annie used to be content, she now spent her days feeling sick with worry. As if she didn't have enough to fret about. The presence hadn't appeared again but that didn't stop her from thinking about it. And there was the fact that she was DEAD and had committed fraud. A criminal offence. If found out, she could go to prison for a long time, and being found out was a real possibility. Had Josie seen her the other day, the game would have been over.

A taxi pulled up. The door slammed and Annie heard a scraping noise against the backdoor. Josh was fumbling with his key. Annie waited. She would not get up and open the door for him. After a few minutes, Josh staggered into the room holding two plastic bags. One carrier was full of food. The other clanked with bottles.

'I bought some halloumi,' he said.

'Where the hell have you been for the last twenty-four hours?' Annie was livid. Although it was the wrong thing to do, she couldn't stop herself from losing her temper. 'I tried your phone and it was switched off. I was worried you had fallen off the cliff or something.'

'Sorry, I got pissed last night then I fell asleep on Ethan's sofa,' Josh was remorseful. 'I had a hangover so I've been playing computer games all day.'

Annie followed him into the kitchen and mechanically unloaded the first bag of shopping. 'Why didn't you call me?' she asked slamming a tin of beans in the cupboard.

'Uh, because my phone was dead?'

'And Ethan doesn't have a phone?'

'I don't know your number,' Josh mumbled. 'And for fuck's sake, what on earth could happen in this dead-end town?' he said. 'I'm fine.'

'You might be fine, but I've been here alone.'

Josh didn't reply, but Annie could tell he was rolling his eyes, even though he was facing away from her. He passed Annie items and she put them away silently. Once the first bag was empty, Josh stuffed the empty carrier in the cupboard under the kitchen sink. He turned just in time to see Annie opening the bag full of bottles.

Annie was alarmed to see there was no wine. The carrier was full of vodka and gin.

'I'll sort that out,' said Josh taking the bag.

'Ugh, you stink of alcohol.' He was inches away from her and the stench was strong.

'So shoot me,' sneered Josh. He carried the bag of spirits into the living room and stored them in the built-in cupboard by the fireplace.

Annie followed him into the room. 'When do I get to meet him? This Ethan? He seems to be the hospitable type.'

Josh sat down and began to roll a joint. 'He's a good guy.'

'Doesn't his wife or girlfriend mind you sleeping over?'

'He's single.'

Annie could see she was getting nowhere fast. She changed tack. 'It's not on, staying out all night like a tom cat. Promise me you won't do it again. I need you here.'

'What's the problem? I am here,' Josh said pausing before licking a Rizla paper.

Annie sat next to him on the chesterfield and looked at

her husband trying to see the man she loved under the veneer of alcohol. 'I'm worried about you, Josh. Your drinking, all the dope.' Her tone was slightly pleading and Annie hoped Josh would see sense.

'You don't seem to drink anymore so I concur, wife, that my consumption might seem excessive. But I can assure you that it is not.'

'You're out every night,' she persisted. 'That is a lot of alcohol. By anyone's standards, not just mine.'

Josh lit the joint. He took a deep drag and blew the smoke out.

Annie made a point of going to the window to open it wider. A gust of cold sea wind blasted in to the room and made the curtains billow momentarily.

'I don't like it, you can't stay out all night,' she repeated, her back still to Josh.

Josh offered her the spliff. 'Toke darling?'

Annie glared at him and sat back on the sofa. She pulled the blanket around her shoulders like a protective cloak.

'Oh yes, I remember. You don't smoke,' said Josh straight faced. 'Miss Goody Two Shoes.'

Her mouth fell open, the comment hurt. 'I have asthma. Smoking isn't good for me. You know that. I've never understood why you smoke in the same room as me. It's incredibly selfish.'

'I have asthma,' mimicked Josh cruelly. 'We don't kiss and we don't fuck either.' He took a deep drag. Annie's eyes filled with tears.

'In fact, we don't do anything. What's the point of us as a couple?'

Annie bit her lip and said, 'I've tried to get you to come

309

out walking on the beach but you hate it.'

'Walking?' said Josh with disdain. 'Who the fuck under the age of fifty goes for a walk? I hate the sea. I even hate the way the air smells here, it's like stale salty chips.' Josh took another deep drag and stood up still holding the spliff in his hand. The smoke curled slowly around his head and made him look like a pantomime villain. He pointed at his wife. 'And the crazy thing is, we can't split up. I killed you and we're shackled together. Forever.'

His cruel words stung her like wasps. 'I thought you loved me.'

'Loved you? I did once. Now you're a millstone around my neck.'

Annie took a sharp intake of breath as though he had pierced her heart with one quick and fatal stab. Surely he didn't mean it?

But he wasn't finished. 'I liked you better when you were fat Brigid obsessed with your crappy job. At least then you were half interesting.' Josh grabbed his coat and wallet and slammed the back door as he left.

Annie leaned back on the chesterfield slowly with tears running down her face. She felt numb. Her husband didn't love her anymore. Her gorgeous Josh had said words that he knew would destroy her. He couldn't take them back and like tar they stuck to her body and burnt her skin. Her heart was beating frantically in her chest. She felt winded and she doubled over in pain. She wondered where her asthma pump was as her breaths grew shallow. What was she supposed to do? She literally couldn't survive without him. There was nowhere she could go. She didn't even have access to any of the money, it was in Josh's account. She didn't exist.

Annie willed her breathing to calm down, determined not to have an asthma attack. Within minutes, she regained control.

She plucked a tissue from the box on the coffee table and wiped her face. She looked around her and came to her senses slowly.

No matter what he said, he had bound himself to her, and he needed to live with the consequences of his actions. Her husband could not just escape into booze and drugs. He needed to wake up, and she needed to take action.

He had already taken one life from her. She would not let him take another.

Darkere

When Darkere pulled up outside Josh Raven's house there was a TO LET sign in the garden. The investigator also noted the self-hire van parked in front of the property.

A woman appeared from inside the house, obviously one of the new tenants. She was slim and wore leggings that made her legs look like black spaghetti. A man came out of the door and chatted to her briefly before picking up a box from the van. He was wearing thick black glasses.

'Fucking hipsters,' thought Darkere with disgust.

Darkere was contemplating chatting to the new tenants, mulling over his cover story, when he saw an elderly woman walking towards his Jaguar. She was pulling a tartan shopper. It was Mrs Flint the old biddy who had blown Josh's cover the last time he'd come to this house. Darkere was out of his car in a flash.

'Nice day,' said Darkere leaning against his car and smiling as Mrs Flint approached.

'Is it?' asked the old woman sharply. Her tartan trolley squealed as it came to an abrupt stop.

The investigator could smell the old woman's stench from where he was standing. The scent of 'Eau de Urine'.

Darkere's nostrils twitched but he pushed on. 'Might rain, though,' he said. The whiff wasn't going to put him off finding out as much as he could from the eyes and ears of the street.

'I've not seen you before,' said Mrs Flint looking Darkere up and down.

'I'm visiting friends,' said Darkere smoothly. 'Have you lived here long?'

'Since 1976.'

Darkere nodded towards the property. 'Looks like you've got new neighbours?'

'Yes. Hope they have better luck than the last.'

'Oh? What happened to the last ones?'

He tried to remain casual but he wanted to pin the old woman down and squeeze every last bit of detail out of her walnut brain.

'It's a tragic story. A couple lived there. The woman, she died. Asthma attack. It was right sad.'

'That is sad,' said Darkere. 'When did her husband move out?' Just then his mobile rang. It was Scott Mac. His first call. Darkere knew it was safe to ignore it. He'd told Little Andy three days ago that he was in hospital for another week. 'Sorry, what were you saying?'

'Few months ago. It was funny,' continued Mrs Flint. 'I was just 'aving a cup of cocoa. The warm drink helps me to sleep. I 'ave terrible trouble sleeping. It's me age you know.'

Darkere smiled and willed the words from Mrs Flint's mouth. He knew that important details would be hidden amongst the drivel, so he stood and let her talk.

'So, there I was tossing and turning and I thought, I'll make meself a nice hot drink. Eee, the kettle was taking ages to boil and I heard a noise outside. It's late, I says to myself. "Who's up at this hour?" I took a little look outside, just a quick scan,' Mrs Flint added proudly, 'There's a Neighbourhood Watch Scheme round here. We look out for one another.'

Despite the jumble of facts, Darkere was keeping up. 'What did you see outside?'

'Josh Raven, that's the man what used to live in that

house,' said Mrs Flint pointing to the rental property. The new tenants were inside and had shut the door. 'Nice polite boy. Very good looking. Eee reminded me of that black and white film star from the sixties. What was 'is name, American, I can't remember it for the life of me.'

Darkere felt his patience failing. But he continued to smile and nod his head to extract more details.

'Anyhows, Josh always said hello,' added Mrs Flint popping a mint into her mouth. 'Well, that night when I was making my cocoa, Josh was getting in 'is car. With a woman.' Mrs Flint mouthed the last sentence near silently to make the point that it was scandalous behaviour.

'Who was the woman?'

'I don't know. But I tell you this for nothing. His wife Brigid was barely cold in her grave. Barely cold, I say.'

This was the gem that Darkere had hoped to find. He would bet his life that the woman was Brigid Raven. He felt it in his bones.

'That's terrible,' he said. 'Shocking.'

'I know. Shocking. I saw 'er, the new fancy woman, briefly. In the street light like,' mused Mrs Flint. 'Slimmer than Brigid and she had short black hair. Same height mind. And you know what?' she added, her voice dropped to a near whisper.

Bingo. Darkere leant in closer and felt his nostrils flare at the stench, 'What?'

'She were wearing a pair of Brigid's boots.' Mrs Flint spoke in her normal voice again, 'I used to tease Brigid about 'em. Lovely girl, liked dogs. Imagine that, wearing a dead person's shoes. What did this fancy woman do? Find the boots in the wardrobe when she 'ad her first sleepover wi' Josh?' Mrs Flint crossed her arms and pursed her lips to show her disapproval.

Darkere felt the excitement leap inside his stomach. But outwardly he kept calm and asked, 'How odd? What kind of boots?'

'Eeh, I think them's called biker boots. Me brother drove a Triumph. He had a pair. Obviously, he was a size 11. Imagine that, wearing a dead woman's shoes.'

'Black boots? Brown?'

'Black and short up to here.' The woman bent down in slow motion and indicated the height of the boots on her own leg. The spot was midway up the calf. 'With a silver buckle on the side. And then there was that house... oh, what do you call them?'

'Cleaner?' offered Darkere helpfully. 'Estate agent?' He wasn't sure what Mrs Flint was talking about or where her conversation would veer to next.

'The people what take away things when someone dies.' Mrs Flint was leaning on her shopper for support.

'A house clearance firm?' suggested Darkere.

'That's it,' said the old woman in triumph. 'I saw them carrying computers out of the house. Potter's on Batty Street, Dewsbury, that's the firm. I know 'em because they cleared me brother's house when he popped 'is clogs. Saw the name on the van. Eee they gave us a shocking price. Shocking price. Anyhows, Potter's came and later that night Josh and 'is mystery woman did a flit.'

'Very bizarre,' said Darkere shaking his head.

'I know. Shocking,' said the old woman shaking her head.

It started to spit. The raindrops were infrequent but big

and left black dollops of wet on the pavement.

'Eee bloody rain,' said Mrs Flint as she looked up. 'Me washing will be ruined.'

The old woman walked away with her trolley squeaking behind her. It was as if she'd never spoken to Darkere at all.

But her words were like golden nuggets. Darkere caressed the words slowly in his mind and rolled the information over and over.

Brigid Raven was not dead. And wherever she was hiding he was going to track her down.

Annie

The bedroom window banged in the wind waking Annie up with a start. As the dawn sunlight filtered through the billowing curtains, she cocked her ear and listened for noise inside the cottage. Nothing.

Annie pulled on her red cardigan over her white nightdress and closed the window. Walking down the stairs, she called Josh's name. The house remained silent.

In the living room, Annie found an empty sofa. She was definitely alone.

Her heart fell. Their latest row had been their worst one yet. Surely he didn't stand by his cruel words about her being a millstone around his neck and not loving her anymore?

'Everyone says things they regret in the heat of the moment,' she told herself pulling the cardigan closer. 'He still loves me and he'll say sorry. He was just off his head.'

Annie went back upstairs and dressed quickly, picking a pair of jeans and a t-shirt off the floor. She despised herself for making excuses for her husband. But what else could she do? Annie knew Josh would only tackle his drinking problem when he acknowledged that he had one. He wasn't stupid, sooner or later he'd have to own the reality of what he was doing to himself and to their marriage. Until then, she had to be the strong one and forgive him for the umpteenth time. She had no other choice.

After a cup of tea and an apple, Annie decided a walk would help her feel calmer. The sea air always made her feel less blue.

Annie navigated slowly along the cliff path that led to the town – mindful of the dangerous drop to the beach below.

317

The air was cool but not cold and the sun was rising fast, its reflection glowed and bounced off the waves.

Stopping to look at the sea, Annie couldn't stop herself and peeped over the cliff edge. She experienced the familiar urge to jump, to throw herself into the sky, but knew she wouldn't do it. Even though the urge was even more compelling today than it had been the previous time, it would be a reckless and stupid solution to her anxiety.

Suddenly, Annie recalled a similar moment, long ago, at the Acropolis in Athens. A French girl, who was staying at the same hostel as Annie, had laughed when she'd told her about the odd experience.

'In French, we have a name for this feeling,' the girl had said with a Gallic shrug. 'We call it *L'appel du vide*. In English, it means the call of the void. It is normal.'

Annie left the cliff, and its siren call, and continued walking along the grassy path. At the bottom of the steps she reached The Ship Inn and the slipway to the beach. In the distance on the left stood the pier, to the right of Annie was the cove with its cathedral cliff.

The sand was cold on her feet and pushed up between her toes. After a while, Annie stopped and looked back at her trail of footprints along the beach. By tonight, her imprints in the sand would be washed away by the incoming tide, wiped away just the same way that her life had been wiped out. She sighed, there was no way she could stop her mind replaying Josh's harsh words. She listened to them again in her memory. The barbed comments made her throat tighten. Her husband didn't love her anymore. She was boring. Sexless.

Fighting back tears, Annie carried on walking up the

beach and climbed the steep steps near the funicular that linked the beach to the town. Without knowing why, she felt compelled to continue walking past the blocks of flats towards The Marine Hotel.

Outside the hotel, which doubled as a pub, she sat on a wooden picnic bench. Annie saw a man and a woman. The man had his back to her and the beach. The woman faced the sea. The woman had cropped blonde hair. There was something about the man that made Annie look again. The broad back. The way the dark hair curled above his collar. It was Josh.

'Why is he sat outside a pub with a woman?' Annie wondered in innocent confusion.

With sickening clarity, the reason became clear when Josh leant across the table and kissed the blonde on the lips. It was a long, seductive exchange.

Instinctively, Annie darted down the small steps that led to the beach. Her breathing was shallow and strained. Ignoring her heaving chest, she ran along the sand back towards the cliff path that led up to the cottage. She wanted to put as much distance as possible between Josh, the woman and herself.

As she ran, nausea gripped Annie but she pushed herself onwards up the beach. When she reached the black legs of the pier she didn't have the strength to continue. Her chest was worryingly tight. Panting, she lowered herself to the sand and sat underneath the pier amongst the pools of shallow water. Annie scrabbled in her bag but in the panic she couldn't find her inhaler. She willed herself to stay calm.

Her breath was coming in even shorter bursts, it felt like the air was being sucked out of her lungs despite her best efforts to remain calm. Her throat was slowly tightening, and soon she felt like the panic would burst out of her chest and rip her open. She tried to focus on the sound of the waves to regulate her breathing but it wasn't working.

Frantically, Annie tipped the contents of her bag onto the sand. There was an old lipstick, her purse, some tissues, but no inhaler. Just then, Daniel appeared under the pier. He barked furiously when he saw her frightened face.

Echo wasn't far behind her dog. She looked at Annie and frowned. 'What's wrong? What are you doing down here?'

Annie tapped on her chest and continued to gasp in shallow breaths.

Echo's eyes widened. She didn't know that Annie had asthma. Why would she? Annie had never had to tell her.

'Do you have an inhaler?'

Annie nodded. She couldn't speak. Her windpipe was being squeezed.

Echo kneeled and quickly checked the rest of the pockets in Annie's bag. She found the inhaler and handed it to her friend. Quickly, Annie took two quick puffs and relief spread through her.

'Just relax. Breathe deeply,' said Echo still crouching down. 'Don't try to talk yet.'

After several more minutes, Annie was calmer and her breathing began to deepen. She felt safe in Echo's care.

Daniel watched quietly. The dog was still and focused waiting for the danger to pass.

Finally, she was able to speak. 'Thank you,' said Annie. 'When I couldn't find my inhaler I panicked.'

Clearly over her asthma attack, and the danger gone, Daniel celebrated by licking Annie's face.

'I love you too,' said Annie kissing the plump of the dog's cheek. 'You are a clever boy.'

'I had no idea you were asthmatic. What brought on the attack?' asked Echo sitting down next to her friend.

Tears came and Annie couldn't stop them. 'I have been asthmatic my whole life, but since moving here, I haven't had any problems until today.' The tears flowed faster. 'It was Josh. I saw him with a woman outside The Marine.'

'Oh shit. I'm so sorry,' said Echo slowly.

'You don't sound surprised?'

'I…' Echo hesitated. 'I thought I saw him the other day going into a house on Albion Terrace. With a blonde. But I didn't want to say anything.'

'I saw them kissing,' said Annie wiping her eyes.

'Bloody hell,' said Echo.

'I would have died for him,' said Annie, the pain ripping through her body.

'Don't die for anyone,' said Echo. 'Live for yourself.'

'Echo, I don't exist without him.' Annie was shaking as she spoke. The full force of Josh's betrayal and what it meant hit her. Her husband was her only link to the outside world. Without him, she would be a refugee in her own life. She badly wanted to tell her friend everything, but the shame of her lies stopped her.

'Come on, you're coming back to my house,' said Echo standing up and dusting the sand off her jeans. 'You'll feel better after a hot bath and some Daniel therapy. He'll squash you on the sofa.'

'You're a good friend,' said Annie forcing a smile.

'Likewise. And aside from me and Harry, you're Daniel's favourite human. So, you'll have to cheer up otherwise you'll depress my dog.'

The women walked slowly and silently up the beach away from The Marine Hotel. As they reached the slipway Annie felt overwhelming heaviness and despair. Josh's betrayal was almost too much for her to carry.

'I feel like my heart's been turned to stone,' she said quietly.

'I know it's too early to say this, but you will get over Josh's betrayal.' Echo put an arm around her friend's shoulders.

Annie looked down and leant into her friend. Daniel whined, he was picking up her distressed energy.

'Some marriages don't work,' added Echo. 'You'll move on. I promise.'

'You don't understand. I really can't live without Josh.'

'Of course you can,' said Echo firmly.

If only her friend knew the truth.

As Annie sat in Echo's kitchen she knew that she was going to have to put up with Josh's infidelity. Or what, leave him? That wasn't an option. Annie knew she was trapped.

'I'm such a fool,' said Annie cradling a hot cup of sweet tea. She'd never been so angry or disappointed with herself. How had she allowed herself to be manoeuvred into a place without power or choice?

Echo leant across the table and gently touched her friend's arm. Her face was full of concern.

'Josh is the fool,' said Echo.

'I'll have nothing if Josh leaves me. Absolutely nothing.' Annie knew that her face was red and blotchy from crying and she didn't care.

'You'll have your self-respect. Are you going to confront him?'

Annie said yes and shut her eyes. When she was very small she believed that if she closed her eyes no one could see her. She disappeared. That's how Annie felt. She was a non-person hiding away from the world.

'Josh cheated on you and you should dump him,' said Echo forcefully. 'End of story.'

In ordinary circumstances, Annie would agree with her friend. But this situation was far from ordinary. Josh couldn't leave her, and she could never walk away from him.

'He has a drink problem, doesn't work and he's not interested in you or anything you feel is important.' Echo put her hands on her hips. 'He doesn't deserve you.'

Annie didn't say anything. Echo was right. But reality was never black and white.

'You need to get him to move out of the cottage,' said Echo loading the dishwasher.

'I don't know… it's just not that simple. I need some space to think.'

Echo suggested that Annie have a hot bath and stay in her spare room tonight. 'Text Josh. Tell him you're staying over. But don't tell him that you know about blondie.'

Grateful, Annie nodded and gave Daniel a cuddle before going upstairs.

Echo and Harry's house was on Ruby Street – one of Saltburn's 'jewel streets'. The terrace had a living room and a kitchen downstairs. Upstairs were three bedrooms plus a bathroom. Echo was a fan of the 1920s and 30s so the house was filled with odd items of Art Deco furniture, pottery dogs made into lamps, and vintage toys.

Annie loved the house's quirky décor and was sat on the double bed in the spare room, which was covered with a paisley quilt. The bath had been soothing. Her face had lost its mottled look. Annie was wearing fresh clothes: grey lounge pants and a grey vest top that Echo wore to yoga. She was musing over her text to Josh. In the end, she decided to keep it simple.

Staying at Echo's tonight. See you tomorrow. A x

As she switched off her phone, there was a knock on the bedroom door.

'Comfort food,' said Echo holding a tray with two mugs and a plate of thick slices of home-made banana bread.

Daniel pushed past her and lay down on the floor. Echo pointed her index finger at the dog like a witch casting a spell and said, 'No begging.' The Lab put his head down with a little whine.

'I don't know if I can stomach food.' Annie tried to hold her smile but she felt it fall from her face.

'You're going to be okay,' said Echo. The bed squeaked as she made herself comfortable.

'I'm not going to walk away from my marriage without trying to save it,' said Annie. What Annie really meant was that she wasn't going to let Josh walk away from her.

Echo offered her a piece of banana bread. Annie had one bite then put the cake back on the plate. Daniel watched her with his eyes but didn't move his head.

Out of nowhere, Echo asked, 'Who were those two women you hid from that day? By the cliff tramway?'

'I thought they were people I used to know, friends I fell out with, but I think I was mistaken,' said Annie.

'Oh right,' Echo said satisfied.

Annie's stomach churned. Her friend was so trusting. She decided to bring the topic back to her present issues. 'I can't believe he's cheated on me,' said Annie with a sigh.

'Why don't you come and watch a funny film?' asked Echo.

'Okay, but no rom coms,' said Annie. 'I can't stomach the happily-ever-after crap. Not tonight.'

'Pop down when you're ready. I'll leave Daniel with you. The little piglet has had his tea so don't let him guilt trip you into giving him cake.'

As soon as Echo was out of the room Daniel gave Annie 'the stare'. Annie said no and realising she meant it, Daniel went to stand by the bedroom door. It was clear that he couldn't bear to be away from Echo for long.

'Josh was once that devoted,' thought Annie opening the bedroom door to let Daniel out. 'More fool me.'

Downstairs Annie found Echo and Harry in the living room. With his buzzcut Harry looked hard, but Annie could see why Echo loved him. He had a beautiful smile.

'What do you know?' Harry asked Annie. It was a typical Northern greeting.

'Not much,' said Annie. No doubt he knew about Josh's infidelity but she didn't want to talk about it with him. It would be embarrassing. She'd never spoken more than a few words to the man.

Harry smiled and said, 'Me neither,' before disappearing into the kitchen with his car magazine.

'A man of few words,' said Echo winking, 'but very expressive with his hands.'

The front door bell rang and Harry answered the door. Annie heard a male voice. It was American.

'Who's that?' Annie whispered.

'That's Duke,' said Echo raising her eyebrows. 'And why

are we whispering?'

A small cog inside Annie's brain whirled. 'Good-looking. Tanned. Looks like a surfer?'

'That's the one. Do you know him?' whispered Echo looking surprised.

'Not really.'

As the American walked past he glanced into the living room, did a double-take and stopped. 'Hello, ladies,' he said.

Duke stood in the doorway and modelled a white T-shirt, unbuttoned checked shirt and faded blue jeans. The man was gorgeous.

Annie was suddenly aware that she was wearing a flimsy vest top with no bra. She looked away from Duke embarrassed.

Duke smiled and said, 'Nice to see you again, Annie,' then disappeared without waiting for a response.

Echo smirked and asked, 'So you don't know him, then?'

'I bumped into him briefly at the retail park ages ago,' said Annie. 'Who is he?'

'Harry's business partner. Duke owns half of the garage.' Echo turned up the volume on the television to drown out their conversation. 'You met him at *the mall*,' Echo imitated Duke's accent. 'And he remembered your name.'

'Yes,' hissed Annie. 'I dropped my handkerchief. He gave it back to me. We barely spoke.'

'How very knight in shining armour. Do you fancy him?'

'Don't be so ridiculous,' said Annie quickly. 'I'm married to Josh.'

'Are you?' Echo folded her arms. 'Last I heard Josh had cheated on you. End of. If Harry did that to me I'd cut his balls off.'

Annie put her head in her hands. She desperately wanted to tell Echo her secret, but knew she couldn't confess. After today she realised how much faking her death had welded her to Josh. It was more binding than being married; at least if they were still legally man and wife she could file for divorce and walk away.

Her friend smiled and pointed to the kitchen and the murmur of deep male voices. Echo made an obscene gesture with her mouth and hand. Despite her dire situation, Annie couldn't help but laugh. Echo could be blunt, but that was one of the reasons she adored her.

Unfortunately, this time she was going to have to ignore her friend's forthright advice about her marriage. Annie knew that she would look weak staying with Josh, but what other option did she have given her nonexistence?

Darkere

It was the kind of day where the unexpected sunshine begged you to stop and enjoy it. But Bennett Darkere wasn't the type to sunbathe or relax.

He was following a lead in the case even though Mander had insisted it was all just a gentleman's bet. Darkere looked forward to winning and proving his boss wrong. He also really needed the bonus.

Darkere arrived in Dewsbury and turned his Jag into a road with a row of terraces. Seconds later, a battered transit van pulled up. The right headlight was missing. The driver parked the van directly in front of Darkere's car and the investigator was able to get a good look at him as he locked the vehicle's door.

The driver was in his thirties, with dark hair, 5ft 9' and his face was pock-marked from acne. A cigarette dangled from his mouth. He wore black trousers and scuffed brown work boots. His denim jacket was too big. The cuffs covered half of his hands.

If he'd still been in the force, Darkere would have organised a warrant to search the man's house and lock-up. He would expect to find stolen goods. But he wasn't a copper anymore. Darkere called a number using his mobile; it had been easy to find the contact details for the house clearance firm on the net. After a few rings, the scruffy man pulled his phone out of his pocket.

Darkere switched his own mobile off. 'All right,' he said getting out of his car. His tone was friendly.

'All right,' said the man cautiously.

'Still doing house clearances?' Darkere spoke as if he

328

wanted the man's help.

'Now and again,' said the man. He wiped his runny nose with his dirty hand. 'Got a job?'

'Maybe. But I wanted to ask about a job you've already done.'

'Why?' The man flicked his cigarette butt on to the pavement. The man's face was expressionless. The face of a criminal.

'I'm a debt collector,' Darkere lied with a smile. 'I'm looking for someone who's disappeared.' He spoke with an even tone.

The man shrugged his shoulders. 'Not sure I can help you.'

'Why not try?' asked Darkere brightly. He took a step closer. 'Could be some cash in it.'

'What do you wanna know?' The man rolled another cigarette.

Darkere noticed the man was calm, which was a good sign. 'Josh Raven. Did you buy any items from him?'

'What street?' The man picked a piece of stray tobacco from his mouth.

'Shepherds Lane, Chapeltown. Good looking bloke, dark hair. Comes across as smart.'

'Aye, I remember him. Fancy MacBook Air, and he was in a rush.'

'When?' said Darkere.

'Around February?' said the man.

'Did you see a woman in the house?'

After taking another drag of his roll up, the man paused. Darkere took out his wallet and gave him a tenner.

'Yes,' said the man. He stuffed the note into his back

pocket.

'What did she look like?'

'Slim. Short dark hair.' The man indicated the length of the woman's bob.

The investigator asked if he noticed anything else. The man went quiet for a couple of seconds then said there was one thing. She had a tattoo.

Casually, Darkere asked, 'Where was the tattoo exactly?'

'On her left wrist. A star. I noticed it because her sleeve was pushed up.'

'Cheers,' said Darkere nonchalantly. He asked if the couple had moved and if they had left a forwarding address. The man shook his head. Darkere walked away, turned back and clicked his fingers as if he'd forgotten something, 'Sorry, what did you do with the computer you bought from Josh Raven?'

'Sold it to that dealer in Horsforth. The one next to the flower shop on Town Street.'

'Thanks,' said Darkere.

The investigator climbed back into his Jaguar and waited for the man to go inside his house. Then Darkere fished inside the glove compartment. He unfolded a brown envelope, tipped the contents onto the driver's seat and searched through the items.

Darkere soon found what he was looking for. The photograph that he'd stolen from Josh Raven's mantelpiece. The couple were smiling at the camera. Brigid looked pretty and happy. Her left wrist was turned out, exposed.

On Brigid's pale skin, etched clearly in a thick black line, was a tattoo of a five-pointed star.

330

Annie

Annie let herself into the cottage. Josh was sat on the sofa rolling a joint, and he didn't look up when she entered.

'Where did you stay last night?' asked Josh casually. All of his focus was directed at running a thin line of tobacco along the Rizla papers.

Annie was surprised to find her husband at home and irked that instead of being happy to see her, he was demanding to know where she'd been. Casually she answered, 'I texted you. I was at Echo's.'

She went into the kitchen and dumped a small bag of shopping on the worktop.

Josh followed Annie and leant against the cooker. 'I was just checking. I was worried about you.'

Annie turned to speak to Josh and saw his face in the full morning light. Her husband looked like a ghoul; his skin was chalk white and his eyes were smaller, darker. This was not the handsome man she'd married, the drink and drugs were eating him slowly from the inside.

Hiding her shock and distaste, Annie said casually, 'Where did *you* sleep last night?'

'I was here,' said Josh hovering by the fridge. 'I played computer games until two. Why do you ask? Where else would I sleep?'

'I don't know, Ethan's maybe?' She forced a smile. 'It's funny, I never knew that women could be called Ethan too. I always thought it was a man's name.'

Josh gulped and looked as if he was preparing a speech.

'Don't,' said Annie bluntly pushing past him into the living room. 'Don't try to deny it. I know exactly where you were last night.' She was close to tears but stopped them from falling.

'Shit. How did you find out?' Josh looked stunned and sat down on the chesterfield next to Annie. He put his head in his hands.

'I saw you with her.'

Josh went to touch his wife's shoulder but she flinched away. Annie couldn't help it.

'Who is she?'

'She's no one,' said Josh. 'No one at all.'

'No one?' repeated Annie with mock surprise. Annie felt the rage boil up in her body like a volcano about to burst. How dare he betray her after what she'd given up? She'd walked away from her life for him. Annie raised her voice, 'You've been shagging someone else, Josh.'

Her husband remained silent and looked down at his hands clasped between his knees.

Annie continued, calmer, 'How long has it been going on?'

Josh shrugged his shoulders and still looking down said, 'A few weeks.'

'Be specific. How long have you been committing adultery?'

'Two months.' Josh inhaled deeply and turned to Annie, 'I feel so guilty. Honestly, it won't ever happen again.' He added in a rush, 'I was in The Victoria one night. She was all over me like a rash. Before I knew what was happening I was shagging the silly cow at her house. She kept texting me and whenever I went out I bumped into her. I couldn't shake her off.'

'God, you're so weak,' said Annie angrily. 'Why didn't

332

you just say no?'

'I should have, but I was pissed and stoned. And you and I weren't…' he tailed off.

'Why did you have to mess it all up, Josh? Why?'

'I need a drink.' Josh found a bottle of gin and poured himself a large glass. As he sat down he said, 'I thought you didn't love me anymore.'

'You thought *I* didn't love *you*? You're the one who said you didn't love me. I'm just a millstone around your neck. Remember?'

Josh winced at hearing his own harsh words repeated.

'I'm sorry, I didn't mean it. I was wasted.'

'You were wasted and you were fucking another woman.' Annie shook her head. 'I can't believe I let you talk me into this insane, stupid, crazy scheme. Josh, I'm dead, I don't exist.'

'The plan worked, didn't it?' he said defensively. 'We got the money.'

'The money means nothing if you don't love or respect me anymore,' Annie said quietly. 'Do you still love me?'

'What an utterly ridiculous question,' said Josh, stumbling over his words.

'Do you still love me?' Annie lifted her chin up slightly. She hated herself for asking the question but she needed to know.

'Yes,' said Josh slowly. 'I was stupid and selfish. But if we're going to get over this bump we can't stay in this Hicksville town. It's too small, I'm bound to see her around.'

'I don't want to move,' said Annie. 'And I'm not the one who's messed up.'

'Okay, we can stay for another month and see how things

pan out,' Josh put out his hand. Annie looked at it and Josh gestured for her to shake on the agreement.

Josh's warm fingers gripped her palm, it was an intimate touch that once would have made her flesh tingle. Annie felt nothing.

'Done,' said Josh. 'Thanks for giving me a second chance.'

'I'm not giving you a second chance,' said Annie. 'I'm giving myself one.'

Darkere

The drive from Wetherby to Horsforth took Darkere half an hour. It was another warm day in May, the sun beamed through the window making Darkere wish he'd worn a short-sleeved shirt.

When he reached the town centre, the investigator found the computer shop with ease. Inside, the shop had white walls, a white floor and a glass counter. The interior was sparse apart from numerous Apple gadgets dotted around in display units. A Gregorian chant played in the background.

'Fuck me,' thought Darkere. 'I'm in the church of Apple Mac.'

A man in a white shirt with long sideburns looked up from a huge desktop screen on the counter and switched the music off. 'Sorry, it helps me to concentrate. How can I help?'

'I'm looking for a laptop. Something second-hand and small.'

'Do you want a MacBook Air. A Mac mini? 13-inch or 15?' asked the man quickly.

Darkere explained that he was looking for a particular laptop, a MacBook Air from a house clearance firm in Dewsbury. The shop owner was surprised and asked Darkere how he knew about his recent purchase.

'I was chatting to a bloke in the pub. The man who sold you the laptop,' lied Darkere.

'Oh right,' said the computer expert. 'Do you want to have a look at it?'

'That would be good. Nice shop,' said Darkere looking around.

The man said thanks as he unlocked a cabinet and fished out the laptop. He switched it on. He spent a few minutes selling the machine.

Darkere asked casually if he could retrieve data from hard drives.

'It's one of my most popular services. You'd be surprised how many people fail to back up their laptops and come to me...'

Darkere interrupted him. 'Do you still have the hard drive from this laptop? It's definitely the one from the house clearance firm in Dewsbury?'

'Yes,' said the man with a quizzical look. 'It's the only laptop I've bought from Potter's in months.'

'How much to retrieve the data from that hard drive? Including a list of all web searches for the past year.'

Darkere felt a flutter of excitement in his stomach. He could smell the kill.

'The past year?' asked the man incredulously.

'How much?' repeated Darkere.

'It depends.' The man rubbed his chin. 'Sometimes the hard drive is damaged although in this case the computer is working perfectly. Why do you want the data? I'm not sure this is legal.'

'I'm investigating a fraud.' Darkere handed the man his business card. 'My client is a high-street bank. Give me a ballpark figure. I don't need the laptop. Just the data.'

'£100, upfront. Cash.'

'Fine,' Darkere said annoyed. He couldn't afford to throw away £100 but the loss was only short-term. He'd win the money back on the horses next week.

The tech added, 'Although with my backlog of work it

336

could take me a few days to retrieve the information.'

'Not a problem,' said Darkere handing the man five twenties. 'Just make sure I get the data. And all of it.'

His mobile beeped. Darkere knew it was Scott Mac's cronie pestering him.

'Sod him,' thought Darkere as he left the shop, 'He can wait for his money.'

Annie

'Josh hasn't been going out,' Annie said to Echo. 'I think he's stopped seeing her.'

The two friends were walking along the seafront. The sky was overcast and it looked like it might thunder.

'Forty-eight hours of good behaviour does not erase what he did,' said Echo bluntly.

'I know,' said Annie with a sigh. 'But I'm not going to throw away my marriage for one mistake.' She paused then added, 'I read somewhere that an affair can make a relationship stronger.'

Echo snorted, 'Really? And who wrote that piece? Some cheating husband?'

'It could have been written by a woman,' said Annie defensively. 'I know you might not agree with my decision, but I'm not going to change my mind.'

'I'm sorry,' said Echo. 'It's none of my business. I just wouldn't put up with it.'

'But I'm not you, am I?' said Annie. 'And Josh isn't Harry.'

The conversation stopped and they continued walking. Annie was too embarrassed, and ashamed, to tell Echo that she agreed with her viewpoint. But she couldn't tell Echo her secret. This invisible status meant she didn't have the freedom to kick Josh out of the cottage. Whether she liked it or not, she was shackled to her husband like a medieval bride with no rights.

Last night, they had lain side-by-side with an invisible electricity fence humming between them. Neither one had stretched out across the silent chasm to make contact. There was no chatting in the dark and no whispered promises. During the day, they had been circling one another being overly polite and courteous. The bond of marriage was fraying, slowly but surely.

Annie kept her thoughts to herself as they turned right onto a road called Glenside, which headed away from the town centre. The detached houses became increasingly larger the further they walked along the tree-lined street.

'Thank you for inviting me to see this intuitive,' said Annie breaking the silence. She didn't want to fall out with Echo because their friendship was too precious. Echo was her only friend and ally aside from Margaret.

'No problem,' said Echo still a little aloof.

Annie couldn't stop herself and blurted out, 'I know you think I'm crazy, but this is the right thing to do for me and Josh. Can we agree to disagree? Please?'

Echo turned to Annie, the friends were stood outside the wellbeing centre, and her face softened.

'I'm sorry, it's only because I care,' said Echo. 'I suppose you never know how you'll react to an affair until it happens to you. I promise I'm not judging you.' Echo glanced at her phone. 'Crikey, we better get inside or we'll be late.'

Saltburn Wellbeing Centre was based in a detached mansion on the outskirts of the town. An orangery leant into the side of the property, and a throng of people were milling about inside the glass extension helping themselves to hot drinks and biscuits.

'I bet this place has been smudged hundreds of times,' Annie whispered as they crossed the threshold and waited in the large hallway.

The walls had been painted a muted green and the original

Victorian tiles on the floor had been restored.

'They might have to smudge it again after tonight,' Echo teased. 'Apparently, this Scottish intuitive can speak to your ancestors.'

Annie laughed briefly but inwardly she was nervous. The dark shadow might turn up in the middle of the evening, in front of everyone. Wasn't she summoning the thing by coming here? Opening herself up to contact? The thought made her take a sharp intake of breath, but a reassuring look from Echo calmed her down.

People were filing into the main room, which was once the ballroom. Annie and Echo found a couple of seats near the front row of chairs. A slim woman in her late forties, wearing a crisp white shirt and jeans, walked gracefully to the front of the room and sat down in a comfortable chair. She was blonde with an elfin haircut and seemed too attractive and normal to be the kind of person who dealt with the unseen world. Yet, without speaking a word, the chattering crowd hushed and their attention became riveted on the woman.

The intuitive, Moira Morrigan, smiled. The hair stood up on the back of Annie's neck. She could sense the woman's powerful energy because it came off her in crackling waves. If anyone could help her with the dark shadow it would be her.

For two hours, the woman talked about the power of dreams and gave detailed interpretations to audience members – even reducing several people to tears when she explained the meanings about their dreams involving dead loved ones. When the event finished, Annie breathed a sigh of relief. The dark shadow had not appeared to the intuitive,

340

but still Annie had no answers because not a single member in the audience had talked about dreams involving strange hauntings, or demons, like her own.

Echo nudged her as people started to leave. Annie followed her friend to the front of the room where the intuitive was chatting to someone from the audience.

'Excuse me,' Echo said. 'I was wondering if we could talk to you in private about a spirit issue my friend is having, it involves strange dreams.'

Annie looked at the intuitive and the woman shivered as if someone had walked over her grave. Her hand quickly went to a large black crystal around her neck, and she held the pendant for a second with her eyes closed.

The gesture of protection scared Annie. She knew the crystal was black obsidian because Josie had a similar necklace. What could the intuitive see?

'I don't normally do one-to-one sessions at short notice,' said Moira quietly, 'but I can feel darkness lingering around you. Is this the problem? Are you aware of it?'

Annie couldn't bring herself to speak and nodded slowly. So, the salt hadn't kept the dark ghost away, it was still with her. Hiding. Waiting. But why?

Echo blurted out, 'Please can you help her?'

'Yes. Just give me a few moments to prepare,' said the intuitive fully composed again. 'I'll meet you in the orangery shortly.'

'Thank you, I really appreciate it,' said Annie finding her voice.

'Let's hope she has some answers,' said Echo as they headed from the ballroom to the orangery. She left her friend sitting by the window and went to get a drink.

Annie's palms were sweating as Moira Morrigan appeared in the vast empty room.

'Let's get straight to it, I have a train to catch shortly,' said the intuitive with a genuine smile as she sat next to Annie. 'I suspect you've been having disturbing experiences. Nightmares?'

Annie nodded and said, 'Yes. I see a presence in my dreams.'

'Okay,' said the intuitive slowly. 'What does this presence look like?'

'At first it was a black cloud, but it's taken on a human shape although there are no features.' Annie hesitated aware of how nutty she sounded. But the intuitive urged her to continue. 'It fills the space with evil, that's the only way I can describe it. And it's jumped into the bathroom mirror more than once. It's turned lights on and off, the television, and thrown books around the room.'

'The presence has jumped through mirrors?' Moira looked concerned.

Annie nodded. 'And the thing, I call it the dark ghost, it pins me down in my nightmares. Suffocates me.'

'Has the presence taken you anywhere unpleasant?'

Annie shifted in her seat. She had to be honest because this was her best chance of solving the mystery. With a deep breath she added, 'It dragged me to the mouth of a cavern. I knew if I fell into the dark hole that I'd die.'

The intuitive asked how she escaped. Annie explained about chanting, 'God loves me'.

Repeating her earlier gesture, the intuitive briefly touched the black pendant around her neck and continued, 'Have you ever taken a hallucinogenic like ayahuasca? Or LSD?

Use of these drugs is on the rise. People believe psychedelics can help with creativity and reduce stress. It's popular in Silicon Valley, apparently.'

Annie said she took acid years ago. Moira Morrigan said no, more recently, around the time of her first encounter.

Annie hesitated, then added quietly, 'I did make a tea with a powerful herb. A sleep aid, but then I made it up much stronger...' She stopped herself for a second then continued, 'The drug slowed my breathing down to a bare minimum, turned my skin cold, and...'

'The Death Herb,' interrupted the intuitive. 'Or *Aconitum mortis* to use its Latin name. Part of the same family as the deadly Wolfsbane.'

'You've heard of it?' asked Annie wide-eyed.

'Yes. It's sometimes used by shamanic cultures as an alternative to trance-inducing drugs like the cactus San Pedro.' The intuitive explained that when she was studying with Norwegian Sami two years ago she even took the herb herself to travel to the Upper World, home of the ancestors and animal spirits. 'What happened, apart from the physical side-effects, when you took the Death Herb?'

Annie explained about being plunged into darkness and the voices. 'It was horrific. The voices took little bites out of me even though I didn't have a body. It was agony, I never want to it experience again.'

'How long were you unconscious for after taking this stronger dose?'

'Three days,' said Annie still speaking quietly. She knew she was giving away too much information but she felt like she could trust Moira and she really needed her help.

The intuitive's eyes widened in surprise. 'Three days. Are

you sure?' She was shocked.

'Yes,' said Annie. 'I felt horrendous when I regained consciousness. I was sick.'

'Black bile that tasted bitter?'

Annie nodded. 'Yes.'

'Was this the first time you have encountered spirits?'

'No, I've seen spirits since I was small.'

'You can communicate with a world that most people don't perceive, yet alone acknowledge, rather like myself,' said the intuitive nodding. 'But three days is a long time to be lost in the Dark World. The realm of evil.'

'You mean hell?'

'I wouldn't call it that, the word is too religious. Let's not get waylaid by semantics, let's focus on what *you* need to do next.' The intuitive held Annie's gaze, 'We all possess a soul, a precious vessel that contains memories from our past lives and the blueprint for this lifetime. Do you believe in the existence of the soul, Annie?'

Annie felt unable to look away. 'Yes,' she said, 'Very much so.'

The woman spoke clearly and with purpose, 'When you took the Death Herb it opened a doorway, and your consciousness travelled through this gateway. Once in the Dark World pieces of your soul were stolen. And the dark ghosts had three days to feed from you.'

Annie felt bile rising in her throat. Could this explanation be true?

'I say ghosts because there's always more than one, but a better description would be malignant entities or what the Greeks called the cacodemons. Or demons,' added the intuitive.

344

Annie felt overwhelmed, 'My husband thinks the experiences are the Third Man Syndrome – you know when an invisible presence appears during a time of acute stress and isolation.'

'Perhaps if you were in the Arctic or on Mount Everest,' said Moira raising an eyebrow. 'But I'm afraid your husband is wrong. When you opened the doorway to this other world you didn't shut it. The cacodemons are travelling from the darkness to feed off your energy in this reality. They are slowly sucking away your life force. Your Prana.'

Annie felt a chill go through her body and shook her head, 'But I feel fine.'

'At the moment. But they're waiting for a time when you will be unprepared. And if they attack you in force, it may well be fatal. You, and the goodness in your soul, will be destroyed forever. You will become part of them. Lost to the darkness.'

Annie was horrified. The intuitive told her to take several deep breaths and asked if she needed her inhaler.

'No, I'll be fine,' said Annie feeling shaky and suddenly aware that she'd not told Moira she had asthma. 'Please continue.'

The intuitive explained calmly that aside from opening a doorway with the Death Herb, other ways people created a link to the cacodemons included: drinking heavily, taking drugs, through perverted sex acts and black magic.

'These types of negative behaviours weaken a person's aura, which allows the dark ghosts, as you call them, to hook into the soul,' said Moira. 'Once a person is fully possessed by a cacodemon, they can carry out horrific acts and often report of having no memory of doing such things.'

'Where did the dark ghosts come from originally?' interrupted Annie still stunned.

'Where does evil come from?' said the intuitive with a shrug. 'They've been hunting humanity for eons,' she explained. 'There are references to them in ancient magical texts with names such as incubus, the shadow people and the cacodemons, of course.'

Annie swallowed hard and asked, 'So what you're saying is that these things, they're real?'

The intuitive nodded, 'And anecdotal evidence suggests that encounters with the dark ghosts are increasing across the globe from Australia to Peru and here in the UK. But the spiritual community doesn't know why.'

'My God, I'd no idea that these creatures even existed,' said Annie.

'Another psychic attack from the dark ghosts could trigger a severe, and sudden, physical illness or leave you in a permanent state of deep psychosis,' added the intuitive gently. 'You need to do a soul retrieval ceremony to protect yourself, Annie.'

'What's a soul retrieval? What if I can't do it?' Annie felt her throat tighten and quickly reached for her inhaler in her bag. This time she took one puff.

'You need to do the ceremony in twenty-two days. On the summer solstice,' said Moira calmly. 'And I'm going to tell you exactly what to do. So, listen carefully.'

Darkere

The grey clouds were threatening rain when Darkere entered the estate agents on Briggate, in Leeds. It was just after lunch on a Saturday afternoon and he was the only customer. Darkere browsed the property details on the wall whilst the middle-aged agent talked on the phone. The woman was wearing too much make-up Darkere noted with disgust.

Darkere had picked up the office's details from the 'For Sale' sign outside Josh Raven's burnt out property. This kind of smash and grab operation was risky, but desperate times called for desperate measures, and Darkere was desperate.

The agent lowered her voice and glanced at him. The conversation was clearly personal and private. The silly cow.

Eventually, the agent ended the call. The woman asked if she could help, Darkere told her he was only browsing. The agent nodded and said she was just popping into the back to make a coffee.

Darkere seized his chance. Quickly, he sat at her desk and clicked on an icon called 'Vendor's Database.' A box appeared.

Taking a punt he typed: JOSH RAVEN into the search box. Incredibly, there was no password and the information Darkere wanted appeared within seconds.

RAVEN, JOSH, 8 Huntcliff Cottage, Saltburn-by-the-Sea, North Yorkshire, TS12 4EF.

Darkere couldn't believe his luck. He memorised the address then closed the database and was just standing up when the agent re-appeared.

'Hey. What are you doing?' she asked. She was angry, but kept her distance. The woman clearly had some sense in her tiny brain.

'I was fed up waiting,' said Darkere who was already by the door.

Before she could question him further, Darkere was outside in the street and had disappeared into the afternoon crowd.

He walked further down Briggate and darted into Harvey Nichols. He snaked his way through the designer handbags and expensive perfumes and walked out of the store's exit into Victoria Arcade.

Soon afterwards, Darkere was inside his Jaguar in the multi-storey car park by the Merrion Centre. He revved the engine. It spluttered and the exhaust coughed.

'Come on,' Darkere said aloud and pumped the accelerator. The car produced a steady hum and he said, 'Finally. Thank you.'

The route from Leeds to Saltburn cut through farmland and small towns. Darkere was thinking about how well the Raven case was going, and how Mander would have to concede defeat, when the exhaust let out several sharp bangs.

Swearing, Darkere pulled the Jaguar into a layby next to a field and put on his hazard lights. He called the AA and told the operator that he was on the A173 and had passed the turn-off for Guisborough a mile back.

Over two hours later, an AA mechanic wiped his hands on a rag and shook his head. 'The exhaust's blown. Sorry there's no way I can fix it.'

'Really? You can't fix it?'

The man shook his head and shrugged. 'I can tow you to the nearest garage in Skelton.'

Less than twenty minutes later, Darkere was given the bad news by the American mechanic at the garage.

'The part won't arrive until Monday and then it's maybe gonna be another day or so before I can fix up your exhaust,' said the American with a shrug. 'Sorry, but we're busy with MOTs and these guys are regulars. You could try another garage. I won't be offended. Even tow you myself,' he added with a white toothy smile.

'Nah. It's fine,' said Darkere swallowing his anger and irritation. 'I can wait. A day or two won't kill me.' Darkere could tell this guy was straight up honest, and he didn't want to take his chance with a rip-off cowboy in this arse-end of a place. He'd just have to find a hotel to hide out in for a while.

That evening, Darkere found himself at a guest house in Skelton, on the outskirts of Saltburn. It was all tartan and velvet, nice if you liked that kind of thing. Darkere didn't particularly but it was rural and quiet, both big plus points.

The mechanic had recommended the place and even booked him a room and a taxi. Darkere hadn't bothered to ask what a Yank was doing near the Yorkshire Coast. He wasn't big on small talk unless it was going to give him information he could use.

But he was certainly looking forward to some small talk with Josh and Brigid Raven. The fun encounter would take place just be a little later than he'd planned.

Annie

In the kitchen, Annie found a piece of half-eaten toast on a plate. Josh had already gone out even though it was still early in the morning. She wasn't hurt by his continued lack of emotional contact just numb. His words about making their marriage work had obviously been meaningless. The shallow little shit.

But Annie had bigger worries than her husband's whereabouts. The summer solstice was in 21 days, and she needed to stay calm and level-headed in order to prepare for her ritual with the dark ghost.

It was a bright breezy day, perfect for a long walk on the beach. Annie slipped on her trainers and headed out of the cottage. She glanced up and saw black clouds far out at sea. Any rain was unlikely today.

The cliff path was empty and the salty air edged into her nostrils. Annie breathed in deeply. In the distance, the beach was already filling up around the pier. At the slipway by The Ship Inn, Annie headed right to her favourite part of the beach – the quiet cove that didn't attract the crowds.

Annie found her rock and with a deep sigh planted her feet on the sand. She let the thoughts spiral in and out of her body while the gulls floated above her in the clear sky. Could she really banish the dark ghost? The intuitive had told her she needed to visit the Dark World to carry out her soul retrieval, but what if she never came back? Or if she failed? What would happen then? Annie wished she'd asked more questions, but then again maybe the less she knew the better. More of the truth would only increase her terror, and she was already scared enough.

Snapping herself out of her reverie, Annie told herself that she was strong enough to carry out the ceremony. There was no choice.

Annie stood up from her rock, rolled up her jeans, took off her trainers, and splashed through the shallow pools that covered the beach. The salt water was surprisingly chilly, it made her feet sting but she continued to walk barefoot towards the pier. In the sea, the surfers floated like bobbing seals waiting for the perfect wave.

Breathing deeply, Annie noticed that her lungs felt clear and at that precise moment it started to rain. Great splashes of water drenched her. Within minutes her clothes were wet through. The lightning came in loud cymbal crashes and jagged forks darted into the sea. She'd been wrong about the black clouds.

The solid imposing structure of the pier was only metres away. As the rain fell harder, the lightning struck the beach just fifty metres from where she stood.

Annie froze transfixed by the power of nature. Adults and children fled the sand for safety. But Annie continued to stand still and let the sky fall around her.

After another loud crack of thunder, Annie noticed someone heading towards her. She soon realised it was Duke.

'Move away from the pier,' shouted Duke when he reached her, the storm was raging around them, 'It's metal.'

'What?' Annie shouted back. The thunder had stolen her hearing.

Duke bellowed against the storm, 'The pier. It's metal. We can shelter over there,' he gestured further down the beach towards the cliff.

Annie followed Duke and they ran to an opening in the cliff base. She was surprised to find that the sheltering spot was a shallow cave, she'd always presumed it was merely a crack in the rock. To get inside the cave, they had to squeeze past a small waterfall that was streaming over the cliff edge. The waterfall normally didn't exist, it had been created by the storm.

The small cave enclosed them like a womb. For a moment, the cave reminded Annie of the coffin. She took a deep breath and told herself she was safe.

'Excuse me, ma'am,' said Duke.

The American adjusted his position in the tight space. Annie felt his firm leg pressing against her own. His warm, bare arm touched her arm and his heat filtered into her skin. She could feel his breath on the back of her neck. Her body tingled, she couldn't help it.

Outside, the storm raged on, flashes of light briefly illuminated the dark space. Annie turned to look at Duke. He was already looking at her. Before she had time to think, he bent and kissed the nape of her neck once then turned her around slowly and kissed her softly on the lips.

His mouth was hot and firm. Duke pressed his body against hers, gripping her waist. Without thinking, Annie kissed him back. It was instinctive.

But before Duke had a chance to snake his tongue into her mouth she pulled away.

'I'm sorry, I can't,' Annie said. She scrambled out of the cave through the waterfall and ran down the beach.

'Wait,' shouted Duke. He sprinted after her and soon caught up. He grabbed her shoulder bringing Annie to a halt. 'I'm sorry. I won't do it again.'

'I'm married,' shouted Annie her wet hair stuck to her face.

'I know,' said Duke. 'And you're soaked. How about I take you for a hot cup of tea so you don't get hypothermia. You English girls like hot tea, don't you?'

Annie shivered and wrapped her arms around herself. 'I'd rather just go home and get dry and warm.'

She turned away and carried on walking down the beach. The rain was slowing up, and the sky was brightening slightly, but all she could think of was how good it had felt to have Duke's body pressed against hers.

'I'll walk you home,' Duke said, staying by her side as they crossed the empty beach.

They climbed up the cliff path. By the time they reached the cottage, the storm had passed and the rain was nothing more than a drizzle.

Annie opened the back door. She was going to send Duke away, but when Annie saw him shivering, she found herself inviting him in.

She found him a towel and some of Josh's clothes, even though she knew they would be a bit on the small side.

Upstairs, Annie had a quick shower and then dressed in warm, comfortable clothes. She was still towelling off her hair when she came back downstairs and saw Duke in the kitchen. He was making them a pot of tea.

He was whistling a tune. Instead of looking ridiculous in Josh's t-shirt and joggers, he looked even sexier.

'Why are you so happy all the time?' Annie asked, draping the towel over the back of a dining chair.

The question was odd, she knew, but the thought had popped into her head. Whenever she saw Duke he was smiling or cracking a joke, usually at her expense. It was also a way to distract herself from staring at his biceps.

Duke held out a mug to her, and then sipped his own. 'No other way to be.'

'That's not really an answer,' Annie insisted.

Duke shrugged. 'God made this beautiful earth. But all people want to do is poison the planet and fight one another. I'm doing my best to bring a bit of positivity.'

'Not everybody wants to fight,' said Annie.

'No, not everybody,' Duke agreed and followed Annie into the living room. 'Certainly not you.'

He gazed at Annie intently. His eyes didn't leave her face. She sat down at the dining table and drank her tea, embarrassed.

'You don't know me, Duke,' said Annie running a hand through her damp hair.

'I do know you, Annie,' said Duke sitting down opposite her and folding his arms. 'You like animals, especially dogs. You're a vegetarian and have good taste in music. I've seen the CDs you've lent Echo. You're loyal even when people don't deserve it. You have flair and style. You're funny.' Duke laughed and said, 'And man you're cute.'

Annie felt the heat in her cheeks. She was flattered by his attention. But it felt dangerous at the same time. She glanced at the clock, Josh could walk in the door at any moment. What would he think?

'Tell me,' said Duke staring at her, 'Why do you stay with that asshole?'

Annie blinked, it was as though he could hear her thoughts. 'We're married. That's what you do. Till death do us part.' She realised that she hadn't defended Josh, and she felt a stab of guilt.

'There's more to it than that,' said Duke leaning forward. 'You're feisty. You don't take shit from anyone. Not even legal vows would hold you back from doing what's right. No, there's another reason.' Duke narrowed his eyes. 'What are you two running from, Annie?'

'What makes you think we're running?' asked Annie trying to add humour to her voice.

She forced herself to maintain eye contact with Duke. A liar would look away or fidget.

'Just a hunch,' he said casually finishing his tea.

'We wanted a fresh start.'

Duke said he knew that feeling and laughed. Annie quickly moved the spotlight from herself and asked him why was he living in Saltburn? Wasn't he originally from Nashville?

Duke stood up, stretched and said, 'I'll tell you some other time. I'd better go.'

Annie nodded and stood up with him. 'I'll wash and dry your clothes and drop them off at Echo's.'

Duke smiled and bowed slightly, 'There's really no need. But thank you, ma'am.'

Annie opened the door, Duke brushed past her as he left making her body tingle. He was nearly at the cliff path when she saw Josh approaching, her husband was stomping towards the cottage in anger.

'What the hell was he doing in the house?' shouted Josh when he was closer.

Annie sighed and went inside, Josh followed her. 'We met on the beach,' she said. 'We got caught in the storm. He's a friend of Echo's.'

Josh stood with his arms folded. 'What is he doing in my clothes?' asked Josh.

'He was soaked through, it was the least I could do,' Annie said patiently, retrieving her damp towel from the kitchen and taking it to the bathroom to hang it up.

Josh followed her. 'Are you shagging him?'

Annie felt a glimmer of satisfaction at his evident jealousy. She spun to face him. 'And that would be your business how?'

She could see her husband's rage building as he decided how to reply.

'I don't want you talking to him,' he said eventually. 'He's a twat.'

'You don't even know him,' said Annie pushing past Josh and heading back to the living room.

'I don't need to know him to know he's a twat, and I want you to stay away from him.'

'Seeing as I have no say over who you're *friends* with, you have no say over who I'm *friends* with,' said Annie unable to stop herself from having a dig.

'Fuck this,' said Josh before he doubled over coughing. He wiped his mouth on the back of his hand. 'I'm going upstairs for a bath and a smoke.'

Annie watched him go, knowing she'd won this round. She settled onto the sofa with a fresh cup of tea, and tried not to think of Duke's muscles rippling under the tight t-shirt.

She had more important matters to focus on than men.

Darkere

Bennett Darkere was bored. He had been holed up in the guest house for two days waiting for his Jaguar to be fixed. He had considered getting on a bus to Saltburn, he was itching to see the Ravens and be proven right, but he didn't want to be stuck with a crappy bus schedule. The place didn't have Ubers, he'd already checked.

He put the TV on mute and picked up his mobile. The shop's phone was answered after two rings.

'Computer Haven,' said a voice.

The investigator didn't bother with niceties. 'It's Bennett Darkere. Any luck with that data from the laptop?'

'I was just about to call you,' said the computer engineer in a friendly tone. 'What synchronicity!'

'Yep, what synchronicity,' said Darkere echoing the man's friendly manner and trying to rein in his impatience. He wished the prick would hurry up and give him the information. Why waste time with chit chat?

The computer engineer cleared his throat. 'I've retrieved the internet search data. It's in PDF format as you requested.'

'Is there a lot?' Darkere was blunt and hoped that the engineer would pick up on his sense of urgency.

'A fair bit. What's your email address, I'll send it to you?'

'Can you fax it?'

The computer expert laughed, 'Fax it? No one's asked me to fax anything since 2001. I don't have a fax machine.'

Darkere kept his voice calm and explained with a laugh, 'Yes I agree it's a bit old school. But I'm away from the office and I don't have access to a secure computer. I do need the information quickly.' Darkere didn't wait for a response and asked, 'What about special delivery?'

'Don't you want me to send it by WeTransfer? It's very quick and…'

'No, post it.' Darkere gave him the address of the guest house and made it clear he needed it by the next day. It would arrive when the car was ready. He just needed to be patient a little longer. 'I have to go. I'm expecting a conference call,' lied Darkere.

'I've put the images and documents I recovered onto a USB stick, I'll put it in with the printout.'

'Thanks,' Darkere grunted before hanging up.

All he had to do was wait until tomorrow. He sighed and unmuted the crappy programme about cars. It was going to be a long day.

The next morning, Darkere dressed in the only clothes he had with him, which were starting to smell a bit, and headed down to the reception desk.

'I'm expecting a special delivery,' he said.

'Ah, yes, it's here already.' The woman handed over the A4 brown envelope. Darkere was surprised. His post never arrived before the afternoon in Leeds. 'Thanks.'

Back in his room, Darkere ripped open the envelope. The printed information was nearly a ream of paper. Each page listed rows and rows of hits ranging from dogs to clothes to music to books to astrology to films to tarot cards to black leather boots to wellingtons to holiday cottages to vintage textiles… the list went on. It also included searches for various social media sites.

'Bloody hell,' thought Darkere. 'I'm looking at the spewed-up contents of someone's brain.'

It was incredible. Even though the laptop's memory had been wiped, every internet search that had been carried out was stored on the laptop's hard drive.

Darkere scanned the list and looked for patterns. His eye fell on a website for free tarot readings. The site was obviously some fortune telling bollocks, and it had been visited regularly.

He checked the extra information that followed the web address. Bingo, it was Brigid Raven. The daft cow had asked questions like: *Should I retrain to work with dogs? Will I ever get a job on a mainstream magazine? Will I get out of debt? Will I get a dog?*

Darkere thought Brigid was stupid for going along with this scheme, but this blind faith in the spiritual world was verging on the idiotic. Consulting a psychic to make life decisions. Christ, Darkere almost felt sorry for her.

And from the date her husband had put in his bogus claim, Brigid had asked one question over and over: *Will Josh and I pull off the insurance scam?*

Darkere smiled. 'Gotcha.'

When the garage called to say his Jaguar was ready, he checked out of the guest house immediately and went straight over to pick it up. He paid with his credit card, praying it wouldn't be declined.

As he cruised down the A174 towards Saltburn, Darkere tapped his fingers on the steering wheel as *Elvis in Concert* blared from his CD player. He was looking forward to what the day would bring; proving beyond all doubt that Brigid Raven was alive. He would finally be vindicated. Though that wasn't quite enough for him anymore. He wanted them to go to prison. To do time. His hatred for that ponce Josh

Raven was illogical and out of control, he knew, and it might cost him his freelance gig, but somehow, it would be worth it.

Then there was Mander, he had to show his boss that he could still do the business. Imagine his face when he proved without doubt that Josh and Brigid Raven had pulled off a huge scam? That he was right and his boss was wrong. He hadn't seen her yet but he knew the woman was still breathing. Why shouldn't he hand the two of them over to the police? He didn't care about their silly little lives. And the world wouldn't cry if they were locked up for life. Mander would still pay his bonus if they got arrested. How would his boss know if he was the one who tipped off the police?

With all his evidence, Darkere knew that the CPS would be able to prosecute. He'd done the leg work for them and even had a positive ID of Raven and her tattoo. Whatever she'd done to her appearance, she wouldn't have lasered off her tattoo. That little star would give a positive match. And their conviction would give him a deep satisfaction.

The sea came into view. Saltburn's smart Victorian terraces lined his route.

'Pretty,' said Darkere to himself. 'And boring. I bet few murders happen here.'

At that moment *Jailhouse Rock* came on. Darkere turned up the volume just as he stopped at a zebra crossing in the town centre. Loud music pumped out of his car.

A boho type was pushing a pram across the road and she glared at him. The investigator revved his engine for a bit of fun and made her dash to the pavement. He drove away laughing. The woman had reminded him of that silly bitch, his psychologist, Dr Augur. Thanks to his heart attack he'd managed to slip off her radar. And he was going to keep it that way.

It didn't take Darkere long to find the town's sea front. In the distance, he spotted the row of cottages perched high on the cliff top on the edge of the town. He drove on towards the cliff and his final destination.

When Darkere turned off the main road he eased the Jaguar down a bumpy farm track near the cottages. Suddenly, he felt his new exhaust hit a rock. He cursed loudly and parked his car by a gate. He walked the rest of the way down the track stopping every few hundred yards to catch his breath.

The row of former coastguard cottages stood alone and exposed to the elements. A small field ran along the back of the properties; wheelie bins and cars were neatly parked outside. Darkere approached the Ravens' cottage slowly.

He tried the porch door at the back of the cottage, it was unlocked. Inside the tiny porch, and in the corner by a pile of logs, he saw the biker boots Mrs Flint had described. He felt a flicker of satisfaction as he knocked loudly on the back door.

'Who is it?' asked a male voice from inside the cottage.

The voice sounded like Josh Raven. The stupid little fucker.

'It's Bennett Darkere,' he replied leaning down to shout through the letterbox.

The adrenaline had kicked in and Darkere could feel his body buzzing. He was ready to meet Brigid, the woman who had risen from the dead.

Darkere heard a noise from the cottage. It sounded like a glass smashing on a stone floor.

'Go away and speak to my solicitor,' said Josh's voice through the letterbox.

'I want to talk to you,' Darkere called back. He was not going to leave without a face-to-face.

'I've already told you, I've nothing to say. Speak to my solicitor,' said Josh.

Darkere moved away from the door and leant against Josh's Land Rover and waited.

To the walkers who passed by soon afterwards, Darkere knew that he looked like a man who wasn't in a hurry, which was true. He wasn't going anywhere.

Annie

'How the hell did he find us?' whispered Annie pulling her knees tight into her chest.

The couple were crouched on the floor in the living room hiding under the table and out of view of the letterbox and window.

'I don't know. But he has nothing on us so let's stay calm,' said Josh quietly.

'You sure?' said Annie. She was scared.

Josh put a finger to his lips. Annie was quiet but at the same time she was thinking that the investigator must know something. But what? They had been so careful. Hadn't they?

After a few minutes of silence, Josh said confidently, 'I think he's gone away.'

Annie crawled out from underneath the table and peeked out of the window. Darkere was leaning against Josh's car. She ducked down quickly.

'He's still outside. He wants something,' Annie said her voice quivering.

She had pins and needles so sat back under the table, stretched out her legs and flexed her feet backwards and forwards.

'The case is closed,' said Josh resting his head against the wall. 'We have the money. I don't understand why he's here.'

'Why he's here is irrelevant. The fact is, he's here, and the man's not giving up. So I'm going to hide upstairs, and you're going to get rid of him.'

Josh gulped. 'Have you seen the size of him? How am I

supposed to get rid of him?'

'By sticking to your story and insisting you have nothing to hide.'

Before he could protest further, Annie slid out from the table and keeping low to the ground, she scrambled upstairs and out of sight. But she didn't hide just yet, Annie wanted to hear what the investigator had to say.

The front door shook violently. Darkere was kicking the wood with considerable force.

'Open the door,' shouted Darkere. 'I won't go until you let me in.'

Annie shrank back into the shadows at the top of the stairs. She heard Josh unlock the door and the heavy footsteps of the investigator on the stone floor.

'Where is she? Where are you hiding her?'

'What are you talking about?' Josh asked.

'Your wife. Brigid. She's here. Bring her out, I want to meet her.'

'My wife is dead.' Annie could hear the fake emotion in Josh's voice. 'How dare you barge in here and accuse me of lying about her death.'

Annie heard the rustle of pages. 'I have proof here that you are lying.'

No one spoke for a while and Annie heard more paper rustling.

'Why did the bank pay up then? If they thought it was fraud?' said Josh loudly.

'Because the idiots didn't let me finish my investigation,' Darkere spat.

Annie wondered what proof he had, and what this meant. Was he going to hand them over to the police? Her chest tightened and she crept slowly to her bedside table to get her inhaler. She took a puff and felt her chest loosen.

As much as Annie didn't want to face him, she sensed that all was lost. Perhaps he would take a bribe?

Annie went downstairs slowly – breathing as evenly as possible. She had tucked her inhaler in her pocket just in case.

'Do you want to speak with me?'

Both Josh and Darkere turned to look at her. Josh's eyes were wide and Darkere just grinned. Josh had been right, he really was unnerving. The investigator's skin had an odd blueish tinge and he was sweating slightly. He was staring at her in a disturbing way taking in the details of her face, her eyes, her hair.

'You're prettier in the flesh,' said Darkere ignoring Josh. 'And smaller than I imagined.'

Annie swallowed, 'People often are.'

Annie took in Darkere's appearance. His hands were huge, strong and lethal. With an inward shudder, Annie saw the man's hands around her neck, squeezing slowly. The image faded away. Annie moved a step closer to Josh.

'This is Annie,' said Josh.

Darkere turned to Josh, as if he was finally aware of him, and with disdain said, 'Oh for fuck's sake. I know it's Brigid. I just showed you the proof.'

Annie wanted to kick her husband. Why was he antagonising the man? Darkere could kill them with his bare hands. 'So what are you going to do?' Annie asked hating the quiver in her voice.

Darkere smiled slowly. 'There's the million dollar question,' he drawled. He appeared to be relishing in their uneasiness.

'You're going to leave,' Josh said. 'The bank has paid out, there's no need for you to finish your investigation. It's over, just let it go.'

Darkere's eyes narrowed. He was clearly a man who didn't appreciate being told what to do.

'Actually, I think I might just accidentally tip off the cops, see where that goes.'

Annie could feel her chest getting tight. 'How much do you want?'

Darkere let out a dark chuckle. 'Oh I like you. Straight to the point. Hmm, let me see…'

Suddenly, without any warning, Josh lunged at Darkere landing a punch on his jaw. Annie gasped and stepped backward. Even though he'd caught him by surprise, Darkere recovered fast, and he grabbed Josh around the throat with both of his hands and slammed him up against the wall.

Josh thrust his hands between Darkere's arms and pushed them apart.

Annie was surprised that Josh had been able to free himself so quickly and she stood frozen as her husband punched Darkere hard in the chest.

Darkere was too slow to react and took the full force of the hit. He staggered backwards onto the carpet and lay panting on the floor.

'It's time for you to leave,' said Josh opening the door.

Darkere stood up slowly and made his way to the door.

'This isn't over,' he growled.

'Yes it is. Go on, piss off.'

Annie's breath caught. Why did her husband have to get one last jibe in?

Darkere turned around suddenly and grabbed Josh by the shirt and threw him out of the house. Josh stumbled onto the grass and Darkere followed landing a punch on the face.

Josh yelled out and launched himself at Darkere. Soon, the two men were rolling around on the grass.

'What's all this racket,' shouted Margaret from an upstairs window.

Annie ran outside, upset that her landlady was witnessing the fray. How would she explain these events?

The men ignored Margaret and continued scrabbling over one another on the earth. Josh, Annie saw, had speed and strength but Darkere had weight and experience. A few manoeuvres later, Darkere had pinned Josh down and was putting pressure on his neck. Josh made choking sounds and tried to wriggle out of the hold.

Margaret appeared by her door and threw a bucket of cold water over the two men.

'Should be ashamed,' she said loudly. 'Fighting in the dirt like navvies.'

The men fell apart. They were both soaked and stood up and glared at one another. Darkere leant over resting both hands on his knees. Josh stood up and rubbed his neck.

Margaret berated Josh, and Darkere took his opportunity to hobble away slowly from the cottage. Annie watched him go from her position by the door.

Josh went to follow the investigator but Margaret blocked his path and asked, 'What on earth were you doing with that man, Josh?'

'Fighting.'

'I know that. Why?'

'A gentleman's disagreement,' said Josh dusting himself down.

Annie watched the exchange with their neighbour and saw that Josh was keeping one eye on Darkere as he disappeared along the cliff path. The investigator was walking slowly.

'Who fights in this day and age?' asked Margaret sternly.

'Everybody,' said Josh. 'Haven't you noticed? The world is at war.'

Margaret tutted and said, 'You're no good for Annie.' She glared at Josh before walking briskly back into her own cottage and slamming the door.

Much to Annie's embarrassment, Josh shouted, 'Sod off, you old crone.'

He picked up Darkere's car keys that had fallen out of his pocket during the fight and gave them to Annie. Josh told her to go inside the cottage and lock the door. Without another word, her husband turned and ran after Darkere.

Annie went back inside the cottage, she was furious. Her neighbour would probably kick them out and they'd be homeless again. And the investigator knew she was alive. Shit. Why had Josh hit him?

All she could do was wait for Josh to come home and hope that Darkere would either just go away and let it go, or accept a bribe to keep quiet.

But what price would they have to pay him? Would he want all of their cash? Then what would they do? Would all of this deceit and loss have been for nothing?

Josh

'Bennett!' shouted Josh when he got within fifty feet of the man. 'Bennett Darkere!'

Josh regretted striking the investigator. He should have listened to Annie and offered the man a bribe. Maybe it wasn't too late? Money talked, after all.

The investigator ignored Josh's cries and continued to look at the sea. The ex-policeman was standing near the cliff edge next to a huge metal sculpture known locally as *The Circle*. It was supposed to be a charm bracelet but Josh thought it was an eyesore.

'What do you want from us?' asked Josh loudly as he neared the man. He stopped on the other side of the sculpture, allowing it to create a barrier. 'I can give you money. How much do you want?'

'That was Brigid wasn't it?' said Darkere still looking out to sea.

A solitary boat bobbed in the water. It was too far away for either of them to see any real details.

'Her name's Annie.' Which wasn't a lie. Her name really was Annie these days.

'Don't fuck with me,' said Darkere, his back still turned to Josh.

Josh didn't say anything. He was weighing up the situation and the man's mental state.

Darkere continued to watch the boat. 'I thought I cared,' he said. 'I thought I had to be right. I thought I needed to meet her, talk to her, see her breathe. I thought it mattered that she was alive and not dead, but I can see it's not important.' Darkere took a deep breath and turned to Josh.

369

'Look at me, at us. I'm too old for this game.'

Both men were still covered in dirt. The damp earth was smeared on their faces, in their hair, and on their clothes.

Darkere continued, 'Keep the bloody money. I don't care. I'm getting out of this fucking country. I'm going to visit Tupelo. You know what Tupelo is, Raven?'

Josh shook his head. The guy was clearly having some sort of breakdown ranting about Tupelo, whatever the fuck that meant.

'Tupelo is the birthplace of Elvis,' said Darkere shaking his head as if disappointed. 'I've wanted to go for years but always been too busy chasing little shits like you.'

Josh let out a sigh of relief. He wasn't interested in Darkere's holiday plans but it was good to hear that he didn't care about the case and they could keep the money. Josh believed the old sod too. Darkere was broken, the old fucker was washed up. Useless. He may as well be dead. Cold air washed over Josh and made him shiver. Josh put it down to the breeze coming off the sea.

'I'm curious,' asked Darkere. 'How did you fake her death?'

'She took this herb that made her look dead,' said Josh calmly. He saw Darkere's surprise and felt powerful.

'Are you serious? A bloody herb?' said Darkere with surprise. 'Honestly?'

'Honestly, it's true,' said Josh frankly. 'I couldn't believe it worked.'

The threat of violence had vanished. Josh knew that Bennett felt it too. The man's body had relaxed and the rage had left his face.

Josh added, 'It's called the Death Herb, she got it from

her gran. The herb slowed down her breathing and turned the skin cold so she looked dead.'

'That's a first,' said Darkere laughing. 'Really?'

Josh spilled the beans. Pride made his tongue loose. 'It wasn't hard to avoid an autopsy thanks to her asthma. The attack on record at A&E was real, by the way. It also helped that she'd seen her doctor days before her death, so no coroner was involved.'

'I know about all that malarkey. What about the coffin?' Darkere had turned away from the cliff and had his back to the sea. Despite the sunny day, there was no one else on the beach directly below them.

'I filled the coffin with wood and it was cremated. All we had to do was sit tight until the money came through,' said Josh with a shrug of the shoulders. 'It was easy.'

Again, he felt a sense of achievement. He'd outwitted the system and won.

'She looks so different,' said Darkere. 'Brigid.'

'I know,' said Josh, 'It's remarkable how someone can change their appearance so much.'

'Does she still have the star tattoo?' asked Darkere off-hand.

'Yes,' said Josh with surprise. 'Why?'

'Just wondering,' said Darkere. He tapped his chest pocket. 'That would be all the proof I need…'

A flock of racing pigeons came out of nowhere and swooped down dangerously low. Darkere, who was standing nearest to the cliff edge, automatically ducked as the birds flew over and raised both of his arms to shield his head. But the combination of the quick movement and the uneven clumpy ground made him stumble backwards a few steps.

371

In a split-second, without thinking, Josh stepped forward and grabbed Darkere's shirt. He could see the relief in the man's eyes, but instead of saving him, Josh plucked the creased photograph from the investigator's pocket and then pushed him hard.

The investigator lost his balance and fell backwards over the high cliff. As he tumbled, Bennett's eyes were full of shock and his arms grabbed wildly at the air as he hurtled towards the beach below. He didn't cry or shout, but Josh heard the sickening thump as Darkere's body landed on the rocks at the base of the cliff.

Josh stood motionless for a second then dropped to his knees. He wasn't asking God for forgiveness, he wanted to look further over the edge. Josh crawled on his stomach and clutched at mounds of damp earth as he inched himself closer to the precipice.

Peering over the cliff, he saw what looked like a broken shop dummy on the rocks below. The legs were bent back at a strange angle.

Josh looked away. He wasn't sure if it was vertigo or queasiness but it took him a few seconds to compose himself. Again, he forced himself to examine Darkere's body. He squinted in the sunlight and could see a halo of blood seeping out of the investigator's head. There was no doubt. He was dead.

Relief and horror swept through Josh in equal amounts. Darkere was dead. They were off the hook. Quickly, he walked away from the cliff edge and started to re-write the events in his mind.

'He slipped and fell,' Josh mumbled to himself as he stumbled back towards the cottage on the cliff path.

In his mind's eye, Josh saw Bennett's final terrified look and his body falling backwards over the cliff. It was madness. Josh felt as if he'd watched someone else push the investigator. He felt like his body had been overtaken and was out of his control. But it had been him, only him.

He had just killed a man with his bare hands. Josh felt sick and broke into a half run.

'What have I done?' He felt breathless. Frightened.

In a daze, Josh stopped at a bench on the cliff path to calm down. He reasoned that no one else had been on the path. The beach had been empty below. No one could link him to the man's death. It wasn't unusual for people to fall off a cliff. Maybe the police would treat it as suicide? Josh looked at his hands and noticed that they were shaking. He had to calm down.

Moments later, a pair of walkers passed him on the path. Both men were elderly and wearing shorts that showcased their white legs. Maps hung from their necks in plastic cases and swung gently like cowbells.

'Hello,' said one cheerful walker when he neared Josh. The man's voice sounded like an announcer from the 1950s BBC.

Josh looked at him wide-eyed. 'Hello,' he croaked back. It felt like someone else was speaking for him.

'Looks a bit peaky to me,' said the other walker as they strolled purposefully away. The rest of the men's chat was lost as they pushed on at a brisk pace.

The air tumbled around Josh and he felt hot and sticky. 'Just get back to the cottage, then I'll be alright,' he told himself. He took slow deep breaths and continued walking.

When he tried to push open the cottage's back door, it

was locked. He knocked and Annie let him in. Her face was deathly white, almost the same shade as when she'd come around in the coffin. Josh heard Annie talking to him but he couldn't make any sense of her words. It was a jumble of sound.

His wife guided him to a chair, pushed a glass into his hand and raised it up to his mouth. The liquid was warm and it burnt his throat. He spluttered. Annie pushed the glass to his lips again.

The brandy hit his stomach and he felt his brain reattach to his skull. But he was still disorientated as if he'd been woken up from a horrible dream.

Annie crouched in front of him and held his hands. 'What happened?' she asked gently. 'Where's Darkere?'

Josh shook his head and moved his gaze from his wife's eyes. He couldn't tell her. But Annie kept her eyes level with his and she wouldn't let him look away.

'Tell me,' she said firmly. 'What happened?'

Josh examined her green eyes and knew that he would never be this close to her again physically. He savoured the moment.

'What happened, Josh?' she asked again more firmly.

Josh took another gulp of brandy and began, 'We were talking by the cliff edge. Darkere seemed fine, he told me we could keep the money. Said he didn't care.' The words stuck in Josh's throat but he continued, 'He asked me how we did it, so I told her. Then some birds flew over and startled him.' Josh stopped speaking and looked down. He took another big slug of brandy.

'Then what?' asked Annie. 'Tell me.'

Josh didn't stumble over his words this time. 'I pushed

374

Darkere over the cliff.'

A look of horror formed on his wife's face and his own heart recoiled with the truth of what he'd done. How could he have murdered another person? What had come over him?

'You what?' Annie stood up. She took a step back from Josh and held out her hands in front of her body as if to protect herself from him.

'Darkere had all the information he needed to frame us. He was going to go to the police.' He was keen to explain his actions. There was a justification. He killed Darkere to protect them.

'You murdered the insurance investigator?' Annie put her hands over her mouth and froze.

'I didn't have time to think about it. It just happened,' Josh said pleading. Both his palms were turned up. 'I don't know what came over me, honestly. It was like someone had stepped into my body and taken over. But it was still me, I was there watching myself but it wasn't me. It was weird.'

'You killed him. Oh my God, you killed a man.'

Josh's stomach flipped. He felt a hole open in his chest. All the goodness that had once linked him and his wife was scooped out and filled with darkness.

'It wasn't premeditated. I swear,' said Josh. 'It all happened so quickly. One minute we were talking. He stumbled and without thinking I pushed him.'

'Is he dead?'

'I think so. He hit the rocks below.'

'You think so?' Annie hissed.

'He was going to go to the police,' repeated Josh quietly. He pulled a photo out of his pocket. 'He had this picture as proof. He must have stolen it when he visited us in Chapeltown. I had no choice.'

Annie took the missing photo from him and smoothed it out. She looked down at their smiling faces. 'Was he moving when you left him?'

'No. There was a lot of blood around his head.'

'I don't believe this is happening.' Annie sat down and put her head in her hands. 'Did anyone see you?'

'No. Not that I'm aware of.'

Annie held his gaze for a second too long. He knew at that precise moment that the little remaining love she'd felt for him had drained out of her. It was over.

'I love you, we can sort this out,' he said desperately.

'You turned me into a liar and a thief, Josh. But one thing I'm not is a murderer. You're going to have to carry that one on your own.'

Annie grabbed her denim jacket and rushed out the back door.

'Brigid,' said Josh quietly. But it was too late. His wife had already gone.

Annie

The tragedy pulled people towards the beach and a crowd had quickly gathered. The ghoulish huddle watched as the paramedics checked the body.

Annie listened to the on-lookers swap information about the death. Her mind couldn't connect Josh's confession with what was happening around her. It felt like she was watching a film.

But she had to see Darkere's body for herself, Annie had to make sure he was dead. When the paramedics covered the investigator's body with a sheet Annie exhaled loudly.

She noticed a nearby policeman talking to a dog walker. His voice reached her on the breeze.

'Are you saying that the man was pushed off the cliff?' the officer asked the dog walker.

She was a young hippy type with dyed red hair. Her dog was a Yorkshire Terrier who barked noisily at anyone who came too close.

Annie's ears became bat-like. She cut out all other sounds and strained to catch the woman's response.

'Yes. I've told you,' said the dog walker. 'Two men were standing on the cliff top. Near the edge. One man pushed the other off the cliff, then he ran away along the path towards the cottages.'

Annie wanted to linger and hear more of the exchange but panic rose inside her. She had to leave, but how to do so inconspicuously? She decided to head toward The Ship Inn. From there she could wait a short while then head back to the cottages. She wanted to run but forced herself to move casually.

As Annie approached the pub, she saw more police cars and a white forensic van coming down the hill from the town centre. She stopped and bought a lolly from an ice cream van and headed for a bench outside the pub.

She sat down and ate the lolly slowly even though it tasted foul and made her stomach churn.

With the panic rising further still, Annie headed back to the cottages. At the top of the cliff she glanced down at the beach and saw that Bennett Darkere's body had disappeared under a tent and the area was being cordoned off.

People in white forensic suits and masks were milling about on the beach along with more police. Annie walked along the cliff path past the row of cottages, up through the fields and towards the farm.

Despite keeping a leisurely pace, her heart was racing and her mouth was dry. She was heading to a bench half a mile along the path where she could sit and gather her chaotic thoughts. But when she reached the bench the area was crawling with yet more police.

'Sorry, miss, but you can't walk here,' said a young officer politely.

He asked Annie if she regularly hiked along this path. She calmly said yes but she hadn't passed this way for a week at least, which was true.

'Been some nasty business,' said the policeman. 'But you'll be able to use this part of the path again shortly.'

'What's happening?'

'Murder investigation.'

Annie was so stunned that she couldn't speak. They clearly believed the dog walker, and possibly other witnesses. She shook her head and mumbled it was shocking. The officer

378

was busy talking to a colleague so Annie quickly slipped away.

As the beach emptied of the onlookers, Annie retraced her steps back along the cliff path towards the cottages. Her mind was frazzled. Would the police come looking for them? But how would they know Josh was the murderer? The dog walker had been a long way off from the action. Surely, the woman wouldn't have seen Josh's face? Should they run? Where would they go next? Edinburgh?

When Annie reached the cottage nearly two hours had passed since she'd originally left Josh. The back door was unlocked, which made her nervous. Annie stepped into the silent living room and shouted, 'Josh?' No response.

Quickly, Annie searched the small cottage. It was empty.

Car keys. She remembered Josh picking up Darkere's car keys after their fight. Annie looked down the path where the investigator's vehicle had been parked. It had vanished.

Turning back to head inside, Annie spotted a wallet on the ground under a neighbour's rabbit hutch. Annie bent down, opened it and saw one of Darkere's business cards. She quickly hid the wallet up her cardigan sleeve.

Inside, Annie stuffed the wallet in a drawer and searched the cottage again. After opening the wardrobe, plus every single cupboard and drawer, Annie discovered that Josh had taken a holdall, clothes, his mobile and passport – all the items that he'd need to disappear.

He'd left his laptop. Her husband had obviously been in a rush. There was no note.

How could he just up and leave her? She didn't exist without him, and Josh knew that. What was she supposed to do now?

Shock set in and Annie laid down on the bed and wrapped herself in the duvet. She watched the light outside slowly turn to dusk.

Maybe her husband had gone for a few days because of the police and would come back once the dust had settled? This thought bounced around Annie's head until she drifted into a fitful sleep.

Annie

A persistent thump on the cottage door woke Annie up. She felt hungover as she staggered out of bed. She glanced down and realised that she was still fully dressed. As she stumbled downstairs, the events of the day before crowded into her mind: Darkere's visit, his subsequent murder, her husband's strange disappearance.

Maybe it's Josh, she thought hopefully, hunting for the keys on the mantelpiece. She had been right after all. He wouldn't leave her in the lurch even if their marriage was all but over. But what if it was the police? With a trembling hand, Annie unlocked the door.

'Just heard the dreadful news,' boomed Margaret Swain. She walked into the living room, stood by the fireplace and rocked backwards and forwards on her heels.

'What news?' asked Annie yawning. She was trying to appear nonchalant.

'The man. Fell over the cliff.'

'Oh, yes, I heard about it last night. Dreadful.' Annie yawned again, 'Tea?'

'Marvellous,' said Margaret following her into the kitchen.

'Late night?'

Annie let the water rush into the sink to give her a few extra seconds to think, then filled the kettle. 'What? Oh, no I was up really early meditating. I must have fallen back asleep.'

'Right oh,' said Margaret brightly. She was always at her perkiest in the mornings. She stood by the cooker. 'Any idea what happened on the beach yesterday?'

Annie shook her head. She busied herself with the mugs and milk.

'Who was your visitor?' asked Margaret. 'Yesterday, that man. He looked ill.'

'Just someone Josh knows,' said Annie. She briefly looked at Margaret before putting crumpets in the toaster. Her heart was pounding and she could feel Margaret's stare on the back of her neck.

'Why were they fighting?'

'A debt. He owed Josh money.'

'Pah,' said the old woman. 'Where is Josh?' Her tone had changed dramatically, she was displeased and stern.

'He's gone to stay with his family. His mother's ill.' Annie busied herself getting peanut butter out of the cupboard. She was surprised by how easily dishonesty came to her these days. It was true that with practice you could improve at anything, even lies.

Margaret nodded slowly and said, 'I see.'

For a moment, Annie felt her heart fall. Her neighbour knew about the murder. Perhaps she'd even seen Josh when he came back from the fight with his face wild like a mad man? Would her landlady call the police? Could she reason with Margaret? Plead their case? Explain how things got out of control? If the police came here and questioned her they'd soon realise she had a fake identity. Fuck.

Margaret tutted. 'Don't bend the truth to me, girl.'

That was it, the game was up. Annie was ready to spill out the whole sorry story. 'Margaret, I'm so sorry and I'm so ashamed. I know you trusted me and…'

Margaret interrupted Annie, 'Gone to stay with family? More likely that blonde tart. Knew he was a bad 'un the first

382

time I met him.'

Annie shut her eyes for a moment in relief. Margaret didn't know about the murder.

'Your husband. He's not been subtle,' said Margaret shaking her head and pouring the tea from the pot into the mugs. 'You deserve better. Seen him skulking about town with that woman more than once.'

'He wasn't always that way,' said Annie with tears pricking her eyes. She was genuinely upset, it was the stress of everything building up, but she was also greatly relieved that Margaret's conversation had veered off on another tangent.

'Plenty more fish in the sea,' Margaret said, adding milk to the mugs. 'Sit down, you look exhausted.' The landlady carried the tray into the living room.

Annie followed Margaret and sat at the table. They drank and ate in silence.

'I could do with going back to bed for the day. I feel peaky,' said Annie eventually, which was true. She didn't have the energy to fake politeness or tell more lies to someone she respected. Her head felt heavy and she needed space to think.

As Annie waved goodbye to Margaret and locked the cottage door her gaze fell upon her psychic protection book, she wondered how on earth she could still do the ceremony when she had so much to worry about. How could she be calm when her husband had murdered someone and gone AWOL? What on earth had come over him? Was she now an accessory? And if the police came asking questions how long would it take them to work out that she had a fake identity?

Slowly, Annie poured more tea, took it upstairs and tried

to quieten her mind. With a sigh, she took off her jeans and climbed into bed. A small dose of the Death Herb would be ideal, just enough to knock her out, but then she wouldn't have enough left for the ceremony. She'd just have to ride out her exhaustion.

Annie spent the day in bed reading. She found herself going over the same paragraphs again and again unable to concentrate. All the while, her ears were pricked for any outside noise suggesting Josh's return. But her husband stayed away. Should she call the police and report him missing? The voice of reason told her no, he'd be back when he knew the coast was clear. And calling the police was out of the question. She risked exposing herself.

It was just past nine and Annie decided she needed a stiff drink to help her sleep. She opened the cupboard in the living room. Next to a half empty bottle of rum was an envelope with Josh's untidy scrawl on the front. She ripped it open and saw two pieces of paper. A note and a print out.

Brigid, the money in this account is yours. The pin number is your day and month of birth, and the login details are on my laptop. I'm sorry. Josh

Annie looked at the print out. It had the name of an online bank she'd never heard of. The available balance was £200,000. She dropped the envelope and its contents as if they were toxic. Trembling, Annie slumped to the floor. But she didn't cry.

He really was gone. And he wasn't coming back. She was free with enough money to last her for a long time. If she was careful.

She could do whatever she wanted. But all she wanted to do was sleep.

Annie

Two weeks had passed since Josh's disappearance, and the local media's interest in the 'Beach Mystery Murder' had fizzled out. A fire at a factory in Redcar had bumped the story off the front page.

Annie was considerably calmer. She'd told a police officer conducting house-to-house inquiries that morning that she'd been reading at the time of the man's death, with her headphones on, and hadn't been aware of any drama until she'd watched the local news.

No one had come back to question her again. Annie would likely be looking over her shoulder for a while yet, but even so she appeared to be off the hook.

At lunchtime, Annie had logged into her online bank account and made a transfer of £10k to the dog shelter in Leeds. A promise was a promise.

But her husband's vows were empty like puffs of air. It was time to accept that Josh wasn't coming back. He hadn't tried to contact her, and his mobile had been disconnected. And she couldn't call his parents because they thought she was dead.

The realisation that she would probably never see Josh again was a relief. The emotion had hit her in the early hours of the morning as she'd waited for the dawn. If she was honest, their marriage had fallen apart long ago. The cracks had appeared when she was hiding out in the rental house in Leeds. He'd left her for hours on her own in that dump. And the scam itself was a strong indication that something was wrong with Josh mentally. Her husband had manipulated her into making this stupid decision, and now she knew they had only stayed together over the last few months because she was 'dead'.

Under normal circumstances, Annie would never have carried on a relationship with an addict. Josh didn't want to help himself and he couldn't see, or admit, how his actions were hurting her. And that's what he was, an addict. Her husband was addicted to alcohol and drugs. He only cared about himself. Sitting on her bed in the cottage, Annie realised with clarity that she didn't need Josh to live a full and happy life.

Yes, things could get complicated for her alone, she knew that, but when she looked at her situation at the most basic level she felt blessed, truly. She was alive. She had somewhere safe and comfortable to live. A basic identity. Friends and money. Annie could, and would, face the future without her husband. The one thing left to do, to close the awful chapter in this period of her life, was to carry out the ceremony to banish the dark ghost. And she was ready.

On the evening of the summer solstice, Annie began to prepare for the ritual. She filled the tub with hot water and added Epsom salt and several drops of Fringed Violet essence. The intuitive's voice played in her mind as she swirled the white crystals and the flower essence around in the water so they dissolved.

'Fringed Violet has been used for centuries as protection against psychic attack. It expels negative energy from the aura.'

Annie immersed herself slowly into the hot bath and stayed in the water until her skin crinkled. She imagined her body being bathed in the heart of a burning violet flame.

'The violet flame will protect you. Keep you safe from the

dark ghosts.'

Fresh from her bath, barefoot and dressed in a long white nightdress Annie continued to collect her tools from around the silent cottage.

'You will need to light a fire to open your ceremony. The fire must burn inside a circle of stones. The size of the stones is not important, nor their colour.'

Annie collected her piles of driftwood into a large eco shopper. Her collection of stones, that had grown over the months and could be found in jars all over the house, went in with the wood. Wood and stones. Stones and wood.

'You will need four items to represent the four elements of fire, air, water and earth. The elements will stand at the four corners of your circle for protection. They will define your sacred space.'

Annie gathered the items to represent the elements and put them in the eco shopper with the stones and wood. She lit more incense, which had been burning since that morning, and the sweet smoke wafted around the room and up the stairs.

'Burn frankincense in your house, when you prepare your tools, to cleanse your space and aura.'

The heavy smell of frankincense reminded her of going to Mass as a child. It was the only time Annie went to a church with her drunken mother, on a Christmas Eve.

But Annie didn't feel guilty about venturing into what some might see as witchcraft. The intuitive had explained that the ceremony could be adapted for any particular spiritual belief. All religions used the four elements in some way during their rituals – even the Catholic faith.

'If you feel comfortable with the concept of angelic beings

387

then call on the four Archangels for help. Each Archangel represents one of the four elements and one of the four directions.'

Annie looked at the picture on the wall of Archangel Michael with his sword. She didn't know if the ceremony was going to work but she had to try. She couldn't spend her life frightened of dark shadows. And even though she hadn't seen the dark ghost in months, she could feel its presence lingering in the shadows, waiting for the right moment to re-attach itself to her.

She whispered, 'Archangel Michael, please help me and protect me when I do my ceremony.'

The sunset faded and soon it was twilight. Annie put on her red cardigan and picked up the eco shopper and locked the cottage.

Barefoot, she walked along the grass path that followed the cliff edge down to the beach and the cove.

'Trust in the Power of the Divine. Trust in Mother Earth. Trust in God.'

No one was sat outside The Ship Inn when Annie made her way past. The night was cool and the drinkers were inside. The beach was also empty.

A light breeze was coming in from the sea. The hood of her cardigan was already pulled up, Annie drew the covering closer around her face glad of its warmth.

The light was fading, Annie knew that she needed to head much further up the beach where she wouldn't be seen or risk being cut off by the tide.

After some time, she found a sheltered spot out of the wind and built her fire of driftwood. The fire took quickly. Annie knew how to coax the hungry flames to life.

'You need to choose a power animal to assist you during your quest. Think of an animal that you feel drawn to. Make it an offering.'

With the fire roaring, Annie walked clockwise around the flames and thought of a black bird. She created a large circle using her offering of flower heads, which she'd picked from the garden.

'You need to create three circles of protection.'

Annie walked around the fire in a clockwise direction again, but this time she placed stones inside the line of flowers. Using salt she made another circle, the third and final ring of protection.

Standing within the three circles, Annie turned towards the south and stuck a three-foot garden candle in the sand and lit it and said aloud, 'The candle represents Fire.'

In the direction of the east she bent down and stuck a white feather in the sand. 'The feather represents Air.'

In the west, she laid the seashells and proclaimed, 'The shells represent Water.'

The bunch of flowers were placed in the north. 'The flowers represent Earth.'

Turning to the east, Annie said:

'Before me Raphael,

Behind me Gabriel,

On my right-hand Michael,

On my left-hand Uriel,

Above me the Father,

Below me the Mother,

Within me the Eternal Flame.'

In a loud and steady voice, she added: 'I reclaim my personal power from all time and all dimensions. I cut all cords and bindings. I RECLAIM MY POWER NOW.'

She continued, 'I decree in the name of the Divine that any of my power and abilities that have been stolen or copied be returned to me. I DECREE THIS HAPPENS NOW.'

Finally, she said, 'I am a divine being. I believe in the power of the Eternal Flame. MY SOUL IS WHOLE AND PURE.'

Annie felt charged, alive. She took out the flask of Death Herb tea, poured some into a mug and quickly gulped down the foul smelling liquid. The flames shot up, she laid down on the sand, shut her eyes and waited.

The fire was warm and the dream came quickly. She was flying on the back of a huge black bird, she could see her fire and the sacred circle below on the sand.

The bird swooped along the beach and dived into the cave that she'd once sheltered in when the sky had rained down. Her tiny hands clung around the bird's neck and her fingers were thrust deep into bird's feathers. Feathers that felt like silk.

Bird and Woman journeyed deep into the cave and travelled downwards through the darkness. Deeper, deeper, following the tunnel of wet rock. Eventually, the tunnel stopped. An opening appeared in the stone. A doorway, an arch that looked like a gaping railway tunnel.

Woman was frightened but she trusted Bird to lead her to the right place. Bird flew through the doorway and they found themselves in a vast wood that had been scorched dry by a raging fire. Blackened tree trunks littered the ground and not an animal or patch of greenery was to be seen anywhere. And it was dark in the burnt forest.

Among the dead and fallen trees, Woman noticed that

below on the ground there were dozens of dark ghosts. Some of the black shapes were semi-human with half a head or a limb missing whilst others were only a swirling mass of inky smoke, not yet fully spawned. These unborns were curling and swirling around the trees and Woman realised that this was why the place was so dark. The beings blocked out the light. They were the darkness.

Terror gripped Woman but she couldn't turn back, she and Bird had to journey to the heart of the darkness. She had to find the missing parts of her soul.

Bird hovered so Woman could get a better look at the dark ghosts below. She noticed that a handful of the beings were fully-formed and were crouched down on their haunches amongst the blackened tree trunks. The group formed an unholy huddle.

All the human-like entities in this group had one thing in common. Inside their chests glowed a golden sphere that was fluttering and trying to escape its dark prison. An aching in her chest told Woman that the golden spheres wanted to be reunited with her, without them she wasn't whole.

Looking up, one of the dark ghosts spotted Woman and Bird. The demon's arm stretched beyond all human possibility and the end formed into a thin distorted hand. The unheavenly limb tried to catch Woman's leg.

But Bird was too swift to be caught, and soared quickly into the dark sky and then dived down low like a Spitfire. Lifetimes upon lifetimes flashed in Woman's mind's eye. Her old soul had been in this battle before, this battle with evil, many times. She was a warrior of the light.

Suddenly, Woman knew why the dark ghosts had haunted her. They wanted her spirit, her power and energy. She was a threat.

With sudden clarity, she saw the events through their soulless eyes. When she'd taken the Death Herb, Woman had entered through a doorway into their world. And while she was in the coma they had tried to take her soul, her power. When she had escaped, the demons followed into her dreams and continued to try and bring her back to the underworld.

The demons had tried to trap her in the darkness. They wanted her to feel hopeless, and without choices. Her fear gave them life. They had been feeding off her unhappiness and misery. Her despair made them no longer a whisper of evil in the darkness but a real thing that had come from the underworld to find her.

Woman saw the dark ghosts had influenced her husband too. The excessive drugs and drink were their doing, their hook into his psyche. They were the reason why Josh had changed so much, beyond recognition, and had descended into addiction.

A fire rose up in her belly. Woman was unable to contain the purifying violet flame any longer. She raised her right hand and a blast of fire shot out of her palm and covered the ground below in a raging inferno of purple light. Screams of pain shot up to her in the sky as the dark ghosts perished in the flames but Woman ignored their cries of agony. It was nothing compared to the agony they had caused her. It was what they deserved. The heat was intense but Bird beat her wings and held her position.

Momentarily, Woman paused in her fury because she'd spotted a slight movement out of the corner of her eye. Bird automatically changed her angle for Woman to get a better look. Woman saw three dark ghosts escaping the inferno. The cacodemon hid behind a large collection of tree trunks, but their tiny golden sparks in their chests gave them away in the blackness.

Woman and Bird gave chase and hunted the dark ghosts. One of the beings stopped and crouched down, then with great force it leapt into the air and was within arm's distance of Bird.

A wail of anger and hate pounded in Woman's ears and was so powerful that she nearly fell, but she clung to Bird who swooped and dived through the thick branches to escape their grasp.

Coming around again, Bird and Woman dived close to the ground. This time, Woman blasted the earth with fire from her heart. All her power, all her anger, all her grief from eons of fighting the darkness was put into the purifying flame.

As the dark ghosts evaporated in the searing heat the golden globes of light were freed and like burning insects they fluttered away. Bird and Woman flew through the wood and followed the golden insects.

As Bird turned her head briefly, Woman saw the creature's yellow eye. The pupil was as large as a dinner plate and Bird and Woman's soul became one instantly. She felt the power of Bird's wings. The freedom of the sky. Bird's strength and perception. Bird's love and care.

Bird and Woman flew on through the forest.

Eventually, Bird reached the edge of the charred trees. Bursting out of the black woodland, Bird entered a lunar-like landscape. Grey rocks and large boulders were littered as far as Woman could see into the distance. A cavern, a large gaping hole, came into view on the ground.

Woman knew this cavern, it was the entrance to the dark world. Past that black mouth was the point of no return.

She hung on to Bird and trembled with absolute terror. She buried her face in Bird's feathers, feathers that smelt of wood smoke and lavender. Bird slowed down and Woman peeped out from the wings. Dozens of the tiny fireflies buzzed around a clump of rocks near the cavern's mouth. Still on the back of Bird, Woman used her bare hands to catch the sparkling flies one by one.

When she caught a firefly, Woman put the insect in her mouth and swallowed the tiny golden sphere whole. But the last firefly that she captured Woman gave to Bird. As Bird ate the insect, Woman rested her cheek on the animal's soft smoky neck.

It was time for the final act. Woman held out her right hand. Fire sprung from her palm one last time and she threw the flame at the cavern. The entrance to the lower world was consumed by a ring of violet fire that burned bright and pure and sealed the doorway.

When the fire stopped burning there was only solid grey rock left. The cavern mouth had vanished.

Woman and Bird journeyed back through the rocky wasteland, away from the cavern, over the blackened forest and through the opening into the long tunnel with the walls of wet rock. As one, they flew through the mouth of the cave, back to the circles of stones and salt and the smouldering fire on the sand.

Annie

The sun was rising. Annie felt the heat on her face but her body was frozen and stiff from having slept on the beach. The fire had gone out and a murder of crows surrounded her in a circle on the sand. When Annie sat up slowly the black birds fluttered high into the air.

With awe, Annie watched the birds fly off in the direction of the farmland on the cliff. On unsteady, numb legs, she unwound the circle in an anti-clockwise direction by picking up the rocks. Once collected, Annie placed the rocks together gently on the tide line and they melted quickly into the other stones on the beach. The charred driftwood, flowers and salt were left for the earth. She packed the candle and her flask into her eco shopper.

Still shaking, her bare feet almost blue with cold, Annie headed back along the sand and up the cliff path. She was exhausted but exhilarated. Her task was complete. She was certain the dark ghosts would not bother her again. The missing parts of her soul, the little golden spheres, were back inside her spiritual body. She was whole again, complete and safe. And the doorway to the other world was closed, finally.

As Annie neared the row of cottages movement caught her eye. She noticed that Margaret Swain was watching her out of a bedroom window – her landlady had always been an early riser. Margaret disappeared only to reappear minutes later by her back door. Her neighbour was wearing a blue fleece over her pyjamas and was walking towards Annie briskly.

When she was within earshot her neighbour shouted,

'What on earth are you doing? You're half-dressed.'

Annie realised she must look odd. Her flimsy white night gown was soaked along the bottom and her red cardigan was covered in sand. She felt her head. Her hair was wet and bits of seaweed clung to the tendrils around her face.

'You'll catch your death of cold,' said Margaret. The old woman flung a blanket around Annie's shoulders. 'What have you been doing? Eh?'

'I've, I've been…' but Annie couldn't get the words out because her teeth were chattering so much.

'Let's get inside. You look deathly pale.' Margaret put an arm around Annie's shoulders and helped her along the track towards the cottages. 'You need warming up quickly or you'll develop hypothermia. Summer or not.'

At her back door, Annie fished out her cottage keys from the eco shopper. Her hand was so unsteady that she couldn't insert the key in the lock.

Margaret took the keys gently and said, 'Here, let me.'

Annie was dazed. She was still groggy from the deep sleep. Margaret took control, ushered her upstairs and told her to step out of her damp clothes. Whilst Annie undressed in her bedroom, Margaret filled the bath.

'Hot chocolate. That's what you need. Get some colour back into those cheeks,' said Margaret loudly outside Annie's bedroom door.

'Thank you,' Annie called back.

Soon Annie was soaking in a tub of frothy bubbles and no longer felt vacant. She could feel her toes and fingers again. She thought about her journey, with the bird, and she recalled the realisation she'd had about the influence of the dark ghost.

She twisted her pearl and diamond ring around her finger and tears filled her eyes.

Josh had never stood a chance against the dark ghosts. After all, how could you conquer something that you didn't even believe in?

But there was no way they could be together. She was a different person and so was Josh. She had to let him go.

A sob rose up in her chest and Annie didn't try to stop it. Her tears dissolved into the bath water as she grieved for her lost identity, her lost marriage and her lost friendships.

She also grieved for her lost honesty. Before taking the Death Herb, Annie had never been deceptive, but she'd become a secretive person with a dark past and this wasn't who she wanted to be.

Taking several deep breaths, Annie let the sobs fade away. As she washed her hair and wrapped herself in a towel Margaret had laid out for her, Annie thought about her future.

Dressed in clothing far too warm for a summer's day, a jumper and jogging bottoms, she went down to the kitchen to join her landlady. She left her pearl and diamond ring on the bedside table.

'So, young lady. What were you doing?' asked Margaret. She put another cup of hot chocolate in front of Annie and sat opposite her at the dining table.

'I went to the beach to see the sunrise,' said Annie.

'In your nightdress?' said Margaret shaking her head. 'What were you thinking?'

Annie stirred the froth on her drink before answering. 'Josh isn't coming back. He's gone. But I'm going to be fine. I just needed to clear my head.'

'Spineless twerp. And yes, you will be fine,' said Margaret firmly.

Even though Annie knew the truth behind her husband's behaviour, she didn't try to defend him. He was no longer part of her life.

In a lighter tone Margaret added, 'Next time you go prancing about on the beach at sunrise please dress appropriately. At least wear a proper coat.'

'Prancing about?' replied Annie her mouth curling into a smile. She loved her neighbour's use of language. No one said prancing about anymore.

'You heard me, madam,' said Margaret faking annoyance. 'Thought you'd lost your marbles.'

Annie laughed. 'I promise if I go prancing about again on the beach in the early hours I will dress more appropriately.'

'Feeling warmer?'

'Yes, thanks.' Annie smiled at Margaret. 'I never had a mother who cared about me. Thank you for making sure I was okay.'

'I never had a daughter,' said Margaret softly. 'Always wanted one. You'll do.'

Her neighbour smiled. Annie smiled back with unspoken words of love and gratitude.

'I nearly forgot.' Margaret pulled a small card out of her cardigan pocket. Her name was printed on the cream square in bold capitals. There was a mobile number underneath. She put the card on the table. 'My mobile if you want anything. Anytime. Just ring.'

Annie's mouth fell open. Margaret, the woman who hated the television, had bought a mobile phone.

'Thought it was time I joined the modern world,' said Margaret smiling. On cue, her mobile rang and Margaret pulled the phone out of her trouser pocket. 'Will be my friend from Helmsley.' Margaret hesitated.

'Please take the call, I'm fine,' said Annie. She could hear Margaret laughing into the phone as she let herself out.

Annie was feeling bone tired and needed to rest. As she slipped under the bedcovers, she glanced at her clock. It was 11.11am. Annie said a silent prayer of thanks to the Archangels for their help.

A dreamless sleep followed. Annie woke up three hours later with her stomach rumbling and her mind clear.

Her red leather journal, with the embossed flaming heart, lay on the bedside table. She picked it up, flipped open to a new page and wrote:

I am free to be whoever I wish to be.

Annie stared at the words for a moment, turned over another new page and wrote a list. Afterwards, she ripped out this page and pinned it on her bedroom wall. She called the list: The Five Rules.

Rule 1: Do not let money rule my life.
Rule 2: Be kind to animals, people and the planet.
Rule 3: Every day do something to make myself happy.
Rule 4: Speak the truth. Live the truth.
Rule 5: I won't die for anyone. I live for myself.

Annie closed her journal and a wave of determination and peace rippled over her. She heard movement downstairs and her stomach flipped. Could it be Josh?

Before she could get out of bed, an American voice

shouted upstairs, 'Annie? You there?'

'Duke,' Annie thought with shock. 'Margaret must have left the door unlocked.'

She jumped out of bed, threw on her dressing gown and ran down the stairs. She halted by the fireplace when she saw Duke's large frame filling the doorway to the living room.

'Why are you here?' she was shocked and delighted.

'I just had this weird feeling that something was wrong. I was worried about you.' He gestured to door, 'You left it unlocked. That's not safe. Especially with recent events.'

'I know. My landlady came to visit earlier, she must have left it open. What do you mean, you were worried about me?' Annie's heart flipped.

'I can't explain it. I felt this weird tug at my chest, and I couldn't stop thinking about you.' Duke laughed. 'I appreciate how odd that sounds.'

Annie was standing in the centre of the living room. She was unsure of what to say or do next.

'No. It doesn't sound odd.' She was nervous and spoke too quickly. 'Josh is gone. He's left me.'

'Sorry to hear that, hell, I'm not actually. He really wasn't good enough for you.' Duke remained rooted to the spot.

Annie shook her head. 'It was more complicated than that, but it doesn't matter. He's not coming back and I'm free.'

Duke continued to hover in the doorway to the cottage but he was smiling. 'Free is good,' he said, taking a step towards her. 'And what will you do with this new freedom?'

Annie smiled back. 'I haven't decided yet, I'm still getting used to the idea.'

'Maybe I can help,' Duke said as he stepped closer still.

He was just a couple of feet away and Annie knew that all she needed to do was step forward and his arms would wrap around her. She knew that she would be okay by herself, she didn't need a man to keep her safe or make her feel whole. But Annie also knew that with Duke by her side, she could do anything she wished.

Could she be with him and not tell him the truth of who she really was?

Rule 4: Speak the truth. Live the truth.

'Just one thing before we go any further,' Annie said looking at the American.

'What is it?' asked Duke taking another step towards her. He was close enough for her to smell his cinnamon scent, and she breathed in deeply. She felt a thrumming in her chest, and could almost see the golden connection between them glowing.

'My name isn't Annie. My real name is Brigid. I am Brigid Raven.'

About the Author

Monica Cafferky worked as a journalist for over 20 years before turning her hand to fiction. She has written for numerous national newspapers and magazines including: *The Daily Mirror, The Daily Mail, The Guardian, Grazia, Red* and *Woman's Own.*

The Winter's Sleep is her debut novel.

She lives in Yorkshire.

MonicaCafferky.com

  @MonicaCafferkyBooks

Book Club Questions

1) Do you prefer Josh's view of reality or Brigid's? Is there an unseen force guiding us through life or is reality just a series of random events?

2) Why is the novel split into four sections of air, fire, earth and water? What role do the elements play in the story?

3) Is the world of nature slipping away as Diana the herbalist believes? If so, does this lack of a connection with nature matter or should technology be fully embraced?

4) What price would you accept to walk away from your life?

5) How important is time in the novel? What does the characters' relationship with time reveal about them?

6) Could you break all contact with the outside world for several weeks – or longer?

7) If a person has no digital identity do they fully exist in the modern world? How important is identity as a theme in the novel?

8) What elements of the novel draw from the fairy tale?

9) Can you identify any aspects of the hero's journey within the narrative?

10) Do you think Brigid/Annie's experiences with the dark ghost are real? Or are the encounters triggered by isolation or even psychosis?

Acknowledgements

A special thank you to Fay Weldon, Peter James and Daisy Waugh; Linda the insurance investigator; Ainsley the policeman; YA the computer expert; shamans Davina MacKail and Chris Krow Summers; intuitive Anne Jirsch; Liz Dean; Jayne Wallace; Kathryn Luczakiewicz from the Saltburn Wellbeing Centre; the helpful friends who gave encouragement or read early drafts of the manuscript especially Carmen Marcus, Andrew Clover, Machel Shull, Deborah Beck, Hannah Eglese, Jen Schofield, Jackie Dennison, Inbaal Honigman, the Holmfirth Bookclub; and all at Jasper Tree Press.

I would also like to thank Terry Tavner who gave me my first big writing break (all those years ago); and Chris Ellis who quietly cheered for me on from the side-lines and never let me give up.

Printed in Great
Britain
by Amazon